THE MANHATTAN JOB

JASON KASPER

THE MANHATTAN JOB

Copyright © 2021 by Regiment Publishing, LLC.

All rights reserved.

No part of this book may be reproduced in any form or by any electronic or mechanical means, including information storage and retrieval systems, without written permission from the author, except for the use of brief quotations in a book review.

Severn River Publishing
SevernRiverBooks.com

This is a work of fiction. Names, characters, businesses, places, events and incidents are either the products of the author's imagination or used in a fictitious manner. Any resemblance to actual persons, living or dead, or actual events is purely coincidental.

ISBN: 978-1-64875-114-1 (Paperback)
ISBN: 979-8-74629-822-5 (Hardback)

ALSO BY JASON KASPER

Spider Heist Thrillers
The Spider Heist
The Sky Thieves
The Manhattan Job
The Fifth Bandit

American Mercenary Series
Greatest Enemy
Offer of Revenge
Dark Redemption
Vengeance Calling
The Suicide Cartel
Terminal Objective

Shadow Strike Series
The Enemies of My Country
Last Target Standing
Covert Kill
Narco Assassins
Beast Three Six

Standalone Thriller
Her Dark Silence

To find out more about Jason Kasper and his books, visit severnriverbooks.com/authors/jason-kasper

To my son, Levi

Welcome to the world.

1

BLAIR

Blair strode purposefully across the rooftop, making her way to the fire escape stairwell.

The night sky over LA was hazy, the stars drowned out by the electric glow of bars and restaurants that would remain open well into the early morning hours. After all, this was New Year's Eve, and the City of Angels wasn't known for restraint when there was any possible cause for celebration.

Reaching the fire escape, Blair took a final glance across the rooftops around her.

Most of the buildings in the Old Bank District had been converted to residential loft apartments, and judging by the thumping bass notes below, more than a few had parties in progress.

But a majority of the occupants, she suspected, were celebrating at the bars along South Main Street. She'd only encountered a few civilians so far, none of whom gave her a second glance. Even from her current location, she could hear the raucous crowds, catch hints of cigarette and marijuana smoke being carried on the calm breeze.

Adjusting her backpack straps, Blair descended the fire

escape toward the empty alley. All in all, it was a perfect night to slip to her destination undetected.

After setting foot on the pavement, Blair began walking down the alley while checking over her shoulder to see if anyone had noticed her. The coast was clear behind her, and she was in the process of turning her head to the front when she collided with a backpack worn by a woman striding out from between buildings.

"Sorry," the two women said, almost in unison.

Blair scanned the civilian's appearance, trying to end the encounter as quickly as possible while simultaneously determining whether she'd been recognized.

Nothing about the other woman's appearance, however, indicated either suspicion or a likelihood to alert authorities. She had darker skin, artificially blonde hair pulled into a ponytail, and accessories that immediately put Blair at ease: skull-and-crossbones earrings, black fingernails, and Converse All Stars.

The woman was likewise taking in Blair's attire, an expression of pity crossing her features as her eyes danced across the hardhat, utility vest, and service backpack.

"They're making you work tonight?"

"Can you believe it?" Blair replied. "Outage on East Third, and we've got to check all the subsidiary breakers. Last night I wanted to be working."

"Seriously," the other woman agreed. "Good luck with that."

Then she was gone, continuing on her way without so much as a backward glance.

When the woman had vanished from sight, Blair transmitted into the radio mic hidden in her shirt collar.

"Ran into a civilian at the base of the fire escape—she's gone now."

Sterling replied over her earpiece.

"*Were you compromised?*"

It was a fair question; without her disguise, Blair would have been one of the most easily recognized faces in LA. So too would Sterling, and for similar reasons.

But both had taken extensive precautions to alter their appearance, and Blair responded, "No. We're good to proceed."

"*All right,*" Sterling said. "*Let's get moving.*"

Blair did, leading the way for her team as they approached JB Porter Federal Bank.

2

STERLING

Swiping a bead of sweat from beneath his hardhat, Sterling adjusted the straps of the massive backpack that may as well have been filled with bowling balls.

He half-turned to the man walking across the rooftop beside him.

"Could you have possibly made this any heavier?"

Alec was similarly attired in a utility uniform, his face dimly visible in the ambient light as he replied in his Boston accent.

"You want a comfortable walk in, or you want this thing popped in record time? Because you can only have one. Besides," he added with a grin, "Marco's got the heaviest pack."

Marco replied a moment later, his Russian lilt more pronounced under the exertion of hauling the weight across their route.

"Don't remind me." He slowed as he withdrew his phone and checked the display.

Sterling asked, "We still good with the surveillance video feed?"

Marco replaced his phone. "And the landline alarm, and wireless, and the cellular. We own it."

With a grunt of approval, Sterling located the fire escape stairs at the edge of the roof. He'd almost reached them when Blair transmitted over his earpiece.

"*I'm one minute out from the target. Last call before I step in front of a camera.*"

Sterling answered, "You're clear, go ahead."

Then he led the way down the fire escape, Alec and Marco clanging on the metal steps behind him. Glancing down, he was pleased to see the alley free of people—and mildly surprised that Blair had already encountered a civilian. He'd intentionally planned this heist to occur when most people would be indoors to ring in the New Year; though unlike any heist he'd ever done before, this one wasn't for financial gain.

No, he thought, tonight's job was about something far more valuable than money could buy, and he intended to see it through at all costs.

Sterling reached the alley and followed the path that Blair had crossed minutes earlier. He soon saw the target building, and even in the alley's murky shadows, it was a sight to behold.

JB Porter Federal Bank was a historic structure, one of the oldest continually operating financial institutions in California. Even the back of the building was finished in the same glorious art deco style of the forward-facing walls, the limestone surfaces adorned with intricate geometric patterns between bold columns. For a moment, Sterling felt like he was in the ranks of the Great Depression-era bank robbers—though men like John Dillinger weren't exactly known for the levels of discretion and technical proficiency that Sterling's crew would be relying on tonight.

Locating the rear entrance, he was pleased to see that Blair had already picked the deadbolt with the help of a covert entry tool tailored to the lock, and was now swinging open the metal door for them to enter.

He swept past her without a word, swapping his hardhat for a headlamp and casting a red beam of light through the bank's dark interior. He moved quickly, eager to drop his pack, breathing the office smells of fresh paper and printer ink and hearing that most treasured sound on any late-night heist effort: silence.

No chiming of an alarm system on a timer, no clanging siren alerting everyone within earshot that four thieves had just entered, and while Sterling wasn't necessarily surprised— after all, Marco's ability to bypass anything and everything digital was the stuff of legend—he still felt immeasurably grateful.

He came to a stop before an obstacle that was decidedly more analog, one that not even Marco could overcome. No cyber-wizardry stood a chance here, and Sterling felt a momentary sense of awe at the sight of the ten-foot circle of armored steel forming the bank's vault door.

The imposing structure was made more so by what Sterling knew remained unseen. Twenty-four bolts radiated from the door to the vault's reinforced concrete walls, locking the enormous metal disc in place against every method of intrusion from acetylene torches to explosives. Modern vault doors were square or rectangular; this circular door was a monolithic throwback to the era of great banks, and the only way to get it open before daybreak was to figure out and enter the correct combination.

And that was where Alec came in.

3

BLAIR

By the time Blair locked the rear door and rejoined her three teammates, they'd already dropped their packs, and Sterling and Marco were retrieving components that they handed to Alec in sequence.

Blair set down her hardhat and activated her headlamp as she took a place next to Alec.

The vault door's central feature was an enormous wheel with eight spokes, with a single latch handle beside it. But the team was currently focused on a small finger dial between these two that was slightly bigger than the circumference of a padlock.

Blair helped Alec mount a heavy metal disc over the dial, clanking it into place with a magnetic backing until the dial emerged through a central cutout. Then they screwed a set of four metal poles into threads on the disc, each two feet long.

Then came the engine, an enormous black box that attached to a forty-pound metal tripod. Both seemed like overkill, but when the clock was ticking and you were detecting internal mechanical deviations down to the micron, both the power and the stability of the combined setup were essential.

Sterling and Marco maneuvered the tripod-mounted engine behind the dial, and Blair and Alec connected the metal poles to the engine's attachment points for additional support.

Then came the sensors: suction-based microphones that would act as stethoscopes, translating vibrations within the vault door to digital signals. Using a tape measure, Alec placed the sensors at strategic points on the vault door, each corresponding to an internal component divined from the original patent specifications.

As Marco prepared a tablet and connected it to the engine, Blair installed the final component on the assembly: a round vise that wrapped neatly around the dial, connected by a horizontal pole attached to the tripod-mounted engine.

Taking the tablet from Marco, Alec consulted the display readout before tapping a green button on the screen.

The engine emitted a thin electric whine before spinning the dial left and right with impossible speed in a whirring series of clicks.

Within seconds, Alec said, "We just struck out on the eleven common factory-default combinations. As old as this bank is, I was hoping we'd get lucky."

Sterling replied, "We don't need to be lucky as long as your robot works as advertised."

"It's an auto dialer," Alec said defensively. "And what's so hard to understand? There's an accelerometer, a step motor, a rotary encoder, and an analog-to-digital converter. Simple. Plus the motor, software to analyze data and reduce permutations, and a lot of sophisticated sensing technology."

Sterling shook his head. "Your knowledge with this stuff is

fascinating. It's like you only have a viable IQ when there's a safe involved."

"What do you mean, *only* when there's a safe involved?"

Marco interjected, "Yesterday you came to work with your T-shirt on backward."

"It was a new shirt, and the cut was...weird."

Sterling placed his hands on his hips and asked the team, "We taking bets on how long the robot takes?"

"Auto dialer," Alec corrected him.

Sterling ignored him. "Because I say four hours, if that—there are a million possible combinations."

Blair said, "Two and a half, tops. This model of vault door has a 'slop' of one, meaning plus or minus one digit from the correct number will still fall within the solution gate, so the auto dialer is probing in multiples of three. That brings us down to under 36,000 combinations."

Alec shook his head. "It doesn't have to run through every possible combo, only determine the location of solution gates."

Marco folded his arms. "You say that like it means something to the rest of us."

"This thing is basically a giant, three-wheel combination lock, right? Each of those three wheels has twelve indents, called gates. Eleven are basically decoys, and only one is deep enough to fit the fence—that's the 'solution gate.' Line up all three solution gates, the fence fits in, and Bob's your uncle."

Blair cringed.

"Did you just say 'Bob's your uncle?'"

"I was watching BBC last night. So the auto dialer is feeling for mechanical deviation indicative of the solution gate, to determine the combo one number at a time. And since we're doing set testing, the auto dialer sets the first two wheels, then searches for the solution gate on the last wheel. Once it finds it, it works backward to the first two wheels so it doesn't zero out the lock and have to start over every time. That drops us down to three hours in the worst-case scenario, but in my testing we usually had the combo by—"

The tablet chimed and Alec stopped speaking, consulting the screen before he looked at Sterling and announced, "Third wheel number is 67, and it's working on the second wheel now. Care to revise that four-hour estimate?"

"No," Sterling said. "Even robots get lucky."

"Auto dialer."

"Whatever. We could still be waiting hours for it to figure out the next two numbers."

"Maybe, maybe not."

Marco interjected, "Seven minutes, thirty seconds."

Alec gave him an appreciative nod.

"Well look who's coming off the top rope with an optimistic estimate. That's a first for you, buddy—making me proud."

"Well," Marco said, "don't be. My faith isn't in you, it's in the software of the robot."

"Auto dialer."

"Because if you were half the lock whisperer you claim to be, you'd be doing all this by hand."

Alec rolled his eyes. "Sure, Marco. Great idea. Let's hang out here for eight hours while I sweat profusely trying to feel for clicks like it's the 1800s."

The tablet chimed again, and Alec continued, "Well look at that—second wheel number is 26, and now we're off to the final one."

Blair blurted out, "Thirty seconds. We'll have the final number in thirty seconds."

"I'll take that bet," Marco said solemnly. "And give you a plus or minus three-second margin of error."

"What are we betting?"

"Pizza for the whole team when we get back to the warehouse."

Blair nodded. "You're on."

Sterling said, "Fifteen seconds left—not looking good, Blair."

She focused on the tablet. "Come on, robot."

"Auto dialer," Alec said.

"Ten seconds," Marco said. "Five...four...three..."

The tablet chimed, a final number frozen on the screen as Blair read it aloud.

"91, and with two seconds to spare. Don't forget, Marco: I like pepperoni and extra cheese."

Marco gave a bow of concession, then detached the horizontal pole and moved the tripod-mounted engine backward with Sterling's help. Blair and Alec went to work detaching the auto dialer from the vault face.

Then Alec cranked the vault door's latch handle ninety degrees, spinning the wheel counterclockwise like a ship captain trying to avoid an iceberg. Blair could hear the steel bolts retracting into the vault door, and with a final, soft clank, Alec pulled the vault door open with the words, "*Sésame, ouvre-toi.*"

Sterling addressed Alec and Marco.

"Start packing up the robot."

"Still an auto dialer," Alec replied, stripping the components from the vault door and handing them to Marco.

Blair was already entering the vault, with Sterling slipping in behind her.

4

STERLING

The vault interior split in two directions, and Sterling followed Blair left to a hinged glass door. Now that they were past the main door, most of the inner locks were simple affairs. Blair was already inserting a tension wrench into the bottom of a keyhole on a door handle.

Then she slid the needle-like extension of an electric pick gun into the center of the keyhole, forcing the lock pins out of the cylinder. She squeezed the pick gun's trigger, causing it to emit a high-pitched buzzing sound as it vibrated against the pins. By simultaneously applying pressure to her tension wrench, she was able to turn the lock cylinder as easily as if she held the key.

She twisted the handle and pushed the door open, Sterling holding it for her as she entered their final destination. The walls glinted with the reflection of their headlamps—floor-to-ceiling safe deposit boxes lined the room, with additional rows of shelving arrayed like bookcases in a library.

Blair made her way to her personal safe deposit box, one she'd reserved while still an active FBI agent. Which was, of course, the last time she'd seen it. The events since then—her transition from law enforcement to heist crew member chief among them—had precluded her return until now.

"Right here," she said, indicating a ten-by-ten-inch box labeled 1159. Beneath the number were two keyholes spaced inches apart, one for the customer's key and one for the bank representative's guard key. Since Blair had long since lost possession of her key, they'd have to pick both locks simultaneously; and since excessive vibration from an electric pick gun could disrupt the pins in the opposite lock, they'd be going manual.

Which was no hardship for Sterling. Sure, there were a few special considerations for safe deposit locks—a hooked pick with a greater tip angle than that required for most pin tumbler locks, a special tension wrench—but they had the tools and had rehearsed this procedure ad nauseum back at the warehouse.

But the warehouse offered no opportunity for suave coolness quite like a heist did, and as they readied their tools, he asked, "You up for another bet?"

She was already inserting her tension wrench into the keyhole, and Sterling did the same as she replied, "When have I not been?"

Together, they slid their hooked picks inside their respective keyholes.

Sterling said, "Go," and the game was on—both of them applying pressure to their tension wrenches and working their picks to set the lock pins from front to back.

Then Sterling asked, "So what do I win when I open my side first?"

"Marco's already buying pizza. How far do you want to push your luck?"

"It's not luck, it's skill," he said. Now the lockpicking process was getting interesting; after setting three tumblers,

Sterling had to release tension on his wrench to move pins deeper in the lock. That risked dropping all pins simultaneously, which would hand Blair an easy win.

Sterling said, "How about a kiss?"

"I've already kissed you. Twice."

"The second was on the cheek. Doesn't count."

"You're on. Unless I win, in which case..."

"Yes?"

"You owe me a bottle of wine with my pizza."

Sterling felt the penultimate pin give way and moved to set the final one. "Done."

Blair bumped him with her hip. "You're crowding me."

"You're crowding *me*," Sterling shot back.

"Well, I guess I'll just get out of your way, then."

Sterling set the final pin, but it was too late—Blair was already turning her cylinder with a click.

"A chardonnay sounds nice, don't you think?" she said in a triumphant voice.

With a dissatisfied grunt, Sterling muttered, "You got it." Rotating his cylinder clear of the pins, he opened the small silver door and recovered his tools along with Blair.

Then he slid the safe deposit box out of its casing—it was surprisingly light for a two-foot-long container— and turned the opening clasp toward Blair.

She opened the lid, revealing a single object: a small black velvet bag, scarcely the size of a pack of cigarettes. It was a small item to go to all this trouble for, he thought as Blair plucked it from the box, held it to her ear, and gave it a shake.

Both of them heard the click of tiny cassette tape cases within, and Blair said, "We're good. I'm out of here."

5
BLAIR

Leaving Sterling to re-pick the safe deposit box and room door into their locked positions, Blair moved past the vault door to see Alec and Marco packing up the myriad equipment components in preparation to move.

Marco pointed to a laundry bag on the floor. "Your wardrobe's in there."

"Thanks," she said, stripping off her utility vest and uniform to reveal the attire beneath: black shorts and a tank top under a blue blouse, along with a ball cap, purse, and nonprescription glasses that she hastily put on. It never hurt to have notable elements that could be ditched if she needed to quickly change her appearance. Together with the blonde wig and green colored contacts she'd worn into the heist, Blair could probably withstand an initial lineup, and didn't fear the passing scrutiny of a largely drunken crowd. The last thing remaining was her footwear, and she quickly transitioned from utility boots to fashionable sneakers.

The combined effect was just unremarkable enough to blend in, while allowing her to run should the need arise.

Stuffing the bag of voice recorder cassette tapes into her pocket, she said, "Marco, am I good?"

He checked his phone, consulting the surveillance camera feed that was now hijacked and streaming to him in real time, all while presenting a pre-recorded version of events to the security office.

"You're clear. Enjoy the party."

"Alec, I'll see you at the car."

"Give me twenty minutes—just need to get the robot out of here."

"Auto dialer," she called over her shoulder.

"See that, Marco?" Alec muttered in her wake. "Now you people even have me saying it..."

Then Blair was off, moving to the bank's back door. She stopped before it and took a final breath before pushing the door open and exiting into the warm night air.

Walking out with her teammates was an option, but not a great one: a single report of a suspicious group of utility workers could result in the capture of her team along with the heavy and expensive equipment used to break into the bank vault. For this reason, the team preferred whenever possible to separate their captured item from all equipment used to obtain it, and get that precious cargo as far from the crime scene as quickly as possible.

Normally, the streets of the Historic Core in Downtown LA at this hour would be a decent place for a recognizable fugitive like Blair to blend in, but when the night in question was New Year's Eve, there was no better place.

She emerged onto the sidewalk to find people sweeping toward the local bars, couples and groups of friends who appeared to have begun drinking at home before hitting the streets. Others were already stumbling back home, having planned to watch the ball drop in Times Square on a bar television but finding themselves unable to sustain the three-hour drinking effort required to ring in the New Year in their local time zone.

Turning right at the corner, she entered the bar strip with a sense of relief. String lights crisscrossed over the street and sidewalk, casting a festive glow to the noisy, largely drunken celebrants below. Blair slipped through the crowds of people stepping outside for bar hopping, cigarettes, and weed, noting as she did so that the LAPD was out in force tonight: she passed one officer strolling the opposite direction, and caught sight of another standing across the street. She could have expected as much: in addition to this being a nighttime hotspot, the LAPD had a community station just a few blocks away on East 6th Street.

But neither officer paid her any mind, and why would they? Even a semi-sober civilian was the least of their concerns amid the New Year's Eve debauchery, and by now, Blair had mastered the art of walking casually in crowded public areas. Contrary to popular belief, the best hiding place for a fugitive was not in some remote small town where everyone knew their neighbors. Large cities like Los Angeles provided a blanket of anonymity because no one knew the vast majority of their fellow residents and most couldn't have cared less, bringing a strange sense of comfort.

She wouldn't have to travel far now, just three more blocks to a parking garage where they'd staged one of four drop cars in preparation for escape contingencies. Blair wouldn't drive, of course: the likelihood of a random DUI checkpoint tonight made that prospect far too risky. Instead, she'd stay in the car until her teammates had dropped the utility equipment in their own vehicle, then wait for them to drop off Alec so he could drive her car home while she hid in the trunk.

That was, of course, if everything went according to plan.

But Blair's first indication that the plan was about to change came when the door to a bar beside her burst open, revealing one man shoving another down to the sidewalk. Blair almost tripped over them, then stumbled backward as a third man darted out of the bar wielding a pool cue like a baseball bat, managing a half-swing downward before being tackled from behind.

Then the melee began, bodies spilling out of the bar and swirling around her. She turned to flee only to find her escape blocked by someone bumping into her from behind, apparently eager to get a view of the confrontation if not join it. By the time Blair caught her footing, she looked up just in time to see a twenty-something man throwing a fist that connected with another man's face.

The volume of noise on the street went from normal to deafening as the sounds of shouted profanities and shattered glass rang out. It was impossible to see through the chaos as a body pummeled into her from the side, shoving her off balance as a cold slurry of liquor and ice slapped her chest, drenching her shirt.

She tried to move backward, then forward, as the mass of bodies blocked her escape from all directions. Someone hurled a chair through the open doorway, and Blair vaguely registered a man on the street grabbing it and throwing it back.

Then she felt the first direct aggression against her—a hand grabbed her right wrist with an iron grip, the perpetrator somewhere to Blair's rear.

A dozen hand-to-hand combat lessons from the FBI Academy fired into her brain at once. Blair instinctively spun toward her attacker, slapping her left hand atop his and pinning it to her opposite wrist. Then she swung her right arm in a counterclockwise arc, twisting the man's body sideways by using his locked arm as a fulcrum. He was spun half away from her as she prepared for her next move: a forceful downward shove of his immobilized arm, a maneuver that would drive him to the ground before she made her escape.

But she never made it that far.

The arm she was gripping, locked at the elbow with the wrist torqued, was covered by a dark blue sleeve bearing the triple chevron patch of an LAPD sergeant.

Blair released him immediately, preparing for a hasty retreat through the crowd, but it was too late—a second officer dove in from the side, threading his arm under hers and placing both hands on the back of her neck in the time it took her to realize what was happening.

By then she was falling face-first toward the concrete, her body absorbing the impact as the officer wrested one hand over her head and hastily cuffed her wrist. Blair didn't resist; the only thing worse than having her hands cuffed was having them simultaneously pinned behind her back, and she narrowly avoided that fate by remaining compliant as her opposite arm was pulled upward.

"You don't understand," she said, panting for breath, "I didn't do anything." That was both true and not true, she thought, as the officer applied the other cuff, restraining her hands together.

"Nice try, lady."

By then multiple cops were converging on the fight, pushing their way through the crowd and pinning assailants to the ground. The officer who'd restrained her grabbed Blair under the arms and hoisted her upright, passing her along a row of officers leading their captives to an LAPD paddy wagon parked on the street. To Blair, it looked like an ice cream truck from hell—the back door was open, revealing seated occupants who'd been detained earlier in the night. This thing had probably been shuttling drunks to and from the local station for hours now, and the officers manning it seemed to be at the peak of monotony for their professional duties as they shoved the accused over the truck's rear step and into the back.

Blair couldn't break free and run, and even if she did, her handcuffs would make escape impossible. Then she was at the loading step, being escorted into the paddy wagon's brightly lit interior. Six cuffed men were already seated on benches inside, with several more following behind her.

"Yeah," one of them called, "we got a woman!"

Blair said nothing, falling into an open seat as her escorting officer called back, "Shut up. You're going to sleep it off at the station."

Except for her, Blair thought. For one thing, she was the only sober passenger, and secondly, she'd barely make it to the fingerprinting portion of her booking procedure before they realized *exactly* who she was. Now that she'd been out of prison for years, she felt a crushing sense of disbelief that of all possible ways to return, it had come down to this: being rolled up in a random street brawl that she had nothing to do with.

Blair whispered into her hidden radio mic.

"Guys...I've got a serious problem."

6

STERLING

Sterling was leading Marco and Alec across the apartment rooftop when he heard Blair's radio call over his earpiece.

"Guys...I've got a serious problem."

"Send it," Sterling transmitted back.

"I got caught up in a bar fight and thrown in an LAPD paddy wagon parked off East 4th and Los Angeles Street."

Alec wondered out loud, "What was she doing in a bar?"

Sterling dropped his pack, patting his pockets to ensure he had his lockpicking tools. Then he said to his teammates, "Get to the truck and stand by for pickup."

He was gone before Marco or Alec could reply, racing back to the fire escape and taking the stairs three at a time on his way to the ground.

Transmitting on the run, he replied to Blair, "I'm coming for you. Let me know if the truck starts moving."

As he hit the alley and began threading his way between buildings, he considered the lunacy of this situation. Sterling was disguised in much the same manner as Blair—different hair and eye color, wardrobe accessories he could don or ditch as needed—but in the end, none of that could withstand an up-close examination.

Turning right onto East 4th, he began running south, pushing past the drunken crowds around him. Sterling felt exalted as he caught sight of the paddy wagon, still parked just off the curb ahead.

To his dismay, though, it began rolling forward.

Blair transmitted a moment later, "*Truck is moving.*"

Sterling didn't reply—he was reviewing a mental map, assessing the route the LAPD truck would take toward the nearest police station on East 6th. They'd turn right on Los Angeles Street, and his only chance now was to catch them at the stoplight with Winston Street.

There was a single alley between buildings to his right, blocked by a seven-foot cast iron fence. Sterling was up and over the top with a leap and two resets of his foot placement, touching down on the far side to a smattering of applause from the drunken civilians he'd just left behind.

Then Sterling was running down the long alleyway's misshapen brick surface, the buildings on either side covered in murals and graffiti as he weaved between parked vehicles, dumpsters, and piles of trash, heading toward the gate standing between him and Winston Street. Before he reached it, the building to his right opened up to a gated parking lot, and he registered a security guard shouting for him to stop.

No luck there, he thought—he was already vaulting onto the final iron gate, planting a foot on the top to send himself into freefall on the far side.

He cut left, racing down the sidewalk toward Los Angeles Street just in time to see the light ahead turn green; and after an SUV and two sedans slipped by his view, so too did the LAPD truck.

Sterling cut right into the street behind it, charging toward the rear panel marked with *LAPD*, *POLICE*, and red text spelling out *KEEP BACK 200 FT*.

A conveniently located rear step bar hovered a foot off the pavement, probably a useful accessory when loading and unloading prisoners from the elevated cargo space. Sterling located a single latch handle on the rear door, the only other purchase to be found on the otherwise flat truck backside, and with three sprinting steps, he leapt aboard the step and clung to the latch handle with both hands.

Now he was an outside stowaway on a moving LAPD truck, and the only thing remaining was to somehow pick the lock without falling from his perch.

Examining the keyhole, he kept his right hand on the door handle and used his left to withdraw an electric pick gun from his kit. Tucking the pick gun under his armpit, he felt for a tension wrench, struggling to locate the thin bent strip of metal amid the vehicle's vibration.

Once he located the tool, he was faced with two conflicting possibilities: either pick the lock, or maintain his only hold on the door handle.

He settled for a hasty compromise, inserting one end of the tension wrench into the keyhole, then transferring control of it to his right thumb while clasping the handle with his other four fingers. Grabbing the electric pick gun from under his arm, he slid the jagged needle attachment into the center of the keyhole, then pulled the trigger to initiate the vibrations that would—hopefully—knock each pin back into its tumbler on the cylinder.

But that was only half the challenge. The other half was maintaining continuous pressure on the tension wrench in order to turn the cylinder at the instant its pins had returned to their keyed position. At present he could only maintain that force through the tenuous contact point of his right thumb, and do so from an awkward angle at the risk of losing his grip.

The door handle wouldn't budge.

Sterling repeated the process, squeezing the trigger of his pick gun as it vibrated in his grasp, all while applying gradually escalating pressure on the tension wrench. Too much pressure and the tool would break inside the lock; too little and he wouldn't open it at all.

Just as he was certain the tension wrench was about to snap, the cylinder gave way and the handle twisted.

The door started to fling open with him on the wrong side of it, and he pirouetted sideways with one foot on the rear step bar. Releasing his pick gun to clatter against the street below, he caught a finger hold on the edge of the door.

But it wasn't enough. He felt his body teetering back on the stair as the truck accelerated through a turn.

At that moment, a pair of hands seized his shirtfront, pulling him upright and stabilizing him against the vehicle. Looking up, Sterling saw Blair.

Her face was strangely tranquil as she held him in place, providing the momentary stability he'd need for his next maneuver.

"Go," she said, releasing his shirt.

Without so much as a second's hesitation, Sterling hopped backward off the rear stair, impacting the street with both knees bent to absorb the impact. He stumbled forward a few steps, then accelerated into a run to support Blair's exit from the moving vehicle.

She landed in the same way he did, launching into a clumsy series of steps with her wrists handcuffed—and just as she began to fall forward, Sterling caught her.

"Come on," he said, giving a momentary glance to their

surroundings before racing toward the best spot his instinct could divine.

Looking over his shoulder, he saw Blair running behind him—and by then, drunks were spilling out of the back of the LAPD paddy wagon as it continued cruising down the street. Most of them hit the pavement and rolled to a stop, struggling to their feet with whooping victory cheers at their newfound freedom.

Returning his gaze forward, Sterling focused on his destination: the ramp entrance of a parking garage. Not, unfortunately, one of the *four* parking garages where they'd staged a drop car, but nonetheless a good place to hide out until his teammates could arrive.

After they'd darted into the shadows of the vehicle ramp, Sterling fished a keyring out of his pocket, handing it to Blair as he transmitted, "I've got her; we're at the elevated public parking lot on Los Angeles Street between 5th Street and East 6th."

Blair had located the ceramic key on his keyring, and used it to spring one cuff by the time Marco replied.

"We're on our way. Seven to eight minutes depending on traffic."

Sterling led Blair up the ramp, where they emerged onto rooftop parking. He assessed their emergency avenues out of the garage, finding a foot entrance into a shopping center and two treetops close enough to make the leap to. Otherwise, there was no shortage of places to hazard a two-story hanging fall onto the pavement below. It wasn't the greatest spot for them to bide their time, but by far the best of their present options.

A sudden chorus of shouts from the streets below startled him, and he grabbed Blair's arm in preparation to bolt.

She brushed his hand away, and he heard the shouting congeal into a unified series of cries.

"*Ten! Nine! Eight!*"

Sterling turned to Blair. "Are you okay?"

"I'm fine."

"*Five! Four!*"

Sterling gave a momentary thought to how ridiculous she looked—blonde wig askew from the escape but fake glasses somehow still in place. He knew he didn't look much better, still panting for breath from his run.

He took her hands as the final cries arose from the streets of LA.

"*Two! One!* Happy New Year!"

A sporadic volley of fireworks soared into the sky above them, exploding into flashes of color as he asked, "So how about that kiss?"

She leaned forward and kissed him on the lips.

"Happy New Year, Sterling." His smile faded as she continued, "You still owe me that bottle of chardonnay."

7

BLAIR

Blair slid into the minivan backseat, joined by Sterling entering through the opposite side.

Then Alec accelerated, steering the vehicle along their route back to the warehouse.

Marco turned around from the passenger seat and asked, "You two okay?"

"We're fine," Blair said. "Safe to say we've never had a simple getaway go sideways quite like that one."

Sterling added, "And we better not have one again."

They had an hour drive back to their warehouse hideout in the industrial district of Moreno Valley, and Alec took a right turn toward US-101 as he asked, "Blair, what were you doing in a bar?"

"What?"

"You said over the radio you got caught in a bar fight."

"Yeah. A fight on the street *outside* a bar."

"That's a street fight."

"Who cares what it's called? And why would I be in a bar?"

"I dunno," he admitted. "You're the one who said it."

Marco interjected, "Alec's not cracking a safe anymore.

Let's all lower our expectations. Blair, tell me you still have the tapes."

Blair pulled the black velvet bag out of her pocket, examining it under the glow of streetlights. "Yeah. That's the one thing that went according to plan."

Sterling clapped his hands together and began rubbing his palms.

"Let's see what we got—time for that scumbag Jim Jacobson to say goodbye to his political career."

She was eager to check on the condition of the tiny cassette tapes, hoping that none of them had broken in the course of the evening's festivities. But all told, she'd collected hours of audio that implicated Jim in widespread corruption, and needed only a small fraction of that to stop his seemingly endless rise to power. Uncinching the bag, she withdrew the first cassette case and cracked it open.

It was empty.

Blair instantly second-guessed her memories of legally visiting the safe deposit box—she hadn't placed any empty cases in the bag, so far as she could remember.

Replacing the case for a second one, she opened it to see that it, too, was empty.

"No," she said. "I'm missing cassettes."

Sterling asked, "Where did you drop them?"

By then she was searching the third case. "I didn't drop them. The cases are all here—the cassettes themselves are gone."

"Jim must have gotten to them first. How could he have known where you were keeping them?"

"He couldn't have," she replied, opening the fourth and final case before halting abruptly.

This case wasn't empty.

Inside was a slip of paper, neatly S-folded to fit. Blair

plucked it out, unfolding it to see the blank side. Flipping it over, she announced, "There's a piece of paper in here. It's not mine."

"Well, what does it say?"

"I don't understand it—it's just a date, a time, and some numbers. February 15, 6:30 p.m. GMT."

Marco said, "Greenwich Mean Time. What are the other numbers?"

"2311647754.onion, PIN 0375."

A stunned silence fell over the minivan, with the exception of Marco, who was nodding knowingly from the passenger seat.

Turning to face Sterling and Blair, he said, "Jim didn't take the tapes. It was someone else—someone who wants to sell them."

"How do you know that?"

"Because those numbers," he continued, "are the login for a dark web chatroom."

8

STERLING

Sterling's footfalls hammered across the treadmill, his breath coming in ragged spurts as he closed in on the five-mile mark. Running had been an enjoyable pastime since he was a kid, and in his current line of work it was a matter of professional necessity.

But at the moment, it simply felt cathartic.

His frustration wasn't so much based on his crew's failure to recover the tapes—he'd been on his share of heists aborted before completion, usually in the interests of preventing arrest. Being outfoxed by a fellow thief, however, was an indignity that Sterling had never suffered before. Adding insult to injury was the fact that he now had no choice but to wait until the appointed time to attend some kind of virtual meeting on the dark web, when this unknown thief would presumably dictate terms that Sterling would be powerless to challenge.

Yet while those thoughts dominated his mind for most of the past week, the treadmill was a sacred place. For the duration of his running workouts, Sterling felt unburdened, his body alive with exertion and his mind cleared of troubles.

He heard Alec call out behind him.

"Hey, boss."

Sterling held up a finger, then throttled the treadmill speed up with two presses of a button. His distance traveled ticked from 4.98 miles to 4.99, and for a moment Sterling feared the embarrassment of being outpaced by the treadmill belt and flung backward.

But his footfalls remained steady, focus steeled on the final stretch as the treadmill emitted a beep and powered down: 5.00 miles in 32 minutes and 12 seconds.

His stride slowed along with the treadmill, his sprint dwindling to a jog and then a walk before he ended the session and let the belt come to a halt. He'd return for a cooldown walk later; Alec had been kept waiting long enough.

Sterling turned first to see himself in the mirror—shirtfront drenched in sweat, face blotched with effort—then across the warehouse gym to find Alec holding up an envelope. The only sound in the room came from a rowing machine churning in the corner, presently manned by Blair as she stroked with a steady, rhythmic pace.

Sterling grabbed his towel and patted down his face as he approached Alec. "What is it?"

Alec handed him the envelope.

"Mail call. Looks like a donation."

Sterling tossed the towel over his shoulder, examining the envelope to see it was addressed to one of the several PO boxes the crew maintained throughout LA using a network of false identities. There was no return address, but the handwriting and postmark told Sterling all he needed to know about the sender.

He hesitated, holding the envelope with sweaty fingertips that saturated the paper.

Seeming to sense his trepidation, Alec asked, "Want me to stick around?"

"No. Thanks."

Alec left, and Sterling glanced in the mirror to see Blair continuing to operate her rowing machine, oblivious to the exchange that had just occurred. He considered whether to read the envelope's contents in private, then felt impatience get the better of him as he tore the flap open.

Inside was a check that he analyzed for a moment before allowing his eyes to tick to its upper-right-hand corner. The check number ended with a nine, and he absorbed that fact as his pulse—still elevated from the run—began to quicken even further. Returning the check to the envelope, Sterling withdrew a handwritten note that he unfolded and scanned, his eyes darting across the text with increasing speed.

Then he re-folded the note and slipped it back inside, the envelope trembling slightly in his hands. Whether that was due to his recently finished workout or the mounting sense of rage surging through his system, he couldn't be sure. But his next actions were calm, routine, almost automatic.

Sterling set the envelope down on a weight bench, then wiped off his face before draping the towel across the bar. He took two steps to the dumbbell rack, retrieved a five-pound weight, and spun to hurl it at the wall.

The dumbbell sailed just over twelve feet before impacting a mirror at shoulder height, creating a circular fracture the size of a dinner plate before clattering to the ground.

Sterling stared at himself in the shattered mirror, blinking quickly as he tried to slow his breathing from the rapid-fire pace that had overtaken his lungs. He felt a hand on his shoulder, saw Blair's fragmented reflection in the mirror.

"Whatever the mirror did to piss you off, you've won. Want to tell me what's in that envelope?"

He took a step back from her, letting her hand fall, and began pacing.

"A donation to the EPS."

Blair shook her head.

"Am I supposed to know what that is?"

"The Eagle Protection Society," he replied, snatching up the envelope and shaking it at her. "The EPS is life after crime."

"I don't understand."

Swallowing hard, Sterling explained.

"It's a shell charity I set up for clandestine communication with my mom. I send her a donation request with the official letterhead, and she sends a check along with a coded response."

Blair lifted her hands. "And?"

"You know about my mom's business?"

"Sure," she said. "The hardware store in Upstate New York, right?"

Sterling nodded, his sweaty grip tightening on the envelope. "Well she started it with my father. For him, it was a means to acquire all the equipment he needed as a thief, and to launder all the money he stole. But my mom had nothing to do with that, and the business has been a hundred percent legitimate since he passed."

Blair's eyes narrowed. She was expecting the worst, and spared him the trouble of breaking the news to her. "So this is about Jim's threat—the one he made while you were in prison?"

"Yeah. The investigation that would tie her every asset—house, car, savings—to my late father's criminal activity. She stands to lose everything, and that's before we consider the possibility of—"

"Criminal charges," Blair finished the sentence for him.

"Right." He nodded. "In which case she's looking at prison time. That threat was intended to strongarm me and her into giving up the crew. But seeing as neither of us did, and you broke me out of prison shortly after that, Jim never had a chance to make good on it. And to be honest, I wasn't sure if he'd cut his losses and forget about her...until now."

"Sterling." She pointed to the envelope. "What did she say?"

"The odd-numbered check means she's replying under duress. And the note apologizes that this is the most she can contribute for the time being, because she's about to fall on hard times." He crumpled the envelope into a tight ball. "That means she's received a warning—Jim is coming after her."

9

JIM

Jim Jacobson was lost in thought in his Albany office, eyes glazing over the talking points on his computer screen, when a male voice spoke from the doorway without introduction.

"Have you read over the white paper yet?"

Jim hadn't even heard the door open, and looked up to see his campaign manager, a well-muscled man seven years his junior.

By way of response, Jim picked up the sheaf of bound paper from the desk beside him, waving it at the door before dropping it.

"'The Future of Sustainable Agribusiness,'" he quoted the title from memory. "Not exactly riveting reading material."

His campaign manager didn't look amused.

"It's riveting to the Chairman of the Albany County Agricultural and Farmland Protection Board, and you speak to him at 2:30. We really need that endorsement."

"Relax," Jim replied. "I read the paper." Then he added hopefully, "Is it a phone call?"

The man shook his head. "Zoom call."

Chris Mitchell was as crisp and professional as they came.

Born in DC, he'd grown up in the political game, yet had never been a politician himself. That much was evident in the way he dressed, because no politician could ever pull off the kind of wardrobes that Mitchell wore to work on a daily basis.

At present he was in a sky-blue suit, dark vest, and paisley tie, with thin eyeglasses perched neatly on his face and a perpetually trimmed goatee with no mustache. Everything from his clothes to his personal grooming was indicative of a life lived with all the precision of a metronome.

Jim leaned back in his seat, gesturing to his computer. "Zoom call...and to do that, I just open the app on my computer?"

Uninvited, Mitchell rounded the desk, leaning so close that Jim could smell his cologne as he took control of the mouse and clicked.

"Just open your digital calendar. Double-click the appointment listing and you'll see the link to connect—doesn't matter if it's video or audio, you'll have the link there. I emailed your talking points yesterday."

"I've got the talking points, just new to all this social media stuff."

"It's a Zoom call, not social media. And you don't need to understand any of it. Just stick to the talking points, seem open and approachable, and make your future constituents feel valued. Your team will take care of all the backside work."

"Thanks, Chris. That'll be all."

But Mitchell didn't leave, a lack of respect that irritated Jim to no end.

"Remember," he said, "that ninety percent of House incumbents get re-elected. You're not only competing in an overwhelmingly Democratic district but in a strategic one—however District 20 falls in November, it's going to impact our neighbors in 19 and 21, and those three make up almost—"

"Half the state," Jim replied. "I'm aware."

"This is the first step in a long-term strategic takeover, Jim, *if* we can pull it off. That's why the National Committee sent me to be your manager."

Jim forced a smile. "And I'm thrilled to have you on board."

Mitchell straightened, seeming to consider whether to rattle off another fact known to both of them already—Jim certainly hoped not—or accept that he'd made his point.

Then he was gone, walking out of the office and closing the door behind him without another word.

Jim slumped in his chair. It wasn't like the election was right around the corner. He had four months until the primary, where he was uncontested as the Republican Party's first and only choice, then another five months to the general election...yet here he was, forty-five days into the new year, working a full-time campaign effort before he'd had time to unpack his moving boxes at the new house.

Checking his Rolex, he saw that he was only minutes away from his call with the county agricultural...whatever he was. Jim always kept the name of his next meeting partner front and center on his computer desktop, and this would be no exception. Also close at hand would be Mitchell's talking points, not that Jim needed them—with the team still crafting his campaign message, anything he said had to be sufficiently vague so as not to be contradicted as his platform continued to grow.

Jim pushed himself up from his chair, grabbed his suit jacket from the back of the seat, and put it on. Then he faced the mirror and tightened his tie knot, checking his teeth for any evidence of his late lunch before resuming his place before the computer.

First, he opened the file with his contact's name along with the talking points. His digital calendar was still open, courtesy of Mitchell helping himself to Jim's workspace and computer mouse, and he double-clicked the upcoming meeting. A breakout box appeared on the screen, and Jim selected the link for the event's video meeting.

A new screen appeared with the words, *Please wait, the meeting host will let you in soon.*

Whatever that means, Jim thought as he inserted his earbuds in preparation for the call. He'd already had a handful of phone calls where he'd had to remain on hold for five or ten minutes, and two in-person meetings to date where the other party had completely stood him up.

But he had to get his start in politics somewhere, he supposed, and Jim was not above working his way up from nothing. He'd done so from a street kid to the second-highest FBI rank outside of their top management, and he'd do the same for his second career—albeit with some outside help garnered along the way.

Finally the Zoom call connected, and after a second of incomprehension at the sight before him, Jim tried to stifle a laugh.

The Chairman of the Albany County Agricultural and Farmland Protection Board was either making a very ill-conceived attempt at a joke, or had forgotten to turn off some stupid camera filter. His image wasn't a camera angle of his face, but a cartoonish avatar of a hooded figure in a black cloak, floating amid a digital background of fire and smoke. The name beneath the image was WRAITH.

Jim cleared his throat. "Mr. Mason, it's a pleasure to meet you...though I seem to be having some technical issues on my end."

As he spoke, his computer screen switched to the standard camera view of himself above the name JIM JACOBSON before flipping back to WRAITH—and then Jim's earbuds transmitted the first sentence of the return exchange, which sounded like a computerized British accent.

"You have issues, Jim, but they are not technical," the voice said. "But it is a pleasure to meet you as well."

Blinking, Jim offered, "Shall we, ah, discuss your concerns for the future of agribusiness in District 20? Because I'd love to get a firsthand account of the real challenges facing your sector."

When the shadowy hood reappeared and spoke amid the backdrop of fire, Jim felt like his stomach was in freefall.

"Up for sale, I have four microcassettes' worth of audio surveillance recordings of Jim Jacobson coercing a subordinate to perform illegal acts in the service of an ongoing criminal case. He admits to the same on multiple previous occasions, citing the assistance of a 'mentor' who has brought dozens of individuals into political power at the state and national levels through long-term cultivation of their careers from various business, law enforcement, and military sectors. A number of these individuals are identified by name, and they span both sides of the political aisle. These tapes represent a skeleton key for virtually any race in the next ten years. If anyone is not interested in participating in the bidding process, please leave the chat room now."

Jim's pulse skyrocketed, a wave of heat flushing across his neck and up his face as he scanned the words. The only source of those tapes, he knew, was Blair—she'd claimed to possess recordings of their private liaisons, though Jim had no way of knowing if that was a bluff.

And frankly, he still didn't.

His first instinct was that this was a blind threat from Blair and her cronies, possibly trying to extort him like the dozen or so crackpots who had come out of the woodwork since he'd announced his Congressional run, each blackmailing him with threats ranging from conspiracy theorists to women claiming they'd raised his lovechild and demanding restitution.

Before he could process what to reply, a new avatar appeared, this one a computerized display of a man in a horned Viking helmet above the name FIXER. It spoke with a synthesized Scandinavian accent.

"What does the bidding start at?"

Wraith reappeared. "Now now. I would not have called you here if I expected instant payment. You will have ten days to raise funds. Then we will reconvene. The highest bid at that time wins the tapes. What say you, Jim?"

Jim knew he shouldn't add to this exchange, but he heard himself replying anyway.

"Nice try, Blair. But I'll save you the trouble: there are no tapes, and everything you're alleging is false."

Wraith answered, "I am not Blair, Jim. Would you like an excerpt to validate the authenticity of my tapes? How about this." An audio recording played then, indisputably of Jim's own voice. "Relax, Blair. My mentor completely buried a mountain of evidence implicating the Chair of the House Appropriations Committee for tax fraud—trust me, neither of us is going to jail."

Jim's throat was closing up now; he vaguely remembered speaking those words, assuring Blair that she'd be protected if she fabricated a report to close a heist investigation. His face on the screen was ruddy with anger as he shot back, "That's a lie. I never said that."

Wraith reappeared. "Combined with your reaction, this audio sample is more than adequate for authenticating the tapes. I will refrain from identifying any specific people mentioned as doing so would significantly lower the value of my offering. However, our final prospective buyer has been quiet so far. Are you in, or out?"

Jim was beside himself with fear at this point. If word of this got out, his career—and his marriage—were done for. That was to say nothing of the criminal charges that would undoubtedly ensue, and if his mentor cut him loose now, he'd have no protection from that.

Things were bad enough with a single competing buyer, whoever this Fixer character was. But with his mentor's funds, Jim had no doubt he would win the auction...unless the third and final buyer had access to a larger bank account, which was doubtful.

There was no immediate response. But when it came, the avatar was a smiling cartoon cloud against a blue sky, and Jim felt himself go pale.

The name beneath the cloud was THE SKY THIEVES, and the single word of response uttered in a digital voice was, "Interested."

10

BLAIR

"'Interested?'" Alec cried. "That's all you could think to say?"

Marco shrugged, spinning his chair away from the two levels of computer screens before him.

"What? We are interested."

Blair looked to Sterling in the seat beside her, seeing her own thoughts reflected in his expression: what, exactly, was going on here?

They both directed their gaze to the largest screen in Marco's office, and Sterling said, "Ask about the next meeting."

Marco typed into a chat box, pressing a key to translate his text into the voice synthesizer that caused the cartoon cloud to speak.

"Date and time to reconvene?"

Wraith appeared. "February 26, 6:30 p.m. GMT at this link. The chatroom will be disabled until then. Once the bidding concludes, the victor will have ten minutes to transfer the funds before bidding re-opens to the other parties. After the money has been received in full, I will set up a meeting to hand off the tapes."

Then the screen flipped to the Viking figure in the horned helmet as Fixer asked, "What assurance do I have that no additional copies will be made or distributed following the purchase?"

Wraith answered, "There will be no copies made. You of all people understand how this game works. I will add for all bidding parties: any mention of this transaction to the media or law enforcement will be met with repercussions against the offending party."

Jim's face flashed across the screen, the only unguarded image speaking in its own voice.

"Repercussions? What's that supposed to mean?"

Wraith answered, "I stole these tapes from the Sky Thieves, which should tell you what I am capable of. This chat is now over."

The screen went black before Marco could type a response, and he directed his efforts instead to typing and analyzing data on a separate screen.

Alec said, "Wraith didn't rob us, exactly. He robbed a safe deposit box, which I feel wasn't that big of an ask as far as—"

"Doesn't matter," Sterling cut him off. "Marco, how are we looking with the trace?"

He spun his rolling chair to face the crew.

"Not good, as I predicted. The base software to access the dark web relies on a suite of plugins that anonymizes the user's IP by routing it through a massive network of other encrypted IP addresses. I could attempt to track the participants if that's all that was used, but it looks like Wraith ran the chatroom setup using the same precautions that I did in preparation for this meeting: by running additional encryption software off a USB flash drive, which provides a self-contained, pre-configured web browser."

Blair raised her eyebrows. "And in English?"

"In English, I can see Jim's IP address in Albany, which means that Wraith deliberately linked to the surface web and probably caught him by surprise with a screen hijack. As for Wraith, Fixer, and us, not even the NSA could trace us. Which brings me to my own question: was Wraith telling the truth—did Jim mention political officials in your recordings?"

Blair pushed a tendril of hair away from her face.

"Sure he did—Jim liked to brag, and would drop names whenever he could. Some were supposed to be politicians, others were kids who got off on ugly charges through political influence. A few coverups of affairs, I think, and some mention of how different people routed money through the Caymans. But what was I supposed to do about it, tell everyone I knew a senator was sleeping with his staffer? By then I was a felon, and the only thing I cared about was making my sentence as short as possible."

Marco replied, "The problem now is that the tapes are extremely valuable. And from what we know about Jim's mentor—whoever he is—financial resources are not a problem. We've already donated half the proceeds from the Sierra Diamond, which leaves us with a depleted account, to say the least."

"Come on, guys," Alec said cheerfully. "If there's one thing we know how to do, it's steal."

Sterling leaned forward. "We need to be smart about this. Ten days isn't a lot of time, and we're not going off half-cocked trying to accumulate as much money as possible."

Alec was undaunted. "I'm not talking about money: I'm talking about the *tapes*. Wraith stole our tapes, so we steal them back."

This statement gave Sterling pause. "But Marco just said we can't trace Wraith's location."

"Maybe not over the computer," Alec conceded, "but that doesn't mean there isn't a way."

"How?"

"Dunno. How did Wraith find the safe deposit box?"

Blair threw up her hands. "I used an alias backed by fake identification, so I honestly have no idea. Best guess? After the media outed me in conjunction with the Sky Safe robbery last year, Wraith started searching my records for anything that would lead him to the Sierra Diamond. Maybe he found...I don't know, a financial record or something that led him to the bank."

"Then we need to do the same thing. Stop worrying about Marco's technical mumbo jumbo and start thinking like Wraith."

Marco's eyes narrowed. "My 'mumbo jumbo' is the exact reason we *shouldn't* spin our wheels trying to locate Wraith. We already know he has the sophistication to cover his digital tracks, and we're kidding ourselves if we think he's going to slip up before the next chatroom meeting."

Blair announced, "You're both right."

The two men looked up at her, surprised.

"Really?" Alec asked.

"We don't know where Wraith is—at least, not right now—and knowing Jim's location doesn't help us. That still leaves one big question to answer."

Sterling completed her thought. "Who is Fixer?"

"Exactly," Blair agreed. "And that's the one question we can find the answer to."

"How?" Alec asked.

"By doing what you said—thinking like Wraith. Let's put ourselves in his shoes. If we had the tapes and wanted to start a bidding war, then Jim and our crew are obvious choices. Jim is easy to find; he's running a political campaign. We're impossible to find; that's why Wraith could only reach us through a note in the safe deposit box. So who's the third party we'd be looking for, and how would we locate them? The answer to that question will lead us to Fixer in the same way that Wraith found him."

Marco sounded skeptical. "But he's bidding against us."

"Exactly. So we turn that around."

"How?"

"Our goals are the same: to put the tapes in the public domain. For us, it's just about making sure Jim goes down in flames. I don't particularly care why Fixer wants the tapes, as long as Jim is exposed to the media."

Sterling nodded. "So we don't compete against Fixer in bidding. We join forces."

"Exactly," Blair replied. "And if we're lucky, that might —*might*—be enough to overcome Jim's mentor."

Marco said, "There are a few things we already know. Fixer's concern was ensuring there were no additional copies of the tape. Pair that with Wraith's mention that either political party could benefit from a selective release of material from the tapes, and we can safely conclude that Fixer represents a political party. And since Jim is with the Republicans, that makes Fixer a Democrat."

Alec clapped his hands together. "Jim's running for a House seat. Maybe Fixer is the incumbent."

Sterling shook his head. "The incumbent has held that seat for ten years running, and New York has voted overwhelmingly Democratic since the '80s. We've got to go higher up the food chain than the battle for House representation over District 20."

"I agree," Blair said. "Wraith probably broke into that safe deposit box hoping to find the Sierra Diamond. The tapes are his consolation prize, and he's looking for a serious payday. So let's start thinking of who would pay more than us for that information—significantly more. We follow the money trail, and that will lead us to Fixer."

11

STERLING

Sterling leaned over the second-story rail, looking down into the main warehouse bay that served as their central rehearsal area.

It was there that he'd practiced robbing the Sky Safe, and where his team had run drills leading up to his jailbreak. He let his view drift across Alec's workshop with all the lock-picking and safecracking equipment known to man, then toward the door to Marco's high-tech epicenter of all things digital. The remaining doors housed the conference room where most of the joint planning occurred and the fabrication shops for engineering required tools, together with a bedroom for each team member and a whole lot of extra space for storing equipment.

This was it, he thought; the warehouse was his kingdom, a humble empire built from the ground up over the course of a lengthy heist career. Sterling had always tried to guide his team through the fray, selecting their jobs with an eye to long-term improvement of their skills—to Alec and Marco, it was about the love of the heist; to Sterling, it was more about legacy. To all three of them, the meticulous preparation and audacious execution of each job was all the motivation they needed.

But all that changed with Blair's arrival.

Prior to that point, things had been clean, linear. They had no personal enemies because nobody knew who they were. But when Sterling crossed paths with Blair, he'd unknowingly become entangled in her past, and that past brought with it the wrath of an incredibly influential and without a doubt *the* most corrupt FBI agent in the country, a man now running for a Congressional seat.

Blair stopped alongside him. "What are you thinking about?"

Sterling smiled.

"About how simple my life was before you joined the team."

"That's funny," Blair replied.

"How so?"

She shrugged, then leaned against the rail, mirroring Sterling's posture. "Because I was just thinking about how complicated *my* life was before I joined the team. Fired from the FBI, recently released from prison, getting hit on by scumbags while bouncing between waitressing jobs."

"Was I one of those scumbags?"

Now it was Blair's turn to smile, a look that never ceased to dazzle Sterling.

"No, you were only interested in hiring me. In a real indirect, messed-up way, but hiring me all the same."

"And since then, I've been to prison, made a mortal enemy out of Jim, and my mother stands to lose everything if we can't pull this off."

"Your mother"—Blair turned to face him—"is going to be just fine. Don't forget, you've got Marco and me standing right behind you."

"What about Alec?"

"Did I forget to mention Alec?"

"You did."

"Fine, then Alec too. And besides, if all else fails, we could take your mom off the grid. Build her an in-law suite right here at the warehouse. Maybe even teach her how to steal."

"Hilarious."

She put a hand on his shoulder, creating a wave of heat that rippled through his body.

"I'm just saying, you're not in this alone. Whatever it takes to put this right, we're going to figure it out. I brought Jim into your life, and I'm going to get him out."

Sterling watched her dark brown eyes, considering a response that would split the difference between his professional obligations as the crew leader, his personal investment in protecting his mother from prosecution, and the romantic attraction he felt for Blair.

As he began to speak, the conference room door flung open and Alec emerged, shouting across the warehouse.

"Hey, boss! Me and Marco are ready to educate you on the shady dealings of the American political system. Bring some popcorn."

"We don't have any popcorn," Sterling called back.

"Well, then, snort some Adderall because this stuff is pretty hard to follow."

Then he disappeared back into the conference room, and Blair gave a halfhearted shrug.

"Guess it's time for class."

12

JIM

Jim walked down State Street, gloved hands tucked into his jacket pockets as his footsteps crunched against the snow.

One thing he hadn't missed about New York: the cold.

This afternoon had barely broken thirty degrees, keeping pedestrian traffic at a minimum. Jim felt like he was treading across the North Pole. Years in LA had thinned his blood to the point that even the warmest days of the month chilled him to the bone, and he came and went from the office building festooned in layer upon layer of cold weather clothing, marking him as a recent import from sunnier climes.

Jim paused beside the New York State Capitol Building, scanning upward to take in the view. To him it looked like the Palace of Versailles, the white granite exterior intricately sculpted into archways and balconies rising up to red spired summits on either end of the massive structure.

Other buildings circled the plaza to his south, most of them far larger. Four identical Agency buildings were spaced out like sentries on the west side, overlooking a huge performing arts venue known as the Egg, all of them in the shadow of the Corning Tower that dwarfed any building in the state outside of New York City.

But it was the Capitol Building that had always held the most intrigue for Jim, for one simple reason: it represented his first concept of power.

He had vivid memories of seeing this building when he was a kid. That childhood had been spent dead broke, with an absentee father and a mother—God rest her soul—taking him and his brother to the plaza to watch other families ice skating or strolling beside the huge central pool and its fountains while eating burgers and hot dogs, luxuries rarely afforded to him in his youth. His mom never said that they were poor, only that all the other families were rich, and Jim would watch them in their carefree abandon and vow that he, too, would be rich.

But as he grew older and learned more of the world, Jim realized that power was far more important. If he could achieve that, he'd get rich as a byproduct—and the further his career progressed, the more Jim's desire for wealth took a distant backseat to the blind and dizzying attraction to *power*. He'd accumulated it however he could, clawed and scraped his way into the back circles of true influence wherever his station, and at every turn in his career found that there was a scene behind the scenes, the true influencers pulling the strings that decreed who would rise, who would fall, and who would be tossed aside.

Power was a double-edged sword, presenting an exhilaration like no other when it was wielded, but inducing fear beyond all fears when it was coming for your throat.

And right now, Jim's head was on the chopping block.

He turned south, crossing into the Empire State Plaza at the epicenter of every significant building in the Albany skyline. This was the place of a thousand memories of his youth, a location he hadn't visited since moving back, and he'd wondered what powerful emotions would pull at his heart upon seeing it again.

But today no idyllic families were gliding across the plaza in Rockwell-esque tranquility; the cold had kept them all away, the fountains were months away from being operational, and now the ice rink was occupied by skaters of a different sort.

The men on the ice were college-aged, though Jim doubted whether any of them had pursued higher education after collecting their high school diploma or—judging by the shouted profanity—their GED.

They were engaged in a hockey game, if you could call it a game, the teams clashing like they were in the NHL playoffs despite the fact that none of them wore protective equipment. Mouthguards got in the way of hurling insults at your competition, he supposed, and when you took to sorting out your differences on the ice, you had to pick your priority.

Jim stopped on the walkway within earshot of the shouts and skates scraping on ice, then checked his backside to see if anyone else was entering the plaza behind him. It was unlikely that anyone in his campaign team would arrive here, and if they did he could easily explain a nostalgic stroll—which, in a way, this was. But Jim felt relieved to see the walkway behind him was empty. He couldn't take any chances of an outside party overhearing the conversation that was about to transpire. That was best left for situations like this: alone, unapproachable, and preferably with some ambient noise. He checked his Rolex, then pulled his coat tighter around him.

His sense of dread while waiting for the phone to ring was so profound that he felt eviscerated, as if all the strength had been drained from him. Here he was, a decorated FBI agent and Congressional candidate, feeling like a helpless child wandering without parents, lost and adrift.

How much to say, to admit to? Every fact he withheld was just as likely to be discovered by some alternate source, and a lack of truth would be met with punishment, swift and severe.

But in this case, telling the truth could hurt him far worse.

In the end, Jim felt conflicted, torn and stranded and utterly defenseless. When his burner phone rang, a muscle in his jaw twitched.

He answered immediately, "I'm here."

A robotic voice responded, with the synthesized baritone of a voice distortion device.

"Your text said 'urgent.' Enlighten me."

Jim swallowed. "You remember the audio recordings Blair threatened me with in the past?"

"Yes."

"Well apparently, they're real."

A brief pause. "Is she selling?"

"No, but someone else is—someone who stole the tapes from Blair."

"How do you know this information?"

Now for the moment of truth, he thought. Time to get this over with.

He continued, "Earlier this afternoon, my computer screen was hijacked by a video chatroom. Someone named Wraith started a bidding war between me, someone called Fixer, and the Sky Thieves."

"Am I correct in presuming that the tapes implicate you in using extralegal means to close one or more cases in the FBI?"

"Yes."

"Anything else?"

"Yes," Jim said hesitantly. "The tapes also mention you."

The pause that followed these words brought with it the most unsettling feeling of Jim's life.

As he waited for the fallout, the shouts from the ice rink escalated. Someone had just administered a hard body check, dropping another man to the ice. Jim plugged his opposite ear against the noise, waiting for his mentor to speak again.

"James, I want you to choose your words very carefully and be extremely precise. More than your career depends upon it, and I will not take kindly to discovering a lie. Now, what did you say about me?"

"Not your name," Jim blurted. "But there may have been some mention of—"

"My network?"

"Yes."

"Names?"

"Possibly," Jim admitted. "This was years ago, and Wraith only provided a small sample. But he said the tape specifies individuals from both parties, and that the evidence could be used as a...a skeleton key in future elections."

The hockey fight that had been brewing broke out as he spoke the last word, a pair of men tossing down their sticks and gloves before throwing blows. Jim turned away from the noise, facing the Capitol Building.

His mentor sounded surprisingly calm. "Is your campaign manager aware?"

"No. I haven't told anyone but you."

"Keep it that way. Who is Fixer?"

"I don't know. He was concerned with what price the bidding would start at, and wanted assurance that no copies would be made."

"A friend from across the aisle. My people will figure it out, in time."

"I can help," Jim blurted. "Leverage my connections at the FBI—"

"You've done more than enough already, James. Interfere any further and you and I are going to have an extremely serious conversation about your future. You're turning out to be a very expensive prospect."

He felt himself nodding impulsively, as if his mentor were watching and trying to gauge by body language whether he was genuinely repentant. "I got carried away with Blair. It was an indiscretion that won't happen again."

"I know it won't. But if you were going to tell someone about me, you could have had the common decency to choose someone I could take care of. Not a fugitive that no one can seem to locate, least of all the police. Where does the bidding stand?"

"We have ten days to raise funds before reconvening. 6:30 p.m. GMT, February 26."

"You've just made my calendar. I'm going to buy the tapes."

"Thank you," Jim said breathlessly.

"I'm not doing this to protect you, James. I'm doing it for me. After you're elected in November, you'll be able to look around the freshman class and see a half dozen other people I put in office one way or another. And when you get to the Capitol Building, you will meet politicians I put in place ten years ago, from the House to Senate. My goal is generational power, the kind that can't be uprooted by one bad election cycle, and to do that I maintain a very deep bench. If you make it to the presidency one day, it will take a billion dollars to get you there. So what's a few million now to recover the tapes?"

Tightening his grip on the phone, Jim spoke with the earnest conviction born of desperation. "I'm not going to let you down again. You've done everything for me, and I promise you I will honor that investment."

"I hope so," his mentor replied, "because thus far you seem to have a fundamental misunderstanding about what you represent. While you are valuable for your potential, you're very, *very* far from essential. I can still cut you loose, and if anything prevents me from recovering those tapes—a mishap, another one of your slip-ups, an act of God—so help me, James, you are going to wish you and I had never crossed paths."

Jim opened his mouth to respond, but it was too late.

The line was dead.

13

BLAIR

Blair followed Sterling into the conference room to find something she'd never seen before.

The room layout was the same: the long table and its attendant chairs were still present, together with the surrounding couches and coffee maker by the sink. Even the clutter atop the table was intact, complete with the assorted toys and puzzles the crew tinkered with while planning.

But Alec and Marco flanked a whiteboard at the end of the room, which was covered from top to bottom in a multi-colored flowchart scrawl of arrows, dollar amounts, and various committee names that were utterly indecipherable.

Sterling casually took a seat, his first indication that he'd seen the board coming when he muttered to no one in particular, "What is that? It looks like a waterfall."

"I was thinking a jellyfish," Blair said, finding her own seat as Alec motioned to the board with two outstretched arms, assuming the pose of a magician preparing for the curtain to be pulled back.

"Ladies and gentlemen, I give you the means of bypassing

campaign contribution laws. And if you thought high school English was hard, buckle up because you're in for a rough ride."

Sterling was unimpressed, pointing toward a bubble of purple marker on one side of the board.

"Fixer runs a super PAC. That's what I thought."

"Not quite," Alec said. "A super PAC is just a Political Action Committee, but it has its limitations."

Marco pointed to a separate circle on the board. "The key is a 501(c) group, which—on paper, at least—is a nonprofit organization exempt from federal income taxes. It's similar to a super PAC in that both can raise and spend any amount of money they want. Here's the difference, and it's a key one: a 501(c) doesn't have to disclose its donors."

Sterling swiped a Rubik's Cube off the desk and began fidgeting with the sides. "So you're saying Fixer started a 501(c)."

"Not quite."

"What do you mean, 'not quite?'"

"I'm saying"—Marco shifted his weight impatiently—"that Fixer started *both*."

Blair gave a low whistle. "That's smart."

"Isn't it?" Alec said.

Sterling set the cube down, giving a slight shake of his head.

"Call me thick, but I'm not seeing how you came to this conclusion."

Marco explained, "So the 501(c) acts as a catch-all for contributions from any number of individuals or corporations, with no donation limits and no requirement to report the donors. Then the 501(c) transfers the money to the super PAC, which only has to report the 501(c) as a donor—"

Alec cut him off.

"And wham, bam, thank you, ma'am, the money trail is wiped clean."

"I'm confused."

"Good." Alec smiled. "That means you're paying attention."

"What I mean is, how has no one put a stop to this loophole?"

"Put a stop to it? The Supreme Court has a major ruling every few years that further reduces campaign finance regulations. The result is called dark money, and it's an arms race between parties: both sides of the political aisle do it, both sides of the political aisle love it. Spending goes up every election cycle."

Blair asked, "How much dark money are we talking?"

Marco said, "High water mark? Between super PACs and 501(c) organizations, the last presidential election spent a hair under $1.5 billion."

"*Billion*? With a B?"

Alec shrugged. "Unless you know another way to spell 'billion.' Then again, I got a C-minus in high school English, so it's not outside the realm of possibility."

Sterling leaned forward and set his elbows on the table. "So the next step is to analyze the top Democratic 501(c)s, and correlate them with the super PACs receiving their donations."

"Already done," Marco said.

"You hacked their files already?"

"Yes," Marco said. "I hacked using an advanced technique called accessing the open records on IRS.gov and checking their publicly listed Form 990s. The top Democratic super PAC in terms of independent expenditures is dedicated to, and I quote, 'maintaining a Democratic majority in the House of

Representatives,' which makes it the logical choice for countering Jim's political ascent. And their top donor is a 501(c) named Decent Democracy."

Blair asked, "And who started those two organizations?"

"The super PAC was started by committee. But the 501(c) was opened by a man named Henry Nordin."

"So that's our guy," she said. "That's Fixer."

Alec pulled out a chair and sat in it, shaking his head.

"No, that is a small, neutered puppy dog they chose to stand in. His background is teaching politics at Georgetown. He barely makes the cut to be a talking head on the B-list networks. We aren't looking for Nordin; we are looking for the man behind the scenes of both organizations."

"Where do we find him?"

Marco rubbed his eyes as he spoke, still standing beside the diagram. "Well, there are two options. One is breaking into Nordin's townhouse in Washington, DC. It doubles as his residence and listed headquarters for Decent Democracy. If I can access Nordin's computers, I can get enough data to analyze and identify Fixer. This is what I would recommend."

"Noted," Sterling said. "So what's the other option?"

"Fixer was undoubtedly selected by a national authority. That means I could also find the information if we broke into the Democratic National Committee headquarters."

Alec leapt out of his chair so fast that it rolled back and hit the wall.

"I've *always* wanted to do a heist with Watergate implications! Marco, you know that. How dare you recommend we infiltrate a paltry townhouse when we can make history by succeeding where those five hacks failed in '73?"

Blair said, "The Watergate break-in was '72."

"Doesn't matter! I just want a heist that we can name with

the suffix 'gate.' And 'Townhousegate' sounds like a straight-to-DVD horror flick."

Sterling ignored the comment, turning his gaze to Marco instead. "Marco, find out everything you can about Nordin's residence. Everyone else, start packing for a mobile job—we're going to DC."

14

BLAIR

Blair and Alec walked arm-in-arm through Northwest DC, breathing the crisp winter air as they tread across a light dusting of snow on the sidewalk.

Already located in one of the most expensive cities in North America, the Dupont Circle neighborhood was a particularly coveted area. Eight-hundred-square-foot apartments went for $500,000, while the narrow townhouses they walked past had sold for one to three million depending on size.

They were beautiful, Blair had to admit, as block after block presented the uniform front of narrow townhouses punctuated only by the occasional gated alley or driveway. But for the most part, vehicles were confined to parking on the street, where they sat bumper-to-bumper along every conceivable stretch of curb.

And yet despite the tightly packed confines, the neighborhood didn't feel claustrophobic—each home seemed to have its own character and individuality, ranging from color and building material to the contents of small gardens planted between stone steps. Trees sprang up from both sides of the sidewalk, some rising higher than the houses. As far as moving with the flow of pedestrians, there were worse places to blend in than Dupont Circle.

With a wide range of restaurants, bars, and grocery stores within a few minutes' walking distance, Blair and Alec drew no attention amid the occasional walker, jogger, or bike rider making their way across the labyrinth of sidewalks.

Even the weather played to their favor: the unseasonably warm February day allowed them to stroll in comfort while retaining winter scarves and hats that provided some visual anonymity.

Blair had to admit that conditions were just about perfect for what they were about to do—all but one, at least, and that one had stuck to his opinion with a resilience that bordered on fanatical.

"A historic opportunity, I'm telling you," Alec said. "We could have called it Watergate, The Sequel. Or just Watergate 2.0, I'm not sure what sounds better."

Blair said, "We drove thirty-nine hours to get here from LA. I think you complained about this for thirty-seven of them."

"And for good reason. I'm very passionate about this issue, Blair, I can't stress that enough."

"I think the Democratic National Committee headquarters would present sufficiently more security obstacles than a personal residence."

"And thus, more glory."

"Well," Blair offered, "look at it this way: your odds of not getting arrested before the auction are up by five hundred percent."

"Hollow consolation. Although I could get used to this."

"This neighborhood?"

"No." He looked down at her arm in his. "You pretending to be my wife."

"Girlfriend. And I'm doing this because people are thirty percent less likely to make eye contact with couples who are holding hands."

"Maybe we should hold hands, then."

"Just be grateful I'm touching your arm. Coming up on 19th Street."

He looked forward as if he'd completely forgotten the purpose of this outing, and they maintained a leisurely pace as they crossed into the 1900 block.

Henry Nordin's home was painted a dull shade of sepia, rising to the three-story height of the surrounding homes as they approached without looking directly at it. Instead, Blair eyed a rectangle of dirt between sidewalk and street that was heavily planted with bushes. Stopping beside it, she released Alec's arm and knelt as if tying her shoe.

Removing her hand from her pocket along with a child's walkie-talkie, she placed the toy out of sight beneath the tangle of bushes, being careful to orient its antenna toward the home to her right.

Then she rose, sliding her arm around Alec's proffered elbow as they continued their stroll. The walkie-talkie was out of sight, and even if someone was to kick through the bushes to find it, the toy would give the appearance of having been tossed from a stroller. Blair had even scraped and chipped the exterior casing to give it the appearance of age—although the innards were Marco's design, and considerably more high-tech than the toy manufacturer had in mind.

Blair texted Sterling to let him know the drop was complete, putting her phone away just in time to witness the only twist to their plan.

She spotted a man in a dark coat coming the opposite way,

speaking loudly into a cell phone. He looked hurried, self-important, barely looking at his surroundings as the call occupied his attention. Blair caught a few words that evoked her suspicion—"the Committee" and "funding deadline" among them—and in the final steps before he swept past her and Alec, Blair recognized the man as Henry Nordin.

15

STERLING

"Drop is complete," Sterling said. "How's it looking?"

Marco, seated to his left, tapped his keyboard. "Standby."

To Sterling, the computer screen before them was an illegible split between a visual representation of a frequency spectrum and a text window filled with what appeared to be HTML coding.

But Marco seemed satisfied with the display. "Looks like a good plant. It's got a read on the baseband data between upconverter circuits, and when the wireless system has activity, we'll know it."

Sterling's phone chimed, and he consulted it to see a new text from Blair.

"Looks like we won't have to wait long," he said. "Apparently Nordin just passed them on his way home."

Then the text window began filling with neat script, which Sterling tried to decipher.

> Packet received from 62 B4 97 03
> Packet type: Entry sensor opened

Data: 20 AC

Packet received from 62 A1 97 03
Packet type: PIN code
PIN bytes: 71 24
Mystery bits: 100

Marco explained, "That's our first event log. He just disarmed the system."

"7124 is his PIN?"

"No, those are just captured data bytes that I'd have to convert. Of course, now we could conduct a replay attack and send that data packet into the control panel to disarm the system...but that would show up on his event log. Same if I spoofed the base station by enabling test mode—easy enough to do, but it doesn't help us get in and out undetected."

Sterling nodded, wishing that Nordin's home could be easier to infiltrate. Most home security sensors transmitted to their base stations at a standard frequency, usually 433.92 megahertz. Something that simple could be blocked with a targeted five-watt continuous transmission, albeit one used with precision: too much power and the base station would detect the interference, and too little would allow the alarm signal to transmit as designed.

But Marco's analysis of security company records revealed that Nordin employed a much more advanced system utilizing 128-bit encrypted sensors. Instead of communicating over a single channel, Nordin's system utilized frequency hopping across a spectral band. This meant the sensors and base station were programmed with a custom code that made synchronized frequency hopping possible—in radio parlance, this code was known as the "key," and the only way into Nordin's home undetected was to decipher it, then program an electronic jammer to block the same pattern of frequencies in sequence.

Sterling asked, "Does this give you enough to start programming?"

"Not yet. I'll need to record the wireless signals from at least ten system events before I can analyze the frequency hopping key."

"How long?"

"Depending on his system settings, how many sensors he has, and how often he arms it, could be by the end of today or it could take until tomorrow."

Sterling felt the nagging wave of impatience rising in him, not for the first time this trip.

They'd left LA under a clear night sky to begin their cross-country drive in two loaded Sprinter vans, both bearing a magnetic logo for a security consulting LLC that existed, of course, only on paper. But it provided sufficient cover for all but the most detailed examination of their cargo, which consisted of the equipment and electronics to install—or bypass—security systems.

There were also various uniforms, costume items, and disguise components for blending in as the occasion required, along with a false-bottom floor panel to hide Sterling and Blair in the event of a traffic stop.

And that risk extended their trip considerably. With only Alec and Marco available to drive during daylight hours, and the necessity to adhere to the posted speed limits at all times, what could have been a two-day non-stop road trip had turned into four. The last of those ended not with recovery, but getting set up in their rental space in the search for Fixer's identity.

Adding to Sterling's irritation at the delay was the fact that this entire effort was merely a tentative first step. They still had to locate Fixer, make contact, and hope that he accepted their proposition to join forces—all with only five days remaining until Wraith auctioned the tapes. And until that happened, every action taken by the team could just as easily turn out to be a colossal waste of time.

Then there was the small matter of going mobile in the first place.

Sterling never liked operating far from their hideout, even for a one-off job. There were simply too many restrictions, too little room for equipment, and too many possibilities of finding out they suddenly needed some item that remained back at the warehouse. Going from their elaborate haven to a couple Sprinter vans' worth of gear was like being forced to run a marathon with your hands tied.

"All right," Sterling announced, "I'm going to stretch my legs."

"You're getting frustrated," Marco replied.

"No, I just need to stretch my legs."

"That's what you say when you're frustrated."

"Can you stop psychoanalyzing me?"

"Only when you no longer require psychoanalysis. We've got five days until the auction, boss. There's time. Even if there wasn't, this isn't the back line at McDonald's. The work takes as long as it takes."

Sterling pushed his chair back, exiting the small office and entering the rental warehouse in which they now resided.

The rental facility was in Hyattsville, Maryland, just east of DC. It wasn't nearly as big as their space back home, but more than sufficient for this job with five thousand square feet, including twelve hundred of office space. With bathrooms, showers, and two oversized drive-in doors, the building had plenty of room for the team's Sprinter vans in addition to a pair of rental vehicles, one of which was currently in use by Blair and Alec. The crew's security consulting LLC had already secured a ninety-day lease on the space, citing a short-term consultation job with a DC-based firm.

Sterling walked between the vehicles, unlocking an exterior door and pushing it open to breathe the chilly air outside.

Beyond the doorway was a paved and fenced storage yard, a row of trees blocking the view of the next complex over. They were on the south end of a heavy industrial zoned park, and while Sterling could probably have loitered outside without anyone noticing, it wasn't worth the risk without a disguise. For now he was content with a momentary reprieve from the desk, from the task at hand, from the endless sequence of delays and obstacles that had followed what should have been a simple safe deposit box robbery.

From the office space, he heard Marco shout.

"Boss!"

Sterling pulled the door shut and locked it, breaking into a run as he threaded his way between vehicles to reach Marco. His mind was racing between two possibilities: that Blair and Alec had been compromised, or that the rental space itself had been compromised. At this point, one was just as bad as the other, but either way, he was going to have to act fast.

Skidding to a halt at the door, he asked, "What happened?"

Marco spun to face him, lowering the phone from his ear.

"Alec and Blair just got back to the car. They need your takeout order."

16

STERLING

Sterling was a block away when Henry Nordin and his wife stepped out of their townhouse, locked the door, and turned left on the sidewalk.

Falling into a casual walk behind them, Sterling said, "I've got eyes-on the keyholders, heading east on South Street."

Alec replied, *"I'm picking up parallel on T Street eastbound."*

Next was Marco from his position at the rental facility.

"They've activated the security system. I've got a clean signal and can intercede in the event of an emergency."

Blair transmitted, *"Got it. I'm ready to move into position once we've got keyholder standoff."*

Standoff had become the operative priority, Sterling thought. Once Blair made entry, they'd estimated ten minutes of "breakdown time"—covering her tracks, recovering her jammer, and resetting locks—before she could exit. Until the Nordins were ten minutes away from their home, any entry was a disaster waiting to happen in the event they turned around for something as simple as a forgotten wallet.

And that's where Sterling and Alec came in, rotating visual on the Nordins to give Blair the maximum possible time inside the house. Her task shouldn't take long, but unexpected delays were the norm rather than the exception in this business.

So that's how he ended up in his current position, wearing a movie-grade fake beard below aviator sunglasses, just another DC resident enjoying the neighborhood.

He watched the Nordins cross the next street and turn left, picking up his pace slightly to keep them in sight.

"They're crossing 18th Street and turning north. Alec, displace to Florida Avenue and be ready to pick them up at the intersection."

"*Got it.*"

The Nordins appeared to be chatting away happily, oblivious to Sterling's presence amid the pedestrians and joggers flitting across the sidewalks. That much notwithstanding, Sterling would have to hand off visual to Alec in the next few minutes to ensure he didn't burn himself in the process.

He checked his watch at the next intersection.

"Crossing Swann Street northbound. Blair, you've got five minutes' notice. You can start moving into position."

"*Got it*," she replied. "*I'm moving.*"

Sterling followed the Nordins as they continued moving up 18th Street toward its next major intersection, a four-way lined with restaurants on all sides. They turned right at the stoplight, passing out of Sterling's view as Alec transmitted.

"*I have eyes-on the keyholders. Sterling, you can wave off.*"

Then Alec crossed the street in front of Sterling, heading right as he followed the Nordins down the sidewalk.

Sterling continued straight, stopping at the corner to await the pedestrian crossing light. Glancing to his side, he saw the Nordins enter a restaurant. Alec wasn't far behind them, transmitting an update over the team net just before he slipped in the door.

"Keyholders are in Keren Cafe & Restaurant off Florida and 18th. Looks like I'm having lunch."

Sterling's light changed, and he stepped onto the crosswalk as he checked his watch and sent his final approval for the covert entry.

"Blair, the keyholders are getting lunch and we've passed the ten-minute threshold for your breakdown time. You're clear to proceed."

17

BLAIR

Blair finished picking the Nordins' back-door deadlock, pausing only to send a final transmission to Marco before testing the handle.

"Making entry. Marco, be ready."

"*Always*," he replied smoothly.

Blair turned the doorknob, ready for the moment of truth.

In theory, the specially programmed jammer in her backpack was now frequency hopping in tandem with the security sensors, blocking each of the rapidly alternating channels in short bursts. If it worked as planned, the entry and motion sensors would still detect Blair's presence and attempt to send alert signals to the system's base station. But since that base station maintained the only event log and link to the keypad with its ability to cue the alarm, blocking the sensor signals would allow the entire system to remain running without any record of an intrusion, allowing her to escape with the data she needed to bring down Jim.

At least, that's how everything was *supposed* to work.

In reality, there was every possibility that she'd push open the door to elicit the chirping countdown of the keypad demanding a PIN be entered or, worse yet, the howl of an alarm broadcasting the intrusion to every neighbor within earshot. If that happened, Marco would remotely disable the system, but Blair would have to flee as it reported the intrusion to Nordin via automated text message.

With a final breath, Blair pushed the door open.

It gave way with a creak, and she quickly entered and closed it behind her, turning the deadbolt to hear only her pulse throbbing in her ears.

"I'm in."

Marco replied, "*Event log is clear. Get to work.*"

She was standing in a kitchen, the proportions seeming oddly distorted—everything in this narrow type of townhouse seemed to be smashed lengthwise between tight walls. To her left was the rear stairwell, which Blair ignored as she slipped through the kitchen and toward the front door. As she moved, she made a mental blueprint of the space around her. Analyzing floor plans from building diagrams or realty records was one thing; painting your own personal picture once inside was completely another, and Blair took in the patterned wallpaper, the orientation of furniture on the hardwood floor, and the position of appliances with an intense focus. Disorientation was fatal to efficiency, and efficiency was the name of the game right now.

Blair entered a tight foyer hallway, passing a formal dining room with glass cases filled with fine china and a sitting room with a marble fireplace. She noted these at a second's glance and then moved on, finding the second stairwell to her left that she continued past in the search for the one object she needed to find: the rectangular white box of the security system base station.

It was located more or less where she expected it, positioned by the front door and below the wall-mounted keypad, between the silver photo frames atop an ornate mahogany side table.

Blair removed the jammer from her backpack. It was the size of a small wireless router, with three stubby antennas that she adjusted before setting the assembly in place behind a photo frame. Only then did she feel the first sense of composure about this job; with the device now positioned beside the base station, the jamming bubble was at its most effective.

Then Blair moved up the picture-lined front stairway, finding its confines incredibly tight even for her size. The stairs were practically shoulder-width, and she had to duck her head to keep from hitting the second-floor abutment. Once upstairs, she moved from room to room, finding first the master suite, then a hallway bathroom beside an unused guest room, its bed immaculately made.

The fourth door revealed paydirt: an office with built-in bookshelves, framed photographs of Henry Nordin smiling with various politicians, certificates and diplomas hanging on the walls.

And most importantly, a desk and computer.

Blair recovered the imaging device from her backpack, this one a self-powered unit scarcely larger than an external hard drive. She plugged it into the computer's USB port, watching a red light illuminate as it began functioning automatically, creating one large compressed file by subversively imaging Nordin's hard drive without alerting the computer that it was doing so. According to Marco, the process was sufficient for him to scan through all saved disc images, including Nordin's previously saved histories and deleted files.

As she waited for the download, Blair couldn't deny her sense of unease. If she were doing this same entry scenario in the FBI, they'd have a dozen or more agents supporting the effort, from surveilling the keyholders to keeping a lookout on the street for any unexpected guests. That wasn't counting the full support of local law enforcement, who were often notified of the effort and standing by to intervene in the event anything went wrong.

Doing the same job with four people in extralegal circumstances felt threadbare by comparison, and yet this crew had never failed to deliver. Sure, there was a lot more improvisation required in this sector than law enforcement, but Blair reminded herself that Sterling's crew was the best for a reason.

The light on the imaging device flicked from red to green, indicating that its upload was complete. Blair quickly unplugged and stowed it in her backpack, zipping it up as she prepared to move. Anticlimactic operations were a *very* good thing in this business, and despite the never-abating tension on the job, Blair reminded herself that sometimes things actually did go according to plan.

At that exact moment, she heard the front door open.

It was an unmistakable creak, followed by footsteps in the foyer hallway below her—and Blair felt a rush of fear as she whispered a transmission.

"They're back in the house. Alec, why didn't you tell me you lost the keyholders?"

"*Because I didn't*," he replied, sounding like his mouth was half-full. "*I'm eating a falafel sandwich about fifteen feet away from them.*"

Marco spoke next. "It's not the Nordins—someone just disarmed the security system using a different PIN."

Then Blair's heart really sank, because the Nordins returning would be the best scenario out of the available options. She could think of exactly three alternatives: it was another burglar, or Wraith himself, or people that Jim's mentor had sent to find the same information.

Sterling transmitted next, "*I'm on my way. Can you get out of there?*"

It was a valid question. There were two stairways leading downstairs, one to the front door and one to the back. She could perhaps sneak down the latter and exit the way she'd come, with one small complication: her security system jammer was still in position next to the base station.

Blair had gotten what she'd come for, but if anyone knew that Nordin's information had been compromised, that data would go from potentially invaluable to beyond useless. Then again, she considered, whoever had just entered the house had come right through the front door—and while she'd tucked the jammer behind a picture frame, it wouldn't take more than a cursory search to find.

But searching the downstairs didn't appear to be on the sudden invader's agenda any more than it had been on Blair's.

Heavy footsteps ascended the front stairs, and Blair ducked behind the desk. She was trapped now, with no choice but to hide until the last possible second, then catch the invader with a surprise attack before fleeing the house. At that point, it didn't matter whether she left the jammer or not—the game was up.

She listened as the footfalls reached the second floor, dreading their approach to Nordin's office.

But instead of advancing footsteps, she heard the heavy thump of a large object being set down in the hallway, and then the intruder began descending the front stairs again. Blair couldn't begin to guess what to make of that, but the sudden wave of relief was almost paralyzing. She rose from behind the desk, slipping quietly toward the office door, and peeked into the hallway.

Positioned at the top of the stairs was a plastic tote filled with microfiber cloths, disinfecting wipes, scrub brushes, and feather dusters—the person who entered wasn't a thief, it was a housekeeper.

Blair heard the front door swing open and then close again, and knew she had only seconds before the housekeeper returned to shuttle her next load of supplies.

Darting into the upstairs hall, Blair vaulted the caddy and began descending the narrow stairs as quickly and quietly as she could. The foyer table came into view, and Blair set foot on the ground floor just as the front door handle began to turn. Instinctively, Blair plucked the jammer from behind the photo frame and wheeled sideways to enter the sitting room.

As she did so, a woman used her shoulder to push open the front door while maneuvering a mop and bucket into the foyer. Blair tucked out of view behind the wall, unsure if she'd been seen as she crept through the sitting area and into the adjoining dining room. Stopping at the final doorway into the downstairs hallway, she listened to the woman rolling the mop bucket into the kitchen, blocking her only avenue of escape out the back door.

With one hand still clutching the jammer, she listened to the woman moving back to the front door to retrieve more cleaning supplies. But then a second person entered, the two exchanging quick words at the front door. Blair paused, feeling a mounting sense of panic as footsteps approached the entrance to the adjoining sitting room.

Tucking herself against the wall beside the dining room doorway, Blair saw the shadow of a person taking the first step into the sitting room, and then strode into the hallway, looking right to see the front door partially ajar. Wherever the first housekeeper had gone, she wouldn't be long.

Blair wasted no time in moving through the kitchen with the stealthiest gait she could muster across the hardwood floors.

Arriving at the back door, she thumbed the deadbolt open with a flat *clack* that made her heart jump. But at this point she was fully committed, and she creaked the door open and slipped into the small, fenced backyard before pulling it shut.

Ordinarily she'd return the deadbolt to its original locked position using the tools at her disposal; but she'd already almost been compromised, had what she came for, and didn't want to risk one of the housekeepers coming to investigate the scratching noises at the back door.

Instead she assumed a casual stroll, tucking the jammer into her backpack and sending a message to her team.

"Sterling, wave off. I'm on my way out." Taking a breath of relief, she added two final words to her transmission.

"Mission complete."

18

STERLING

Sterling took a sip of beer, watching Blair as she did the same from her seat on a foldout chair across from him.

She set down her can and asked, "So what were you going to do today?"

"When?"

"When I told you someone was in the house with me, and you were on the way."

"Other than sprinting three blocks in an itchy fake beard before you told me you were fine? I don't know."

"I'm serious."

Sterling drew a long breath, then took another sip before he replied.

"Depended on the situation. If I found the front door ajar, I would have gone in. But if I saw it was just housekeepers coming to clean? Well, that's easy. I could have created some kind of a distraction at the front door. Distraught pedestrian looking for a lost dog, that type of thing."

"Doesn't sound like you had much of a plan."

"Some of my best work is improvisation."

She pulled her jacket close to her body, considering the

statement. The rental warehouse was climate controlled, but the open warehouse bay got chilly at night nonetheless—and Sterling wasn't about to invoke the suspicion of Alec and Marco by retiring to one of the closed offices with Blair.

She'd emerged from her foray into Nordin's home a little shaken up—that much was normal. There was no easy way out of the heart-pounding encounters where you came within seconds or inches of getting compromised. Once they'd returned to the rental facility, Sterling treated her like he would either of the other members under such circumstances: told her to relax, have a drink, take the night off. After all, there was no crisis at the moment, and Marco would need time to sift through the imaged files of Nordin's hard drive.

But the cluster of beer cans next to her seat had gone from one to four in the time it had taken him to polish off his second. That wasn't a problem, professionally speaking, so long as it wasn't a multi-day trend. Decompressing from jobs was particularly important when you conducted some of the highest-pressure jobs imaginable, and as long as his crew members were switched on when it came time for work the next day, Sterling wasn't going to begrudge anyone a few drinks.

The concern he felt was more for himself. In the past hour Blair had gone from tense to relaxed to flirtatious, and Sterling had a harder time focusing on the mission at hand with each bleary-eyed stare he caught her throwing his way.

Passing flirtatious comments when they were back at their hideout alone was one thing; Sterling had been all about that, and would have leapt at the chance to escalate things between them from the current stagnation at three kisses, one of which was on the cheek. But now they were in Maryland, sharing a living space with Marco and Alec.

And it wasn't just Blair's current lack of composure that concerned Sterling—it was also his own.

Blair swallowed and said, "Well, thanks for coming after me, just the same. It would have been really embarrassing if you had to save me two heists in a row."

"Not really," he replied. "No matter what happened, I'd still owe you."

"For Supermax?"

"Some would consider that a slightly more involved rescue than breaking into a moving LAPD truck."

"Meh." She suppressed a belch. "That was nothing. That was...fun."

"Glad it was fun for one of us."

She threw her head back. "Don't lie, you enjoyed yourself."

"Once I was safe, sure."

"Not that." Blair took another sip of beer without taking her eyes off him. "When I kissed you. Our first kiss."

An office door swung open, and Marco strode into the warehouse bay.

Sterling quickly stood, spinning to face him.

"Hey, Marco. Find anything interesting?"

"Yes," Marco said. "Alec is pulling through the gate—we need to let him in."

The three made their way to one of the rolling drive-in doors, detaching the lock and sliding it upward to a cold gust of night air spilling inside. It was followed by the blaze of headlights as Alec's rental sedan pulled past them and onto the concrete floor, advancing a few meters before he parked and killed the engine.

Sterling and Blair slid the rolling door shut, locking it as Alec stepped out of the driver's seat.

"It wasn't easy, but I battled traffic to make it back before the food got cold, and—" He squinted at his female teammate. "Blair, are you drunk?"

"Yes," Sterling and Marco replied simultaneously.

Blair shook her head. "Just a bit lightheaded from the exhaust fumes when you pulled in."

Sterling said, "She needs food. Fast."

Marco was already yanking open the passenger door and removing a stack of pizzas. He flipped open the top box, scanning the contents as his face turned to a grimace. "What exactly is this?"

Alec took the box back from Marco, who made no effort to stop him.

"This, my friend, isn't just pizza. This is Maryland-style crab pizza, seasoned in Old Bay spiced alfredo sauce with fresh-cut scallions."

"Crab pizza?" Sterling asked. "You getting homesick for Boston, buddy?"

"Maybe. Doesn't change the fact that this is awesome."

They converged on the circle of chairs arranged before the two Sprinter vans, taking seats as Blair said, "Well, keep your awesome pizza and hand over the pepperoni."

Alec shook his head, holding out the box to her. "Just give it a shot, Blair."

Sighing, she accepted a slice, sniffed it, and reluctantly took a bite.

"Wow," she said, chewing. "Wow. Alec, this is...you are...*wow*."

"I hear it all the time," he professed.

Sterling replied, "You hear it all the time from women in Blair's state, which is to say, drunk. Marco, beer me."

Marco reached into the cooler and tossed a can to Sterling.

Alec asked, "So what'd I miss? We find out who Fixer is?"

"Not yet," Marco said. "I'm still analyzing, and there is a lot to go through. I have, however, determined the significance of Jim's campaign as it relates to our fellow bidders trying to get his tapes."

"Yeah?" Alec said. "What's that?"

"It can wait until tomorrow."

Blair shook her head.

"Don't be a tease, Marco. If we're waiting on Fixer's identity, we may as well know the bigger picture."

Marco set down his pizza box, brushing the crumbs from his hands.

"California is a perennial Democratic state, and the RNC doesn't assess that taking it over is in the cards anytime soon. The focus then shifts to the next three most important states for the electoral college: Texas, Florida, and—you guessed it —New York. Those three alone add up ninety-six electoral votes out of 270 required to win the presidency."

Sterling asked, "So what's the relevance of New York? Why aren't they having Jim run in Texas or Florida?"

"Texas always votes Republican, so there's not much investment needed there. Florida is a swing state that represents a battleground for both parties with each election. And that's where the current strategy comes into play. New York borders significant electoral vote counts in Pennsylvania, New Jersey, and Massachusetts. By shifting the political tides in New York, it becomes a foothold for the National Committee in spreading their influence across the northeast."

Sterling asked, "Okay, but how does this apply to Jim?"

"Exactly the same way, but at the state level. Jim is running for Congressional District 20, which has voted Democratic since forever. It borders Districts 19 and 21, both of which voted largely Democratic up until the last presidential election. The Committee sees New York as critical to winning the next presidential seat, and District 20 as critical to winning

New York. So it's not about Jim per se; he's the figurehead they're backing with immense support, including a veteran campaign manager to help craft his message."

Blair set a beer can on the ground next to her empties.

"Well," she asked, "what's Jim's message?"

19

JIM

"It's about *integrity*," Jim said, thumping the heel of his hand against the podium. "Because my opponent has demonstrated that he lacks the moral compass to stand up to those who would do irreparable damage to law enforcement. He's worried about votes and his political legacy. Me? I'm concerned with doing what's right, no matter the cost—just like the brave officers of Council 82."

A flurry of applause rose from the crowd, roughly eight hundred current and former cops from the state Law Enforcement Officers Union. This room represented the most influential people in the organization, gathered for their annual convention in downtown Albany.

Jim continued, "For someone who never spent a day in law enforcement, my opponent seems to have some strong views about cutting funding for the men and women who leave the safety of their homes to defend their fellow citizens from violent criminals who would do them harm."

Giving speeches had always been second nature to Jim, though most of his experience in that area consisted of dealing with the press. He was pleased to find that the carry-over into the political dimension was virtually seamless, and the assembled crowd had been eager to receive Jim's message.

Of course, it was easier when the audience consisted of fellow officers of the law.

Jim wore his FBI Medal of Valor over his shirt collar, a distinction his campaign manager would only allow when addressing an audience of law enforcement. To them, it represented the very essence of their highest ideals. To Jim it was instant credibility, perhaps Blair's greatest gift to him—because while she may have defeated him in the aftermath of the Century City heist, Jim and his mentor could control the only narrative that mattered. His defeat had thus turned into a documented act of heroism on his part, one that erased any possible suspicion of wrongdoing in the court of public opinion.

He placed a hand over his chest, feeling his wedding ring tap against the gold star medallion.

"Now I'm often asked about this medal. And the truth is that it doesn't belong to me; it belongs to everyone who wears or ever has worn the uniform, everyone who earned their badge not by graduating from the academy but by representing our profession with honor, bravery, and integrity.

"Now my opponent doesn't seem to know too much about honor or bravery. But what really troubles me is his lack of integrity. What troubles me is how for the past ten years, he's taken to the podium to say one thing to his constituents, then voted another way as if no one would hold him accountable. Well, with your help, that will all change this November."

Jim turned his shoulder from the podium, pointing to the banner hanging on the wall behind him.

It was a four-by-five picture of his face, the official photo taken against the backdrop of an American flag. Below it was the campaign logo, spelled in a custom font with a flourish of stars and stripes: *Jim Jacobson for Congress: It's About Integrity*.

"Integrity isn't just a word to me. It's the backbone of my entire tenure in law enforcement, and if you give me the chance to represent you, it will be the backbone of my future service to the interests of District 20 and its citizens."

The audience began clapping, and Jim gave a gracious nod of thanks and scanned the room as he waited for the applause to die down.

Most of the men and women seated before him were in suits and blazers, though a few dozen wore local or state police uniforms. Council 82 had thirty-five hundred total members, of which only a thousand resided in Jim's district. But those thousand had families who would vote as well, and the more passion Jim aroused in them, the greater his reach.

Besides, he thought, this was just the beginning.

Jim was running unopposed in the primary election, so it was time to set his sights on the easiest dominos to tip before going head-to-head with the current incumbent. That process would snowball in momentum until November, when the Congressional seats—and the presidency—would be determined.

As the applause tapered off, Jim delivered his final comments.

"It gives me hope to see you coming together for change, to make a difference not just for our profession but for the future of the communities we serve. Ladies and gentlemen, let's make it happen. God bless New York, and God bless the United States of America."

Jim shot a thumbs up to the cameras flashing from his front-row photographers, then smartly marched away from the podium to shake hands with the Council 82 president.

The president then took his place at the microphone, making his announcement to a partial standing ovation.

"I'm proud to announce Council 82's official endorsement of Jim Jacobson's run for Congress."

Jim gave a final wave to the crowd, exiting the stage through a back door to find his campaign manager waiting with a ledger in hand.

Chris Mitchell was impeccably attired as always, not a thread out of place.

The difference, Jim thought, was that his expression was now a stone-faced look of anger, if not outright rage.

"We need to talk," Mitchell said, gesturing to an open doorway.

Jim followed him inside, noting that Mitchell closed the door with a few more pounds of pressure than were necessary.

He asked, "What's wrong with you, Chris? I thought that went pretty well."

Mitchell tossed his ledger on a table and folded his arms. "I'm not concerned about your ability to give stump speeches. You said you came completely clean with me when I agreed to come on board with you."

"I did," Jim replied defensively. "And I'm not sure I care for your tone."

"The Dems are raising funds for some piece of blackmail against you. Something that has implications for the entire party."

"Oh really? According to who?"

"It doesn't matter how I know. I know. You don't make it as far as I have without having friends on the other side."

"Sounds like your friends are misinformed. I told you I'm clean because I *am* clean."

Mitchell tilted his head toward Jim in an unsettling gesture reminiscent of a schoolteacher scolding his pupil.

"Out of all the politicians I've met, I can count the number with spotless backgrounds on three fingers. None of them made it very far. I don't care what's in your past, only what can affect us."

"It's being handled," Jim said firmly.

"If I'm finding out from my plants in the DNC, it's not being handled. Now you tell me what they have on you or I announce my resignation from this campaign tonight and the Committee chooses another candidate to fill your ballot slot within the week."

Jim felt the heat of blood rushing to his face. Mitchell's threat wasn't an idle one; he had more than enough pull with his party to end Jim's political career before it began. And while Jim's mentor had demanded that any word of the tapes stay between the two of them, clearly the word was spreading and neither of them would benefit from Mitchell publicly falling on his sword.

Jim lowered his voice. "There are audio recordings at large. Someone is selling them in a bidding war between me, the Sky Thieves, and an unknown person working for the Democrats."

"What's on the tapes?"

"They pertain to some of my work in the FBI. That's all you need to know."

"Can we do damage control if they get out?"

Jim shook his head. "Not a chance. But I have a buyer who's going to ensure we get the tapes."

"Who's buying them?"

"Someone with the finances to win at all costs. That's all you need to know."

"No, Jim," Mitchell said in a low voice, "that's not all I need to know. You say this person can buy them back, that's fine. But I need to be informed every step of the way so we've got a chance to get ahead of any political blowback. If we can't agree to that, then we're done here."

"There are four days until the final bidding. I'll advise you of the outcome, but I'm telling you it's a guaranteed win. I'll handle acquisition of the tapes myself, and let you know when they've been disposed of. Okay?"

"Okay," Mitchell agreed. "But I'm going to ask you one more time: who's your buyer?"

Jim took a half-step toward Mitchell, answering the question in his most severe tone.

"Someone who could destroy both of us. And if anything goes wrong with getting those tapes, that's exactly what's going to happen."

20

BLAIR

Blair awoke to a dull headache and the coppery taste of beer.

Squinting in the sunlight streaming through the blinds, she realized she was lying on the cot in her room, which was in actuality just an office she'd appropriated for a living space during their stay at the rental facility.

Blair sat up on her cot, felt the lightheadedness of moving too quickly for her current state, and lay back down with a grunt. She needed a few minutes to compose herself, and in that span of time, she found her mind slogging through the previous night's events, trying to recall everything that happened.

She recalled flirting with Sterling, the pizza being amazing, and Marco's discourse on the particulars of national political strategy as it pertained to Jim's campaign. Beyond that things got fuzzier. They'd stayed awake another hour or so, no one had drunk as much as her, and then...she recalled being the first to go to bed. A foggy recollection of closing her door, lying down, and then lapsing into a bottomless, drunken sleep.

That much was a relief, and she felt reasonably confident

she hadn't said anything too outlandish to her crew. The real problem wasn't that she'd had too much to drink in front of the others—the four of them had been working together for too long to be insecure in one another's presence—but rather that she'd impaired herself for today's work, whatever that may be.

She sat up again, mustering the strength to rise and make her way to the door. Pausing, she opened it, expecting to hear Sterling, Alec, and Marco bantering as they went about their business as usual.

Instead, she was met with silence.

Blair shuffled into the warehouse bay, noting first that one of the rental vehicles was gone, and second, that the sound of someone typing on a keyboard was coming from Marco's office. When she made her way there, she found not Marco at the computer but Sterling. A half-eaten breakfast burrito was on the desk, and the screen before him was filled with the satellite view of city streets.

He looked up as she entered, taking in her appearance with a sympathetic gaze. Then he grinned and said, "Well good morning, Sunshine."

Blair rubbed her eyes. "Is there any water in this place?"

Sterling handed her a plastic shopping bag from a convenience store, and Blair found two bottles of Gatorade and a bottle of Tylenol.

"You're a lifesaver. Thank you."

"You can thank Alec. He picked this up for you when he went out for breakfast. You hungry? We've got two breakfast burritos left."

"No, thanks."

"Sure? You should eat something."

"Sterling, I've never been more sure of anything in my life." She dropped into a seat beside him, opening the Tylenol and shaking two pills out of the bottle before washing them down with a swig of Gatorade. Then she asked, "Where are Alec and Marco?"

"DC. Marco found the identity of the mysterious Fixer."

Blair, drinking again, almost choked.

She swallowed hard. "Really—who is he?"

"A Wall Street financier named Eric Dembinski. On paper, he manages private equity firms with assets in the twelve-billion-dollar range."

"What about behind the scenes?"

"That's where it gets interesting. When banks like Goldman Sachs, JPMorgan Chase, and Morgan Stanley want to influence politics, Dembinski is the guy who masterminds funneling cash from A to B without violating a labyrinth of campaign finance laws. He's the brains behind using the collective cash of American finance to determine which political officials get elected."

Blair capped her bottle of Gatorade and set it on the table.

"I would've thought they'd be worried about overregulation from the Democrats. Why are they donating to them?"

"Because the Republicans have started gaining traction in controlling both chambers of Congress. Right now, Wall Street just wants to make sure Washington stays divided to prevent any major industry overhauls."

"So they don't care about the politics, just business."

He clapped her on the shoulder. "Now you're getting it. I used to think we were top-notch criminals—turns out we've got nothing on the dynamics of American campaign financing. We could learn a lot from these people."

Blair nodded, then found herself shaking her head. "Wait a minute—if Fixer is a Wall Street guy, then why did Alec and Marco go to DC?"

"Because Dembinski is here. At least, for a little bit longer

—he flies back to New York the night before the auction. In the meantime, he's taking meetings with the American Bankers Association on Connecticut Avenue. But if we want to make contact while we're here, it better be soon."

"Should be easy enough. We could get into his hotel room, have a private meeting there."

"Should be," he agreed, "but it's not that simple. He's staying at the Thomas Jefferson Presidential Suite at the Willard InterContinental."

"So?"

"So the Willard is at 1401 Pennsylvania Avenue. Sound familiar?"

"Wait, isn't—"

"Isn't the White House at 1600 Pennsylvania Avenue? Yes, it is. If this hotel were any closer, you could hit the Oval Office with a tennis ball. And even if it weren't under round-the-clock surveillance, take a wild guess what additional security measures you and I need to be concerned with."

"Ah," Blair groaned, "of course."

Then, simultaneously, they said the same word.

"Biometrics."

They both leaned back in their chairs, and Blair realized why Sterling had remained behind at the rental facility.

The truth was, moving about in public as a fugitive was simpler than it seemed. With a bit of rudimentary disguise work, and avoiding the traps of TSA checkpoints and the like, known criminals could move about quite comfortably in heavily populated areas like DC. The more people, the more anonymity—right up until you started messing with the Secret Service.

Facial recognition technology was nothing new, having made its way into the pockets of almost every civilian in the world via smartphones.

But that technology went to a whole new level in the security sector, where computer recognition could search real-time video feeds against an endless database of photos depicting criminals-at-large. And in the case of protecting the leader of the free world, that same technology could equally flag any passersby whose faces were determined to have been deliberately obscured, even by subtle methods like temporary facial prosthetics.

Blair said, "So that means neither of us can be involved in contacting Fixer."

"Exactly the opposite. One of us will *have* to make the pitch."

"What? Why?"

He raised his eyebrows at her. "How else is he going to know we truly represent the Sky Thieves?"

Blair's lips parted in silent contemplation. She wondered how she could have missed it—only Blair and Sterling had been associated with America's most famous heist crew, their faces plastered over every major news outlet. In the effort to assure Dembinski that they were who they claimed to be, the only way to guarantee instant credibility was to expose themselves.

Looking back at Sterling, she said, "So we have to miraculously find a way to reveal ourselves to Fixer, but no one else, in order to pitch him on joining financial forces with us in bidding for the tapes. All while escaping before we can be arrested if he decides he doesn't want to play ball."

"That's right."

"Well, how are we supposed to do that?"

Sterling stretched his arms, bringing his hands to rest behind his head.

"I have no idea."

21

STERLING

The crew had lined their chairs before a wall in the rental facility's warehouse bay, where Marco rigged a projector to display an enlarged overhead view of Washington, DC. Alec pointed to the hotel and began his brief.

"Daily routine begins here at the Willard InterContinental Hotel. At eight a.m. sharp, a chauffeured Rolls Royce pulls up to the Pennsylvania Avenue entrance. Driver stays in the vehicle, and the hotel valet opens the rear passenger side door. Dembinski gets inside, and then they're off like a prom dress —up the block to 15th Street Northwest, right turn and head north for five blocks to I Street."

He traced his finger along the route. "Left turn, west for five blocks to a right turn on 18th Street, then north for two blocks to the west parking garage entrance of 1120 Connecticut Avenue. Route is 1.2 miles, and we clocked it at six to twelve minutes depending on traffic."

Sterling asked, "Drop-off?"

Alec tapped the ABA headquarters.

"Rolls Royce stops at the third-story landing in the parking garage, where a group of two men and one woman from the

ABA are standing by to walk him through security and into the headquarters office."

"And pickup?"

"Same spot as the drop-off, at six p.m. Return route is a little different because 18th Street is one-way, so they head north to Connecticut Avenue"—he swept his hand upward on the wall—"and follow it southeast to 17th, then H Street east past Lafayette Square, 14th Street south to Pennsylvania, up the block to the hotel entrance. Valet opens the rear passenger door, Dembinski gets out and waltzes up to his 2,300-square-foot suite on the sixth floor and does it all again the next day."

Then he went silent, waiting for the next inquiry, until Blair asked, "How's the security at the American Bank Association?"

"Based on our initial passes, it's pretty tight. They represent a lot of insider information that they're less than keen to have stolen, what with trying to forestall the collapse of the American economy."

Marco added, "Could we get inside if we had to? Absolutely. Could we smuggle one of two known fugitives inside for a one-on-one meeting with Dembinski in broad daylight with no one being any the wiser? I think not."

"And the hotel—"

"The hotel is even worse," Marco cut her off. "Forget about their employed security. Proximity to the White House means they're within range of every imaginable camera, sensor, and thermal imaging system. Any or all of which could be hidden in plain sight and probably are. I ran a signal sweep from the car and picked up on so many encrypted wireless signals being transmitted that smoke started coming out of my computer."

"Really?" Alec asked.

"No, not really. I am making a point. And it goes without

saying that there is biometric technology in place that would not take kindly to Blair or Sterling showing their face. Unless we want to wait until Halloween, it's a no-go."

Sterling leaned his chair back on two legs.

"Does Dembinski go anywhere besides the hotel and the ABA headquarters?"

"Meals are variable between the hotel and fine dining options, but he never goes alone. And we have about forty-eight hours before he flies back to his job on Wall Street, after which life becomes considerably more difficult."

Then Sterling let his chair drop forward, waiting for a good idea to occur to him. None did.

Alec offered, "Sterling, you could disguise yourself as a homeless man."

"No."

"Blair, you could disguise yourself as a streetwalker."

"Excuse me?"

Sterling said, "Entertaining, but no."

"Then how about I disguise myself as you, Sterling?"

"Your ideas are getting worse." He rose. "I'm going to stretch my legs."

Marco looked up.

"That's what you say when—"

"I know," Sterling shot back. "Leave it alone."

He stalked off into the warehouse bay, cutting between the Sprinter vans on his way to the door. But he stopped short of going outside—it was broad daylight, and being spotted wasn't outside the realm of possibility. Frustrated, he turned and began pacing along the wall holding the roll-up doors, turning at the corner and hitting his knee on the bumper of a rental car.

Sterling had more motivation than anyone to take down Jim, save maybe Blair herself. And for every step forward in that effort, they seemed to take two steps back. First the tapes were stolen, then they'd traveled clear across the country only to find that Fixer was perhaps the most elusive man on earth.

Turning at the next corner, he bumped his shoulder into a Sprinter van, and then stopped abruptly.

He ran his eyes over the team's vans and the two rental cars, and had a sudden realization that made his heart beat faster.

Striding back toward the team, he found them engaged in a minor argument about whether the hotel or the ABA headquarters would be the easier target.

Sterling called out, "What type of car picks him up?"

The crew stopped talking and looked up at him. "I already told you," Alec said, "it's a Rolls Royce."

"No, I mean what model."

"The Cullinan. It's their SUV."

Sterling was nodding thoughtfully, a smile playing at the corners of his lips. "And where, exactly, does it come from?"

22

BLAIR

"You're invisible," Marco said, consulting his computer screen to verify the call routing. "And Alec will be back from Philadelphia any minute now. Let's get this over with."

He slid a phone across the desk to her, and she picked it up, careful not to unplug the wire connecting it to his computer. Consulting the screen, she dialed a number before holding the phone to her ear.

A man picked up by the second ring, speaking in a courteous tone.

"Executive City Charter Services. How may I help you?"

"Good evening," Blair said, "this is Jenna Palkovic. I'm Mr. Dembinski's personal assistant."

"Of course, Ms. Palkovic. How can I help you this evening?"

Blair swallowed. "Mr. Dembinski has had a change of plans for tomorrow's itinerary. He'll breakfast with the ABA Vice Chair and his staff at the Willard, and ride back with them to the headquarters building. We'd like to cancel our morning charter."

"Understood. And will Mr. Dembinski require transportation back to the Willard at close of business?"

"Yes. Evening transport should remain as scheduled."

"I will make the arrangements. Unfortunately, we are not able to make adjustments to the daily rate for cancelations occurring within twenty-four hours, so tomorrow's bill will remain at $5,200 for the day."

She smiled.

"That won't be a problem for Mr. Dembinski. Thank you for your help, and have a wonderful night."

"You as well. Thank you for trusting Executive City Charter with your transportation needs, and please don't hesitate to reach out if we can be of further assistance."

"Thank you. Goodbye."

She ended the call and saw Marco holding a thumbs up.

"Easy enough," he said. "Ready?"

"Born ready."

They walked into the warehouse bay, where Sterling was ending a call on his cell phone. "He's pulling into the industrial park now. Let's get this lifted."

Sterling and Marco wheeled the roll-up door on its tracks, and Blair cleared the section of concrete floor in front of it. They'd shifted the cars around to make room for one more, and within the next thirty seconds, blinding headlights marked its arrival.

The enormous vehicle that rolled inside was stark white, looking like a cross between a luxury SUV and a tank with a pantheon grill. Blair felt the rumble of its massive engine shaking the air around her until the car shut off, and as Marco and Sterling closed the rolling door, Alec exited the vehicle in a state of near-delirium.

Blair asked, "How was the City of Brotherly Love?"

"Forget that," he said, eyes wild. "Right now I'm concerned

with something much more powerful—the love I have for this vehicle, which borders on erotic."

"Alec," Marco asked, "are you okay?"

"Okay? I feel like I just got out of a day spa. Did seventy miles an hour on I-95 and I could've heard a pin drop on the lambswool floor mats. Felt like I was riding a magic carpet." He gave a wistful sigh. "I guess it's true what they say. You don't drive a Rolls Royce, you *experience* it. For $3,500 a day this thing really is worth every penny."

"Cool," Sterling said. "And don't get too attached, because we *will* be returning it to the rental agency. Let's get—"

Alec cut him off, sweeping a hand toward the car.

"Look atop the bonnet—that's British for car hood—and you'll find the little lady that makes every Rolls Royce a Rolls Royce."

Blair examined the hood ornament, a gleaming silver sculpture of a woman leaning forward, billowing cloth forming wings from her outstretched arms.

"That's the Spirit of Ecstasy, rightfully named because that's what driving this vehicle is: sheer ecstasy."

"Sure," Sterling said. "That's great, and I hate to cut you short, but we've got a long night ahead."

He walked over to the boxes of supplies they'd spent the better part of four hours acquiring: scissors, magnets, propane torches, polyester gloves, masking tape, squeegees, and a cluster of tall cylinders bearing the 3M logo.

Sterling grabbed one of the cylinders and tapped it against his opposite palm.

"Let's get to work."

23

STERLING

As Sterling drove toward the Willard InterContinental the following morning, he was almost overwhelmed by a single thought: Alec was right.

Driving the Rolls Royce Cullinan wasn't like driving at all. It was like being swallowed into a cocoon of conditioned leather, then gliding across a surface of polished glass where every bump in the road vanished amid the vehicle's self-leveling air suspension. The sound insulation was so magnificent that he'd driven by a construction site without hearing so much as a faint burble from the jackhammer, the vehicle's cabin a universe of tranquility unto itself. There was simply no noise, whether from wind, tires, or engine.

Until he depressed the accelerator. At that moment, the Cullinan reminded him of the power under the hood. And lo, Sterling thought, how there was power.

The 6.75-liter V12 applied its 563 horsepower so effortlessly that Sterling had to keep a laser focus on remaining at the speed limit lest he blow by a speed trap on the way to DC. He'd initially balked at the vehicle's near-half-million-dollar-with-options price tag. After driving the Cullinan for thirty seconds, he thought the price was an absolute steal. The road melted away as languidly as ice in bourbon, the sheer sensory pleasure of operating this vehicle making Sterling momentarily consider retiring to a non-extradition country so he could drive on endlessly. But retirement wasn't on the horizon for him or his crew, and unless they were successful in the auction tomorrow, for Jim either.

Sterling considered that he was now driving through the center of leadership in the Land of the Free. That meant a lot for a fugitive, particularly one who'd seen the dark underbelly of the American penal system. But he'd chosen this life, made no excuses for who he was or what he did, and if he was arrested in the course of that, then so be it.

Jim, by contrast, was a fugitive of a different sort. He was a man who'd never been caught, and only rarely suspected, of what he'd done for his entire career: masquerading as an agent of justice while engaged in every sordid corruption that would advance him up the ladder of power, and crushing underfoot whoever he had to in the process. Backed by the seemingly limitless finances of his mentor and characterized both by ruthlessness and the ability to lie as easily as he breathed, Jim had been a bulletproof vessel of deceit rising up the ranks with ease.

Granted, Sterling was no agent of reform for abiding by the law, much less enforcing it. But Jim had become a personal enemy the second he threatened Sterling's widowed mother as a means of achieving his own ends, and Sterling intended to do whatever it took to bring the world down around Jim Jacobson, corrupt FBI agent, master manipulator, and current Congressional candidate.

Sterling approached the intersection with 14th Street,

catching his first glimpse of the Willard InterContinental ahead. It was a grand, twelve-story structure of cream granite, surrounded on all sides by trees and street lights bristling with trios of American flags drifting lightly in the cold morning breeze.

He pulled up to the curb beside the main entrance, receiving a friendly wave from the valet who remained at his station. Sterling was two minutes early, and that was apparently an acceptable margin of error in occupying this prime parking spot for the time being.

In contrast to Sterling, Dembinski appeared right on time, almost down to the second. Sterling got his first in-person look when a doorman pulled the door open for him. Dembinski approached the car without so much as a sideways glance, and Sterling thought, why wouldn't he? Here was a jet-black Cullinan at the appointed time, by now a routine that even the valets knew by heart.

The valet approached the rear passenger door, pulling it open as Sterling looked over to see his new passenger muttering a word of thanks to the valet and entering the backseat.

Eric Dembinski was a large, solidly built man, one whose posture implied a great deal of natural strength despite the presence of a rotund belly stretching his shirtfront. He had longer hair than Sterling imagined was common on Wall Street, gelled back in spiky peaks as he set his briefcase on the seat beside him.

But his eyes were his most notable feature: dull, half-closed, lifeless. They were the eyes of a shark, and in that moment, a shark was exactly what Sterling needed.

The valet closed the door. Sterling activated the rear door locks and said, "Good morning, Mr. Dembinski."

Dembinski pulled the seatbelt over his chest and replied in a low monotone. "Where's Carl?"

"Carl got the morning off." Sterling pulled out onto Pennsylvania Avenue, gliding into the right turn lane as Dembinski checked his phone and said quietly, almost to himself, "I don't have reception. Why don't I have reception?"

Sterling wasn't about to mention the cellular jammer in the console, a provision in case Dembinski tried to alert the authorities mid-trip. Instead he asked, "Do you recognize me?"

"No."

"I left you some reading material in the seatback to your front. If you wouldn't mind."

He checked in his rearview and heard the rustle of paper as Dembinski plucked the printout of a news article with the headline, *THIEF CAPTURED AFTER ROBBING THE SKY SAFE.*

Beneath the headline was the mugshot that had made Sterling famous.

Turning his head to look at Dembinski, he said, "How about now?"

Dembinski didn't sound threatened or even surprised, replying instead in the same deep, monotonous voice as before. "Huh. It's really you."

Sterling turned right and saw the Treasury Union building spanning the length of a city block, shielding the White House from street view.

He began, "We don't have much time, so please listen carefully. You want the tapes for the same reason we do: to ensure they make it into the public domain. Now I'm reasonably confident you want to trim some content that implicates whatever political party the finance sector is trying to back at present, and I don't care about that. I just need one guarantee, and that's to make sure that everything implicating Jim Jacobson for criminal charges gets leaked to the press. Since I understand Wall Street is supporting the Democrats this election cycle, that shouldn't be a hardship."

"You need that guarantee in exchange for...what, exactly?"

"Jim has a powerful backer, the one he refers to in the tapes as his mentor. Whoever that individual is, he has deep pockets, and it's going to take my people and yours to stop him. I want to combine our finances for a single bid."

"How do you propose we do that?"

Sterling had caught a series of green lights that reduced his time in the car with Dembinski, and was crossing over H Street as he continued.

"It's in our best interests to avoid scaring off Wraith, so I'll compete in the bidding until my funds tap out. After that, you increase your bid to account for my crew's contribution." Sterling turned left on I Street. "You win the auction, and I wire you the money instantly, to whatever account you want. Then you arrange receiving the tapes from Wraith, and once you get them, make sure the media knows how much of a corrupt scumbag Jim is in addition to whatever other content you want leaked. And after that, we're done."

"How much can you contribute?"

Sterling tightened his grip on the steering wheel. "Twelve million."

"Twelve?" Dembinski scoffed. "The Sierra Diamond was worth twice that."

"It was *valued* at twice that. I want Jim to go down more than anyone, and if I had more to offer, I would. I'll spare you the specifics of fencing stolen property and my crew's donations to charity."

"Charity? What do you guys get, a tax credit?"

"Well," Sterling said, seeing Farragut Square's open grass

to his right, "we all have our idiosyncrasies. Do we have a deal, or not?"

Right turn onto 18th Street, and they were now only two blocks from the destination.

And yet, Dembinski was silent.

"Well?" Sterling asked.

"I'm thinking."

"This is free money, helping you get what you want. What's there to think about?"

"Oh," Dembinski said, the final minutes on their trip ticking away, "I don't know. The legal implications of not reporting a wanted fugitive, the professional implications of doing business with thieves, the personal implications of being blackmailed and discredited in the press."

"Blackmail isn't my style," Sterling said firmly, advancing up the final city block. "And if you think you're assuming risk by saying yes to this deal, consider what I've already gone through just to offer it. If that's not a show of good faith, I don't know what is."

Dembinski remained silent, and Sterling checked his mirror to see the banker with his lips pursed, lost in thought.

And then Sterling was crossing over L Street, seeing the parking garage entrance to his right beneath a black sign that read, *WELCOME TO 1120 CONN. AVE, NW*.

Wheeling the Rolls Royce inside, Sterling said, "We're out of time. What's it going to be?"

"Okay," Dembinski said as they passed into the dark recesses of the garage. "Okay. Let's do it. My cap prior to this was ten, but I'll dip into my own pockets to match you at twelve. I'm presuming there's no sales tax on this auction, so I'll go head-to-head with Jim with a ceiling of twenty-four million."

Sterling almost shuddered with gratitude, carving a left turn toward the ramp to the third level.

Then he said, "I need you to go about your day as normal. Your normal chauffeur will pick you up this afternoon, and if he asks, you had breakfast with the ABA Vice Chair at the Willard, and he took you to headquarters this morning." He reached the ramp and began ascending. "Any questions?"

"Just one," Dembinski replied. "How do I contact you?"

Sterling hesitated—while select contact with the outside world was easy enough to maintain through the team's network of PO boxes, those were all based in Los Angeles, and that ruled them out for the timely communication required for the task at hand.

So they'd had to come up with something easy and foolproof, so much so that Sterling felt ridiculous mentioning it.

"Set up a new email account and drop us a line. Address is theskythieves@gmail.com."

"You're kidding."

Sterling frowned as he reached the third level and wheeled toward the drop-off point. That email address had been Alec's bright idea, citing they needed something easy for Dembinski to remember and every other form of shorthand had been taken. By the time Sterling could argue, the damage was done.

Sensing that Sterling wasn't going to answer, Dembinski said, "Okay, you're not kidding. All right. I'll be in touch."

"Thank you," Sterling said, braking before a glass door where three people awaited Dembinski's arrival.

Dembinski pushed a button to open his door, then grabbed his briefcase and slid out of the vehicle.

Another button push caused the door to close, and Sterling watched Dembinski approach his reception party as he slowly accelerated forward. Once they had disappeared inside the building, he increased his speed, turning down the ramp as if he were making a hasty exit from the building.

But instead of continuing his descent to the ground floor, he departed the ramp on the second parking level, cutting to the farthest row of cars and speeding toward the back corner of the garage.

24

BLAIR

Blair heard Sterling's black Cullinan approaching, proceeding past the road cones and yellow tape the crew had used to fence off a section of the parking garage for "construction repairs."

He pulled the massive vehicle past the plastic sheeting they'd erected from floor to ceiling, then parked in the open spot before leaping out and moving to the rental sedan that was parked with the engine running.

Sterling shot her a thumbs up and then hopped into the driver's seat, slamming the door and pulling forward as Blair lowered the plastic sheeting to conceal the remaining work.

Then she knelt before the Rolls Royce's rear bumper, using a handheld drill to remove the fabricated DC license plate and replace it with its original Pennsylvania plate. The sound of the drill was obscured by the chatter of a police transponder over her earpiece, which she monitored for any indication that Dembinski hadn't taken kindly to Sterling's pitch. By the time she'd finished, Alec and Marco were already making serious progress on the Cullinan.

Applying the jet-black wrap film had been difficult—first

the crew had to wash and dry the vehicle, then use torque wrenches and screwdrivers to remove the door handles and dental floss to pull the badges. Once the Cullinan was naked, they'd secured sheets of wrap film over the vehicle's surfaces with magnets, cutting it roughly to shape and folding it back to remove the liner and expose the adhesive side. Then it had been a matter of pressing it to the car paint with light tension before smoothing it out with handheld squeegees, removing air bubbles to give the appearance of a painted surface.

Removing the film, by contrast, was a rapid procedure: Alec used a plastic card to separate the seams of the black 3M wrap film as Marco blasted the surface with a giant propane torch, rapidly heating it to create elasticity before Alec peeled off the sheets one at a time to expose the vehicle's white paint.

Blair rushed to the front of the SUV, removing the temporary plastic bracket they'd attached to secure a DC license plate there. Then she tossed both plates into the open trunk of their waiting rental vehicle, now being filled with the discarded sheets of wrap film that Alec had already pulled off.

Once the wrap was fully removed, Alec drove the now-white Cullinan out of the garage, bearing legal plates and legitimate paperwork. It only took Blair and Marco minutes to clean up the rest, packing up the traffic cones, yellow tape, and plastic sheeting before getting in the final vehicle.

Marco was at the wheel and Blair rode shotgun as they swept out of the garage, onto Connecticut Avenue, and on their way back to the rental facility.

25

STERLING

Sterling squirted detailer spray onto the Cullinan's hood, wiping down the pooled liquid with a neatly folded microfiber cloth.

The crew's hasty wrap removal had been sufficient to restore the vehicle to its factory white color, but to avoid any suspicion on behalf of the rental company, they'd had to go back over it with a fine-tooth comb, using detailer spray to remove any sticky spots and searching for remaining scraps of black film under badges, in the door jams, and under the handles.

Now they were finishing their final cleaning process, a last safeguard in the event the authorities started looking for a mysterious Cullinan used to impersonate Dembinski's usual transport—but it didn't appear that would be the case.

There had been no mention of the morning's interdiction on the police transponder, and while Dembinski hadn't yet contacted them over their email address, they had no reason to suspect that Sterling's pitch had been anything but a massive success.

And now that the vehicle was fully cleaned, it was time to do what Alec—and Sterling—dreaded.

"All right, Alec," Sterling said, tossing his microfiber towel in the bin with the others. "It's time to take her home."

Alec looked to him with pleading eyes.

"I've bonded with this vehicle in a way that I have with very few human beings. She *is* home, Sterling, and...so am I."

Sterling lowered his head, speaking mournfully.

"It's not going to be easy for any of us. But Rolls Royce giveth, and Rolls Royce taketh away. I'm sorry, buddy. It's time to say goodbye."

Alec walked to the front grill, leaning forward to gently kiss the Spirit of Ecstasy hood ornament.

"I'll miss you the most, girl," he whispered. "We'll always have DC."

Marco emerged from his room, carrying a jacket.

"Where are you going?" Sterling asked.

"What do you mean, where am I going? To Philadelphia."

"Alec can handle that."

"I don't care about his emotional support; I care about getting behind the wheel of this beast. I'm the last one on the crew who hasn't driven it yet—"

"And me," Blair corrected him.

Marco rephrased, "The last *guy* on the crew who hasn't driven it yet, and it is highly unlikely I'll have the opportunity ever again. Besides, we haven't heard from Dembinski yet, we have less than twenty-four hours until the auction, and as enjoyable as it is to watch Blair get smash-hammered while eating crab pizza, I could use a change of scenery. No offense, Blair."

"None taken."

As they prepared to depart, Sterling felt suddenly uncomfortable about being alone with Blair in the rental facility for the next five hours. He wasn't exactly sure why—after all, they technically lived together at the warehouse back in LA. But that was a much larger space, their respective bedrooms spread sufficiently that each may as well have been living alone.

Here at the rental facility, the confines were much tighter. Adding to Sterling's apprehension was the fact that there was nothing to plan, no equipment to prepare, nothing to do but wait until the auction tomorrow. He'd never done well with sitting still and waiting for events outside his control, and today was no exception.

Blair and Sterling lifted the rolling door for the great beast to depart, locking it after Alec and Marco had begun the trip.

Then Blair said, "Congrats on the job this morning."

"Oh. Thanks."

"I mean it. I know I would have been terrified, driving around the streets of DC, giving a business pitch to a passenger who may or may not want to have me arrested. And your face is just as recognizable as mine out there. That takes guts, and you pulled it off."

"Yeah," he agreed. "It got a little hairy there, after he made it clear that we picked the dumbest email address imaginable."

"Doesn't matter if it's dumb, only memorable. That being said... theskythieves@gmail.com is both."

"Agreed."

Her sparkling eyes met his. "What do you want to do while they're gone?"

"Dunno," he said, feeling suddenly flushed. "Hadn't thought that far ahead."

"Well, it's been a long day. I'm going to shower."

26

BLAIR

Blair toweled off from her shower, dressing in a T-shirt and sweatpants before following the sound of voices into the warehouse bay.

When she arrived, she found that Sterling had reappropriated the projector to play his all-time favorite movie.

As she approached, Robert DeNiro was taking a seat at a cafe counter, ordering coffee and asking a woman beside him to pass the cream.

"I don't know why I'm surprised every time I catch you watching *Heat*."

Sterling took a sip from the can in his hand. "It's a classic. You want a beer?"

"My body is still processing the alcohol from last time." Taking a seat and crossing one leg over the other, she remarked, "We met in a coffee shop too. Remember Greaney's?"

"How could I forget? But in *Heat*, Eady doesn't assault DeNiro by spilling coffee on him."

"Waitressing never did suit me."

"It was for the best." He waved his can toward the screen,

and Blair studied his features as he said, "Can you imagine having to research a score like that?"

"Like what? The precious metal repository they hit before the bank?"

"No. No, I mean the way they had to research it. Like, go to a bookstore, find a book about stress fractures in titanium, then have to shotgun coffee while you try to figure it out. It's a wonder anything got robbed before the internet."

"This is true."

She looked at the screen. DeNiro and his date were now overlooking a panoramic view of Los Angeles at night while he ruminated on its similarities with the iridescent algae in Fiji.

Sterling lifted his beer toward the screen-slash-wall and said, "Maybe that'll be us at some point."

"Drinking in LA, talking about how lonely we are? Get real, Sterling. That was every day before we came to DC."

"I mean going to Fiji. Someplace we don't have to hide our faces."

Blair countered, "But after the bank heist, he tries to escape to New Zealand. I never got that—both countries have extradition treaties with the US. He'd still have to hide."

"There probably aren't many good options."

She shook her head. "Not to correct you, but there are some beautiful countries without extradition to the US. Indonesia, Madagascar, Nepal, Vietnam...and don't forget the UAE. Dubai sounds like a good time."

"You've given this some thought."

"Have you not?" she asked, half-wondering if he was serious. It was hard to believe anyone in this profession hadn't considered their long-term options for avoiding prison. "I mean don't get me wrong, I'm not ready to hang up my spurs by a long shot. But what about when you want to retire? Why stay in a country that wants you behind bars when the statute of limitations is active?"

"I guess I've never seriously considered retirement. And I just..." He shrugged helplessly. "I guess I just love America."

In that moment, Blair felt a tug of emotion as she considered Sterling's almost childlike enthusiasm about the job. They'd both been to prison, but while Blair felt forever changed by the experience, Sterling had quickly returned to his normal self: audacious, optimistic, certain of success against the most overwhelming odds.

Onscreen, DeNiro and his date clutched one another in a kissing embrace. The scene cut to him rising from bed, bringing his sleeping partner a glass of water wrapped in a napkin so he wouldn't leave fingerprints.

Blair knew, of course, what happened later in the story. Hollywood seemed to prefer a tragic downfall for its thieves in all but the most comedic heist films. She gave a momentary thought about how her own story would end one day, or for that matter, her crew's.

And in the end the only thing she knew for certain was that she was doing what she loved, and as DeNiro said in *Heat*, that life was short.

Then the cinematic moment was over, cutting to Al Pacino and his LAPD partner in a separate part of the city, preparing to shake down an informant.

Blair didn't know why she did what she did then; there were no thoughts, just the view of Sterling's face lit by the projector's glare.

She said, "Give me your beer."

He handed it to her, and she set it on the ground before taking his outstretched hand in hers.

Blair stood first and Sterling followed suit, neither of them speaking as she led the way to her room.

27

STERLING

Sterling spent the following morning in a dreamy state of disbelief.

After all the jobs they'd done together, him saving her and her saving him, Sterling telling Blair that he'd loved her moments before being arrested, and a first kiss during a jailbreak, they'd finally slept together.

Sterling wasn't unhappy about the development—he'd been attracted to Blair long before the feeling was reciprocated—but he couldn't help but wonder what implications it held for the crew. They'd have to maintain a professional relationship in addition to a romantic one, and there wasn't exactly a playbook for that in the realm of high-stakes heists. If an office fling could be complicated, what about one within a small crew of thieves?

None of this seemed to concern Blair, who showed up for work that morning bright-eyed and bushy-tailed. The only indication of what had transpired the night before was a softness in her step, a lingering gaze when she looked at Sterling.

And while Sterling had felt a vague sense of anxiety about

Alec and Marco leaving for Philadelphia, now he couldn't wait until he and Blair could be alone again.

Marco said, "You worried about this, boss? Only ten minutes."

"Until what?"

He heard the creaking of chairs, looked up to see the other three crew members turning to face him. They were clustered around Marco's computer, now watching him with expressions of disbelief.

"You kidding me?" Marco said. "The auction. We've only got ten minutes until the auction, and it's been radio silence on the account."

Sterling flashed to the present moment, recalling that the effort to pitch Dembinski had gone off more or less without a hitch and the crew now had a shot at winning Wraith's auction.

There was just one problem: Dembinski had never contacted them.

Sterling blinked.

"Right. I know that."

Alec asked Marco, "You're sure it works?"

Marco closed his eyes and spoke slowly. "Yes, Alec. I am sure that Gmail works."

"I mean you tested it?"

"Yes, I tested it."

"I told you all from the start," Sterling insisted. "We should've picked a better email address."

Alec groaned and threw his head back. "There *isn't* a better email address. It's literally our username in the chatroom. If anything went wrong, Sterling, it's that you screwed things up as usual. Bet you told Dembinski the sky thief, singular. Poor guy is probably pulling his hair out trying to reach us at the wrong address."

Sterling rubbed his temples. "I didn't misspeak, and Dembinski is a smart guy. If he hasn't contacted us yet, it's because he doesn't want to. Let's just hope he's going to bid on his own, because I don't think our money is going to last long against Jim's mentor."

Even if Dembinski contacted them at the last minute, Sterling wasn't thrilled about paying twelve million for tapes that should have been theirs to begin with. Despite the high-yield scores they'd taken, their profits were bound by rules that had been in place since the crew's inception—half to charity, five percent take-home split equally, and the rest retained for planning and executing future heists. In that way they'd scaled their efforts much like a business that had little concern for profit, expanding their research and development until they could take more technologically advanced scores than anyone else.

In that way they'd also broken through a threshold that few other heist crews in the world had. At the upper echelon of security technology, there existed a catch-22: any thieves skilled and wealthy enough to break in probably wouldn't, because they'd already made enough to retire. This effect was embodied by the most secure vault ever built, the Sky Safe. No one but Sterling's crew would have even attempted to crack such a magnificent testament to protection, and their success in robbing it had earned them the media-proclaimed moniker of Sky Thieves.

Sterling accepted that nickname with pride, and that pride had been seriously wounded when he'd found out that someone had stolen the tapes that incriminated Jim. He resented having to participate in this charade of an auction in the first place—he shouldn't have had to spend his crew's hard-earned winnings buying anything from another thief.

They were arguably the most skilled heist crew in the world; they should have been able to *steal* it.

And yet they had no choice other than to play Wraith's game, although Sterling's meeting with Dembinski appeared to be all for naught.

Then, at the moment this thought occurred to him, the double chime of an incoming email sounded from Marco's computer.

The team responded with a collective gasp of relief, and Marco read the contents of Dembinski's email aloud.

"He says he's ready to bid, and is asking if we're ready to transfer our share immediately upon winning." Marco typed the team's response in the affirmative, and it was met with an almost immediate reply stating that Dembinski would send wire transfer instructions upon winning.

Alec nodded at Sterling. "You think we really got a chance at this? I mean if Jim's mentor has so much money…"

"It's not about how much money Jim's mentor has," Sterling replied. "It's about how much money his mentor is willing to spend on a corrupt scumbag he's already had to bail out of trouble multiple times before now. And there has to be a threshold where it's cheaper to cut Jim loose and do damage control with the press than to buy the tapes in the first place. With a ceiling of twenty-four million, we've got a chance."

Before anyone could debate the issue, the computer screen filled with Wraith's avatar and the computerized British voice spoke.

"Welcome, and thank you for coming. Is everyone ready to bid, with funds available to transfer immediately?"

Marco replied first, the smiling cartoon cloud speaking the single typed word. "Ready."

Then the Viking in the horned helmet appeared, Dembinski's response emitting as a digital Scandinavian accent. "Ready and waiting."

Sterling wondered what Jim's avatar would be—surely by now he'd educated himself in the absurdly simple particulars of replacing his own image and voice.

And when Jim answered, Sterling wasn't disappointed.

The next avatar to appear was a digital white man in a Colonial tricorn hat, appearing against the backdrop of a waving American flag.

Sterling shook his head. Of course Jim would choose something so vain as an American revolutionary.

A neutral digital voice answered on Jim's behalf, "Let's get this over with."

Wraith took the screen again. "Today's one and only auction lot consists of four microcassette tapes that contain, without exaggeration, exhaustive evidence of corruption not only from Jim Jacobson, but from high-ranking members of both political parties. You all understand the significance of this information or you wouldn't be here, so let's get started. The bidding starts at one million dollars, proceeding in increments of the same."

Dembinski's Viking said, "Five."

Wraith asked, "Five? Five million?"

"Yes. Five million USD."

"I have a starting bid of five million. However, we have two additional buyers, and six million is next."

The cloud representing the Sky Thieves spoke. "Six."

Jim quickly answered, "Seven."

"Eight. Whose money are you spending, Jim?"

"Someone with deeper pockets than you common criminals. Nine."

Sterling spoke his response to Marco, who typed quickly.

"Ten million. Do you consider yourself an uncommon criminal, or not a criminal at all? Asking for a friend."

Jim replied, "Eleven. And you're the only ones here who have been to prison."

Sterling shot back a verbal response, and his words were translated into the cloud's digital voice as quickly as Marco could type them.

"Winning this auction will change that, and we look forward to seeing you join the ranks. Prison isn't so bad, Jim—you'll meet plenty of people just like you. Twelve million."

"History is written by the victor. Thirteen."

Sterling felt two conflicting emotions at the sight of the number thirteen. On one hand was a sense of embarrassment that he was being outbid by Jim—or, more properly put, by Jim's mentor—and on the other was an almost delirious sense of relief that Dembinski had agreed to their plan, a contingency that was about to come into play.

He spoke to his team.

"We're out—let's see if Dembinski can do any better."

28

JIM

Jim felt a rush of exaltation when his bid of thirteen million was not met with an immediate response from the Sky Thieves.

Sitting in his personal office within his campaign headquarters, a corporate suite rented for the purpose, he'd locked his door and drawn the shades in preparation for this auction. He'd informed his campaign manager to ensure total privacy for the duration of the auction, at least from his campaign staff.

Jim had no such privacy from his mentor, who was understandably monitoring the auction over a phone connection as Jim kept a single earbud tuned to the auction proceedings.

He typed quickly as he informed his mentor, "Sky Thieves are out at thirteen."

Onscreen, Jim's patriot avatar spoke. "No pithy comeback after my bid? What's the matter, did you already spend everything you stole?"

The grinning cartoon cloud answered, "Umm..."

"That's what I figured," Jim replied.

Wraith's hooded figure appeared. "The tapes are now with Jim at thirteen. Any advance, Sky Thieves?"

Once more, the smiling cloud said, "Umm..."

"I will take that as a no. Fixer, how are you doing?"

The Viking took the screen. "Fourteen million."

"I have fourteen from Fixer. Jim?"

Jim, who had been narrating the proceedings to his mentor, faced the unenviable necessity of having to deliver this latest update.

"Fixer is back in at fourteen."

He expected a swift rebuke, some underhanded comment implying future consequences tantamount to being crushed under the heel of his mentor's considerable influence.

To his surprise, his mentor's synthesized voice replied, "Get this over with. Take it to twenty."

Jim's mouth went dry. The starting bid of one million was an outlandish sum of money; now they were reaching stratospheric amounts that made his head spin. But he couldn't deny the sense of gratitude he felt as he typed his response.

"Twenty million."

Wraith replied, "Twenty million...I actually cleared half an hour for this, but it looks like the massive bids are speeding up the auction considerably."

The Viking said, "Twenty-one."

Jim countered, "Twenty-two."

"Twenty-three."

"Twenty-four."

After Jim's latest bid was met with a pause, Wraith's avatar spoke.

"Fixer, I have the tapes with Jim at twenty-four million. Do you care to challenge that?"

There was another brief delay before the Viking answered, "24.5."

Wraith said, "Out of respect for these important tapes, I will accept smaller bid increments."

Jim typed a response for his patriot. "Twenty-five."

Fixer replied, "25.2."

"25.4."

Wraith appeared. "Fixer, I have the tapes going to Jim at 25.4 million. If it is your last bid, I will take 25.5."

Fixer answered quickly. "25.5."

Jim typed eagerly, feeling the exhilaration that he was about to outpace his opponents.

"25.6."

Wraith said, "25,600,000 for Jim Jacobson. It is now or never. Fixer, can you support 25.7? I will give you a moment to consider. I think we are all in agreement, these tapes are worth the wait."

29

BLAIR

Blair watched the auction proceedings with the vague sense of guilt that had plagued her since discovering her safe deposit box had been robbed. She'd taken precautions to hide any link between it and herself, but those precautions had proven to be insufficient to stop Wraith.

And now, entering into the final stretch of bidding as it dwindled down to a conclusion that now seemed inevitable, Blair knew this was all her fault. The feeling reached a distinct peak of emotion as Dembinski's Viking avatar replied.

"I'm out."

Those two words were the nail in the coffin for the team's hopes of purchasing the tapes, the final admission of failure from which there was no return. Jim's rise was proceeding unabated, his ascent to power having spanned the FBI's rank structure and now continued into national politics.

She put her head in her hands, feeling a supportive squeeze on her shoulder. Blair looked up to see Sterling shaking his head slightly, as if to say, don't worry about it. Glancing back to the monitor, she read the new messages filling the screen.

Wraith said, "Jim stands alone as the winner, unless anyone else is raising their bid paddle. Sky Thieves, have you been holding out on us? Care to rejoin the bidding at this altitude?"

Marco typed without waiting for input from Sterling or anyone else, and the cartoon cloud cheerily replied, "You suck, Jim."

Then Wraith was on the screen, the fire and smoke drifting behind his black cloaked figure.

"The gavel is up...Fixer, Sky Thieves, I am selling to Jim at $25,600,000 USD. Fair warning, the only set of audio tapes, last chance. It is now or never."

Dembinski's Viking replied, "Still out."

Then the cloud answered on behalf of Marco, "Jim still sucks."

Wraith said, "Do not despair just yet. If I do not receive the funds in full within ten minutes, I will accept your bid of 25.5. Barring that, I am selling officially for 25.6 to Jim Jacobson. Jim, you will see a private pop-up window with the account information. Your ten minutes to deliver the complete payment begin now."

Jim's ridiculous patriot figure replied, "Information received. Transfer initiated."

Wraith's response was almost immediate.

"Funding received in full. Sky Thieves, Fixer, this auction is history. Jim, congratulations on your victory, and I will be in touch regarding transfer of the tapes. You will receive instructions from me within five days. This chat is now over, and this link will be permanently disabled. Good day."

In the seconds before the screen went black, Blair felt a seismic shift in her mood.

Sterling, Marco, and Alec immediately lapsed into excited

chatter, debating everything from whether or not Jim would ever receive the tapes to how they could identify and locate Wraith for a heist of vengeance.

But Blair felt serene, almost tranquil—an abrupt moment of clarity that brought with it the calm certainty that she knew exactly what to do.

"Guys," she said calmly, "we can still get the tapes."

They went silent, their eyes fixing on her as they awaited an explanation.

She continued, "Wraith told Jim he'd receive instructions within five days. Why that amount of time?"

Sterling answered, "Because Wraith isn't going to mail the tapes. He'll travel to Albany to hand them off, either in person or using a dead drop."

Alec shook his head. "How do we know Wraith will give the tapes to Jim at all? For all we know, he could've said five days just to get a head start on wherever he's taking his newfound twenty-five million dollars."

"I don't think so," Blair said. "I think Wraith will deliver exactly what he promised."

Marco smiled at her. "Your faith is quite endearing. But you haven't explained why you believe this."

"Let's look at what we know about Wraith: he's highly skilled, because he managed to trace that safe deposit box to me and then got into the JB Porter Federal Bank same as we did. Having found surveillance tapes implicating both Democrats and Republicans, he chose to establish a bidding war between the three most well-funded parties who'd be willing to bid on them. That means he's apolitical, because a zealot would have leapt at the chance to discredit whichever party they didn't support. I think we're dealing with someone smart enough to make a legal living in any number of ways, but choosing to be a thief because he loves it. In short, I think we're dealing with—"

"Someone like us," Sterling finished.

"Exactly." She paused to gather her thoughts. "And if it had been us taking such elaborate measures to run a dark web auction of stolen property, what would we do after being paid?"

Alec said, "We'd deliver."

"That's right. And Wraith will do the same, mark my words. We don't need to find Wraith; we need to picket Jim's communications and wait for Wraith to contact him."

Sterling looked to Marco. "How about it, tech whiz?"

"Based on the timing of Jim's entry into the first chatroom, and his initial suspicion that Blair was behind the sale, it's safe to assume that Wraith hijacked Jim's computer screen at work. So that balance of probability is that the next contact will occur in a similar manner, while he's at his campaign headquarters. In short, we would need total transparency over his communications, including everything that comes through his business computer, phone, and personal cell, and that is going to require physically tapping all of it."

"Physically tapping," Alec began. "You mean like breaking into his campaign headquarters?"

Seeing where the conversation was headed, Marco sighed wearily.

"Yes, Alec, we can call the heist something that ends in 'gate.'"

"Not Watergate," Alec replied quickly, "that's taken. But Albanygate, or Campaigngate, or…"

"Or Jimgate," Sterling said.

Alec's eyes lit up, and he jabbed a finger at Sterling.

"*Jimgate*," he said breathlessly. "That's it."

Marco cautioned, "We're getting ahead of ourselves. Let's

say we went to Albany and succeeded in tapping everything that Wraith could use to contact Jim. What's our next move?"

Blair said, "Then we monitor, and wait for Wraith to establish contact and set a handoff for the tapes."

"Yes, but then what?"

"Then we do what we do best—steal them back."

30

STERLING

Sterling piloted the lead Sprinter van north on I-95, watching a white sign reading *Welcome to Delaware* slip by outside his window.

He checked his side-view mirror, seeing that the trail Sprinter van remained fifty meters behind him. That one was driven by Alec, allowing Blair the luxury of staying out of sight from other drivers as the crew made their way toward Albany. Sterling had no such advantage, resorting instead to a ballcap with the logo of their security LLC and the itchy, fake beard that he desperately wanted to remove and set on fire.

Operating a motor vehicle as a fugitive wasn't the wisest move, but they were on a serious time crunch now. They had committed their final hours in the Maryland rental facility to a "pack and hack," meaning everyone packed the team equipment into their Sprinter vans while Marco hacked information for their upcoming job.

He was now sifting through that data in the back of the van, a digital vault of open- and closed-source information ranging from local fire codes to building insurance policies, both of which carried far more specifications as to entrances, exits, and security measures than most people knew.

But the building's onsite management database had provided the most useful clues of all, and Marco began speaking as soon as he'd finished analyzing it.

"Well," he said, "I've got good news and bad news."

Sterling nodded, adjusting his grip on the steering wheel. "I figured as much. Let's start with the bad."

"Jim's campaign headquarters is on State Street in downtown Albany. It's a twelve-story building with a three-story underground parking garage and four high-speed elevators, all split up into subdividable office space for rent. About three-quarters of the building is currently in use by a total of eighteen businesses."

Braking behind a slow-moving semi-trailer, Sterling said, "With that much foot traffic from that many businesses, getting in and out without being noticed should be a cinch. I thought we were discussing bad news."

"Yes," Marco agreed, "but it's *because* of all that foot traffic that we're running into a different obstacle. The building management can't rely on hair-trigger motion sensors or even surveillance cameras when they rely on providing 24/7 access to their occupants, so the balance of security is with physical keys issued to authorized parties. Because of that, and due to how subdivided the building is, we're looking at a highly complex key assignment structure combined with each door being individually locked at the close of business. Moving through the building while picking a lock every thirty seconds will be difficult. Given the narrow window for entry in between the janitorial and staff schedules of each business renting office space there, it becomes a nightmare."

Sterling considered this information, reminding himself there was always a way. No secure space was truly impenetrable, but the amount of time, effort, and funding required to penetrate a facility rendered many of them too much of a pain to bother with. That was where the most complex and exhaustive security measures succeeded—not by eliminating every imaginative means of bypass, but by making entry so inconvenient there was no reason to bother with such a difficult target when there were so many easier ones out there.

But in this case, it wasn't a matter of target selection. They had one goal, and would either find a way or die in the attempt.

Glancing over his shoulder at Marco, Sterling asked, "Then what's the good news?"

"The entire building is grand master keyed."

Sterling thumped a victorious fist on the steering wheel. "What's the hierarchy?"

"Each floor of the building is split into quadrants. Those each have their own change keys that won't operate in any other quadrant, so forty-eight sets of quadrant keys for the building. They are organized with one master key per floor."

"And above those twelve master keys, we have a grand master."

"One key to rule them all. It will open every door in the building."

"Easy," Sterling said. "We make a copy."

"The grand master key is located on the 10th floor. Access is restricted to authorized personnel using a detailed sign-out roster and backed up by routine key audits. It's so deep in the building that getting to it is worse than getting to Jim's office, which defeats the purpose. That's why I'd propose—"

"Don't tell me." Sterling cut him off. "You're thinking we go with a cylinder swap."

31

BLAIR

Blair reclined in the back of the trail Sprinter van, studying the map of Albany on the tablet in her lap. She was certainly no Marco, but with over four hours remaining in their trip, she could accomplish plenty as a passenger.

She announced to Alec, "There are five public parks surrounding downtown, and if I were making the drop, I'd choose one of those. Enough people to blend in, and enough ways out to make a quick getaway. I can't rule out the Riverfront Preserve, but it's doubtful—highway access is terrible, and Wraith wouldn't risk isolating himself on a speedboat."

Alec replied from behind the wheel.

"You really think Wraith will hand off the tapes right there in Albany?"

"Hundred percent. He'll probably give extremely short notice to a nearby location, probably one within Jim's normal pattern of life. That drastically reduces Wraith's exposure time and the chances that Jim would be able to arrange backup."

"Backup?" Alec asked. "If he's getting the tapes, why bother?"

"To make sure he's got the *only* tapes. I wouldn't put it past him to try and roll up Wraith and find out if there are any copies. Or to learn Wraith's identity to get some leverage to threaten him with, to prevent any copies from surfacing. Jim's ruthless, and he'll cover his tracks however he can."

Before Alec could respond, Sterling's voice transmitted over the van's radio speakers.

"All right, sports fans, looks like we'll need a heist before we can tap Jim's office. His campaign headquarters is in a subdivided office building with a complex grand master key system. In order to get in and out on a narrow timeline, we're going to have to pull a cylinder swap. And that leads us to the obvious problem."

Blair leaned forward. "Alec, what's a cylinder swap?"

Alec pressed a switch on the steering wheel and transmitted back, "Standby, I've got some explaining to do. Apparently this kind of thing isn't common knowledge at FBI TacOps."

Ending his transmission, he said, "You understand the grand master key system?"

"Of course," Blair replied. "Compartmentalized access according to a hierarchy of keys, with a grand master key at the top of the chart and able to open any lock in the building."

"Right. Well there's nothing special about the locks in and of themselves—they're pin tumblers with double-detainer action. The magic happens at the factory where they're produced, and the machines are programmed to generate one-off hierarchical access locks to order, together with the labeled key sets."

"Okay. So?"

"So if you were to disassemble a set of those locks, say two or three from different parts of the building, you could examine the tumblers and—"

"And reverse-engineer a grand master key," she concluded for him.

"That's exactly right," he said. "But that's a meticulous process, far too intensive to complete in an occupied building. Hence the 'swap' part of 'cylinder swap.' You steal the lock cylinders you need from easily accessible doors—say public restrooms—and temporarily replace them with identical-model cylinders that you've modified to function with any key. Once you've built your grand master key offsite, you swap the cylinders back."

She asked, "So what's the 'obvious' problem Sterling mentioned?"

"Well, the disassembly and examination of grand master-keyed lock cylinders is a painstaking process—we'd need to analyze measurements down to fractions of a millimeter, then reassemble to functional condition without leaving a trace. That requires a lot of specialized equipment that isn't exactly in the average locksmith's arsenal."

"Let me guess," she said. "We have the equipment in LA, but we didn't pack it for DC because we didn't anticipate any need for it."

He bobbed his head in agreement. "And there's no time to make a round trip to get it. Even if Marco or I made the cross-country flight, we'd eat into too much of Wraith's time window."

Keying the transmit switch on the steering wheel, Alec said, "All right, boss, we're all caught up back here."

Sterling replied, "*Since we don't have the equipment, we're going to have to find it one way or another. Alec, you think you could procure that stuff locally?*"

"Might be a few shops in New York City that would have the kind of stuff we'd need—but it would take days of shopping to spread out the purchases so as not to raise suspicion. By the time we get it done, we're as likely as not to have missed the contact from Wraith. So we're going to need a better plan."

"Yeah. Any bright ideas?"

Alec replied, "You tell us. Didn't you grow up outside Albany?"

"I did. Unfortunately no one in my high school class chose the same career I did, so not a lot of professional contacts in the area."

"I'm not talking about your contacts," Alec said. "I'm talking about your dad's."

32

STERLING

Sterling considered Alec's comment, blinking quickly as he kept his eyes on the road.

His dad had been a doting and attentive father, a committed and loving husband, and a brilliant master thief.

It wasn't that Walter Defranc had stumbled into a life of crime out of any desperate necessity. Instead, that particular skill set had been forged by Sterling's great-grandfather, a devoted career criminal who'd learned much of his trade the hard way and picked up the rest on his way in and out of trips to Sing Sing. By the time he had his own son—Sterling's grandfather—high-stakes robberies became the family trade.

Sterling's grandfather fared slightly better, cutting his teeth alongside his dad before venturing out on his own. He accumulated three convictions along with a snowballing universe of knowledge on how to execute heists, and the cycle continued with Sterling's dad.

By then Walter Defranc had seen the cycle of prison and its impact on the family, and he had no intentions of being in a cell for any duration of Sterling's youth. Instead, he combined a brilliant analytical mind with his family's devotion to thievery, making the smart plays at every turn and distinguishing himself as the first Defranc man to *not* go to jail in the course of his professional duties. Walter figured out how to do more with less, restricting his crew to a small team of professionals while both laundering and investing his earnings in a legitimate business that fed back into his illegal affairs: a hardware store, where all the necessary equipment could be obtained without raising an eyebrow.

There was another reason for the store—Walter had wanted to hand it down to his son, breaking the family tradition and setting the Defranc course into lawful waters.

But whatever gene was responsible for the allure of elite robbery, Sterling had inherited it as much as his father's wristwatch.

Gripping the steering wheel tightly, he transmitted back.

"There might be a way. It won't be easy, but...I could move on it tomorrow night. Alec and Marco could pull the lock cylinders from Jim's office while I chase down the only lead I've got."

Alec replied, *"Blair wants to know what she's supposed to do."*

Sterling felt a wave of heat flush across his neck.

"For this to have the slightest chance of working, I'll need Blair to come with me."

33

JIM

Jim hit send on the last email of the day, then checked his Rolex to note with pleasure that he'd managed to finish up early.

He was shutting down his computer when he heard a double knock at his office door.

"Enter."

The door swung open to reveal Mitchell. Jim still didn't know what to make of the man—whereas Jim liked to remove his jacket, loosen his tie, and roll up his sleeves when the door was closed, Mitchell remained impeccably attired as if press cameras had invaded the inner sanctum of their campaign.

"Staff's all cleared out for the day," he said, looking at Jim expectantly.

"Great. See you tomorrow."

Mitchell slipped inside, closing the door behind him.

"You owe me an update, Jim. Did the auction proceed as planned?"

"Yes," Jim replied, assuming a self-satisfied grin as he waited for Mitchell to probe for more information.

"And did you win?"

"I told you I'd win, and I did."

Jim spoke with smug conviction, but his mood had been very different prior to the final bid. The effects of those tapes reaching the public would have been devastating on many levels; instead, Jim was about to be free and clear forever. He'd previously evaded every internal investigation launched by the FBI, and now the tapes were a small obstacle to be disposed of. With Fixer bidding into the twenty-million range, Jim had begun to sweat his mentor's commitment, but all had turned out well, and now there was nothing to hold Jim back.

Mitchell, however, remained unconvinced.

"You still have enemies, Jim."

Rolling his sleeves down and buttoning the cuffs, Jim replied, "None that can touch me."

"I'm talking about the Sky Thieves."

"So am I. They bid on the tapes as well—and they lost."

"Jim, if they facilitated a breakout from Supermax, I'm concerned about them interfering with your recovery of the tapes."

"That breakout," Jim said, rising and donning his suit jacket, "made Sterling an international fugitive. Blair already was. They're not traveling all the way across the country to try and discredit me. It's simply too dangerous for them, and more importantly, it doesn't earn them a dime. These people are greedy, Chris. If messing with my campaign resulted in a payday for them, I'd be concerned. But it doesn't, so I'm not. It's that simple."

Jim snatched a business card holder from his desk drawer, a move that didn't go unnoticed by Mitchell.

"Where are you going?"

"To celebrate."

"Your first engagement is at eight tomorrow, Jim—I can't have you attending hungover."

Jim smiled. "Relax, Chris. I'm just off to raise a little community awareness on my way home."

34

BLAIR

Blair dropped her bag on the dusty floor of her new room, kneeling to unzip it and retrieve the cold weather clothing she'd desperately need in the coming hours.

Donning a winter coat, she considered that the new rental facility wasn't new at all—while it was listed as available for a month-to-month lease as "industrial space," that was a kind term for this building.

The exterior was plain red brick, as unimposing a veneer as she could've imagined. Upon entering, Blair realized the exterior's greatest service to the world was concealing the building's interior.

The floors—what Blair could see of them, anyway—were a circa-1940s surface of battered and scarred hardwood planks, visible in patches between debris from the warehouse's previous occupant.

And what that previous occupant did with the space, Blair wasn't exactly sure.

There was a pallet stacked with bags of concrete powder, a pile of empty orange gas cans, and a graveyard of metal planks whose original purpose she couldn't begin to divine. Two metal ladders covered in so much rust that she wouldn't climb them without a tetanus shot, five glass window panes leaning askew against a corner, and a forklift that looked like it hadn't been operated, much less dusted, since the mid-eighties.

But there were side rooms for Marco's office and team lodging, a single vehicle door to conceal the Sprinter vans in addition to the pair of rental cars they'd acquired since arriving, and due to its location in Menands, New York, less than a ten-minute drive to downtown Albany.

Besides, Blair thought, much of the negativity she felt toward their new temporary home had nothing to do with the structure—she'd once spent months in a prison cell, after all—and everything to do with nerves. Both about tonight's foray and the knowledge that Jim Jacobson roamed the landscape a few miles to her south.

Steadying her nerves with a few breaths, she emerged from her room into the main warehouse bay to find Sterling waiting for her.

"You nervous about tonight?" he asked.

"Yeah. Like never before."

"If it's any consolation, I'm probably more anxious than you."

She shot him a glare. "I severely doubt that."

Sterling smiled reassuringly. "Just follow my lead. If I'm right, everything will go fine."

"And if you're wrong?"

He shrugged, then clapped her on the shoulder—a buddy maneuver that gave her the slightest tinge of irritation under the circumstances.

"We'll cross that bridge when we come to it."

Alec and Marco were loading their gear into the trunk of a rental sedan. Paradoxically, theirs was the easier of the two jobs tonight: posing as maintenance people, they'd infiltrate

Jim's building and swap a few cylinders with duplicates at the total cost of two minutes per door. While their task required considerably more planning than her own, they'd probably make it back to the rental facility long before she and Sterling did.

Alec announced, "All right, boss, Team Cylinder Swap is ready for duty."

"Godspeed," Sterling replied. "Don't wait up for us—we're going to be a while."

"We won't. Good luck, you two."

As they entered the car, Blair asked Sterling, "Think we're going to need it? Luck, I mean."

He shrugged. "Probably. Let's go find out."

35

BLAIR

The moon burned bright, causing every snowy branch to glow white amid the otherwise black forest. This was like something out of a fantasy novel, Blair thought, as the soft calls of owls rang out over the sweep of wind through the trees. Between the moonlight and the abundant snow, she covered most of the way with her naked eyes, only occasionally peering through the night vision device in her hand.

Sterling didn't appear to be using his night vision at all; he was moving as easily as if it were broad daylight, navigating the intersections of game trails with a quickness that told Blair he either knew exactly where he was, or he was totally lost and too embarrassed to tell her.

She truly hoped it was the former, because apart from her anxiety about the proceedings ahead, Blair felt like she was freezing to death.

The temperature was in the twenties, and no amount of movement could warm her up despite the winter clothing. How Sterling appeared so at ease in the cold despite years in LA was beyond her.

At one point in their journey, he turned around to check on her, asking in a low voice, "You cold?"

Blair's jaw fell open, trembling with the chill. "Is that a serious question?"

He put his hands on her shoulders and rubbed up and down. "Don't worry, we're almost there."

She leaned in toward his face, as if for a kiss, but instead whispered, "Then let's go, because I'm freezing to death."

They proceeded to another junction between game trails. This time Sterling paused, scanning both paths before following the one to the left. It wound downhill to a stream bed long since frozen over, and Sterling followed it twenty meters until he found a string of rocks to cross.

"Careful," he warned her, "going to be a bit slick."

Then he led the way, choosing his footfalls carefully and pausing on the far bank to help her up.

Blair almost slipped off at several junctures, her final step a quick leap to take his hand as he steadied her.

"I feel like a city girl," she whispered.

"You are a city girl. Try not to worry about it too much."

They picked up another game trail, this one threading uphill until she could make out the distant security light of a house through the trees.

And at that moment, Blair heard a sound that made her heart stop.

It was a shrill, howling cry, the scream of a woman in mortal danger, coming from the woods to their right.

Sterling stopped in his tracks, and Blair raced alongside him to whisper, "We need to go help."

"Blair," he whispered back, "it's a fox."

"What?"

"Red foxes scream like that. Listen."

She panted in the cold night air, her breath puffing clouds

of white steam as she waited. Within twenty seconds the cry sounded again—the exact same tone and pitch, with precise repetition that couldn't have possibly been a human voice. A moment later it was answered by the shriek of a second fox, this one more distant.

Sterling turned to her and whispered, "But if you want to abort this job and go see if the foxes are okay, I'm cool with that too."

She punched his arm. "I hate you."

"Noted," he said as they neared the house. "We're going to enter through the back door. If we have to leave in a hurry, just stay behind me and follow my lead."

"Well there's no way I'm going back through those woods without you, so that shouldn't be too much of a problem."

The house's security light filtered through the trees around them, and Sterling tried to remain in the shadows as much as he could as they approached.

Blair's first glimpses of the house revealed a two-story structure with panel siding, an elevated back deck with an outdoor dining set covered in snow, and darkened windows that revealed no trace of an awake occupant. But the brick chimney told a different story: hazy streaks of smoke floated lazily upward. Stacks of firewood were lined up a short way from the house, the distance between them covered by a fresh trail of footprints in the snow.

Her heart was hammering away now, though Sterling showed no signs of hesitation or discomfort. Whether he was genuinely calm or just good at hiding the telltale signs, she had no idea. Blair suspected that under the circumstances, either option was possible.

Sterling darted under the elevated porch, and Blair followed him into the shadows for lack of a better place to hide. She watched him run his hand along a side beam, feeling for a nail protruding from the wood that held a spare key.

Retrieving the key, he turned to her and nodded toward the stairs.

She followed him to the deck, where he swiftly unlocked the back door. Sliding it open, he stepped inside and waited for her to enter before closing it behind them.

Blair stepped atop a mat, doing her best to quietly wipe the slush and snow from her boots before following Sterling into the house.

She could faintly smell burning wood from a fireplace, though the interior design cues drew her attention more. With popcorn ceilings and laminate wood paneling on the walls, walking through the house felt like stepping back in time.

Sterling moved slowly, cautiously, until freezing at the sound of a 12-gauge shotgun slide racking.

He was hit by a blinding light a moment later, raising his hands in submission as he turned to face the defending homeowner.

Squinting against the glare, he muttered two words.

"Hey, Ma."

36

STERLING

"Sterling!" his mother exclaimed, lowering the shotgun as he gingerly took it from her.

"Let's...just set this to the side, okay, Ma? I know you're excited to see me, but let's not turn your house into a crime scene."

Ensuring the shotgun's safety was on, he set it against the corner, barrel pointed down, the weapon-mounted taclight providing a pool of light for them to see one another. Then she embraced him forcefully, and he returned the hug.

When she finally stepped back, it was as if Sterling didn't exist anymore—his mother was fully focused on his partner-in-crime, taking Blair's hands as she spoke breathlessly.

"You must be Blair."

"It's nice to meet you, Ms. Defranc."

"It's Kathryn to you, dear. Always Kathryn to you."

Then, without warning, she wrapped her arms around Blair.

Sterling flinched in anticipation of Blair's reaction, but to his surprise she embraced his mom as if they'd known each other for years.

His mom's voice was choked as she said, "Thank you for getting my son out of that terrible place."

"It was the least I could do," Blair whispered back.

Now Sterling understood the bond between the two women. Having never met before, they were nonetheless united out of concern for him spending the rest of his life in prison. The thought made him feel a pang of guilt that no crime he'd committed ever had, and before he could examine the emotion any further, his mother released Blair and cut her eyes to him.

"The last time I caught you sneaking a girl into this house, you were sixteen years old."

Sterling grinned. "Molly Denninger. Heard she's got four kids now."

Blair asked, "Any of them yours?"

"Ha ha," Sterling said in a deadpan voice. "And it's great to see you, Ma, but we've got to ask…"

He trailed off mid-sentence, seeing that neither woman was listening to him.

His mother had taken Blair's hand and was leading her down the hall with the words, "Come on. Let's go into the living room so I can get a good look at you."

Then they were gone, forgetting about him entirely.

Sterling shrugged and muttered, "Sure. Why not."

Turning off the shotgun taclight, he slipped through the hall of his childhood home to join them.

37

BLAIR

Kathryn led Blair into a modest living room whose dominating feature caused her to sigh in relief.

The huge stone fireplace spanned much of one wall, logs crackling and snapping on the hearth. Entering the room was like stepping into a cozy orbit of immense warmth, and Blair felt the clammy coldness on her skin recede at once.

"Take off your jacket and have a seat right here next to the fire," Kathryn said, directing Blair to one of two couches facing each other across a small table with a tea set. "You must be freezing."

Blair gratefully obeyed, shedding her coat to feel the fire's warmth radiating through her chest as she took a seat. Kathryn was drawing the curtains over the windows, giving her fugitive guests some measure of privacy as Sterling entered, took a seat on the opposite couch, and waved a hand for his mother to join him.

But Kathryn sat next to Blair instead, then reached over the table and poured a cup of tea that Blair eagerly wrapped her hands around, letting it warm her palms.

"Thank you," she said, sipping from her cup as she took in Kathryn's features.

Her auburn hair was shoulder-length, showing threads of gray that had probably increased after her son's incarceration. But there were hints of Sterling in her face; the two shared the same nose and cheekbones, a similar subtle sense of grace that permeated their expressions.

But Kathryn's most notable feature was her eyes, sparkling in the fire's glow and fixed on Blair with an intensity that would have been uncomfortable under any other circumstances.

"My God," Kathryn said, "you're beautiful."

Blair blushed. "So are you."

Kathryn swatted a hand at Blair, as if the very notion were ridiculous, then asked, "Are you two hungry? I can heat up some beef stew and cornbread."

Sterling answered, "We're fine, Ma."

"Unless I'm mistaken, you don't speak for her."

Blair gave a gracious smile and said, "Just the tea is perfect, thank you."

"I can't imagine all the trouble you went to getting across the country just to see me. Thank you for coming."

"It's great to meet you at last. I'd like to say Sterling has told me a lot about you, but you know how he is: ninety percent of his brain power is focused on heists."

"He's always been that way," Kathryn agreed, "but it's great to see he's finally doing something useful with the other ten percent. How long have you two been together?"

Sterling and Blair responded simultaneously.

"Ma, we're not exactly..."

"About a week," Blair said, assuming control of their collective response. "Officially, at least. Our first kiss was during his prison break."

His mother bristled with pride.

"And what a first kiss that must have been. Again, Blair, I can't thank you enough for getting my boy out of that place. When I left that visitation room and saw all the chaos erupt at the prison, I knew exactly what was happening. I just sat there praying, 'please let my son make it out.'"

Blair adjusted her hands on the teacup, its warmth eroding the remaining numbness from her fingertips. "It was the least I could do. Believe it or not, Sterling rescued me during that Century City heist."

Sterling looked conflicted. "Technically you were a hostage."

"Technically," Blair went on undeterred, addressing Kathryn. "I was in a bad spot that was getting worse by the day. Your son got me out of it and gave me a fresh start..." She glanced at Sterling. "And I couldn't be more grateful for that."

Kathryn smiled warmly, as if this were the most normal conversation in the world, and Blair thought that between marrying one thief and raising another, the woman must be pretty hard to shock at this point.

She asked, "But you guys are doing okay? Wherever you're staying, you're safe?"

Sterling nodded. "We've been safe, Ma. Everyone's fine."

"Well I'm glad to hear that. Your father never had to go into hiding, thank God. But I know things are a bit different for you these days. And speaking of your father," Kathryn continued, holding out her hand to Sterling, "let me see it."

38

STERLING

Sterling unclasped the vintage Omega Seamaster from his wrist and handed it to his mother.

She accepted it as if it were a magic talisman, appraising the dial in the firelight. Sterling watched her eyes glisten as countless memories of her husband washed over her. His father had worn that wristwatch continuously right up until his death, and after that it had passed on to Sterling.

He said, "Blair kept it safe when I got arrested. And it was back on my wrist within an hour of my escape from prison."

She handed the Omega back to him, looking bitter. "Jim lied to me about this. Said it was sitting in an evidence locker."

"Never," Sterling said, accepting the watch and strapping it back on his wrist. "Jim is a liar; it's what he does."

Leaning forward and focusing intently on his mom for emphasis, he continued, "But that doesn't mean he can't hurt you. I got your letter in the mail—what happened?"

She forced a thin, nervous smile. "One of your father's old contacts keeps an ear to the ground at the state attorney general's office. They've been given a heads-up that I'll be on their docket this December."

"This December," Sterling replied bitterly, "because Jim gets elected in November."

Kathryn waved an indifferent hand.

"You don't have to worry about me. You two stay out of handcuffs, and I'll be just fine."

Sterling insisted, "That's not good enough. Jim has to be exposed, he has to account for his corruption. And we've got just the way to do it." Seeing his mother's eyes narrow with suspicion, he cleared his throat and continued, "We just need a little help."

"What do you mean, 'help?'"

Sterling cast a sideways glance at the fire before looking back at his mom.

"Ma, I need to get in touch with Uncle Wolf."

Kathryn's gaze hardened as she responded in an angry hiss.

"Absolutely *not*."

Opening his hands as a visible peace offering, he said, "I know he still checks up on you. Just tell me how to reach him."

But his mom crossed her arms tightly and shook her head.

"I don't presume to tell you how to live your life any more than I told your father. But I will not be a party to it. I will not help you risk prison again."

"Ma, everything Jim Jacobson said to you last year was a legitimate threat. He's going to be elected to Congress, and he's going to use his many connections to have you investigated. They're going to tie your business to money laundering for Dad, they're going to fabricate any evidence they can't find, and they're going to take everything from you before sending you to prison."

She looked genuinely hurt.

"Sterling...don't you think I know that?"

He didn't mean to raise his voice, had spoken more forcefully than he intended.

"Then why won't you help us?"

"You really don't get it, Sterling. I'm fine with going to prison, as long as *you don't*."

Blair reached out and touched his mom's hand.

"Kathryn, Jim is a dangerous man. There's no telling how many people he'll hurt if we don't expose him, and we need your help to do that."

But she was indifferent to Blair's plea. "A mother's first responsibility is to her child. I don't care how old Sterling is now—nothing about that responsibility has changed."

"Ma," Sterling offered, "I've only been caught once."

"And if Blair hadn't saved you, you'd still be rotting in a cell at Florence. What do you think is going to happen if they get you a second time?" She shook her head again. "I'm sorry, but my answer is final. I don't want you anywhere near that man."

"Ma, you don't understand—"

"Sterling," Blair cut him off. "It's her choice. We'll just have to find another way."

Kathryn appraised Blair with a newfound sense of respect. "I didn't think I could like you any more, sweetheart, but it seems I was wrong. You really get it." Her eyes crinkled with a smile. "You're going to make a fine mother someday."

That final comment somehow transmuted Sterling's mounting anger into a chest-seizing jolt of absolute sobriety, leaving him at a loss for words.

Then his peripheral vision registered a new light in the room, not from the fire but a pale yellow beam shining through a seam in the curtain overlooking the driveway.

Sterling was on his feet, grabbing Blair's hand. "There's a car coming!"

39

JIM

After putting his Suburban into park and killing the engine, Jim crossed a short, snowy path to the front entrance of a modest country home.

Knocking on the front door, Jim only had to wait a moment to hear the deadbolt working before the door swung open.

"Hi," Jim said, extending a business card with his campaign slogan. "My name is Jim Jacobson, and I'm running for Congress this November to bring real change to District 20. I wanted to see if I could count on your vote."

Kathryn Defranc replied, "You've got a lot of nerve coming here." Her eyes lasered into him at maximum force as she snatched the card from his hand. "And if you came to threaten me, save your breath. My son is free and I couldn't be much happier about that."

Jim glanced in the living room behind her, the old law enforcement instinct that would never die, but saw only a roaring fire. Then he met her gaze again.

"I'm not here to threaten you at all. Please don't misunderstand. You see, Kathryn, I only *threaten* when there's an alternative to offer. When we met at Supermax, I delivered a threat. I also gave you a way out—tell me everything you know about your son's crew, and then persuade him to provide their identities and hideout as a small concession to justice. If you had, I would have ensured you were never investigated for the links that would otherwise be found between your business and money laundering for your late husband's addiction to thievery. I was willing to honor my end of that agreement—"

"We never had an agreement," she spat back.

"—but now, I'm afraid all that remains is for me to direct a few subtle inquiries into your business affairs. And since I know your son has the means to support you—after all, stealing other people's wealth seems to run in the family—it seems to me you're quite the flight risk. I'm not going to stop until you're in prison. Given your son's breakout, I think the State could make a strong case for maximum security confinement. I told you this would happen when we met in Colorado, and I'm a man of my word."

Jim delivered a wry smile as he waited for the vitriolic response, the accusations of corruption or simply outright irrational female rage. The more she lashed out, the better; Jim harbored a penchant for delivering on his promises, and reinforcing the power balance to anyone who refused to submit. Kathryn had refused, and she was going to pay dearly for that.

But his mood went from celebratory gloating to befuddlement when Kathryn Defranc did the unthinkable.

She smiled.

It wasn't a derogatory sneer, or even a forced expression to make him second-guess himself. He'd come here to intimidate, and Kathryn was genuinely smiling at him.

"You know what?" she said, looking at the business card in

his hand. "Best of luck with the election. You can count on my vote. Politics suit you, Jim—you fit right in."

Then, before he could summon a response, she slammed the door in his face.

He took a step back, blinking as the deadbolt clicked shut. Without further options, Jim returned to his truck, firing the engine and reversing down the snowy driveway and onto the country road.

Then Jim drove home to his wife, his mind spinning with questions on exactly what, if anything, he was to make out of Kathryn Defranc's response.

40

BLAIR

In the wake of Jim's departure, Blair heard the faint rumble of a vehicle engine recede down the driveway.

She and Sterling had been in the back hallway, listening to Jim's words while waiting near the rear door in case they needed to flee.

But it was clear that Sterling had no intention of abandoning his mother. The short interaction between her and Jim had passed with Blair resting a hand on Sterling's fully tensed bicep, listening to his breaths becoming shorter with barely suppressed anger.

Now they had to assume Kathryn was waiting at the window for some verification that Jim was gone and no one else was coming before sounding the all-clear. And despite Blair's restraint while providing a comforting hand to Sterling, she found her head spinning with the implications of what had just occurred.

Jim had crossed the line from his previous opportunistic encounters with Kathryn—first outside the LA courthouse, and then at the Supermax visitor center—to a predator seeking her out in her home for no other reason than to shatter a widow's existence, to flaunt his own victory after securing the tapes at auction. And since he couldn't gloat to the crew for lack of a means by which to communicate, he'd settled for the closest person he could.

Kathryn called from the living room, "It's all right, he's gone. You can come back out."

As she and Sterling re-entered the living room, Blair was shocked to see tears streaking down Kathryn's face.

"Ma," Sterling said, moving in to hug her. "We heard everything. I'm sorry I—I'm sorry I couldn't do anything."

Blair watched mother and son embrace, her heart turning to stone. She regretted so many things at that instant: becoming involved with Jim in the first place, keeping silent about his corruption so as not to extend her own sentence, not securing the tapes as soon as she could upon being released from prison. This was all her fault, even if she hadn't intended it, and Blair vowed to set everything right. She would restore order to the universe no matter the cost, and ensure Jim Jacobson got what he deserved.

Kathryn pulled back from her son, holding up a slip of cardstock in one hand. Sterling took it from her, examined the print, and shook his head. He handed it to Blair, and she saw that it was Jim's campaign card, bearing his face and the motto, *It's About Integrity*.

"You don't deserve this," Blair said, pocketing the card. "I'm so sorry."

Kathryn wiped away her tears and nodded.

"You know what? I don't. And I want to stand by my motherly duties, but sometimes things gotta get ugly. That snake wants to visit my house while I'm seeing my son and future daughter-in-law? I've got something for him."

She turned her gaze to Sterling, her voice raw with emotion.

"You want to contact Uncle Wolf? Be my guest."

41

BLAIR

The sun had risen by the time Blair and Sterling made it back to the rental facility.

Upon entering the dingy interior, Blair was cold, tired, and wanted nothing more than to change into dry clothes, crawl onto her cot, and pass out for five hours.

Which made it all the more irritating when Alec burst through the door holding a box of coffee to-go in one hand and an enormous bag of food in the other.

Without introduction, he began speaking in a singsong voice. "I got coffee, I got donuts, I got bacon, egg, and cheese biscuits. What's that, you prefer sausage? Boom, got those too. And my God, Sterling, you never told me how beautiful Albany is. The buildings, the people, the weather...it's making me nostalgic for the northeast, man. Felt like I was back home without the risk of running into anyone who bullied me in high school."

He paused, examining their blank faces. "What's wrong with you two? Thought you were returning from a trip to Momma Defranc, not a funeral."

Sterling answered, "We had a surprise visit."

"Yeah?" Alec asked, setting down his cargo. "From who?"

Blair removed Jim's campaign card from her coat pocket and handed it over.

Alec examined it in disbelief.

"What'd that scumbag want?"

Sterling's jaw tensed. "To threaten my mother."

"No way. You guys get compromised, or is Jimgate still on?"

"Blair and I were hiding. Jim didn't know we were there."

"So..."

"So we're not compromised." Sterling approached the box of coffee, filled a disposable cup, and offered it to Blair. She shook her head, instead searching through the bag to find a breakfast sandwich.

Alec repeated, "So..."

Seeing that Sterling wasn't going to answer, Blair cut in.

"Yes, Alec, Jimgate is on. Okay? It's still on."

Alec pumped a fist in silent victory. "Good, 'cause me and my Russian colleague got not three, not four, but *five* lock cylinders. All from separate change key areas in Jim's office building, all swapped with any-key duplicates."

Sterling sipped his coffee and asked, "Any concerns about getting spotted?"

"Not after we took control of the cameras. Other than that, the building's a free-for-all. Getting up to Jim's office will be considerably trickier, mind you, but as for getting the cylinders...it was like taking candy from a very docile, well-behaved baby."

Marco emerged from his room, long hair in disarray, and shuffled across the warehouse floor while rubbing his eyes.

Alec lit up at the sight of him, and began his breakfast speech in the same singsong voice as before.

"I got coffee, I got donuts, I got bacon, egg, and cheese—"

"Don't care," Marco yawned, "about anything but the coffee."

Sterling filled a second cup and handed it to him. Both men toasted, tapping their paper cups together before taking a sip.

Alec tapped Blair on the shoulder. "So what's Sterling's mom like?"

"She was nice."

"You're positive she wasn't, like, a robot? One designed to raise the ultimate thief from an orphaned newborn as part of an experimental government program?"

Blair took a bite of her sandwich, savoring the taste of bacon amid the layers.

She mumbled with her mouth half full, "Reasonably confident that wasn't the case."

"Was his bedroom covered in swimsuit centerfolds?"

"I didn't go to his bedroom."

Alec lifted his eyebrows. "Better luck next time, Sterling."

Then he announced to the group, "Well, I'm not letting Blair have all the fun. I call dibs on going with Sterling to meet Wolf."

Blair grinned. It was, of course, Sterling's choice on who should accompany him, and based on how interesting that meeting would be, she hoped he'd once again choose her.

But her grin faded as Sterling set down his cup of coffee and spoke the words she never thought she'd hear on this crew.

"I'm not taking anyone. For this meeting, it has to be me alone."

42

STERLING

Rounding a corner in the trail, Sterling looked up the next stretch and continued making his way uphill.

There wasn't much of a visible trail to speak of at present, merely a two-foot width of unbroken snow threading between trees. The dirt path below wouldn't be visible until the snow melted off sometime in April, and by then Sterling hoped to be back home in LA, back to life as it was before meeting Blair had shifted his world on its axis.

Navigation was easier with the benefit of sunlight, waning though it was in the late afternoon hours. Sterling had certainly hiked in the Catskill Mountains throughout his teenage years, though this particular route was new to him. After parking his rental car at a ski resort, he'd followed a trailhead at the edge of the parking lot west, away from the lodge and deeper into the Catskills.

An hour and a half of hiking had reminded him how much he'd taken these views for granted in his youth. All this had been normal then: the endless labyrinth of whitewashed forest, the snow-drenched pines, the jagged rock faces with their surfaces obscured by the countless razor icicles of waterfalls frozen over until spring.

It had taken years in the relatively flat, perennially warm vistas of Southern California for Sterling to see this landscape with some measure of objectivity. Now, the winter universe seemed both strange and familiar, as if two separate identities had converged here, one from a younger, pre-LA version of Sterling, and the other from the older, perhaps wiser, man who had returned home at last.

Ascending to a ridgeline crest, Sterling took in the view to his side while panting a few visible breaths in the glacial winter air.

The rolling expanse of mountains was alternately bathed in shadow and light, a few rays of sun beaming through the misty layers of cloud cover drifting overhead. He could make out a body of water snaking across the horizon, so distant that he couldn't begin to imagine which it was. It should have been a quiet moment of reflection, a beat of silence between the otherwise feverish efforts to further the task at hand.

But Sterling had a hard time focusing on the view.

The truth was, he felt as if he were in an existential dilemma ever since Jim's interruption last night. He'd been reduced to a fugitive hiding in the dark in his childhood home, listening to Jim threaten his mother while impotently waiting for the threat to pass. Here he was, a so-called master thief at the apex of his profession, and yet unable to do anything at present for the two women he wanted most to protect: Blair and his mom, both subjected to the continual indignities inflicted by a corrupt FBI-agent-turned-aspiring-politician.

Sterling wondered what his father would think of him now. For every dazzling heist success, there had been an equally gut-wrenching low point, and while he loved his job the same as his father had, Sterling was facing challenges that Walter Defranc never did. His father had never squared off against an archnemesis, never had to hide from the public eye following a prison escape, never had to disguise himself before venturing into civilization.

That much was just as well, Sterling thought as he continued down the trail. Maybe his dad would have dealt with these issues better than he did, or maybe worse. Either way, his father couldn't help now, but his friend Steve Wolf could.

At least, he could if Sterling ever reached his destination.

The trouble in linking up with a paranoid recluse was that the path from A to B was never simple. Wolf was concerned—justifiably, perhaps—that Sterling would be unwittingly trailed by some surveillance effort searching for the fugitive from California or, alternately, the retired New York thief currently waiting for a few dozen statutes of limitation to expire.

Sterling was tired from his all-night foray to his mother's home, and would have loved few things more than sleeping through most of the day. But until he could produce a grand master key for Jim's building, the crew couldn't install their surveillance measures, and until he personally visited Wolf, he wouldn't have that key. With Jim awaiting contact from Wraith at any moment, there was no time to waste, and so Sterling continued trudging along the trail, searching for his rendezvous point.

When the trail finally gave way to a plowed stretch of paved road, Sterling checked his watch to find he was only a few minutes early despite having been on the move for just over two hours. He scanned left and right for traffic and, seeing none, descended a final slope toward a yellow diamond sign indicating curves in the road ahead.

Removing a strip of red cloth from his pocket, Sterling tied it in a loose knot halfway up the signpost. Retreating to the high ground, he dusted the snow off a low rock and took a seat, stretching both legs out as he fished in his coat pocket for a PowerBar.

He only had time to chow down half of it before hearing a truck engine approaching. Pocketing the remainder of his bar, Sterling rose to a knee, keeping his body tucked behind a wide tree trunk to observe a black quad-cab pickup roll into view, braking beside the sign and turning on its four-way flashers.

Sterling scrambled downhill, untying his red cloth from the signpost and lowering the tailgate to let himself beneath a tarp stretched over the pickup bed. He barely had time to close the tailgate before the pickup lurched forward, causing him to fall on his side in the darkened cargo space as his driver accelerated to their final destination.

43

BLAIR

From her seat in the warehouse office, Blair tried to decipher the feelings of betrayal and deceit she hadn't been able to suppress.

After all the trouble they'd gone through to make contact with his mother, Blair could only assume she'd be able to join Sterling on his expedition to see Wolf—after all, visiting a thief who was lying low in his home state wasn't exactly a high visibility assignment. She should have been the clear choice to go with him, and Blair had been the most surprised of anyone when Sterling said he had to go alone.

He had his logic, of course. Wolf had a long career for a reason, and it wasn't because he was prone to recklessly letting anyone visit him at his current hideout. Sterling knew him from his father, and that gave a certain level of credibility that Blair couldn't match, wanted fugitive or not.

But Blair knew Sterling, and she sensed there was another reason altogether. Something he wanted to discuss without her around, or something he was afraid Wolf would say in front of her that was better left unheard.

Though what that might be, she had no earthly idea.

"Blair."

Marco's voice was impatient, spoken with the tone of having repeated himself.

She glanced up to see him facing her from his seat at the computer, looking stoic, with Alec slouched in the chair beside him.

The black, Styrofoam-lined case with her surveillance kit was open on the table next to her, brimming with wires and tiny electronics that she needed to prep before entering Jim's office.

"Yes?" she asked.

"We need to execute asap once Sterling gets back with the key. The tech side needs to be ready to go now. I was asking about Jim's level of countersurveillance."

Blair groaned at the mention of Jim, the one person she wanted to forget above all others. He was like a low-grade headache that wouldn't go away, every relief from him proving to be a temporary respite before he re-entered her life.

She said, "Jim's role on the FBI task force was management and command, not technical implementation. He's got some basic knowledge of the tech side, so it's safe to say he has his office swept for bugs. And he's definitely being cautious with his comms plan—I know for a fact he communicates with his mentor through a burner phone, probably a number of them used on a rotational basis." Pulling her hair into a ponytail and securing it with a tie from her wrist, she asked, "Can you access his office communications remotely?"

"Maybe. I've already initiated the data scrape for a CALEA exploit."

"Well, that should be half the battle, right?"

"Maybe," Marco said. "Maybe not."

Alec pushed himself upright in the chair. "Not to break up

the meeting of the nerds, but there's still one analog brain in the room. What's CALEA?"

Blair answered, "Communications Assistance for Law Enforcement Act. It's the government's built-in digital wiretap on all telephone, broadband internet, and voice over IP activity in the US. That way once the police get a court order to conduct surveillance, the telecommunications service providers simply transmit the data. No physical entry required."

"So you can just hack the service provider and presto, we see it all?"

Marco pinched his eyes shut and sighed, the expression of an adult about to explain something to a very small child.

"Not quite so simple," he began. "I will have to research the technical specifics of legal mandates ensuring CALEA compliance. For telephone, that's easy—since the Act was passed in '94, every voice switch on the US market now has built-in intercept capability. But broadband and VoIP weren't added until years later, so they rely on deep packet inspection software that differs per provider. I will have to determine what that software is, then set up a mirror port on the network switch to relay the data to an IP probe that I establish. It won't be easy, but...well, I'm me, so it is not impossible."

Alec shook his head as if waking up from a deep sleep.

"Sorry, what was that last part? The tech nerd dissertation got so boring I started to nod off."

Blair crossed her legs and intervened to save Marco the trouble.

"Bottom line is yes, we can remotely loop into Jim's office phone, cell phone, and computer. That gives us audio from his calls plus stuff like IP address, programs he's running, URLs visited, and email usage."

Alec gave a halfhearted shrug.

"I feel we should install listening devices in the phones anyway. You know, just to remain truer to the original Watergate break-in."

Marco shook his head. "Technology has come a long way since the '70s. There's no need to bug the phones manually."

"Then aside from having an awesome name, why do we need to conduct Jimgate at all?"

"Because there's also a lot that CALEA information doesn't give us."

"Like what?"

Blair said, "Conversations over his burner phone, for one. You better believe he uses it in his office, and until we know what that phone number is, our only chance of catching even a partial conversation will require continuous audio surveillance."

"But if we don't have that number, how could Wraith?"

Blair lowered her hand and countered, "I don't know—maybe Wraith wouldn't. But we can't underestimate him. And even if Wraith doesn't transmit the meeting specifics over the burner phone, anything Jim discusses with his mentor is of use to us. We'll need physical entry to tap his office."

"I thought he has it swept for bugs. What if he finds our surveillance?"

"He won't find it with a sweep, because I'll use a fiber optic strand." Seeing Alec's eyes glaze over, she clarified, "Debugging crews search for electronic emissions of surveillance devices sending encrypted transmissions to outside receivers. So we'll install a bug that sends its data on a fiber optic strand leading to another room that doesn't get swept, where we'll have a wireless transmitter broadcasting back to us. Then there's the matter of keystroke logging."

Marco added, "Which is non-negotiable, because certain applications will prevent deep packet inspection software from recording what was typed. I'll need to install keylogger software that will tell us everything Jim has typed, including hidden passwords. And let's not forget that Wraith could feasibly bypass CALEA screening by sending a message via a screen hijack of Jim's computer—for that I'll need to install an additional piece of spyware that will capture his monitor display and broadcast it along with the key logging data via the wireless connection."

Alec nodded as if finding no fault with the plan thus far. Then he stopped, his head movement turning to a slow shake as he spoke.

"So if Marco is going to be whacking out Jim's computer..."

"Yes," Marco said.

"...and Blair is going to install the bug in his office..."

"Yes," she replied.

"...then what exactly are me and Sterling supposed to be doing during Jimgate?"

Blair uncrossed her legs, leaning sideways in her chair and extending a hand toward him, palm up.

"That depends," she said. "Let me see the building blueprints."

44

STERLING

When the pickup finally rolled to a stop, Sterling heard the engine go silent and then the low rumble of a garage door closing.

Once it had, the truck door opened and footsteps rounded the vehicle before stopping at the tailgate. Sterling had spent the last forty-five minutes curled up on the piles of blankets haphazardly tossed into the tarp-covered cab, and was relieved when the tailgate opened, followed by the tarp being thrown aside.

Sitting up and squinting against the sudden light, Sterling looked at the figure standing before him.

Steve Wolf had aged considerably since Sterling had seen him last—his features were creased with stark lines, his trim beard more gray than black.

But Wolf bore the same thick, perpetually furrowed eyebrows over his ever-squinting eyes, and when he spoke, it was with the same menacing whisper that had always served as his baseline voice.

"Welcome to *mi casa*, whiteboy."

Easing himself off the truck and onto the concrete floor, Sterling replied, "Good to see you, Mexican Clint Eastwood."

Wolf offered his hand, giving Sterling's a quick pump before turning away and walking up the steps to his home entrance.

Following him through the door from the nondescript garage, Sterling felt like he'd stepped onto another planet.

He was entering the great room of a majestic log home, a huge open space with a floor-to-ceiling stone fireplace and a wall of windows that rose thirty feet high. The outside boasted an enormous deck, elevated over a stunning view of sunset over the Catskills.

Sterling breathlessly remarked, "If this is lying low, Wolf, sign me up."

"I'm retired, not dead." Wolf's voice came from a distant corner, and Sterling looked over to see him pulling open the fridge in a gourmet kitchen. "Beer?"

"Yeah." Sterling nodded, turning back to the windswept view that extended for miles without a neighbor in sight. "Thanks."

Wolf walked to his side carrying two cans, handing one to Sterling before cracking open his own.

Sterling took the cold can, recoiling at the label.

"PBR?"

"It's a classic for a reason," Wolf replied testily. "Besides." He gestured to their surroundings. "I blew it all on the house."

Then he pointed to a door in the corner. "You want to critique my beverage selection or you want to show me what you've got?"

Sterling cracked his can open, following Wolf first to the door, then down a narrow staircase that ended in a closed metal door with a keypad-protected entrance. Wolf looked over his shoulder at Sterling and, seeing that his visitor wasn't going to look away, proceeded to block the view of the keypad with his body before entering the code.

Sterling knew he should keep quiet, but he couldn't help himself.

"Come on, Wolf," he said, throwing back a sip of beer, "like that's going to stop me."

"Old habits," Wolf conceded, turning the handle and pushing the metal door open.

Flipping on the light, Sterling saw a veritable thief's paradise. The basement had been converted into one meticulously organized workshop, every side lined with tables or workbenches and the walls stacked with shelves, drawers, and tools. There probably wasn't a locksmith business in the state that could compete with the sheer volume of equipment that Wolf had accumulated over his decades of operation, and Sterling took in the sight with the same sense of majesty that he'd felt when gazing out the great room windows.

Wolf flipped on an ultraviolet light over a workbench, tapping the wood surface twice with his middle finger. "Right there."

Sterling set down his beer and recovered the padded case from his jacket pocket, unzipping it and laying out five cloth-covered objects that he unwrapped one at a time. Within were the lock cylinders, each bearing a piece of numbered white tape.

Wolf took a seat, picking up one and examining it under the glare of the light.

"Schloesser IG-72. Not bad. I assume you're putting these back after you're done?"

"We are. The fewer marks, the better."

"I got the magic touch, boy. Any marks I add will be indistinguishable from the existing wear and tear."

"That's what I was hoping to hear. Want me to get started on another bench?"

Wolf had prepared his tools and was already going to work on the backing of the first lock, using a tiny screwdriver to spin the cylinder retaining screw.

"No offense," he said as he worked, "but I like to do a job from start to finish. Not saying you'll screw up your measurements, but if we hit sunrise and my best guess isn't working, it's easier for me to see what went wrong when I've laid eyes on all sixty pins."

"Sure, Wolf. I understand."

Turning his attention back to the cylinder, Wolf asked, "So how are things?"

"Not bad," Sterling replied, finding his beer and downing a sip. "And it looks like you've got it made up here in the mountains."

"Thought I'd be done with this stuff forever. Should have counted on Walt's boy keeping me busy."

Sterling suppressed a grin. "Well, some of us have to carry the torch."

"You're not carrying the torch, you're setting the world on fire."

Sterling frowned, setting down his beer.

"Excuse me?"

Wolf patiently extracted the cylinder's collar before moving on to the mounting plate. "What you've done with your crew...things have changed, forever."

"How so?"

Continuing his meticulous disassembly, Wolf explained, "Used to be a time we worked in the shadows. Maybe the robberies would make the paper, maybe not. But you guys are front and center in the media spotlight in a way that hasn't happened since the '30s. Bonnie and Clyde, Dillinger, Al

Capone. They were all thieves in the same way a sledgehammer is a tool. You guys are the scalpel. Robbing people who need to be robbed, and I know your father raised you to kick half of the proceeds over to charity. If that's not the case, then I don't want to know about it."

"It's still the case," Sterling assured him, watching Wolf extract the keyway cylinder.

"I've never seen a crew turned into celebrities in my lifetime. Doubt I will in whatever time I've got left."

"That wasn't intentional."

"Son, it doesn't matter if it was intentional or not. It happened. Everything's on camera these days, and you're too high profile to remain obscure. Rappelling down an LA high rise in broad daylight, the high-speed chase, that stunt you pulled at the Sky Safe—don't even get me started on your prison break, which was as fine a piece of heist art as I've ever seen."

Sterling smiled, trying to sound humble. "Thank you."

"It's not a compliment," Wolf said, looking over his shoulder at Sterling. "It's a warning. Know what happened to Dillinger, Bonnie and Clyde, Capone?"

"We're not killing people. They were."

"Doesn't matter if you're killing or not. What matters is you've captured the public's imagination, and the powers that be won't let that slide."

"We survived the federal task force in LA. Even recruited one of its former members with Blair."

Wolf set down the cylinder, retrieving his beer and spinning the chair to face Sterling.

"That task force was just the beginning. They're gonna keep coming at you until they find you, and with one prison break under your belt, I don't believe you can count on a second."

Sterling shrugged. "I'm not taking on any action I can't manage."

"No? Then let me ask you a question you don't know the answer to."

"Shoot."

Wolf raised his eyebrows and asked, "What's your exit strategy?"

Sterling said nothing, feeling the heat rise up his neck.

"That's what I thought. And you better figure out the answer quick, because in this business either you manage your retirement or the law does it for you."

"I understand the risks."

Wolf spun back to the workbench, inserting a blank key through the front of the lock and a thin metal shim through the rear.

"You understand the risks of doing *a* heist, sure. The fact that you can't answer my question tells me you have no idea of the risks involved in an entire *career* of doing heists. You know the pilot saying? 'There are old pilots and there are bold pilots—'"

Sterling finished, "'But there are no old bold pilots.'"

Wolf nodded slightly, conducting the process of rear shimming by extracting the key slowly while advancing the metal shim in its wake, separating the key pins from the driver pins inside the lock's pin stacks. "That's right, son. Now you're a bold pilot, there's no question. Scores you've been taking down are beautiful things and I'd be lying if I said I wasn't proud, or that I can't pick out a Defranc job from the headlines whether the media realizes it or not. Problem is, you need to start thinking about that getting-old part. In your case, getting old outside of a prison cell."

"Even if I retired," Sterling said half-jokingly, "what else is there?"

Turning the key, Wolf succeeded in opening the first lock. Now he'd begin the painstaking task of removing the pins in sequence, measuring each down to a thousandth of an inch before meticulously reassembling the lock.

But rather than remove the pins, Wolf looked over with a measured intensity that made Sterling's blood run cold.

Then he grunted and turned his gaze back to the lock cylinder. "Oh, I don't know. You tell me. Maybe get back to your crew, look into the eyes of that beautiful brunette you've got onboard, and figure it out."

45

BLAIR

Blair turned the gray handheld box over, setting it on the ground and flipping the switch to turn it on.

The transmission device was the size of a paperback novel, a bulky proposition but well worth the trouble of concealing it. As a self-contained unit, the transmitter had a thirty-day power supply, along with the ability to transmit encrypted wireless transmissions back to the crew. Besides, what the transmitter lacked in finesse was made up for by the bug she'd be planting in Jim's office—a potent microphone that could pick up a whispered voice from across the room, all while weighing less than three ounces and packed into a cylinder shorter than a pencil—and the fiber optic cable she connected now.

The strand leading out of the room was almost as narrow as a human hair, easy to miss with the naked eye but capable of relaying data to the transmitter almost as quickly as it was received. By shifting the electronic signal to a remotely located transmitter, the cable setup would pass the most thorough surveillance sweep completely undetected.

Blair attached the connector to the transmitter, ensuring it was inserted fully and then crossing the room to an open laptop on the table. Taking a seat and donning a set of noise-canceling headphones, she opened the audio recording program and heard the faint white noise of the distant room where the microphone was positioned.

After adjusting the volume, she heard Alec speaking through her headphones, leaving no doubt that the three-part setup of surveillance bug, fiber optic cord, and transmitter was functioning as intended.

Alec was speaking in a throaty, pretentious voice.

"My name is Jim. Jim Jim Jim, I could say it all day. This mirror has never been kinder to me—look at these stately silver locks, this rugged jawline. Yet despite my countless advantages, something is amiss...and in my heart, I know it's Blair."

She was going to shout through the walls that he could stop now, that the unit was functioning just fine, thank you, and then decided against it. Sometimes it was better to let Alec wear himself out.

Within ten seconds, she regretted the decision.

"Blair is so hot, I don't know how I ever let her out of the FBI. It's hard work sublimating my attraction to her into a nefarious plan to hide my own corruption by villainizing her crew. I know she's working with Sterling and probably some tech geek to pull off these scores, but there's got to be someone else...someone with rakish good looks, an abundance of wit and good humor, and a freakish ability to crack any safe known to man. That's the real mastermind, I just know it. If I could only figure out who it is..."

She yelled at the wall, "You can stop now! It works fine."

But Alec's voice continued over the headphones, *"Guy like that could have done anything he wanted in life. Astronaut, president...but he was drawn to crime like a brilliant moth to the flames of heist glory. That's my real archnemesis, the brains behind these brilliant robberies that have befuddled the best and brightest minds in law enforcement..."*

"I said you can stop!" she shouted.

"...and if I ever find him, I don't know whether to have him arrested or buy him a beer and ask for the privilege of cowriting his memoirs. If there's one thing I find more compelling than Blair's svelte figure and smoky, smoky eyes, it's the thought of this safecracking rogue somewhere out there in the great big world, working his magic for fame and fortune..."

Before Blair could shout through the wall again, Marco strode into the room like he was marching up to an award podium. She removed her headphones, Alec's voice fading out as she watched Marco come to a halt, place his hands on his hips, and announce, "We're in."

"Pump the brakes," Alec said, entering the room behind Marco. "I'm still fine-tuning my Jim impersonation. Though I think Blair can agree I've come a long way in the past ten minutes, and within an hour I should be able to record campaign messages for him."

Blair considered whether a direct response would encourage Alec further, decided it would, and instead addressed Marco.

"What have you got?"

"The CALEA tap, of course," Marco said. "For starters, we are now receiving all the metadata for a standard 'Trap and Trace.' Time logs, incoming and outgoing numbers dialed as well as the cell towers relaying the calls, which will be useful if Jim decides to leave Albany for any reason. Then we've got everything that would be granted to law enforcement for a Title III wiretap on his office phone and computer, as well as his personal cell. That will give us the actual voice recordings and content of his text messages, and any real-time computer usage."

"What about prior computer history?" she asked.

"That's beyond the scope of CALEA infrastructure. Once I get physical access—"

Alec said, "During Jimgate."

"—during Jimgate," Marco agreed, "I'll image his hard drive and be able to go through his previous activity. Though I dare say anything of use to us will occur from this point forward."

Alec set his hands on his hips, mirroring Marco's posture. "So what now?"

"Now," Blair said, "we need Sterling to get back here with a working key."

46

STERLING

Reaching inside the fridge, Sterling retrieved two more cans of Pabst Blue Ribbon and turned toward the doorway in the corner. The view outside the wall of windows was now darkness, a sheet of black save the stars and a few twinkling lights in the distance. Sterling slipped through the doorway and negotiated the narrow staircase to Wolf's basement workshop.

As he descended the stairs, Sterling considered the implications of his conversation with Wolf. Anyone could provide vague and ominous warnings that a crew needed to slow down if not retire altogether. But Wolf's premonitions were troubling on two fronts. First, Wolf possessed a tremendous amount of experience and wasn't prone to being overly dramatic.

And second, the old thief may have been right.

Passing through the metal door, Sterling hoisted the cans and said, "Your bartender has arrived."

Wolf didn't reply, or even acknowledge that he'd heard.

Instead he was hunched over a notepad on his bench, scrawling a final annotation before setting down his pen and turning his eyes to Sterling.

"I think we've struck gold."

"Really?" Sterling set the cans next to the carefully separated components of the final lock cylinders. The other four had been reassembled with a speed and dexterity that Sterling could never hope to match. He guessed it would have taken him all night to disassemble and reassemble each lock down to the key pins and drive pins, much less reverse out and decode the full bitting values for a grand master key that could open all five. Wolf seemed to have produced those values in just over three hours, all while drinking the cheapest American lager ever produced.

"Only one way to find out." Wolf tore the sheet off his notepad and handed it to Sterling. "Want to run off a key while I reassemble this?"

Sterling examined the paper, which was filled with three-digit numbers corresponding to the sixty pin measurements. Each cylinder was from a part of Jim's building that required its own key for entry, but Wolf had used a Schloesser factory chart to derive the sequenced code values for a key pattern that would open all five.

"Okay," Sterling mumbled, analyzing the circled numbers at the bottom of the page and then looking up at the array of key cutting machines in the workshop. "What do you want me to use?"

Wolf gave him a Schloesser blank key and then gestured with his thumb. "The Jarmon is in the corner."

Sterling turned to see a sheet-covered mass lined up against the far wall. As he approached it, he asked over his shoulder, "This the 240?"

"I'm not destitute, Sterling. It's the 320."

Sterling pulled off the dust cover to reveal a pinball-sized machine with a touchscreen that glowed to life with the flip of a switch.

The real marvel was the backlit cutting assembly beneath the glass cover.

These mechanical portions looked almost like a vehicle engine, a tightly assembled mass of gears, knobs, and cylinders machined from heat-treated aluminum and steel. Even the last-generation Jarmon—the one Sterling had back in LA—could cut anything from a letterbox key all the way up to a high security key, and do so to a greater degree of accuracy than most factories that produced the locks, all the way down to the half-thousandth of an inch.

But the 320 model was even more precise, automating the process to remove any human error.

Sterling hesitated before speaking again. "Can I ask you a question?"

"You're already here," Wolf replied. "Do you have to ask if you can ask?"

"It's just...my father had a rule against sharing job specifics with anyone outside the crew."

Wolf shot back, "Your father is dead, God rest his soul. And it appears his son threw that rule out the window the second he needed help deciphering a grand master key from a quintet of lock cylinders. Rules are just preferences chosen when you have the luxury of a choice."

Sterling smiled at this, inserting the blank key into a slot and selecting *SCHLOESSER* from the screen's drop-down menu. A second menu presented every production variant of Schloesser locks, grouped by type, and he followed the submenus until he located the IG-72 model that Alec and Marco had pilfered from Jim's building.

The machine calibrated itself for the starting cut and spacers in its digital memory of Schloesser's factory depth and space manual, and the screen flashed a keypad with the prompt, *ENTER BITTING CODE.*

Then Sterling said, "There are two things I'd like your opinion on."

"So start with the first," Wolf called back.

Sterling consulted the paper in his hand and typed in the sequence that Wolf had decoded: 051283.

The machine sprang to life, advancing the key's bitting surface across a spinning wheel with a high-pitched series of metallic grinds that produced specific depth values. An internal fan suctioned excess metal particles away from the machinery, and within seconds his key was deposited into a padded slot with all the fanfare of a vending machine depositing a candy bar.

Sterling reached inside and took hold of the key.

It was hot in his hand, and he swept his thumb across the cut. It was so clean that he didn't even have to brush it, every particle of metal smoothed and sharpened to perfection. He now possessed a key more finely machined than the ones Schloesser had provided to Jim's building, and there was only one thing left to do: test whether it worked.

Crossing the workshop back to Wolf, he found the veteran thief patiently completing his assembly of the fifth lock cylinder.

Placing the key beside him, Sterling said, "The current job involves politics, and I've got some ethical concerns."

Wolf set down his lock, then picked up the key and waved it at Sterling as he spoke.

"Politics?" He laughed. "You think *we're* criminals? Sometimes breaking the law is more noble than mastering every loophole while pretending to obey it."

Sterling nodded. "Injustice masquerading as justice."

"At best," Wolf remarked, picking up the first lock and inserting the key. It clicked open. "At worst, you get what happened with Nixon."

"That's my point. Nothing I've done has ever coincided with politics, but it is now."

"What's your concern?"

"That I'm interfering with democracy. That I'm going down the same road Nixon did."

Wolf extracted the key and took hold of the second lock. "Not that politicians don't manipulate those levers at every opportunity, but I don't see how anything you could be interested in stealing would have an effect on the democratic process."

The second lock clicked open with a turn of the key, and Wolf gave a grunt of satisfaction.

Sterling continued, "The thing I'm interested in stealing can bring down someone powerful."

Wolf replied at once.

"Jacobson."

Sterling didn't respond, nor did he have to. Wolf inserted the key into the next lock and asked, "Is this for your crew's protection, or a vendetta?"

After a moment of thought, Sterling said, "It's both."

"Vendettas are a dangerous thing in this business. Any time you stick your neck out, it had better be for a good reason." He turned the key and unlocked the third cylinder. "Petty grievances don't qualify."

"And protection?"

"If it's truly a matter of protecting your people, then you don't need my opinion."

Sterling watched as Wolf withdrew the key.

Sterling reached for his beer, touching the can without lifting it. "That brings me to my second question. I'm worried that if I succeed in taking this guy down, it's going to bring in a worse threat."

"Another politician?"

"Someone who creates the politicians."

"A puppetmaster."

"Yeah," Sterling said. "I think so."

Wolf reached for the fourth lock. "With the resources to take down your crew?"

"With the resources to take down any crew."

"Then why aren't you starting with them? Why bother with the puppet when you can cut the strings?"

"Because I don't know who the puppetmaster is, and the puppet is about to go after my mother. If that happens, it doesn't matter whether my crew is safe or not—we've already lost."

Wolf inserted the key, then set down the cylinder without opening it.

"If the house is on fire, you don't worry about your mortgage payment. You put out the fire. Sounds like Jacobson's your fire, so put him out. Forget about democracy, forget about the greater good. Protect your family—you do right by that, you do right by everything else in the world."

"But then what? What happens when the puppetmaster comes after us?"

Wolf lifted the cylinder and turned the key, unlocking it with a half-spin.

"Same rules apply. You can't affect that right now, so why are you worrying about it? When the time comes, you'll know what to do. Remember whose blood you have in your veins. Your father would have wrapped this entire conversation up in three immortal words."

"Yeah," Sterling agreed, quoting his dad's favorite saying. "'Figure it out.'"

"Exactly. So douse the fire and then worry about the mortgage."

Sterling gave an exasperated shake of his head. "So many metaphors."

Wolf moved on to the fifth lock, which clicked open as easily as the previous four.

Handing the key to Sterling, he said, "That's what happens when I drink PBR. I get all whimsical."

Sterling took the key, analyzing it in the glare of Wolf's workbench light as his friend watched him with a bemused expression.

"Thanks, Wolf. I can't tell you how much I appreciate your help."

"And you don't have to. Just remember to return the favor if the time ever comes."

Lowering the key, Sterling felt his eyebrows furrow.

"I thought you were retired."

Wolf broke his eye contact, reaching for the unopened can beside him.

Cracking the tab open, he took a sip of beer, nodded at the flavor, and said nothing in response.

47

BLAIR

Blair strode into the warehouse area of the rental facility, seeing the rolling door ajar. "Sterling is almost back," she announced. "Alec, you're ready to brief the air vent system?"

Leaning back in his chair, he said, "As ready as I'll ever be."

"Diagrams? Schematics?"

Alec tapped his laptop. "All right here."

"Okay. I'll cover the overall scheme and then dial into the specifics of our recording system. Marco, you've got the CALEA setup and then the keylogger and spyware—"

"All of which I will brief," Marco said, seated across from Alec with his own laptop open, "and none of which Sterling will understand. Why are you nervous?"

"I'm not." Blair's eyes darted sideways to make sure that her surveillance equipment was properly laid out for Sterling's review. "It's just that I want Sterling to have confidence in our plan. I mean, we did this all without him around."

Marco gave a nod of concession, then pointed out, "We planned his prison break without him around, and that worked out just fine. I would contend that getting into Jim's building will be considerably easier. Now calm down—you're scaring the kid."

Alec, who was fidgeting with his notes, stopped abruptly. "No, she isn't."

Blair heard Sterling's rental car a moment later, and bypassed the piles of warehouse debris to stand beside the door to the drive-in bay.

The car rolled inside, and Blair pulled the door down before the idling engine had cut out.

Sterling stepped out of the vehicle in his hiking attire, pausing to stretch his back before slamming the door shut. "We've got a grand master key. Actually, we've got four—I made a copy for each of you."

"Great," Blair blurted, quickly rounding the car to stand beside Alec and Marco. "We've gone over the building layout and have the mission plan worked out. You and Alec will go topside and feed the fiber optic down to Jim's level, where I'll receive the cable and set the surveillance device while Marco works the computer. Then we all replace the lock cylinders and recover our duplicates. Provided there are no issues requiring us to hide inside the building, we should be installation complete within forty-five minutes and have everyone off the target within two hours max."

"Yeah," Sterling replied. "Sounds good."

Blair waited for him to say something else, and when he remained silent, she continued, "Don't you want to see the blueprints? Make sure you're good with our plan?"

"Of course. I mean, I trust you guys. Let me get changed first, and then you can get me up to speed."

Blair watched him closely, trying to discern what was going through his head and coming up empty. Usually Sterling was eager to dive into a plan, scanning for fault lines in their logic and anticipating the myriad ways in which things could go wrong.

Now he looked tired, his expression vague and oddly distant. Sterling looked troubled by something he wouldn't name—and that bothered Blair more than any risks in the mission ahead.

But Marco and Alec seemed satisfied with this dismissal, allowing Sterling to leave the briefing area without so much as a word of objection. Whether that was because they didn't see anything wrong with his halfhearted response or merely knew better than to say something, she wasn't sure. Unable to let the matter rest, Blair followed Sterling to his room.

She stopped him outside the doorway, speaking quietly so Marco and Alec wouldn't hear.

"Hey. What happened with Wolf?"

Sterling gave a nonchalant shrug that seemed forced. "Nothing. He practically shot the key code out of his fingertips."

"Then why do you seem like something's wrong?"

"No reason. Everything's fine. We just talked about my dad, stuff like that."

Blair crossed her arms. "You may be able to brush off Alec and Marco with that, but not me. You don't get this worked up talking about your dad. What else did Wolf say?"

Sterling's eyes darted sideways, assuring her that she'd found the gap between what he'd chosen to say and what he was trying to hide.

Undeterred, Blair gave Sterling her most forceful glare until he continued, "I mean, we talked about our crew."

"And?"

Another shrug, more forceful than the first. "He thinks we're good. High profile, but good."

Blair let her eyebrows drop, giving him a suspicious look.

"I'm guessing there was an emphasis on the 'high profile' part."

"A little bit, yeah."

"Does that mean you're going to Fiji after this?"

Sterling smiled at the reference to *Heat*. "No."

"New Zealand, then."

"Blair." He dropped his voice to a near-whisper. "I'm not going anywhere without you. But I don't think retirement is going to be an option for a while."

"Why not? We lost the bidding war, after all. Even if we left with what we've got, it's more than enough."

"It's not about the money. It's about Jim's mentor."

Now Blair felt a pang of guilt in her chest. Here she was trying to shake him down for information, and the conversation had once again circled back to the topic of Jim—a curse she'd brought along with her when she joined the crew.

She managed a noncommittal response. "Oh?"

"Once Jim goes down, we have to assume his mentor will come after us. Maybe even after my mom."

"I see. So you're worried we'll get rid of one threat only to piss off an even bigger one."

"Something like that."

"Well," she offered, "as far as Jim goes, I don't see any other choice."

"Neither did Wolf. It's what comes next that concerns me."

Blair nodded, seeing the logic in his point but no immediate way to mitigate the risk.

"And how do you think we should deal with that?"

Sterling blinked twice, then slid his hands into his pockets. "I have no earthly idea."

48

STERLING

Unlocking the office door with his grand master key, Sterling turned the handle and entered with Alec close behind him.

The interior was dark, the only light provided by the windows across two walls. Sterling's first priority was to make sure the office was empty; the worst-case scenario was to stumble upon a workaholic or an office space affair in progress, in which case he'd mumble a hasty excuse before retreating. Upon seeing the room abandoned, he closed the door behind him and locked it.

Then he transmitted, "We're in. You guys doing okay down there?"

Blair responded over his earpiece. "*No. There are campaign posters with Jim's face everywhere. It's like we've entered the seventh circle of hell. Other than that, no issues—ready when you are.*"

Sterling grinned at the comment as he moved to the far wall.

There was an oddly voyeuristic element to entering someone else's office, a sacrosanct space they believed would be unoccupied until their return save perhaps a janitorial sweep. This one was large with dual corner windows overlooking the Hudson as it stretched north, lined on both sides by the lights of riverside civilization. Sterling wouldn't see Jim's office tonight, but he didn't need to—according to the building's floor plan, this room was an identical layout. That much figured, Sterling thought; Jim was the type of guy to take the corner suite over everyone else on his staff.

The view of the Hudson River was erased as Alec hastily lowered the shades, adding a quick explanation.

"Let me get these for you, boss. Don't want someone to see our lights and call the cops. That's how the Watergate burglars got busted, you know."

"No," Sterling replied, "that's how they got busted in *Forrest Gump*." Kneeling before the air vent in the floor, Sterling put a red lens penlight in his mouth to illuminate it. Retrieving his screwdriver, he shifted the penlight to a corner of his mouth and mumbled, "In real life they taped the door locks shut like idiots, and a security guard noticed."

"Pretty sure the lights were spotted too, though."

Sterling removed the first of four screws holding the vent to the wall, shaking his head.

"No, the security guard removed the tape and those amateurs had the audacity to re-tape them." He moved on to the second screw. "Security guard noticed that too, finally called the cops, and their lookout was watching TV so he didn't notice when the responding officers arrived. His first warning to the entry team came around the time they were getting arrested."

Sterling had transitioned to the third screw before Alec replied.

"But the lights woke up another guest at the Watergate complex. That part was based on fact."

Sterling lined up the extracted third screw next to the rest, then set to work on the fourth. "The lights didn't wake anyone up."

Still unconvinced, Alec said, "I'll check Wikipedia when we get back."

Then he knelt beside Sterling, setting down the transmitter to be affixed inside the vent by a magnetic panel. Once installed and connected, it would provide their continuous link to the 24/7 audio of Jim's inner sanctum on the floor below.

By then Sterling had removed the final screw. Carefully separating the vent from the wall, he laid it down and sat cross-legged to begin the next phase of his role in tonight's job. Retrieving a small lead weight from a spool on his belt, he began lowering the fiber optic cable through the vertical air shaft beyond the wall.

The thread of cable was so thin that he had to pinch his fingers together to feel it at all, and it unspooled cleanly from the reel as he worked hand over hand to lower it down in the center of the vent, doing his best not to clang the lead weight against the sides. Within forty seconds, he heard the next transmission over his earpiece and immediately stopped.

"*You can stop feeding the line,*" Blair transmitted. "*I've got it.*"

49

BLAIR

Blair closed her hand around the lead weight, pulling it through the vent opening and into the glow of her red penlight.

From her position on the floor of Jim's darkened office, she detached the weight and stowed it in a shirt pocket. Then she reached for the cylindrical microphone, connecting it to the attachment point at the end of the fiber optic cable.

Her next step was to attach the microphone to the vent on the floor beside her. Seeing that the length was insufficient, she transmitted, "Give me another two feet of slack."

Another section of cable dropped into a loop below the vent opening, and Blair recovered the excess as she prepared to attach her surveillance device.

The tiny cylinder in her hand was a directional boundary microphone, and she oriented the slit running down its length with the bottom vent opening. If she misaligned that slit, the mic would record little more than the churning howl of air pouring through the air duct behind it—but by facing the receiver through the vent, the microphone would capture every noise in the office.

Once the device was positioned, she connected the magnetic attachment clips to fix it into place. Then she replaced the vent over the wall opening, recovering the loose screws one at a time and spinning them back into their original positions. Once the vent was secured, she transmitted again.

"Vent is fixed, you can proceed with installation."

Sterling answered, "*Proceeding.*"

In the office overhead, Sterling was recovering the slack in the fiber optic cable; otherwise, the building's ventilation could cause it to tap against the duct, creating a barely perceptible tapping noise that no one wanted to risk. Once that was complete, he'd attach it to the transmitter box and install that inside the vent opening.

Blair retrieved a handheld keyboard vacuum, thumbing the power switch to elicit a thin whirring noise as she raked the brush end across the floor to pick up any plaster dust that had fallen during the vent removal.

Then she worked the handheld vac across the vent itself, using her penlight to ensure there were no finger marks across the dust. You could never be too certain when working under low-light conditions, she thought, and the last thing any of them needed was for Jim to notice something amiss.

Satisfied with her work, she stowed the vacuum and stood, turning to see Marco.

He faced away from her, sitting at Jim's desk as he uploaded the keylogger and spyware while simultaneously imaging the hard drive. It was easy to forget Marco was there at all; aside from the periodic click of a USB port being plugged or unplugged, he hadn't made a sound since they'd entered.

She whispered, "I'm almost done. Any issues?"

"None," he replied. "One minute, maybe two remaining for the upload."

Then Alec transmitted over her earpiece.

"*Transmitter is installed and broadcasting. Ready for mic check.*"

Blair knelt before the vent and spoke without transmitting. "Point blank."

Alec replied, "*Crystal.*"

Rising and walking alongside Jim's desk, she said, "Halfway."

"*Still crystal.*"

Walking to the closed door, Blair reached the farthest point she could achieve from the air vent while still remaining in the office.

Turning to face the hidden microphone, she spoke quietly. "Max range."

"*And we're good. Crystal sound, no distortion.*"

Marco unplugged a device from the computer, quickly stowing the gear as he whispered, "I'm done...and Jim's chair is the most comfortable thing I've ever sat in. How come we don't have any chairs this comfortable?"

Alec transmitted, "*Tell the tech nerd to stop complaining.*"

As Marco rose from the chair and replaced it to its original position, he said to Blair, "Tell the glorified locksmith to stop eavesdropping."

"*I want you both to know I found a desk drawer full of candy bars, but out of respect for everyone in this building but Jim, I didn't take any. This despite the fact that there were multiple Almond Joys, the greatest candy produced by any nation in the free world.*"

"No one cares," Marco transmitted back.

"*Maybe you didn't hear me. I said there were* Almond Joys. *Still, I didn't touch them.*"

Then Sterling's voice came over the frequency.

"*Alec. Marco. Knock it off or so help me, I will call off Jimgate right now.*"

Neither man replied, and Sterling continued, "*Now let's get to work replacing those lock cylinders so we can get out of here.*"

50

STERLING

Sterling was the last one to reach the Sprinter van, sliding into a backseat as Marco fired the engine and pulled out of the space.

Alec turned from the passenger seat, his face lit by the orange glow of the parking garage lights. "Was it just me, or did that all go according to plan?" He sounded alarmed.

"Yeah, Alec. It did."

Alec looked to Blair seated across from him, hands behind her head as if she was quite satisfied with the night's proceedings. They exited the parking garage, bathing the van interior in darkness between street lights as Marco accelerated.

Alec continued, "Well I'm just saying—it was Blair's plan. Let's briefly go over the differences using the Scale of Destiny."

He turned one palm upward. "Blair's plan: everything goes off without a hitch. Back to the van fifteen minutes ahead of schedule."

Then he held up the opposite palm, level with the first.

"Sterling's plans: police showing up, high-speed chases, arrest and imprisonment."

Alec shifted his hands as if they were a scale, with Blair's side outweighing Sterling's. "So as we see on the Scale of Destiny, Blair's plans are like a light, refreshing romantic comedy that restores your faith in humanity. Sterling's are more of a horror movie that makes you regret ever going to the theater and leaves you feeling terrified and alone, glistening with your own cold sweat."

Sterling snapped, "You done? Can we discuss the next phase now?"

He looked to Blair for support, but she merely gave a light shrug and said, "He's not wrong."

Leaning back in his seat, Sterling rubbed his forehead. It was late, he was tired, and they had a way to go before sleep was an option—while the rental facility wasn't far, Marco wasn't driving a direct route there. In the rare event a heist went off according to plan, as this one ostensibly had, any return to a hideout would be preceded by a surveillance detection route.

This consisted of a circuitous path with multiple changes of direction, stretching out the distance and effort required for a pursuer to stay on their trail and thus cause them to expose themselves. It was a simple but effective insurance policy to mitigate the risk of police surveillance tailing them from the scene of a crime. Marco wheeled the Sprinter van meticulously along their predetermined route, aided by a GPS display.

Alec asked no one in particular, "Awful quiet back there. Is Sterling still sulking?"

Marco glanced at the rearview mirror. "It appears so."

"No," Blair said, "that's his 'lost in thought' face. And he's right, we need to discuss the next phase. As I see it, we've got two possibilities, and the first is a dead drop."

"Please, elaborate," Marco said.

She continued, "In that event, Wraith tells Jim where to recover the package, then watches it from a remote location until it's recovered. Transaction complete. If that happens, we hit the drop site before Jim gets there."

Marco braked for a stoplight and asked, "What if Wraith tries to stop us?"

"Then we stop Wraith."

"Right," Alec said. "I'll start shopping for a hand cannon."

Sterling spoke in a flat voice. "No guns."

"A .44 Magnum isn't a gun, Sterling. It's much more than that. Have you ever seen *Dirty Harry*?"

"Irrelevant," Sterling said as the light turned green and the Sprinter van lurched forward. "There are four of us and one of Wraith—we'll figure it out when the time comes. Remember, Wraith has no idea we've hacked into Jim's computer and phone; if it's a dead drop, Wraith will be safeguarding against an accidental discovery, not expecting a full heist crew to be moving in a step ahead of Jim."

Marco nodded from behind the wheel, checking his mirrors for any sign of pursuit. "I agree that a dead drop is a no-brainer. What's the next option?"

Blair said, "A direct handoff."

"You think Wraith will be that brazen?"

Sterling answered before Blair could.

"I think he'll be exactly that brazen. With a dead drop, there's always a risk of someone else discovering the tapes first, but if he does a direct handoff, the transaction is complete the second the package touches Jim's hands."

Alec countered, "But then Jim would recognize Wraith."

"I don't think so," Sterling replied. "Wraith isn't going to risk appearing on surveillance, and he'll probably pick a public place. As we know by now, big groups of people are the best anonymity. Even then, Wraith would appear in disguise and, if the level of skill we've seen so far is any indication, be acting no different than anyone else. He could be a tourist, delivery guy, jogger...all he has to do is direct Jim to sit on a park bench facing a certain direction, and drop a shopping bag next to him before taking off in the crowd."

Blair was nodding slowly. "And once that handoff is made, we get the package from Jim."

"Yes. Response time will be critical—if I were Jim, I'd destroy those tapes at the first opportunity."

"Unless he wants to check their authenticity," Blair pointed out.

"Why would he?" Sterling replied. "Let's say the tapes turn out to be a decoy. Jim has no recourse to ask for a refund. Remember, he's already secured millions from his mentor. He's got no choice but to hope the tapes are real, destroy them at once, and report to his mentor that the job is done. If Wraith burns him after that, he's screwed anyway. If not, then his career is back on track. He has nothing to gain by keeping those tapes in existence long enough to verify they're real."

"Okay," Marco said, "so let's say Wraith hands off the tapes to Jim. How are we supposed to get them?"

Sterling shrugged. "Ideal situation? We pickpocket him."

Blair looked incredulously at Sterling and managed, "Without him noticing? Unlikely."

"I said 'ideal,'" Sterling pointed out, "and it's not as unlikely as it sounds. If this goes down in a crowded public place like I think it will, getting the tapes could be easier than we think."

Marco didn't disagree, but responded in a cautious tone, "It's been a while since we've practiced pickpocketing."

"Well, get ready for the refresher course of a lifetime, because we're not rehearsing anything else until Jim gets the call from Wraith. The band is about to get back together. We'll work as a four-man canon: me and Blair are the first steers, Alec is the hook, and Marco is the second steer. Then Blair and I transition to third and fourth steer until everyone's gone."

"Hang on," Blair said. "I don't understand what you just said."

"What part?"

"Any of it."

Alec rolled his eyes. "What's the matter, you forget all that pickpocketing training at the FBI Academy?"

"As best as I recall," Blair shot back, "there wasn't any. What's a steer, a canon, a... What did you say, a hook?"

Sterling answered, gesturing with his hands.

"Canon is the pickpocketing team. The first steer IDs the mark—in this case, Jim—and more importantly, where he's stored the cargo. First steer signals the hook, Alec, with the location the mark has stashed the cargo—let's say a certain pocket. Then the hook goes in to take the cargo, and immediately hands it off to the second steer, who goes in an opposite direction."

Marco added, "That way, if Jim feels the bump and confronts the hook, the cargo is already safe."

"Exactly," Sterling agreed. "And by the time he confronts the second steer, the cargo has already transitioned to the third or fourth steer."

Blair frowned.

"Well, why does Alec get to be the hook?"

"Because his dip is the best of any of us."

"His dip?"

"Reaching in and grabbing the cargo." Sterling hooked a thumb toward the passenger seat. "Alec is really good at dipping pockets."

Alec turned slowly, holding up his palms to Blair and

wiggling his fingertips. "Turns out these hands aren't just good for cracking safes. Is your team phone still in your pocket, Blair?"

"Yes," she answered flatly.

He raised his eyebrows at her.

"Are you *sure*?"

"Yes," she said again, pulling her phone from her pocket and holding it up. "It's right here."

Alec shrugged, turning to face forward as he muttered, "Well that's because I haven't tried taking it yet."

Blair sighed and put her phone away. "This is all well and good, but let's say we can't pickpocket him. What then?"

"Then." Alec reached under his armpit and drew a finger pistol. "I whip out my .44 Magnum and tell Jim he has one second to—"

"No guns," Sterling said.

Marco looked over from the driver's seat. "Plan B is we take the tapes from Jim using rougher means."

Sterling nodded.

"Preferably, me punching Jim in the face as hard as I can. And we'll carry tasers as a backup."

"Well," Blair conceded, "I've tased him once before. I could do it again."

Sterling clapped his hands together. "So it's decided. We go home, get some sleep, and start tomorrow morning bright and early. Alec, you get Blair up to speed. Marco and I will join you for pickpocketing rehearsals after we've finished packing up."

Blair tentatively asked, "Packing up for what?"

"To get out of New York. Once we get the tapes, there's no need to wait here—we'll need to go home and get the content into the public eye, asap."

51

BLAIR

Blair paced in the rental warehouse after sunrise the next morning, awaiting Alec's return. And while he'd been gone for several minutes—to where or for what purpose, she had no idea—Blair contemplated the odds of success for the upcoming pickpocketing effort.

Like Sterling, she was reasonably certain that Wraith wouldn't risk a dead drop. That put the crew's odds of success firmly in the hands of their pickpocketing ability or lack thereof, and it felt like more of a gamble than she was comfortable taking. As much as she detested Jim on a personal level, he was nothing if not smart and cautious. A long career of corruption and power mongering had endowed him with a healthy sense of paranoia and suspicion, the continual process of covering his tracks and mitigating his own accountability in criminal activity serving as a vaccine of sorts to being caught by surprise.

Once Jim got the tapes in hand, he'd undoubtedly stuff them into a pocket until he was ready to destroy them. Until then he was unlikely to fall victim to any possible spectacles aimed at distraction. Whatever the outcome of his transfer with Wraith, Blair imagined they'd succeed in only one way: physically restraining Jim and taking the tapes by force.

Alec finally strode into the warehouse carrying a small item in one hand. "Welcome to Pickpocketing 101," he said, tossing the object to Blair with the words, "Think fast."

The projectile made a long arc toward her, and Blair intercepted it with both hands. It was four tiny cassette cases with the tapes inside, each taped together to form a single unit.

Alec approached her, explaining, "We'll use that to simulate our cargo. If it's in a larger container, that makes our jobs easy, and if we're really lucky, Wraith will pass it off in some kind of a satchel so we can do a simple bag snatch. But we'll plan for the worst, so put that in your pocket."

Blair pocketed the tapes as Alec continued, "So let's take it from the top. The Sign is when you alert the mark that there's a pickpocket—"

"Intentionally?"

"Of course intentionally," he said. "You call out that there's a pickpocket in a crowd, and nine times out of ten everyone including the mark will reach for their most valuable item to make sure they've still got them. In Europe, the canons put up signs saying to watch out for pickpockets—then they hang out by the signs, watching for someone who looks like they've got something they don't want to lose. Then the hunt begins."

Blair nodded. "The Sign. Got it."

"Now if you don't know where the cargo is, you can bring in the Fan. That's where you brush by the mark to feel his pockets without actually taking anything."

To demonstrate, he walked past Blair as if they were in a crowded public place, sweeping the backside of a hand delicately across her leg and announcing, "Felt it."

She turned to face him. As she did, he bumped into her as he moved in the opposite direction.

"Sorry, ma'am," he said, stopping to see her patting down her pocket to make sure she still had the tapes.

He pointed to her hand. "So *that's* where you have the cargo. What I just did is called a Bump, to see what you pat down afterward. Now I'd keep walking, because by then a steer or a hook has identified where you're storing the cargo and can follow you into a Transition Zone."

"What's a Transition Zone?"

"Anywhere the mark has to adjust to new surroundings, which maximizes distraction. Could be getting onto or off of a subway, in or out of a building. Best bet is if it correlates with a chokepoint like a doorway or park gate, where it's natural to brush into people."

Peering over her shoulder with a look of annoyance, he called out, "We're in the middle of class, Marco. What do you want?"

Blair turned to see the room was empty, and by the time she looked back to Alec, he was gone, brushing past her opposite shoulder.

She instinctively reached for the tapes, feeling they were still there as Alec continued circling her.

"When you're pickpocketing, distraction is key. It's the same principle as magic tricks: direct the focus one way, then exploit the gap in another. Stage a fight. Or ask the mark for directions, then hand him your phone map so you have to lean in to see."

"Makes sense," she acknowledged.

Alec sauntered up to her and said in a seductive voice, "Hey, girl, you got plans tonight?"

She took a step back, stopping him with a hand to his chest.

"What are you doing?"

"Making a point," he said, stepping back. "You had that

reaction because you know what I'm trying to do, but most women would be overwhelmed by my physical attractiveness, welcome my advances, and allow me to get close enough to make a dip. Sex sells in pickpocketing just like anything else."

She shook her head. "I don't think Jim is into guys, Alec."

"He's never met me. But let's flip the script." Alec looked her up and down, making a momentary assessment. "Say you did something with your hair, wore a little makeup for once. Put on a nice silver high-slit party dress with some strappy heels that accentuate your calves and brush up against the mark outside a bar, have a little liquor on your breath to make it convincing—"

He advanced on her again, and again she pushed him away.

"I get it," she said. "But Jim would recognize me, and also I'm not going to do any of that."

"Well, that's a little selfish and narrows our options, but I'll play your game. You can also go for the Compassion play—drop your purse, spill stuff everywhere, and get the mark to help you pick it up while the hook dives into the exposed pockets."

"Jim's not going to help anybody."

"Or the Reverse Compassion." He took a step toward her, pretending to carry a cup as he stumbled. "I am SO sorry. Here, let me help you clean up that coffee—"

He reached for her as she stepped away, turning the pocket with the tapes away from him.

"Too suspicious," she said. "I wouldn't fall for that."

"You might if I had one of my people spray your shoulder with fake bird droppings, and then I pointed it out and turned all Good Samaritan with a handkerchief, trying to wipe it off you. By then, you've got that guy standing behind you."

He pointed behind her and she looked over her shoulder, seeing no one as Alec brushed lightly past her.

"Boom," he said, "hook just moved in while you're worried about your clothes. And here's another one: the Sandwich."

"The Sandwich?"

"Turn around and start walking."

Blair reluctantly did as she was told, halting abruptly when Alec said, "Now stop!"

He bumped into her from behind, and she whirled to face him as he explained, "Surround the mark when he's passing through a choke point. Person in front becomes the stall, stopping suddenly like they just dropped something or realized they were going the wrong way. Mark bumps the stall, hook bumps the mark while making the dip."

Blair sighed. "I appreciate all the theory, Alec, but I think I need some actual practice."

"We're not done yet: I haven't told you about the jacket and the newspaper."

"What's that?"

"Exactly what it sounds like: a jacket and a newspaper." He removed his jacket to demonstrate. "Point is to have something to conceal what your dip hand is doing. Draping a jacket over one arm works wonders, as does a partially folded newspaper."

Bending one arm at the elbow, he said, "See what I'm doing?"

"No."

Alec turned to the side, lifting his jacket slightly to reveal his other arm reaching beneath it, the opposite hand reaching past the elbow in a move that would be imperceptible to outside view.

"I see," she said.

Alec put his jacket back on. "Your chances of success go up exponentially if you can hide the dip from outside observers."

"Got it," she said impatiently. "Now can we get started?"

Alec reached into his jacket pocket, removing the tapes and holding them up for her to see. Blair patted her pants pocket, noticing for the first time that the cargo was gone.

"I got started five minutes ago," Alec said with a mischievous smile. "Time for you to catch up."

52

STERLING

Sterling carried a box to the Sprinter van, looking sidelong at Blair and Alec's rehearsals. The sight cut through the tension and anticipation of the upcoming exchange between Wraith and Jim, bringing a smile to Sterling's face.

Alec was critiquing Blair's form with the intensity of an Olympic shot put coach, gesturing wildly as he gave his pointers, then snatching a newspaper from her to demonstrate. At present they were covering handoff of the cargo from one steer to another, a transfer that had to be both seamless and invisible to the outside observer.

Repositioning himself, Alec walked past her, pretending to glance at a half-folded newspaper in one hand while the other swept beneath the opposite arm, dropping the cargo into an open pocket of Blair's coat. Once she nodded that she understood, Alec handed her the cargo and the newspaper, and they reset their positions for another walking pass.

Sterling deposited the box into the van, feeling reasonably confident in Blair's ability to perform in her first real-world pickpocketing team effort. She was a quick study in technique, and performed well under pressure so long as no heights were involved. Even then, he couldn't fault her for one irrational childhood fear, and the odds of this exchange occurring at altitude were slim to none.

He turned and walked to the next box to be loaded, this one inside Marco's office.

The tech expert was analyzing his screen with the same laserlike focus that he did everything at a computer. *Better him than me*, Sterling thought. Jim's first communications and surveillance recordings had been subjects of fascination to the crew; it was a real-time bird's-eye view into his political campaign. But within an hour, the allure had faded and no one but Marco was interested in the least.

The problem wasn't with the audio quality or the comprehensiveness of Marco's hacking efforts—both were superlative. Instead, Sterling, Alec, and Blair had simply found the content far too boring to be of interest. Most of Jim's communications had been absurdly banal: vague promises to various interest groups in his district, assurances that he'd represent their interests better than his opponent regardless of which side of the party line they stood on. Sterling thought the leering web of deceit fit Jim perfectly—promise everything to everyone, then serve your own self-interests behind the scenes. Jim had come here to accumulate power; he didn't care about the constituents here any more than he did the principle of integrity that he campaigned atop. And yet here he was, branding himself as some kind of moral crusader returning home after decades of fighting criminals for the FBI.

So it was with an air of irony that he asked Marco, "Anything interesting yet?"

Sterling had already begun lifting the next box when, to his surprise, Marco replied in the affirmative.

Dropping the box, Sterling moved behind Marco's chair and asked, "What is it? They set up a meeting?"

"Relax," Marco drawled in his Russian accent. "Nothing so dramatic. But there is this."

He pulled up a software-generated transcript of a conversation from Jim's office, then pointed to the first line of dialogue.

"This first speaker is Jim. He refers to the other speaker as Chris, so I'm fairly confident it's Chris Mitchell, his campaign manager."

Sterling scanned the lines of dialogue as Marco scrolled down. Everything appeared to be what he'd expect of two men discussing their ongoing campaign plan, until Marco stopped near the bottom.

"Right here," he said, pointing again. "Mitchell references two days remaining, and Jim assures him he's got it, quote unquote, 'taken care of.' Then Mitchell demands resolution once the item is in hand, and leaves the office."

Marco spun his chair to face Sterling, folding his hands across his stomach. "The specified time remaining correlates with Wraith's deadline to contact Jim, and I find that interesting indeed."

Sterling nodded. "So do I, buddy. Why would Jim ever tell his campaign manager?"

"Maybe he didn't have a choice."

"You think his mentor made him?"

Marco leaned against the headrest of his chair, sounding like Sterling had missed something blatant. "Just the opposite. I think our favorite Rolls Royce-riding political fixer may have leaked information about the tapes."

Sterling's eyebrows shot up. "You think *Dembinski* told Jim's campaign manager? What would he possibly have to gain by doing that?"

"I don't know. But remember two things." Marco held up his index and middle fingers. "One, this election cycle is an exception: Wall Street usually supports the Republican party, not the Democrats."

"And two?" Sterling asked.

Marco lowered his hand.

"You know the saying, boss: politics makes strange bedfellows."

53

BLAIR

Alec sat facing the wall, using a letter stencil to meticulously address the last of four padded manila envelopes.

Blair directed her gaze to the jacket pocket on his right side, where she could make out the corner of the cargo: four tiny cassette tapes wrapped as a single tantalizing package, ripe for the picking.

She closed with one quiet footfall, then two, before slipping her fingers into his pocket.

He spoke without looking up. "Nice try, Blair."

She withdrew her hand, snapping her fingers in disappointment.

"Too much pressure?"

"You used three fingers, didn't you?"

Blair sighed. "Yes."

"Next time, go for index and thumb only. You're trying to gently manipulate a small object, not stuff a Thanksgiving turkey." He compiled the envelopes into a neat stack, which he handed to Blair. "One per pile, doesn't matter which."

She did as she was told, spreading the envelopes evenly

across the stacks of individual gear spread across the table behind Alec.

With only one day remaining on Wraith's timeline to contact Jim, the entire crew was on edge, but especially Blair. The entire future of this operation, if not their crew, rested in that contact, and once it occurred, they'd have only minutes to respond and react. If they succeeded, it would erase the endless threat that Jim represented to their team, to say nothing of Sterling's mother.

Blair didn't want to consider what would happen if they failed.

Sterling entered at a brisk stride.

"We're all packed, other than Marco's surveillance setup that we can break down in a few minutes. How are you guys doing with the equipment prep?"

"Good to go," Blair replied. "It's all right here."

Sterling inspected the contents of the table, seeing that everything was parceled into a pile for each crew member.

There were four tasers in the event Jim couldn't be pickpocketed, plus the assorted props for concealing their faces as well as handoff of the cargo. These included pocket-laden jackets, scarves, magazines, and newspapers. And, of course, some additional hardware to help cover their escape if they were spotted.

But there was another item in each stack that seemed to surprise Sterling: padded manila envelopes complete with postage, each addressed to a separate PO box maintained by the crew in LA.

Sterling pointed to the table. "What's with the envelopes?"

Alec responded enthusiastically, waving his hands as he spoke.

"In *Entrapment*, Catherine Zeta-Jones executes a daring high-rise robbery to steal a priceless Rembrandt. Rather than take the painting out with her, she secures it in a shipping tube and puts it in the building's mail chute."

"And?"

Alec hesitated. "I thought if we get the tapes, but cops are getting too close or whatever, we could seal them in an envelope and put them in a post office collection box on a street corner somewhere. Ship the tapes back to ourselves, and if we get searched, we come up clean. And no one can steal the tapes back because they'd be in the mail."

Sterling was quiet for a full thirty seconds after that, his brows furrowed in concentration. Alec watched him expectantly, waiting for a response.

Finally, Sterling said, "Alec, that's—"

"Oh sure," Alec replied, "let me have it. Dumb idea, Alec. Movies aren't real, Alec. I've heard it all before."

Sterling shook his head. "I was going to say—"

"That in *Entrapment*," Alec cut him off, "Sir Thomas Sean Connery just robs the first-floor mailroom anyway, thereby negating Catherine Zeta-Jones's brilliant scheme."

Sterling spoke quietly. "No, Alec. This is a *great* idea."

"Sure, because—wait, what?"

Sterling shrugged. "It's a great idea. If anyone's in danger of getting caught with the tapes, they book it to the nearest mail drop box. Worst-case scenario, someone gets caught with an envelope and we burn a PO box, but they're all secured through fake identities anyway so that doesn't matter. And if we do need to mail the tapes, these envelopes are the difference between total failure and total success. I should have thought of this myself." He placed a hand atop Alec's shoulder. "Well done, Alec."

Then Sterling walked out of the room, leaving Alec to stare at Blair with a dumbfounded expression.

"You think he meant all that?"

She nodded slowly.

"Yeah, Alec. I do."

Alec gave his best attempt at a nonchalant shrug, but Blair could make out the look of pride on his face as he turned back to the table, this time analyzing a map of Albany in consideration of possible exchange venues.

With a compliment from Sterling fresh in his mind, Alec would be at his maximum distractedness.

Blair slipped close behind him, gently lowering each footfall across the grimy floor so as not to alert him. Slipping her index finger and thumb inside his jacket pocket, she felt the slick surface of the stack of tapes and began gently, almost imperceptibly, lifting it out.

"Nice try, Blair," Alec said without looking up.

She snapped her fingers in exasperation. "But that was only two fingers this time!"

"With me sitting up, you didn't have a chance—pocket is too taut to make that dip without bumping me. Next time, wait until I'm leaning over the table, see?"

He leaned forward, and the jacket pocket formed a crease that provided more room to manipulate the tapes out.

Blair pressed her lips together, then sighed angrily.

"Yeah," she said, "that makes sense."

Then, attempting to push through her frustration to focus on the task at hand, she said, "Find any other exchange sites that look promising?"

He never had a chance to answer.

At that moment, Marco sprinted into the room, shouting his announcement in a tone somewhere between urgency and panic.

"We've got to move now—Wraith just announced the meeting!"

54

JIM

Jim stepped off the elevator with his suitcase in hand, following a corridor toward the suite of rented offices serving as his campaign headquarters.

He'd just gotten back from morning coffee with a wealthy private donor, a meeting that had occupied thirty minutes on his schedule and then stretched an hour and a half, with Jim maintaining a strained patience as his long-winded benefactor extolled the greatness of the Republican party with the fervor of a Soviet propagandist.

Now he was happy to be making it out of traffic before the lunch rush hit, so far behind on his workload that he'd have to skip eating altogether just to leave the office by five o'clock.

He arrived at the door of his office suite, shuffling his keychain to sift out the numbered key the building management had assigned. Unlocking the handle with a sense of irritation at his campaign manager's unwavering "locked door" policy, he made his way inside and thumbed the handle lock into place behind him.

Entering the office suite felt like stepping into a pseudo-reality where he was a celebrity of sorts—his name and face were everywhere, from campaign banners to stacks of yard signs being stored in assorted corners ahead of major publicity pushes.

Given the visual fanfare, an outside observer could easily assume that Jim entered the suite every day to a standing ovation from his campaign staff.

The truth was that they barely noticed him—and Jim couldn't blame them at all.

The staff was too busy furiously pecking away at keyboards, making phone calls in rapid succession, or preparing strategy documents for Jim's approval.

Personally, Jim thought the full staff this early in the campaign effort was overkill—after all, he still had two months until his filing deadline and wasn't even running against anyone in the primary—but his mentor had been adamant that no chances could be taken. Apparently when you were disrupting a long-term Democratic stronghold and a ten-year incumbent, a bit of overkill was just the ticket.

Still, the effort going into his campaign planning was mind-boggling, almost equal to his federal task force in LA. He had a volunteer coordinator, political director, combination social media strategist and web designer, communications director, database manager, plus an elections lawyer on retainer.

All of these people formed a comprehensive network supporting Mitchell's guidance. Which was just as well to Jim, because he'd have no idea what to tell these people to do in support of his campaign.

Mitchell, by contrast, was a tyrant. The levels of micromanagement he was capable of on a daily basis, even this early in the election year, were so staggering that Jim worried whether half the staff would quit by the time November rolled around. If he wasn't in his office, Mitchell was making his rounds among the staffers' workstations, asking pointed questions and following up on assorted minutiae from his eerily comprehensive memory.

The man didn't miss anything. Even after Jim's quiet entry and stealthy maneuver toward his corner suite, Mitchell managed to appear from behind the doorway to the political director's office, tilting his chin upward by way of inquiring how the meeting went.

Jim shot him a thumbs up, and Mitchell vanished to continue...well, whatever it was he had to do with the political director. Jim didn't have any idea, nor did he have a burning desire to know—by the time any campaign decisions reached his desk, they'd been sifted through Mitchell's vast filter of political experience. Aside from appearing at group events or meeting with the leadership from various local interest groups, Jim's biggest contribution so far had been fundraising from his network of former colleagues and law enforcement organizations. While both Jim and his campaign manager knew full well that the money would flow in however it had to, Mitchell explained both the nuances of campaign spend accounting and the importance of maintaining a grassroots appearance for the benefit of their media coverage. At this point Jim was largely a figurehead, the smiling face of an ever-growing effort to put District 20 into Republican hands.

Jim entered his office with a weary sigh, closing the door and going through the process that had followed his return to work for the majority of his professional life. The only variation was to begin by taking off his overcoat, courtesy of the Albany weather he hadn't missed since leaving. Everything else was the same: remove suit jacket, loosen tie, roll up sleeves, drop into the chair, and fire up the computer to continue the day's work.

His screen refreshed itself from Jim's lengthy absence, and

he clicked his email app to see what fires needed to be put out before he could return to his normal routine. Half his incoming mail seemed to originate from Mitchell, each subject line a task to be completed, every message sent with a colored flag indicating priority along with a read receipt so he could tell whether Jim had opened it yet.

Then a strange thing happened—Jim's screen flickered, then froze before the email app had fully loaded. Jim tapped his mouse twice against the desk, slid it around to see if he could move its arrow. Nothing worked.

Great, Jim thought. Another computer issue worthy of summoning his web designer, who'd invariably explain some software update before rebooting his system and taking another twenty minutes out of his available workday.

But a moment later, Jim saw the real reason for his screen freezing—the familiar chat box window appeared, a single message dancing into view.

WRAITH: *Albany Institute of History & Art. Lansing Gallery. Noon. Come alone.*

Jim checked his Rolex, then typed his response.

Got it. See you there.

His screen flickered again, and then all functionality resumed —his email app was open and loading new messages from

Mitchell, the computer mouse once again directing the tiny arrow on screen.

Jim hurriedly drew his burner phone and dialed his mentor, tucking the phone between his ear and shoulder as he locked the computer, then shucked his sleeves down to the cuff and buttoned them while waiting for the call to connect. Switching the phone between hands to slip into his suit jacket and overcoat without buttoning either, he knew he'd have to hang up within seconds—with the imminent surge of people flushing out of every building in downtown Albany for their lunch break, even a small delay could cost him the linkup. But his mentor had insisted on knowing the very second the meeting was announced, and Jim had no choice but to make the effort.

The ringing stopped as the call connected, and Jim spoke without waiting for a response.

"Noon, Lansing Gallery, Albany Institute of History & Art."

Ending the call, he swept out of his office, making his way to the office suite door. Ever vigilant, Mitchell stepped into view and was about to cast a verbal query when Jim silenced him by mouthing the word *showtime*. Mitchell gave a solemn nod, and Jim hurried out the door on his way to the elevator.

55

STERLING

Sterling uncapped the bottle, extracting the brush top and nearly spilling the adhesive across himself as Alec carved the Sprinter van through a sharp right turn. Steadying himself in the back, Sterling strained to hear Marco's analysis of the museum floor plans on the official site.

"Aside from entrances and a library," Marco said from the passenger seat, "the first floor is mostly offices and collection storage. Second floor has a museum shop, cafe, and seven galleries."

Sterling asked, "Is the Lansing Gallery one of them?"

"No. It's on the third and final floor. There are seven interconnected galleries—Lansing is at the dead end, accessible through three other exhibits. It's the farthest possible point from the building entrance."

Blair was in the back of the van, applying the particulars of her own disguise. "Why would Wraith risk that for the exchange?"

Sterling shook his head. "He wouldn't. And choosing a dead end on the highest floor tells me he's going to make the exchange as Jim is on his way to or from the gallery. If it were my drop, I'd aim for an opposite-direction drop on a stairwell or passing through an exhibit. Wraith may just plant the tapes in Jim's pockets with a reverse pickpocket, knowing that Jim will find them eventually."

Then Sterling focused his attention on the bottle in his hand, using the brush cap to apply a layer of silicone-based adhesive across his cheeks and jawline. He repeated the process on his upper lip before capping the bottle. His eye color had been concealed by brown contacts since he'd woken up that morning, but the irritation of fake facial hair was one he wasn't willing to bear until it was absolutely required.

Since escaping from prison, he'd become seasoned at the nuances of changing his appearance. It was, to an extent, a demeaning necessity— no boy ever grew up dreaming of having a wig collection worthy of a Hollywood movie set—but he'd done what he had to, assembling a wide variety of head coverings in addition to beards, goatees, eyebrows, mustaches, and sideburns in every conceivable color.

Marco added, "Don't forget that Jim placed a call to relay the meeting time and location. Since there's no record of the call on his personal cell or office phone, it means he used his burner, and there's only one person he calls with that."

Alec accelerated through a yellow light. "Why would Jim inform his mentor?"

"Worst case?" Blair asked, fixing her wig into place. "They're trying to roll up Wraith."

"Jim wouldn't risk informing police about the tapes."

"Who said anything about the police? It could be a team of hired guns, former cops, or mercenaries."

Alec sounded mournful as he replied, "I knew I should have brought a .44 Magnum."

Then Marco said, "The message said to come alone. You don't think he's worried about scaring off Wraith?"

Blair, finished fitting her wig into place, spoke with conviction. "Believe me, Jim might not even know."

"What do you mean?"

"If his mentor simply demanded the meeting info as soon as Jim received contact, then as far as Jim knows, he *is* going alone. His mentor could be the one trying to get Wraith off the playing field, to make sure no other copies of those tapes are at large."

Sterling probed his cheeks with a fingertip, finding that the adhesive had dried to sufficient tackiness for the next step of his application. "If that's true— if there is a team of thugs moving in—we're at just as much risk as Wraith is. Once we get the tapes, they won't know us from Wraith. And if they get their hands on me or Blair, we'll be a pretty big consolation prize for Jim and his mentor."

A collective moment of silence followed this statement. Grasping the fine Swiss lace backing of his hand-tied beard, Sterling lifted the mass and prepared to apply it. While his wigs were one hundred percent real hair, the facial pieces were, for reasons that were beyond him, a combination of human and yak hair.

That last detail gave Sterling a moment of pause as he laid the beard across his face, tapping it to adhere the lace backing without getting hairs stuck in the glue.

Marco cleared his throat. "Maybe you two should sit this one out. Let me and Alec handle the dip."

"No way," Sterling and Blair responded in unison.

"We could do it, I'm telling you."

Sterling applied the mustache to his upper lip and said, "What, with a single steer and a hook? We're only going to get one shot at this. Four people is the bare minimum."

Then he used a comb to blend the two hair pieces until they were virtually indistinguishable from the real thing.

"How do I look?" he asked Blair.

"Like you just walked out of a truck stop diner. How do I look?"

He scanned her ingenious disguise. "Like you just stepped off the cover of *Ladies' Home Journal*."

"Exactly what I was going for."

Braking for a stop sign, Alec looked over his shoulder and said, "Boss, maybe Marco's right. It's rare, but it happens. I mean, at least consider waiting outside the museum with Blair."

Alec was not often the team's voice of caution, so his comment gave Sterling pause. The risks of entering the museum as a known fugitive under these circumstances were daunting, to say the least. That was exactly why, amidst all the uncertainties surrounding the exchange, Sterling had felt certain of one thing: Wraith would choose an outdoor venue.

If you were looking to make a handoff and escape unidentified, it was the only way to do business. Buildings meant limited points of entry and exit, increased security, and the ability for police to lock them down and question occupants with little more than an anonymous tip.

And anything that played against Wraith would apply doubly so to Sterling and Blair.

Then Sterling shook his head.

"We don't know how this will play out, and we're not going in half-cocked. Our crew does this together or not at all. But since we've got three floors to cover and a probable exchange in passing somewhere along the way, we'll have to switch up our roles. So here's the plan."

56

JIM

By the time Jim finally found a parking spot, he whipped his Suburban into it and put the vehicle in park as its frame was still rocking to a halt.

Then he exited into the frigid air, the sun's blaze overhead doing little to tame the early March freeze. Checking his Rolex, Jim strode across the snow and slush covering the parking lot toward a stairway leading up to the crosswalk.

Jim hadn't been to this museum since he was a kid, and doubted the area was usually this busy. In his search for a parking spot, it occurred to him that everyone in Albany must have converged on this area in one fell swoop. The museum's tiny parking lot was out of the question, already fully packed along with all four streets lining the block. And since the Albany Institute of History & Art wasn't exactly an international tourist destination, Jim knew at once that some big event was going on and Wraith had chosen to exploit it as his camouflage among the masses. Though what that event could possibly be, Jim had no idea, and after circling the block, he had found the only available parking in a cash-only public lot next to Sheridan Park.

He pulled his overcoat tight around him, swinging his gaze left and right for anything out of the ordinary as he considered Wraith's greater strategy in selecting the museum.

The surrounding area was a melting pot of privately owned retail stores, residential areas, government buildings, and restaurants. Each provided its own nuances of access and attire, and combined into a veritable labyrinth through which Wraith had surely layered a multi-tiered entry and escape route. There was also the very real chance that Wraith was watching him at this very moment, a prospect that Jim welcomed—with such a narrow margin to make it to the museum, the last thing he needed was for Wraith to declare him a no-show and abandon the exchange.

Reaching the stairs, Jim trotted up toward the corner crosswalk and caught sight of his destination.

The Albany Institute of History & Art had an odd layout consisting of two staggered buildings connected by a central atrium with an entrance on either side. The three-story museum of pale brown bricks struck Jim as a bizarre location for Wraith to choose—of all places in Albany, why here? To Jim, there was only one explanation: whatever event had caused the influx of cars and people at this time of day, the museum was its focal point.

And when viewed in that regard, choosing such an unlikely exchange venue was a stroke of genius on Wraith's part. Not even Jim had considered the museum as a possible meeting location, and even if he had, he could have taken precious few precautions if the Institute was at maximum capacity, a situation compounded by lunch hour's sidewalk foot traffic to the surrounding restaurants.

Jim's suspicion was confirmed when he reached the museum's back door only to see a printed sign that read, *DOVE*

STREET ENTRANCE CLOSED FOR PRIVATE EVENT. PLEASE PROCEED TO WASHINGTON AVENUE ENTRANCE.

Now the selection of this building seemed even smarter. With fifty percent of its pedestrian access cut off, the main entrance would be overtaxed with processing law-abiding visitors—and it wasn't as if the closed entrance would stop Wraith in the slightest. Jim could already make out fire escapes and staff doors on the northwest side of the museum, along with a loading dock presently blocked by a box truck. As an elite criminal with time for advance preparations, Wraith was working with a three-dimensional map where nothing was off limits and no response by law enforcement would go completely unanticipated.

But Jim had his own problems to negotiate at present. With the Dove Street entrance closed, he now had to circumnavigate the block to reach the main entrance, costing him another minute and a half in his dwindling time reserve.

He rounded the corner onto Washington Avenue, scanning the flow of vehicle and foot traffic for signs of physical surveillance: out-of-place electrical equipment on the streetlights and powerline posts, a car parked with an occupant inside, someone standing stationary with an orientation to the museum entrance.

By all appearances, however, this was an extremely busy Albany weekday lunch rush.

Jim proceeded to the museum entrance with the sense that only minutes remained before he had the tapes in hand; once that occurred, he was a bottle of lighter fluid away from ending this nightmare once and for all.

He pulled open a glass door and strode into the lobby, coming up short when he saw that it was packed with people, ranging from clusters of high school students to senior citizens, their voices echoing off the marble floors. The Dove

Street entrance he'd had to bypass was blocked by a banquet spread, food platters and seating for some closed event that took up nearly half the lobby.

Jim stopped before the ticket counter and removed his wallet.

"One adult," he said, handing his credit card to an enthusiastic clerk who smiled at him from behind thick eyeglasses.

"That'll be ten dollars," she said, accepting his card.

"Can you tell me where the Lansing Gallery is?"

"Third floor, all the way in the back."

Jim considered this for a moment—by selecting the farthest point from the museum entrance, Wraith could have been planning for a brush pass while Jim was on his way to or from the gallery.

There was no time to speculate about it now, however, and Jim nodded to the crowd behind him and asked, "What's going on today?"

The clerk brightened. "Fort Nassau Day."

"Excuse me?"

She ran his credit card, explaining, "On this day in 1614, Hendrick Christiaensen built a fur-trading post on the banks of the Hudson. It was the first structure in the area, and the start of Albany as we know it today. Every year the museum hosts group visits by the Historic Albany Foundation, the Capital District Genealogical Society, and the Berne Historical Project."

Finally the ticket printed, and the clerk handed it over along with his card and receipt as she continued, "And the field trips from local schools, of course—three in progress, and two more arriving this afternoon."

Jim pocketed the items, mumbling a word of thanks before turning toward the elevator. He quickly ruled it out after seeing the line of senior citizens waiting for its return, moving toward the stairs instead with a growing appreciation for Wraith's strategy. The entire museum was packed, and someone looking to hide could move with impunity among every floor in the building.

He'd made it halfway to the stairs before a rotund man in an ill-fitting blazer and sweater vest emerged from the crowd, approaching with a sense of purpose.

"Excuse me," the man asked, "are you Jim? Jim Jacobson?"

Jim squinted at the man in confusion, unable to reconcile the overt contact with any conceivable strategy by Wraith.

Then it hit him: Wraith could have selected someone in the crowd to hand off the tapes, giving the man a hundred bucks in order to maintain anonymity as he watched from a distance.

Jim quickly scanned the crowd for someone watching the interaction, his law enforcement instincts attuned to the slightest discrepancy. But nothing caught his eye, the swirling flow of civilians proceeding without indication that anyone but this man noticed Jim's presence.

"Yes," Jim said. "That's me."

The man glanced about as if suddenly embarrassed, then summoned his courage and extended his hand, fingers spreading, as Jim held up his palm to receive the tapes.

But instead, the man clasped Jim's hand, pumping his arm in a furious shake.

"I just want to shake your hand, sir. My son is a deputy with the Montgomery County Sheriff's Office, and saw you speak at the Officers Union. He's told the whole family about it, and you better believe you've got our vote come November. And let me tell you, sir—it'll be nice to have a Republican in office for a change."

Jim gave a forced smile, tried to extricate his hand, and found himself unable to do so for another three solid shakes.

"So what brings you to the museum today, Mr. Jacobson?"

Jim gestured to the marble sculptures in the lobby. "To plan for Albany's future, I believe it's important to connect with its past. And nothing reminds me of our heritage quite so much as being surrounded by the history of this amazing region, especially on Fort Nassau Day."

Jim was proud of himself for his off-the-cuff response, a parlay worthy of an aspiring politician, but the feeling only lasted a moment before he realized it was the worst possible thing he could have said if he wanted to end the conversation.

"Boy, Mr. Jacobson, I couldn't agree with you more. My family first settled in the Upper Hudson Valley in 1845, when the Troy and Greenbush Railroad was chartered and—"

"If you'll excuse me," Jim interrupted, "I've only got a brief time before I have to return to the office."

The man turned red. "Of course. You must be a real busy man, Mr. Jacobson. Well if there's anything I can ever help you with, don't hesitate to reach out."

He dipped his hand in a pocket, and Jim felt his interest pique—either this man was an ignorant dolt in the crowd, or the best method actor he'd ever seen.

When he withdrew his hand, it was with a business card that Jim accepted greedily, expecting some further instructions from Wraith to be printed on it.

But the card read, *Phil Dexter, President. Dexter & Sons Plumbing—Serving the Capital Region Since 1939.*

Jim flipped the card over, seeing the backside was blank, and grinned at the man.

"Thank you so much, Mr. Dexter."

"Please, call me Phil."

"Thank you, Phil, for all your support."

Turning to watch him leave, Jim caught a glance of another man entering the museum—and unlike Phil Dexter of Dexter & Sons Plumbing, this new visitor was no accidental bystander.

His coat wasn't unusual given the weather, but the fact that it was unzipped as he entered in from the cold told Jim a gun was concealed beneath it. Anyone experienced with concealed carry would be well-rehearsed in the process of lifting a coat or overshirt with their non-firing hand as they drew a pistol; those who felt they were about to require the quickest draw possible tended to leave their jackets and overshirts open for easy access.

And while all this was speculation on Jim's part, presented in the form of a split-second gut instinct, what he saw next assured him that he was right. Upon entering the museum, the man had found Jim Jacobson staring directly at him, and his reaction was to look away, averting his eyes a bit too quickly as he walked to the ticket counter.

Wraith wouldn't be so bold—or stupid—as to carry a weapon into the exchange, nor would he react overtly to the sight of Jim. That left only one explanation: his mentor had sent reinforcements to tail Jim, either in an effort to oversee the exchange or capture Wraith altogether.

Judging by the appearance of this man—and who knew if others were on the way, or already present in the other exhibits—his mentor had sent what the dark side of the law enforcement community referred to as "cowboys." They were off-duty cops who worked for the highest bidder as hired guns, conveniently positioning themselves wherever the combination of firearms and legal authority could benefit their employer. More often than not they were also adrenaline junkies who wanted a situation to escalate, looked for any reason to draw a gun, and were happy to fudge an official report in the aftermath to protect themselves from legal ramifications.

And sending people like this was the worst possible thing his mentor could have done.

Wraith had told Jim to come alone, and he could only assume that the thief would be able to spot an armed contingent from a mile away.

Jim turned and hurried to the staircase, grasping the rail as he ascended two steps at a time, making his way toward the Lansing Gallery before some overeager gunslinger managed to screw up his exchange.

57

STERLING

Sterling perused the art in the Martin Gallery on the museum's second floor. Pausing before an 1830s oil painting of a small boat crashing over the rocks of a stormy Hudson, he admired first the drama of the sky and water, and then a smaller detail that almost went unnoticed—an angel on the cliff, watching over the boatsman.

His crew had barely beaten their quarry inside the building, having to illegally park the Sprinter van just to make it past the ticket counter before Jim got there. A traffic citation would be a small price to pay, and besides, no matter what was about to transpire here, his crew would be on their way out in the next few minutes.

Against all odds, they'd managed to position themselves a full ninety seconds before Jim entered the building. Marco was first steer, trailing Jim and watching for the exchange. Alec was behind Marco, waiting for him to signal that Jim had the cargo along with where it was located on his person. And while Blair was currently stationed on the third floor, both she and Sterling would transition to third and fourth steer to accept the cargo handoff from Alec as soon as he had it in hand.

Merely making it into their designated positions had been no small feat, especially considering that every history buff in Albany had descended on the museum today in honor of Fort Nassau Day. That minor detail made Sterling understand a lot more about Wraith's logic in staging the meet at this time and place, and he couldn't help but scan the myriad faces around him with the oddly curious notion that one of them was the thief who'd started this entire mess to begin with. As frustrated as the entire debacle had been, Sterling couldn't help but feel a begrudging respect for Wraith.

Marco transmitted over his earpiece in a whisper.

"Jim is moving up to the second floor."

Blair replied, *"I'm still in position, but it's getting packed here. I'm going to need support to keep eyes-on without getting too close."*

Marco transmitted, *"I could displace, but I'd miss an exchange-in-passing."*

Sterling moved toward the stairwell, gazing at the paintings and murmuring softly as if commenting to himself on the beauty of the art.

"Marco, hold course as first steer. Alec, keep trailing as hook. I'm headed up."

Then he reached the atrium and ascended the stairs to the Lansing Gallery.

58

JIM

Jim climbed the marble stairs, scanning the descending civilians for any indication that one of them was Wraith. Each passing second brought a mounting sense of surprise that no one had brushed past him to deposit the tapes into his coat pockets, which he'd spread open for the purpose.

But he reached the third floor without physical contact of any kind, and turned to enter a gallery titled *Traders and Culture*. The first two galleries to his left were a gridlock of amateur historians gawking at the displays; he continued to the final one before heading toward the rear of the building, toward the Lansing Gallery.

The path took him through the Ancient Egypt gallery, where a central glass display held a wrapped mummy in an open sarcophagus. Jim bypassed a family of four staring at three-part shelves supporting the top and bottom of another sarcophagus, the central shelf bearing a second mummy. These seemed to draw most of the crowd's attention; the rest of the exhibit was filled with pottery and jewelry from some raided tomb, all neatly labeled with signs and lengthy historical notes that Jim didn't have time to read and wouldn't care about if he did.

His sole focus was getting through the doorway leading to the Lansing Gallery. Jim checked his watch, seeing that he'd arrive with less than two minutes to spare—given the dearth of parking spots and the number of people in the museum, Wraith had calculated Jim's travel time with uncanny precision.

He entered the gallery at last, looking over the crowd of people to see the walls lined with baroque portraits in gold-leaf frames, the stoic portrayals of men and women gazing out at the room, expressionless. Then there were the usual art museum fluff pieces—still life paintings of bowls of fruit, riverboats, men on horseback hunting foxes. Choosing the museum's most remote corner without making a drop en route seemed to indicate that Wraith would plant the tapes as Jim was on the way back to his vehicle, but he couldn't rule out the possibility that the master thief was simply brazen enough to hand off the cargo right here, exactly as he'd said.

So Jim scanned his surroundings, considering where exactly he should station himself.

The Lansing Gallery was larger than the three galleries that bordered it, the trio of open doorways representing the only ways in or out of the windowless room. Which one of these people, if any, was Wraith? He ruled out the senior citizens and the high school kids, and was left with a dozen or more candidates of varying races and genders, none of whom paid him any mind.

Jim looked for a bench, then realized none were empty—the only one with space for him to sit was partially filled by a blonde breastfeeding her baby beneath a blanket. Definitely not Wraith.

Without a place to sit and wait, he made for the most open

corner of the room, hoping to remain as visible as possible until he was approached. He worked his way there, squeezing past the bored high schoolers and museum guides discussing paintings before clusters of onlookers.

Jim neared the corner only to spot a man he'd never seen before but recognized as surely as the incoming visitor on the ground floor: a second "cowboy," an off-duty cop called in by his mentor to oversee the proceedings and be prepared to intervene if necessary. Everything about the man screamed *cop*, from the high fade haircut to the unbuttoned flannel shirt concealing a handgun to his wide stance, hands clasped in front of his waist for speedy weapon recovery. He was scanning everyone in the room but Jim, a standout in a packed assembly of civilians. Amateur.

Jim's first thought was that he needed to distance himself from this cowboy before Wraith saw them together and determined that the "come alone" clause of his instructions had been violated. By the time he'd spotted this man, of course, he was already within a few feet—and Jim spun a quick 180, changing direction so rapidly that he feared his sudden reaction would spook Wraith as much as the sight of an off-duty cop.

But those thoughts faded from his mind as Jim recognized a face in the crowd—not looking at him, but perusing the paintings just like everyone else. So why did he stand out? Jim couldn't be sure at first, but his instincts were ironclad and he knew in his gut that this face was of great significance, even before he knew why.

He looked away from the bearded man, his mind racing until he finally realized who it was, along with the fact that his exchange was about to get sabotaged.

Reversing direction, he approached the cowboy and spoke in a low tone.

"Black jacket and beard, twelve feet behind me—that's Sterling Defranc. Arrest him, now."

"Sir?"

"He's here to sabotage the exchange. You know who I am, and I know who sent you. Arrest him or I'll have your badge."

To his credit, the cowboy advanced quickly into the crowd, drawing his weapon.

Then he shouted to Sterling, so loud that the room momentarily went silent. "Police! Show me your hands."

Sterling turned his palms up as screams arose in the crowd, every civilian making a panicked bid for the adjoining exhibits.

Except for one.

Jim watched with a detached sense of disbelief as the seated mother cast aside her nursing blanket, which fell to the ground along with her baby. She leapt to her feet in a solid two-handed shooting stance, firing the twin barbs of a taser that struck the off-duty cop in the leg and abdomen, causing him to collapse backward as the paralyzing electrical current surged through his body.

Sterling had drawn his own taser the instant the man began to fall, aiming first toward Jim.

Instinctively, shamefully, Jim threw up his hands, flinching in anticipation of the shock.

But Sterling then swung his taser toward one of the exhibit entrances, and before Jim could sweep his gaze toward the intended target, the first off-duty cop being tased by Blair—the breastfeeding mother—finally hit the ground.

His shoulders struck hard, the impact causing his pistol to fire with a deafening blast.

The bullet impacted the ceiling, gunshot fading to renewed screams from the fleeing crowd—and only then did

Jim register a second cop charging into the room, bringing his pistol to bear on Sterling.

It was too late. Sterling fired his taser and sent the second cop into a freefall to the rapid clatter of electrical current. He hit the ground a moment before Blair vaulted his body on her way out, and with Sterling seconds away from dropping his taser to flee, Jim saw his one and only chance to capture a Sky Thief.

Jim sprang into a run—by the time he recovered a pistol from the fallen officer, Sterling would be gone. Likewise, Sterling wouldn't be able to reload his taser before Jim tackled him into the wall...which was exactly what he planned to do.

As Jim closed the final few feet, he saw Sterling release his taser from his grasp, exactly as expected. Driving forward, Jim prepared to alter his course to intercept Sterling's attempted escape.

But astonishingly, Sterling didn't try to escape at all; his taser was mid-air on its way to the ground when the thief instead spun toward Jim, one fist cocked back for a wild haymaker blow that launched into motion as Jim feverishly attempted to reverse his momentum.

It was too late—he was irrecoverably moving toward Sterling, whose fist grew large in Jim's vision while he tried to bring up his hands to block the blow.

The *crack* of knuckles against Jim's temple sent his vision spiraling, blotches of color blazing into view, head ringing with a high-pitched bell noise as he tumbled sideways.

Jim's shoulder struck the ground, his body bouncing once before rolling onto his back. He blinked hard, trying to orient himself; two abandoned tasers lay on the ground before him, two men struggled to their feet as they recovered from being electrocuted, and the Lansing Gallery was otherwise empty.

Sterling and Blair were gone...and then he saw a silver

projectile soaring into the room from the door, a metal cylinder that bounced and rolled to a stop before him. He had just enough time to see the printed words—*RIOT CONTROL, CS*—before it emitted a low *pop* and began spraying a long hiss of white smoke.

Then Jim closed his eyes, tucked into the fetal position, and felt the real pain begin.

59

BLAIR

Blair and Sterling ran past Marco and Alec, both in the process of hucking their third volley of tear gas grenades into the vacated exhibits between the Lansing Gallery and the atrium stairs. No words needed to be spoken; the visual accountability of their crew was enough. For now they were executing their contingency plan for an emergency retreat, and aside from following the groundswell of civilians surging down the stairs after the sound of a gunshot, only one step remained.

Arriving in the atrium, Blair turned left and pulled down on the slotted handle of a wall-mounted fire alarm.

An earsplitting, buzzing shriek sounded in three-round intervals, white emergency strobes flashing on every floor as she descended the stairs two at a time with Sterling close behind her. Blair reached the second-floor landing before hitting the rear vanguard of retreating civilians, mostly senior citizens being assisted by good Samaritans, and she glanced back to see Alec and Marco closing the distance with them.

The crew threaded their way into the ranks of the descending seniors, appearing for all the world like selfish and able-bodied museum visitors who were ruthlessly leaving the old and infirm behind. But Blair knew that she and her crew—particularly Sterling—were in the only real danger, and they quickly blended in with the evacuating civilians. For now, their protection was amidst the people.

Two men were pushing their way up the stairwell, both fit and determined and very likely late arrivals in the effort to interdict Wraith or the Sky Thieves. Blair made way for them to pass, crying in a panicked voice, "Go back—there's a fire on three!"

The men pushed past her, and Blair felt an immeasurable sense of gratitude for the riot control grenades. She had no idea if those men had radio contact with their counterparts on the third floor, but if so, they wouldn't regain the power of speech for at least another minute. For now they were unable to see, struggling to breathe, and coughing salvos of mucus onto the carpet they were probably trying to crawl across in the effort to find clean oxygen.

As she led the way down the final flight of stairs, she caught her first glimpses of the lobby below—people were streaming out of both exits, having forced their way through the private lunch that previously blocked the Dove Street door. It was a churning maelstrom of bodies fighting toward the exits, and for a moment Blair saw a figure that stood out—pausing to look at the stairs, seemingly right at her—and then it was gone, lost in the flow of bodies.

And in that instant, Blair knew she had just caught a fleeting glimpse of Wraith.

With nothing she could do about it now, she reached the ground floor and followed the crowd. She tried to freeze frame the scene in her mind, to recount any details about the figure, but there were none; it was just one more person in a sea of people and clothing, and nothing more.

They made their way outside, emerging into the wintry air and onto the walkway. The crowd was dispersing, a few uniformed cops trying to flag people down for questioning but mostly being ignored. If the police had made any effort to contain the crowd, that had stopped the moment the fire alarm began wailing.

The first fire engines were already arriving on Washington Avenue, blocking the street as the crew cut east across the lawn toward their illegally parked van. No one spoke as they boarded the Sprinter and resumed their original seating—Alec at the wheel, firing the engine as Marco took the passenger seat and Blair and Sterling slipped into the back.

Then they were off, accelerating down Dove Street before turning right on Elk. Alec pulled over and stopped to allow a procession of emergency vehicles past—two fire trucks, a police cruiser, and an ambulance, all with sirens blaring—before continuing back to their hideout.

Looking over his shoulder, Alec said, "Well, guys, look at the bright side."

Blair faced him with disbelief as he pointed to the windshield and continued enthusiastically, "No parking ticket on the Sprinter."

Blair felt her face go tense with anger, an expression mirrored by Sterling. Marco looked over at Alec, shooting him a death glare that needed no words.

"What?" Alec asked innocently, sensing the tension. "I'm just saying, we parked illegally to make it in time and didn't even get a ticket. We could be out two hundred dollars on top of the tapes."

Marco replied, "Alec, maybe let's pass some of the ride in silence while we all process what just happened. How does that sound?"

60

BLAIR

Blair huddled alongside her team, now crowded around Marco's computer to watch the streaming local news broadcast.

A blonde news anchor in her fifties was commenting, "Breaking news on the ongoing disturbance at the Albany Institute of History & Art. While we've been covering the appearance of emergency vehicles and interviewing eyewitnesses outside the scene, Caroline Paquin joins us live now with more on just what happened. Caroline?"

The image flipped to a younger brunette standing before a green screen with a graphic of handcuffs and the title, *FRIGHT AT THE MUSEUM*.

She began, "Kate, it was certainly an interesting afternoon at the museum and not just due to today's annual celebration. As a large group of visitors from various schools and historical associations gathered to commemorate Fort Nassau Day at the Albany Institute of History & Art, a team of thieves attempted to steal a painting just hours ago. What they didn't count on was an off-duty police officer present in the gallery with them."

Then a familiar face appeared, speaking into a microphone thrust into the bottom of the screen. This was the man who had attempted to arrest Sterling. Below his image, a banner caption read, *Sergeant Troy McKinley, Albany PD*.

"I witnessed a white male attempting to remove a painting from the wall. At first I couldn't believe it—the gallery was packed with civilians—and then I realized this was actually happening, that the thief was taking advantage of the attendance to attempt a heist in broad daylight."

Caroline Paquin reappeared, teasing the upcoming interview segment. "Officer McKinley attempted to take the suspect into custody—but the thieves had other plans."

McKinley spoke confidently. "I drew my sidearm, declared myself as a police officer, and the next thing I knew I was hit by a taser from another suspect." He shook his head. "Now I've been tased in the Academy, so there was no doubt in my mind what was happening."

"But Officer McKinley wasn't alone," Caroline went on. "Another off-duty police officer, this one a state trooper, moved in to back him up."

The next man who appeared on screen was the second to arrive in the gallery, brought down by Sterling's taser moments before the crew escaped. His banner caption read, *Trooper Sean Connolly, New York State Police.*

And if Blair thought the first cop was full of it, Connolly redefined her parameters for the art of lying with extreme conviction.

He looked directly into the camera, an amateur movie star in the making.

"When people are running the other way, screaming for their lives, well, as a cop, that's exactly where you need to be. I didn't hesitate, and no police officer in my position would have either."

Caroline's intermission was spoken with compassion and a hint of injustice.

"But Trooper Connolly faced the same challenges as his fellow off-duty officer."

Then Connolly continued, "As soon as I came through the door, they were waiting for me. The taser struck before I could identify suspects from innocent bystanders, and I went down."

That last bit was particularly infuriating, Blair thought. The innocent bystanders had fled the gallery into the three adjoining exhibits, so the only civilian he saw was Jim, a man he surely recognized as part of his job.

Caroline gave a concerned frown. "The thieves weren't finished: they used what police describe as riot control grenades to spread tear gas, incapacitating the two officers before fleeing the scene."

Then it was back to McKinley for his personal account of being tear-gassed, and he laid it on thick.

"My eyes were on fire, my lungs were on fire...you just can't breathe, can't see, all you can do is gasp and cough. It's about as miserable as it gets."

The screen cut to Caroline to deliver her conclusion to this breaking report.

"The thieves are believed to have pulled a fire alarm on their way out of the building, and are currently at large. Fortunately, museum officials say that no art was permanently harmed by the tear gas, although the affected exhibits will undergo cleaning ahead of schedule to remove any lingering smell. We'll keep you posted on further updates and the police department's search for the missing thieves in our later newscast. Live in the studio, Caroline Paquin, CBS 6 News."

Marco ended the streaming broadcast, then turned away from the computer to look at the rest of his crew.

Sterling was shaking his head bitterly.

"Don't you ever just wish we could tell the media what actually happened?"

"Last I checked," Marco intoned, "they don't consider career criminals as reliable sources."

Alec, per usual, had a different perspective. "I don't want to hear any complaints from you, Sterling. You got to punch Jim, which is more than any of us can say."

He nodded. "That's true. But I'm a little concerned that he wasn't mentioned in the coverage."

Blair groaned. "He wasn't mentioned because he got his story straight with those two cops, along with using whatever connections he has to keep his name out of the news."

"But I thought that would be some good publicity for him. You know, hero Congressional candidate attempts to stop the infamous Sterling Defranc."

"If he acknowledged that the Sky Thieves were in Albany," Blair said, "it would indicate we came for him. That's bad press because it implies blackmail. Which, of course, is false: we don't want or need Jim's money, just his career. But don't worry, he'll find a way to spin this in his favor. He just hasn't figured out how."

"Well," Alec said, "at least someone will benefit from that cluster at the museum."

Blair considered staying silent, but was driven by an impulse that bypassed her sensitivity to her teammates' skepticism.

She blurted, "I saw Wraith today."

Marco looked up. "What? When?"

"Moving out of the lobby exit before we reached the ground floor."

Alec slapped a backhand across his opposite palm. "Details, woman. What did he look like?"

She gave a slight shake of her head. "I couldn't tell. It was just one figure turning to look at us on the stairs, and then he was gone. There were so many people, I couldn't make out details. But everyone else was trying to get out, and I'm pretty sure he recognized us. I just knew in my gut it was him."

Blair couldn't tell whether anyone believed her, but it didn't seem to matter. A moment later, Sterling spoke up.

"Well since you're apparently the Wraith whisperer, let's discuss his next play—because everything we do hinges on that."

Blair said, "Wraith will set up a new exchange."

Marco tilted his head, watching her through narrowed eyes.

"You sound certain of that."

"I am," she said.

"You have some information we're not aware of?"

Sighing, Blair considered how to word her argument. Sterling, Marco, and Alec had grown up in a life of crime; Blair had chosen it as her second career, and that seemed to grant her a certain perspective that wasn't shared by everyone on the crew.

"If Wraith wanted to take Jim's money and run," she said, "he could have already. Look at everything he's done so far: stealing the tapes, the bidding war, traveling to Albany to make the exchange. Whoever Wraith is, he's not just doing this for a payday. He's doing it because he enjoys the cat-and-mouse game, he likes the thrill of outwitting everyone else. Wraith isn't just a thief, he's a chess master. Now that the stakes are raised, he won't be able to keep away. Even if he took his twenty-six million to the beach, he wouldn't be able to think about anything else until he'd delivered on his end of the deal. He promised the tapes, and he's going to get them to Jim."

Marco asked, "What if you're wrong?"

Sterling answered for her, though Blair's response would have been largely the same.

"We don't have to concern ourselves with what happens if Blair is wrong. If that's the case, there's nothing we can do unless Wraith surfaces again. But if Blair is right, the question isn't if Wraith is going to make contact with Jim. The question is *how*. So if you were Wraith, how would you establish contact after what happened at the museum?"

Marco began ticking off the fingers of one hand as he said, "Off the top of my head, brush pass, dead drop, live drop, car toss, cut out, or—since we've tipped our hand about Jim's office being tapped—something as simple as a piece of physical mail. It'd be quicker to list the places where Wraith *wouldn't* contact Jim, which, by my estimate, consist of his office. As for his route to work and the parking garage, both are in play. And let's not forget about—"

"His house," Blair said.

"Right," Marco agreed, nodding slowly. "His house."

Alec glanced from one teammate to the next. "So we need to figure out how Wraith could contact Jim, and tap in."

"Not just tap in," Blair replied, "but do it as quickly as possible. This is going to be a race. Wraith knows that the longer he waits to contact Jim, the more time we have to anticipate his next move. Mark my words, he'll do everything he can to beat us to the punch. And if Jim hasn't started sweeping for bugs yet, he will now. That's going to limit our options. I don't see any way around physical surveillance—we've got to start tailing him."

Sterling agreed, "You're right. And since you and I are recognizable to Jim—even in disguise, apparently—that means Marco and Alec are going to have to pick up the bulk of those duties. So we keep monitoring his computer and phone until he pulls the plug, and begin tailing him everywhere he goes to watch for the exchange."

"Don't forget his home," Blair said. "That's an easy fixed position for Wraith to make contact somehow, and we need to know what's going on inside."

Alec reminded her, "He'll be getting it swept for bugs."

"I agree. That means we need to tap it in a way that won't be detected."

Marco said, "You sound like you have something in mind."

Blair looked across her teammates in sequence, settling her gaze on Sterling.

And then she smiled.

61

JIM

It took Jim nearly four hours to return to work, by which time most of his staff were departing for the day.

Police questioning had taken most of the first hour, and due to the grace of God, both Jim's and his mentor's connections had sufficed to suppress his name from any public connection with the incident at the museum.

But the real time suck had come from the aftermath of the CS gas—Jim smelled like a walking chemical burn, having to return home to deposit every stitch of clothing into sealed bags for dry cleaning before slipping into the shower amid his wife's grand inquisition about why he'd come home reeking of pepper spray, as if it were another woman's perfume.

The shower water had felt like sandpaper against Jim's irritated pores, and his eyes, nose, and mouth were instantly aflame as much as they had been in the Lansing Gallery. That was to say nothing of the tender swelling on the side of his head, an additional indignity courtesy of Sterling's punch. Jim had never felt so resentful of his mentor as he did in that moment. Rather than trusting Jim to handle the exchange, his mentor had second-guessed him and sent in cowboys to oversee everything.

But the most troubling aspect of that disaster was the presence of the Sky Thieves, who'd apparently traveled to the farthest limits of the continental US to pursue those tapes. Jim had identified Sterling on sight, and Blair only after she discarded her pseudo-baby to draw a taser—how bold could these people be? Either of them would be jailed for the rest of their natural lives if spotted, and rather than leave Jim alone, they'd put everything on the line to end his career.

After exiting the shower, Jim had re-dressed in the closest approximation to the same suit, shirt, and tie that had been gassed at the museum, hoping that none of his staff would notice the change in attire.

By the time he finally entered the office suite, his communications director and social media strategist were on their way out. Jim waved a friendly goodbye, analyzing their glances to see if they noticed anything out of the ordinary about his appearance.

If either of them did, they gave no indication; each murmured a polite goodbye on their way to the elevator, and Jim felt pleased with himself as he entered the office suite, locking the door behind him.

And there, of course, was Chris Mitchell. Perfectly attired as always, feet wide and arms crossed as his eyes scanned Jim from head to toe.

"Everyone's gone," he said at once, "and I see that you changed clothes."

"Astute observation."

"From the news, I take it the exchange occurred at the museum."

"The Albany Institute of History & Art. And yes."

Mitchell shrugged. "So what happened?"

Jim stripped off his overcoat, setting it across the back of a chair. "The exchange got interrupted."

"What do you mean, 'interrupted?'"

"The Sky Thieves were there. I saw Sterling and Blair, plus a few others I couldn't identify."

Mitchell's eyes widened, as if Jim must have been joking. "The Sky Thieves?"

"Yes."

The campaign manager thoughtfully stroked his cheek, voice in awe as he said, "*The* Sky Thieves? As in the ones who robbed the Sky Safe, and broke one of their people out of—"

"Chris." Jim slapped a palm on the conference table. "If you're going to make me repeat myself every time I try to fill you in, then we're just going to have to stop talking altogether."

Mitchell recoiled slightly, as if Jim had threatened to hit him.

Then he responded, "Remind me, Jim—isn't the FBI supposed to pursue the thieves across the country, and not the other way around?"

Jim felt his jaw going firm at the retort. "Very funny. I've had a long day, so please spare me the attempt at humor."

"So what happens now?"

Throwing up his hands, Jim said, "Do I look like I have any idea? I wait for the seller to get in touch again. What choice do I have?"

Jim moved to his office before Mitchell could respond, closing the door behind him. After this afternoon's debacle, he needed some time alone to think through his next move.

Most of all, he needed to hear from Wraith.

Settling into his office chair, Jim booted up his computer and waited for the inevitable screen hijack.

To his surprise, nothing happened—his computer functioned normally, betraying no indication that the thief sought to contact him. Instead, he responded to emails for ten minutes, then fifteen, before his screen image warbled and the chat box appeared.

WRAITH: *I told you to come alone.*

JIM: *I DID come alone. Blair and Sterling were there. They were trying to steal the tapes, don't you get it?*

Jim felt his throat tighten as he awaited the response; he wasn't about to mention that his mentor was responsible for the gun-toting maniacs in the museum, and he couldn't be sure if Wraith would piece that together.

WRAITH: *If that is true, then you are missing the first problem.*

JIM: *Which is...?*

WRAITH: *They did not find out about the meeting from me. Your communications have been compromised, Jim. And if you are serious about getting these tapes, you had better figure out how.*

The chat window disappeared, and his computer screen resumed its normal function as Jim sat back in his chair. He felt the blood draining from his face, a prickling sensation spreading across his back as he thought, *of course*. He'd been so focused on the encounter at the museum that he'd missed its implications. Had the Sky Thieves been in this office? He looked over his shoulder, wondering if he was being watched at that instant.

They certainly had taken hold of his computer feed, because the meeting invitation had been through a pop-up window on his screen. Jim rose and looked to the corners of the room, then the walls themselves, searching for any imperfections that would indicate a bug or camera.

But ultimately, Jim knew this was useless—Blair's former FBI TacOps unit made covert entries and installed surveillance as a way of life, and from what little he knew about them, they had practically turned it into an art form. Blair had once told him she'd installed microphones into the drywall of a suspect's home, using an algorithm to mix paint on the spot and covering it up down to a pinhole so small you'd need a magnifying glass to see it.

Whatever the Sky Thieves had done here, Jim was unequivocally burned. They surely held every thread of communications passing through his computer and work phone at a minimum, possibly even his cell and anything spoken within his office.

There was only one line of communication they couldn't possibly have tapped, selected specifically because it was untappable.

Jim withdrew the burner phone from his pocket and sent a text message to his mentor.

Then he folded his hands in front of his face, waiting for a response with the knowledge that he was about to have a very long night.

62

BLAIR

Blair adjusted her footing on the forked tree limb, reaching forward with her pruning shears to clip off a small branch and depositing it into the drop pouch on her belt.

As much as she didn't care for heights, doing this at night seemed to mitigate the fear that being thirty feet off the ground would normally evoke in her. She hadn't climbed trees since she was a kid, and in a sense this wasn't much different —other than being at night, in a highly illegal context, and for the purposes of emplacing close to a hundred thousand dollars of equipment.

The laser microphone array now strapped to the branch beside her was, after all, quite easy to install. The tough part came after that, when calibrating each of the invisible infrared laser beams to a corresponding window on the back of Jim's house and ensuring its return beam aligned with a receiver consisting of a photodiode array complete with a signal processing chip. That process took considerably more finesse, and as she underwent the painstaking adjustments to each laser, trimming branches when necessary, she considered that Jim had, financially speaking, done pretty well for himself.

The custom home on the three-acre lot in Loudonville had a sprawling wraparound porch overlooking the back lawn along with its inground pool, currently concealed by a winter cover barely visible through the leaves. The sheer number of windows in the two-story home made this laser array the first of two she'd have to install tonight, and that was just to cover the backside—Sterling was currently performing the same task in a wooded patch across the street, albeit at a closer range than she had to deal with.

The real problem wasn't the lasers' range, which could reach a maximum distance of four hundred meters. They'd only need to reach windows located at a fraction of that distance, though aligning each laser and its corresponding receiver required every ounce of patience that Blair had acquired during her years in the FBI's Tactical Operations Section.

Blair had caught fleeting glimpses of movement through the house windows as Jim's wife turned out the downstairs lights one at a time, unaccompanied by her husband, who remained at his office into the night. She felt sorry for this woman; if all went according to plan, Jim was about to be exposed for all the things he'd hidden from her for years, and the myriad lies wouldn't bode well for his marriage. Then again, Blair thought, in the long run, her crew was probably doing Mrs. Jacobson a favor by revealing to the world exactly what kind of monster she'd married.

By now Blair's entire team was aware of Wraith's last communication with Jim a few hours earlier, during which he alluded to proceeding with the tape exchange despite the interruption at the museum. That confirmation had lifted Blair's spirits considerably. Of course, that would likely be the last they heard from Wraith for some time, and she hoped that the current installation would be a key factor in intercepting the next communication.

With the final laser in the receiver properly aligned, Blair withdrew the last piece of kit for this assembly and plugged it into the unit's power source. It was a long-range video camera, a key step in completing the surveillance picture now that placing internal bugs was out of the question.

With the camera in position, Blair prepared to descend and make her way to the next tree with a good line of sight for the remaining windows on the backside of Jim's residence. She still had a second laser array and camera to affix before her job was complete, and she tried not to consider the height as she clambered across the tree limbs on the way to her rope.

63

JIM

The man arrived shortly before midnight, having made the trip through New York City traffic on his way upstate.

He was escorted into Jim's office by Chris Mitchell, who wordlessly opened the door without knocking.

Jim rose to greet the man, only to see him press a finger to his lips in a request for silence. Of course, Jim thought. What introductions could possibly be necessary under such circumstances?

He was a pudgy man in his mid-fifties, face covered by the scrawl of black stubble under thin eyeglasses. Unslinging the satchel from his shoulder, he withdrew a small dry erase board and wrote on it with a marker. Then he held the board up to Jim, revealing sloppy handwritten script: *turn off your cell phone*.

Jim complied, first turning off his personal phone and then the burner.

The man cast a knowing and skeptical gaze at the cheap prepaid phone. Jim couldn't have cared less what a counter surveillance specialist thought about his moral decisions—the man had probably seen more dirt on various high-power individuals and companies than most people could imagine.

Next, the man closed every shade in Jim's office, erasing the nighttime view of downtown Albany leading toward the Hudson. Then he extracted a compact laptop from his satchel and set it on Jim's desk, opening the screen before using a USB cable to connect it to the computer and disabling Jim's Wi-Fi. As the screen showed the progress of a hard drive scan, the man began a walking patrol of Jim's office, scrutinizing every crevice and vent with a practiced eye.

This visual inspection seemed like a game to Jim; this guy had more equipment at his disposal, so why not use it?

But Jim said nothing, letting the man complete his visual sweep. Only then did he finally retrieve a tool, this one a black device with a flip-up screen that looked like a small, ruggedized laptop with an array of antennas. This was, Jim knew, the object that would detect Wi-Fi and RF signals.

The man waved it like a water dowser directing a forked stick over the desert, albeit perpendicular to every surface in the room with a determined focus on outlets, vents, and electronics. When the indicator lights flashed, he turned a knob to reduce the device's sensitivity, then moved it closer to determine whether the signal was malicious or simply due to electronic interference from the opposite side of the wall.

Ending his frequency scan, he set down the device and flicked off the office lights, and then progressed to the next phase of his search. Producing a second device at the end of a telescoping pole, he turned it on to elicit a glowing red glare and then extended the pole to full length.

Then he swept the light across every surface, scanning for the signature twinkle of a hidden camera lens. The process took long minutes, during which Jim stood impatiently in the darkness, and by the time the man finally flipped the lights back on, his face bore an expression of mild disappointment.

That soon changed when he consulted his laptop display, which was churning out the results of its scan of Jim's computer. And while Jim could make no sense out of the coding script that appeared line by line as the scan progressed, the counter surveillance specialist gave a thin smile, then looked about the office once more before settling his gaze on the wall vent.

Recovering a screwdriver, he knelt before the vent and carefully extracted each of the four screws. Then he lowered the vent face-down on the carpet, scanned it closely, and waved Jim over.

Jim knelt beside him, following the man's index finger to a thin black cylinder affixed to the vent's backside. At first it seemed like part of the vent itself, and as Jim wondered how a bug could have escaped the electronic scan, the man moved his fingertip to indicate a length of barely perceptible wire disappearing into the air duct.

Then he detached the wire from the device, laying the excess across the carpet before rising and moving back to his dry erase board.

Scrawling quickly with his marker, he showed the board to Jim once more.

Govt/corporate-grade espionage eqpt. Who did you piss off?

Jim shot him a glare, and the man wrote a new line of text.

Office is burned. I need to check your house ASAP.

64

STERLING

Sterling adjusted his footing against the forked tree limb, manipulating a laser microphone through a gap in the branches as he heard Marco's voice over his earpiece.

"*Keylogger and spyware programs are offline, along with our audio surveillance. Jim is on the move with a second vehicle tailing him—unless I'm mistaken, he's bringing a counter surveillance technician back to the house.*"

Releasing his grip on the laser, Sterling asked, "Do we need to displace?"

"*No, continue the installation. I'll turn off the laser arrays remotely for the duration of his sweep, then reactivate after he's gone. It looks like our CALEA taps are still running for the time being.*"

Great, Sterling thought. Those CALEA taps were beyond useless now—they only covered Jim's computer activity, along with his office and cell phone audio. This was of little consolation considering that Jim would discuss nothing official over them, but for the time being, it was all the crew had to go on. They'd continue to monitor, but Sterling had no doubt the effort would be futile.

"Pick up something good for us, baby," Sterling whispered to the laser microphone between his fingertips, aligning it with a corner window on the second floor.

Then he heard Blair transmit, *"Backside of the house is complete. I'm coming down and moving to the link-up point."*

She'd tried to keep her voice neutral, but Sterling detected the undercurrent of pride. Of course she finished first, he thought, even though the back of the house was the more complicated install by far, dealing with longer distances and a greater number of windows. He'd been assigned the easier of the two installs, and would be lucky just to finish by the time Jim arrived. Sterling was an expert thief, objectively speaking the best on his crew.

But when it came to surveillance equipment, Blair was the undisputed champion.

He pushed the thought aside and continued working. This was the first time in his heist career that he'd ever had to climb a tree like an eight-year-old in his parents' front yard, and Sterling hoped it would be the last.

It wasn't that the climb up using spikes was particularly taxing, nor was the descent on a double-looped rope that he could pull down by one end after he was done. Instead he felt unsettled by the thought of monitoring the goings-on in a personal residence, which would include not just Jim's spoken interactions—that much, Sterling could live with—but his innocent wife's as well.

This entire installation had an oddly voyeuristic aspect to it that made Sterling feel like a petty thief. In the past he'd targeted people and corporations that deserved to be robbed, diverting a hefty portion of the proceeds to charity to offset the moral ambiguity of what he did. But now his mother's freedom was on the line, not just his own, and Sterling couldn't afford an attack of conscience when it came to bringing down Jim once and for all.

Sterling adjusted a laser microphone in the array, homing in on the last window as he replayed Blair's instructions in his mind—a head-on laser shot was worthless, while ten to twenty degrees of variation would yield sufficient results.

Once the laser was aligned, he checked the reception of its corresponding optical detector. There was a variation in the angle of the return beam, and Sterling relied on a percentage indicator to gauge the signal's strength before deeming it adequate for the crew's purposes. They'd have to analyze the return laser current remotely, demodulating the photocell variation from the window's vibration to produce sound files of every word spoken inside Jim's house.

Sterling finished aligning his final laser, testing the reception not a moment too soon—headlights became visible through the trees, and Sterling tucked himself tight against the trunk. But the tree density was sufficient enough that nothing short of a flashlight search through the woods would expose him at this point, and he doubted that kind of legwork was on Jim's current agenda.

Sure enough, Jim's Suburban pulled into the circular drive followed by a black Lincoln sedan.

Sterling transmitted, "Jim and the tech are arriving now."

Marco responded, "*I need to shut down the laser arrays for the duration of the sweep. You'll have to finish after the tech leaves.*"

"No need," Sterling replied. "All I've got left to install is the camera. You can shut the lasers down now."

"*Copy, shutting down.*"

Jim exited his Suburban, and Sterling peered through the branches at the second figure, a portly man carrying a large satchel who was following Jim up the cobblestone walkway to the front door. Sterling took in the opulence of Jim's house and was once again struck by the disparity in surroundings: both he and Jim were criminals, albeit of a very different sort, the difference in their living situations not due to any moral high ground but rather what the public knew. Sterling had been arrested and uncovered as a thief; Jim's corruption had existed in the shadows for his entire career. Sterling lived in a warehouse, hidden from view, and Jim lived in an elaborate custom home.

How those circumstances would change, Sterling thought, once the public knew what his crew already did.

Jim was at the front door, unlocking it and waving the man into his home with an elaborate sweep of his hand, as if this were some grandiose housewarming party and he was eager to show off his new accommodations.

Keep smiling, Jim, Sterling thought as he began setting up his surveillance camera. Keep smiling, and see what happens once we get those tapes back.

Because Sterling would get those tapes, and for the time being, he pushed aside any concerns about what—or who—his crew would have to deal with once that occurred.

65

BLAIR

Blair was lying on her cot the following morning when she heard Marco yelling from the warehouse bay.

"Showtime, people!"

It was odd to hear him belting out cheerful words. Usually he was quiet, or brooding, or pointing out the many possible shortcomings of a plan-in-progress.

But all that changed when he was at the helm of a massive data effort, a time when he happily became the center of the storm. And now that effort was about to begin anew, Blair thought as she swiftly rose and left her room, making her way to Marco's office.

Sunlight was filtering in the facility windows, each taped over by wax paper to keep the interior blocked from view. She checked her watch—it was just after eight in the morning—then saw Sterling stumbling out of his room wiping sleep from his eyes. Apparently he'd managed more rest than she had, and the two met behind Marco's computer in time to take in the view of the surveillance feed outside Jim's house, where a black Lincoln sedan was backing out of the driveway and vanishing from view.

Marco clapped his hands together and then rubbed his palms in eager anticipation.

"Tech specialist is gone," he said cheerily. "Time to fire up our laser microphones and test the system."

Ordinarily Blair would be geeking out right alongside him, but the tech had spent well over five hours sweeping Jim's house, presumably without results—if he found any bugs, they certainly weren't from her crew. During that time, she, Sterling, and Marco had monitored the camera feed in shifts, waiting for the counter surveillance specialist to leave so they could fire up their laser microphones while Alec waited in a parked rental car along Jim's work route.

Blair had only been able to manage fitful sleep, troubled by the reality of their current predicament.

She hadn't oversold the notion of setting up laser microphones around Jim's house. They were an incredible tool, capable of monitoring audio inside a structure without entering or even coming near it, but they hadn't been able to test the system without hearing anyone speak inside the house—Jim's wife hadn't had even a telephone call before they had to shut down the setup in anticipation of a surveillance sweep.

The physics behind translating laser reflection off audio vibrations on windows was ironclad, but a hundred variables could complicate deciphering the return signal into anything resembling a human voice. Preeminent among these was the fact that if the critical verbal exchange was conducted sufficiently far from a window, the crew would never know about it. Added to that was the uncertainty of whether that critical exchange would occur in Jim's home in the first place; and if it didn't, they'd be reliant on the unlikely possibility of a CALEA tap revealing some clue, perhaps paired with the physical surveillance of a crew member following Jim whenever he was on the move.

Ultimately, these efforts represented the crew's best attempt at intercepting a communication from Wraith. It was entirely possible, probable even, that Wraith would find a way to sidestep every measure in getting the tapes to Jim, who would destroy them before they had any idea he'd received them in the first place. In that event, their first indication of total mission failure would occur when Jim made some gloating proclamation to Sterling's mom, probably just before he pursued his vendetta against her to its inevitable conclusion.

All of this seemed lost on Marco, who was merrily pecking away with his computer mouse, bringing the laser microphones online as they began recording.

Then he turned to look at them, asking in a quizzical tone, "Why are you two so quiet?"

"Because we've been up all night," Sterling said groggily. "What's your excuse?"

Marco turned back to his computer. "Well wake up and then cheer up. I am pleased to report that *all* laser beams are reflecting off their respective windows, returning to their receivers with the vibration data, and being converted to audio signal, which is broadcasting back to us with only a ten-second delay."

"Well," Blair replied, "let's hear it."

Marco selected an audio feed, then trimmed a sample clip and clicked play.

The noise that projected over the computer speakers wasn't a human voice at all; instead it sounded like distorted music in slow motion, an eerie rattling groan.

Sterling's mouth fell open.

"What in God's name is that? Unless Jim is possessed, these pieces of crap aren't working at all."

Blair put a hand on his shoulder. "Relax. Jim's house has

double-paned windows. Return audio is garbled from the air gap between the panes of glass."

Marco began adjusting the audio software settings. "She's right. I just need to calibrate the interferometer to a modified set of intensity variation before the audio will be recognizable."

He finished his inputs and pressed play again, and the clip repeated at a slightly better tone—though it was a low, deep monster growl of words, barely discernible as a human voice.

"This is terrifying," Sterling said. "I'm going back to bed. Let me know when—"

Marco cut him off. "Just a second, boss." Altering the audio levels again, he played the clip a third time.

Now it was indisputably Jim's voice, the words crisp aside from a slight warble in pitch.

"I'll be back around noon for a few hours of sleep before my interview tonight."

The audio sample ended.

"What interview?" Sterling asked.

Blair shrugged. "Who knows? But given that we're talking about Jim here, I'm sure it'll be entertaining."

Before they could contemplate it further, the surveillance feed showed Jim leaving his house and rounding his SUV to enter through the driver's door before pulling out of the circular drive.

Marco picked up a radio mic and said, "Jim is on the move in his Suburban, heading east on Crumtie Road toward Loudon."

"*Got it*," Alec responded over the frequency. "*I'll let you know when I have eyes-on.*"

Marco set down the mic as Sterling concluded, "So now all we have to do is wait. Super. I'm going back to sleep."

But at that moment an alert chimed from Marco's computer.

The team hacker clicked to open a window that had been minimized, then leaned in and squinted at the contents.

"Perhaps not, boss." He glanced up from his computer. "We just received an email to theskythieves@gmail.com. Dembinski says he's found a solution." Looking at Sterling with pursed lips, he continued, "He wants to meet with you."

66

JIM

Jim straightened himself in the chair, adjusting his pant leg in the glare of studio lights as he took a final glance at the three-camera setup going live any moment now.

A man with headphones and a clipboard announced, "Going live in five, four." He held up three fingers and counted down the remaining seconds in silence, his hand turning to a fist as a green light flicked on behind him.

Seated in the chair opposite him, Caroline Paquin stared at the lens of the central video camera and began, "Here in the studio we have Albany native Jim Jacobson, who after decades of service with the FBI returned home for a new challenge: to run for office as the House representative of New York's capital district."

Jim had to admit that Caroline looked resplendent in a form-fitting jacket and skirt, her legs crossed over red heels. Her brunette hair cascaded down her shoulders, ending in loose curls. Only her cosmetics seemed over the top—Jim had underestimated the amount of makeup used in the brightly lit studio settings, receiving his first reminder upon meeting

Caroline in the green room and his second when he had to go under the brush himself.

The studio's makeup artist had to earn her pay to hide the dark circles under his eyes, the result of a sleepless night trying to ferret out all of Blair's efforts to bug him. In spite of that—or maybe because he reveled in the desperation he was about to inflict on Blair and her crew—Jim felt powerful, upbeat, almost loopy with excitement. Mitchell had always implored Jim to exude passion during his political engagements, noting that the public responded to enthusiasm before they ever reacted to the details of the spoken content.

And tonight, Jim didn't have to fake it.

Caroline continued, "But when he entered his campaign headquarters yesterday, his instincts from a career in law enforcement told him that something was wrong—and tonight, he shares his story in an exclusive interview with CBS 6 News." She turned to him. "Jim, thank you for coming on the show."

Jim gave her a fetching smile. "Thanks for having me, Caroline. It's a pleasure to be here."

"When I first heard your story, I felt as stunned as you must have. Could you tell us what led you to the shocking discovery in your campaign headquarters?"

Drawing a breath, Jim adjusted the cuff over his Rolex and said, "When you've worked in the FBI as long as I have, you deal with some unsavory characters. Maybe it was my past experience or maybe it's the healthy dose of suspicion I've developed, but I was entering my office yesterday when something felt off.

"Now ordinarily I'd be too busy running my campaign and planning real change for the hardworking citizens of District 20 to think much of it, but I couldn't shake this feeling. I examined my office and noticed some plaster dust on the carpet beside an air vent. Trusting my instincts, I unscrewed it from the wall and found a device attached to the back. Now I've had my fair share of surveillance experience while commanding the federal task force chartered to stop the high-profile heists in LA, and I immediately knew I was looking at a directional boundary microphone. At that point, I called the Albany Police Department."

Caroline's face transformed into an aghast expression for the benefit of the camera.

"And what else did they find?"

Jim raised his eyebrows. "A pretty sophisticated setup, actually. The microphone was attached to a fiber optic cable routed through an air duct to the office directly overhead, where a transmitting device was broadcasting wirelessly. Whoever put it there was trying to avoid detection in the event of a counter surveillance sweep of my office—which, after this event, I may have to start doing on a regular basis."

Caroline gave a good-natured laugh. "That kind of equipment can't be cheap."

"Absolutely not."

"Who would have the finances or motives to do such a thing?"

"Well," he replied, "I can only speculate that it was someone trying to gather information about my campaign plan."

"A modern-day Watergate?"

"I suspect so, but I can't—and won't—level any accusations. Any guilt in this matter is for the Albany PD to determine, and they've assured me that their investigation is ongoing. It seems clear to me that the perpetrators were either trying to sabotage my Congressional campaign or discredit me personally. Any information they collected, of course, would do nothing but validate what I've said in public—otherwise you'd be hearing it in the press by now. And I hate to disappoint these criminals, but you don't campaign under a slogan of 'It's About Integrity' if you've got something to hide." He directed his gaze to the central camera and concluded, "Next time, they should choose an easier target."

Caroline's follow-up caught him off guard.

"You mentioned working on a federal heist task force in LA."

Jim hesitated. This wasn't on their list of topics for tonight's discussion, and he didn't know where she was headed.

"That's correct, Caroline."

"Any comment on yesterday's events at the Albany Institute of History & Art?"

"I'm sorry," he stammered. "The...events?"

His head was spinning now, trying to get ahead of what was about to come. To his knowledge, his presence at the museum had been hidden from the public, but if someone had come forward claiming Jim was present in the Lansing Gallery at the time of the failed exchange, then he was going to have to think on his feet.

She said, "These people weren't exactly the Sky Thieves, were they?"

"What?"

Caroline was taken aback by Jim's confusion, and she gave him a reassuring smile as she explained, "I mean, this just seems so unskilled."

Jim relaxed, a relieved grin springing to his face as he realized that the comment had been innocent.

"That's exactly right." He gave a short laugh. "Broad daylight in front of a crowd doesn't put these thieves in what I'd call the 'master criminal' bracket. But what you have to understand is that while you and I live our lives by a moral code, a backbone of values that guides our actions day to day, the kind of people who steal for a living are driven by one principle: greed. And that greed can blind them to everything else, including logic and common sense. The law will catch up with them, as it always does. In the meantime, I'm just glad that no one was seriously hurt, particularly the two brave officers who protected the citizens of Albany that day."

Jim felt a resurgence of confidence as he considered the new development: Blair and Sterling's attempts to get the tapes had just been rendered null and void whether they realized it or not. Jim's mentor had arranged something that couldn't fail—two things, actually—and not only was Sterling about to be in custody, but the tapes would be in Jim's hands with no chance for the crew to intercept them.

Straightening his suit jacket, Jim continued his banter with the most gratifying feeling of all, that of absolute and total victory over his enemies.

67

BLAIR

Blair was huddled around Marco's computer with Sterling and Alec—Marco had left to physically surveil the man they were now watching onscreen.

Jim Jacobson was at the conclusion of his interview with Caroline Paquin, detailing his stance on the museum debacle.

"...I'm just glad that no one was seriously hurt, particularly the two brave officers who protected the citizens of Albany that day."

Blair ended the playback, eliciting a groan from Alec and Sterling.

"What are you doing?" Alec asked. "I wanted to see how he'd close out the parade of lies."

Sterling added, "Seriously."

She shook her head firmly. "I'm sorry, I just can't watch anymore. We need to get prepped for the Dembinski meeting, anyway. Though I must say, I'm reluctantly grateful to Jim for not mentioning our involvement."

"About that," Alec began. "Jim knows good and well that we installed that device. Why's he blaming the Democrats?"

"Because everyone knows the only reason we'd infiltrate

his campaign headquarters is for the purposes of exposing him, which implies he's guilty of something. By shifting the attention to his political competition, he can play the victim card all the way through the November election."

"Huh," Alec remarked. "That's smart. I'm starting to like this guy."

Sterling was the first to rise from his chair.

"All right, I'm going to get in costume."

"Godspeed," Alec replied, turning to watch Sterling depart the room.

As he was turned away, Blair deftly slipped her index finger and thumb into Alec's jacket pocket.

"Nice try, Blair," he said, turning in time to catch her pound a fist onto the table.

"Man!" she exclaimed. "My fingertips touched the cargo that time—that's a first. You know, I actually fanned you to locate the tapes back when—"

Alec interjected, "When I came in off my surveillance shift and you brushed past while getting supplies from the Sprinter van. It wasn't bad."

Her jaw settled.

"I *will* get that cargo off you, Alec."

Alec looked at her quizzically. "Why do you think I'm still carrying it? You're a competitive freak and I'm a gifted instructor with a fine eye for talent. No one learns how to pickpocket overnight. You'll get there, young padawan. Now forget about the cargo for now and go express your concerns about this meeting to Sterling."

She tried to sound innocent. "What concerns?"

Alec's eyes narrowed. "I told you, Blair, I've got a fine eye. And it doesn't take a master detective to see you're worried."

Blair's shoulders slumped. "Fine. I am. Aren't you?"

"Of course I am; I just don't think we have a choice. So go

talk to Sterling and get all those complicated she-emotions off your shoulders so you can focus on the job we got coming up, savvy?"

He rose to leave the room, and Blair spoke to his back before he cleared the door.

"Thanks, Alec. You're a good friend."

"And an even better pickpocketing instructor," he replied, turning to face her as he pointed to a sheaf of papers stacked on Marco's desk. "You could have knocked those over while reaching for something. Chivalry would have gotten the best of me and Sterling, and you could have had both of us helping to pick them up. Better pocket gap for you to get the cargo."

She snapped her fingers in frustration.

"The compassion play. Of course."

He nodded. "Don't worry, you'll get there. And when you do, I'll take you out on our first date."

"Very funny."

Alec shrugged. "Worth a shot."

Then he left Blair alone in Marco's office to consider the job they were about to set off on.

There had been no small debate on the team over whether such a meeting was worth it; after all, what could Dembinski possibly have to offer on top of the current surveillance efforts? They didn't know and he wouldn't say, insisting only that the information couldn't be sent via email. That much made sense, she supposed—given Wraith's demonstrated technical sophistication, the risk of data compromise was high.

But now Sterling wasn't just a member of the crew, he was someone Blair felt a protective impulse over ever since his arrest during the Sky Safe heist. And while she could have done nothing to prevent that at the time, she felt a sense of guilt then and now that she hadn't anticipated Jim's response, that she hadn't seen that heist for the well-laid trap that it was.

Rising from her seat, Blair went to Sterling's door and knocked twice.

"Come in."

Blair opened the door to find Sterling in jeans, pulling a shirt over his bare torso, the elements of his disguise laid out on the table before him. He'd already moved his father's watch to his right wrist, donning the digital chronograph on his left—this was his routine before every operation, not relinquishing the vintage watch in favor of one with split-second precision, but merely shifting its location.

Upon seeing her standing there, he quickly buttoned his shirt.

"Hey," he said, "what's up?"

"Can I talk to you for a minute?"

"Of course. Come in."

He seemed unsettled when she closed the door behind her, a look of apprehension crossing his features.

"Relax," she said quietly. "Alec knows I'm coming to talk to you. Matter of fact, he told me to."

"About what?"

Blair studied his face to see if his ignorance was genuine, and decided it was. Alec had been able to pick up on both her unease and its source, while Sterling seemed blissfully unaware that anything was wrong.

She said, "I'm worried about you."

"Blair." He stepped forward and took her hands in his. "We don't have the luxury of choice in this. If Jim doesn't go down, then my mother will, and we're next, whether we know it now or not. We knew from the start that Jim and his mentor bring too much to the table."

She released his hands and looked away.

"Even if we get the tapes, it does nothing to stop his mentor."

"I know that," he said with a sigh. "But we can't control everything, at least not yet. In the meantime, we just have to take this one step at a time."

"I'm not disputing that. I'm just saying, I'm not sure this is the right step."

"You have a bad feeling about the meeting?"

"Yes. And I'm not sure whether I'd have that feeling if it were Marco or Alec heading into the meet. What do you think about it?"

"I'm not emotional about it one way or the other. If Dembinski's offer is legit, then we have everything to gain. If it's not...well, I've only been caught once."

She took a step back.

"That's one time too many. This crew can't run without you, Sterling."

"This crew *has* run without me. The guys told me how you took over the reins to break me out of prison, and I'm forever grateful for that. But we can't just stop this operation in its tracks, not when we're this close. We don't know if the laser mics or CALEA taps or anything else will pay off, and if they don't, then Dembinski may be the last shot we have left to end this thing for good."

She shook her head. "It's just that—"

Sterling cupped her face and kissed her.

Blair tried to pull back, but found herself returning the kiss instead. And then she completely forgot what she was going to say.

68

STERLING

Sterling jogged through Washington Park, each step landing on footprint-laden snow. He jogged only because his cover dictated it—he wore cold-weather running clothes in line with an unsuspicious male exercising in the park at night—but other than that, his pace was the easiest he could maintain without slowing to a walk. Because while Sterling was a naturally proficient runner, at present he needed to conserve his energy. If the meeting with Dembinski went bad, he was going to desperately require all the speed he could manage.

A light snowfall was in progress, large flakes floating past the glowing lamp posts as he felt a sense of déjà vu on the park trails, the faint childhood memories of various festivals and concerts on this eighty-acre spread of land. Washington Park was Albany's answer to Central Park in Manhattan, complete with a large lake, gardens, and sports fields. The trails and roads were lined with crab apples and elms, their branches heavy with snow. Sterling considered that this was more or less what he'd expected Wraith to pick for the exchange with Jim: an open park with lots of foot traffic and egress options in every direction.

He continued jogging, his light exhales forming puffs in the chilly night air. The meeting he was about to embark on was something of a last resort—while Sterling had downplayed his feelings with Blair, he was deeply reluctant to meet with Dembinski and said as much in his response to the email.

Prefer not to meet. Maybe you don't watch the news, but my last public foray didn't end well.

But Dembinski had been adamant, saying the information he had couldn't under any circumstances be shared online. Sterling had to admit that the political fixer had a point; after all, who knew how sophisticated Wraith was, or whether the information would be rendered meaningless if it fell into the wrong hands.

His trail led into a circular clearing, where four paved paths converged at a single monument. Its official name was the King Memorial Fountain. Despite Sterling growing up outside Albany and visiting this park many times, he only became aware of that title while planning the meeting. To him and all the other locals, the monument was known as the Moses Fountain.

He learned a great deal more in his research—the tall hillock of stone rising from the center of the monument was taken from Old Storm King Mountain on the Hudson, the water flowing down it inspired by a verse from Exodus where at God's instruction, Moses smote the rock to produce water for his people to drink.

Sterling had looked up the verse out of sheer morbid

curiosity, unfamiliar with both the Bible and smiting, and found a certain symbolic justice in Dembinski's choice of this location for their meeting.

Preceding the Bible verse on which this monument was based, Moses had led his people toward a pillar of cloud and fire only to find the rock at Horeb, where the lack of water caused them to question their faith. And while Albany was certainly not a desert in the archetypal or literal sense, Sterling had taken his crew as far from their LA hideout as he could without crossing an international border, all in the hopes of freeing them—and his mother—from the threat that Jim represented.

Sterling swept his gaze across his surroundings as he jogged into the clearing, looking for anything out of place. The statue of Moses was lit from below, a tall figure with arms held upward, one hand clutching a staff.

After the journey to the East Coast, identifying Fixer and making the initial contact, a little assistance from his father's friend Steve Wolf, and a failed interdiction at the museum, Sterling had arrived at a dead end at his own personal rock of Horeb—and here, he would either produce some mission-altering information, or very possibly be resigned to failure.

But no water flowed from the fountain now; it had been shut down for the duration of winter, and when he caught his first sight of Eric Dembinski standing before it, Sterling got his first indication that no information would flow from the political fixer either.

Dembinski was standing as instructed, facing the fountain with his hands in his pockets to indicate that he hadn't been followed, and Sterling should approach as planned.

Sterling noticed a certain stiffness in Dembinski's shoulders that seemed to be due to more than the cold. Still, he approached to make contact—after all, if this was a trap, he was already deep inside it, and there was only one way to be sure.

Stopping alongside Dembinski, Sterling spoke quietly.

"You rang?"

The Fixer looked over, his dull shark eyes repentant.

"You have no reason to believe me, but I didn't have a choice. I'm sorry, Sterling."

Breaking left, Sterling began to run.

69

BLAIR

Blair saw the figures appear just as Sterling began to sprint toward her.

From her position in a car along the park's southwestern boundary, the first men in pursuit of her fleeing teammate appeared as little more than wisps of movement fluttering in the dim light between trees. How long they'd been lying in wait was a mystery—the crew's thermal sweeps hadn't uncovered an ambush, but that was more or less to be expected during snowfall.

She rolled down her passenger window, transmitting, "He's on the run, need you at the emergency pickup."

Over her earpiece, Marco's voice was calm and measured.

"On the move."

Marco leaving his position meant they were about to lose their only physical surveillance over Jim, creating a gap where Wraith could initiate contact with them being none the wiser, but that was better than Sterling being overrun by the men chasing him.

Blair made out five at first glance, each moving at full speed. Washington Park had just transformed into a football field, with Sterling as the receiver trying to avoid being tackled until he made it to the end zone. A single misplaced footfall or errant stumble would be sufficient for the lead runner to tackle Sterling, and the rest would dogpile atop him in short order.

Sterling, for his part, hadn't hesitated in the slightest. He didn't waiver from his straight-line run, every step executed at a breakneck pace as he darted along a preordained path toward Blair's car, his eyes scanning sideways for a particular tree before he took a running leap.

The move was slight enough to go unnoticed by an outside observer, and that was more or less the point. Unbeknownst to his pursuers, Sterling had just vaulted the first and almost absurdly simple blockade—a braided steel cable notable for its slim diameter and incredible tensile strength.

The cable had a white lacquer coating and was strung up over the unbroken snow across a thirty-foot gap between trees, making it virtually invisible at night. It created a devastatingly effective chokepoint that the nearest runners were now funneling into as fast as they could sprint.

The first two men to cross it did so at the same instant, shins clipping the wire before their bodies were flung parallel to the ground in a brutally short flight path.

They were still airborne when the three men behind them noted the discrepancy in their teammates' movement and spent the final moments of bodily control attempting to reverse all forward momentum. It was, of course, impossible: the first two struck the wire almost as violently as their predecessors, while the third made a valiant effort to blindly leap over the unseen obstacle—but that effort came a second too late to save him, one ankle hooking the line and slinging his head downward in a violent front flip.

Even at this distance, Blair heard the percussion of bodies

striking the frozen ground in a rapid *thud-thud-thud* cadence, which brought with it a certain level of exultant satisfaction. But the escape wasn't over yet, and Blair saw the aftereffect playing out even as Sterling gained ground. The downside of such an effective measure was that once the cable had taken out the first wave of pursuers, it was impossible for anyone else to miss it.

That predictable eventuality was reached when the men with a more distant starting point saw their predecessors fall and were joined by those stationed beyond the range of the cable in the first place. Their combined effort resulted in an additional four men eagerly giving chase to Sterling, creating a second wave of pursuit that required a more precise countermeasure.

And Blair held that countermeasure in her hand.

These men were probably expecting for the crew's previously deployed measures—namely tasers, which had to be fired at close range, or tear gas, which would disperse quickly in the open air. But what Blair aimed out the car window was neither; it looked and felt like an oversized pistol, save that the forward receiver was a blocklike structure that emitted a brilliant neon green spotlight when she pulled the trigger.

The swath of emerald light was an erratically pulsed laser that had immediate effects, including temporary blindness, loss of situational awareness, and in some cases, nausea.

Intended for long-range vehicle engagements, this particular model was admittedly overkill for the situation at hand. Blair felt remarkably free of remorse, however, as she swept the beam across the pursuers, sending the nausea-inducing, retina-searing beam over everyone running toward her except Sterling.

The laser had been developed for police departments and military units, and had even been FDA approved—though that seemed lost on the men now stumbling while blocking their eyes or sprawling across the snow as Sterling proceeded, now uninhibited by immediate pursuit. The victory would be short-lived, Blair knew, as there were surely peripheral security elements beyond the park who were being called to converge upon the fleeing suspect.

But for the time being, Blair was burned; anyone within a three-block radius could have seen the phosphorescent green beam blaring out of her vehicle's open window, and it was time for the next wave of Sterling's escape plan.

Putting her car in drive and accelerating forward, Blair cleared Washington Park and headed to her next standby location.

70

STERLING

Sterling vaguely registered Blair's car pulling out of view as he sprinted across Washington Park Road, hearing her voice over his earpiece.

"You've got a twenty-second lead; I'm moving to standby."

Sterling didn't need to respond and wouldn't have had much breath for the effort if he'd tried; his lungs were already raw from sucking icy air, adrenaline speeding him along as he crossed a barrier and caught sight of the road before him, currently his next major obstacle to escape.

Whereas Washington Park Road was a minor access route into the park, Madison Avenue was a major thoroughfare that he wasn't lucky enough to catch during a lull in traffic.

Headlights flew past in both directions, and Sterling only had a moment to squint into the glare of oncoming traffic before trying to cross. Hesitate for too long, and his pursuers would catch him; move too fast, and they wouldn't have to hurry because he'd be laid out with a shattered pelvis or worse.

Sterling raced into the road just behind a passenger van, so close he almost hit the rear bumper as he inhaled its hot exhaust. He succeeded in threading the needle without being struck by the pickup behind it, whose driver slammed on its brakes and horn at the same instant. Then he came to a full stop atop the first of two yellow stripes cordoning off the two-way turn lane, a sedan screeching past so close that he had to push himself off its rear quarter panel to remain upright. As that driver added his contribution to the rising symphony of car horns, Sterling pirouetted into the far lane and darted between a gap in cars that hadn't bothered to stop.

He cleared the traffic and was mere feet from the curbside parking when he collided with a cyclist ripping through the bike lane, the impact sending both men sprawling and the bicycle crashing into a parked car.

Sterling hit the pavement hard, his knees and elbows stinging as he struggled upright and limped over the curb.

Shouting, "Sorry!" over his shoulder, he heard a decidedly less polite response shouted at his backside. He didn't bother looking back as he turned right on the sidewalk, resuming his run and gaining momentum against the throbbing objection of limbs still reeling from hitting the street.

The row of townhouses to his left formed an impenetrable barrier, and he sprinted to the corner, cutting left down New Scotland Avenue and crossing to the opposite side at the first opportunity. More car horns sounded on Madison Avenue behind him, then the screeching of brakes and crunching metal of a vehicle collision alerted him that his pursuers were making their way across the road with equal determination.

The men chasing him were no doubt expecting Sterling to head for some pre-staged getaway vehicle, but he had no such plans. The last thing he needed now was an APB out on one of the team's rental cars, and he had a much more airtight getaway in mind—though to execute that, he'd need more than running ability.

Feet pounding on the sidewalk, he transmitted breathlessly, "Two blocks out from Morris."

Alec's response was immediate, sounding almost casual about the whole affair.

"Ready and waiting, boss."

As Sterling reached the corner of Morris Street, he ducked behind a building corner to see his twin—Alec fully attired in identical running gear. He took off at a sprint to the east as Sterling moved in the opposite direction, crossing the street and entering an alley between buildings. The plan would hopefully draw Sterling's pursuers further away, but at best, that would only buy him thirty seconds to a minute. After all, Alec would have to stop at the first police order, when a second's glance at his Asian features would reveal that he was not the fugitive they sought.

By then, if all went according to plan, Sterling would have entered a refuge that not even his pursuers would anticipate.

As he ran down the alley, Sterling stripped off his jacket and tossed it toward a dumpster. Next came his tearaway pants, which he ripped apart at the buttoned seams during three stuttering steps before resuming his run.

By the time he crossed Myrtle Avenue, the night air was freezing against his skin— Sterling was now wearing only medical scrubs, a forged identification badge bouncing off his chest as he cut right up a short ramp at the Albany Medical Center Hospital. He could make out spinning red lights at the ambulance access point ahead, though not until the emergency room entrance came into view did Sterling remember to remove the final element of his first-layer disguise.

Pulling the fleece beanie off his head and stuffing it into a pocket of his scrubs, he recovered a disposable surgical cap and pulled it on. Unclipping a handheld radio from his belt, he turned it on to hear the chatter of an EMS frequency. Sterling held the radio to his ear, entering the ER through glass doors that parted on his approach.

The room was fully packed with non-critical patients waiting to be admitted, and Sterling kept his head low, appearing to be focused on the radio transmissions as he moved to a staff entrance beside the reception desk.

After he swept his identification badge across the card reader on the wall, the door clicked open and Sterling pushed his way through, easing it shut with his foot on the chance that any of the men chasing him had come this far. The door locked into place, and Sterling moved halfway down the corridor before glancing back to see that he hadn't been followed.

Alec transmitted, "*They just stopped me in a catch-and-release on the corner of Knox Street. Five plainclothes officers, now headed back west and spreading out in a search pattern.*"

"It's all right," Sterling said. "I'm already in. Marco, I'll be at the staff parking lot in three minutes."

Marco replied, "*I'll be there in five.*"

His transmission was followed by Blair's voice.

"*Alec, run a surveillance detection route and then meet me at the laundromat for pickup.*"

"*I'm on it,*" he replied.

Sterling's earpiece went silent, yielding to tinny voices on the EMS frequency. Sidestepping a gurney being pushed in his direction by two nurses, Sterling took a left turn down the hall and proceeded toward his linkup.

71

JIM

Jim stepped off the elevator into the office parking garage and made his way toward the Suburban.

Swinging his briefcase as he walked, he was halfway down the rows of cars when his burner phone vibrated in his pocket. Jim continued walking, taking a breath with the silent wish that Sterling Defranc was already in police custody.

Instead, he checked the display to see a single text.

Quarry escaped.

Jim put the phone away and flung open the driver's side door. Throwing his briefcase on the passenger seat, he entered the vehicle and slammed the door shut, pinching the bridge of his nose between thumb and forefinger as he wondered how in God's name a single thief could have both shown up for a meeting with Dembinski and then escaped unscathed. He'd either gotten extraordinarily lucky or his mentor was employing cowboys who were incapable of the simplest conceivable task.

They couldn't inform the Albany PD, of course, without burning Dembinski for communicating with a known fugitive —and while Jim was perfectly fine with that, his mentor seemed to have other considerations. What could have been more important than catching a Sky Thief was beyond Jim, but knowing his mentor, the explanation was preceded by a dollar sign.

He was about to start his truck when a phone buzzed again in his pocket. Jim pulled out his burner, only to see that the display was blank and the buzzing continued—this vibration was from his personal cell phone, probably his wife asking when he would be home. But he checked the cell to see an incoming call not from his wife but a caller labeled as *GUESS WHO?*

Jim paused with the phone in hand, considering whether Blair or Sterling was calling to gloat about escaping capture. With a frustrated sigh, Jim answered.

"Yes."

The voice that responded was male and spoke in a British accent, the syllables deep and disjointed as the result of some computer modulation software.

"I have a package for you."

"Who is this?"

"Wraith, of course."

Perhaps, Jim thought, or perhaps it was the Sky Thieves posing as Wraith. Jim's personal cell number doubled as a work listed phone, and it wouldn't take a genius intellect to find it after sifting through a basic hack of his campaign's data.

He said cautiously, "As I'm sure you're aware, this line isn't safe."

"It does not have to be."

"How do I know you're Wraith and not the Sky Thieves?"

"Because if you follow my instructions, you will receive the tapes. Not even the Sky Thieves can promise that."

Jim swallowed hard. "I'm listening."

"Exit your vehicle and go to the far back wall of the garage, underneath the sign for row B2."

Jim did as he was told, locking his vehicle and looking around the empty parking garage. He had no doubt that Wraith wasn't present, and instead scanned for any sign of a camera. Rows of concrete support pillars stretched from floor to ceiling, the bottom half of each painted bright yellow as a safety provision that hadn't protected them from sustaining countless scrapes from bumper impacts over the years.

In the end, the attempt was little more than idle curiosity—every possible surface in the garage, or every vehicle in it, could have held cameras feeding Wraith a real-time view of Jim's actions. He reached the wall, stopping beneath the B2 sign.

"Now what?" he asked.

"You see the fire extinguisher?"

Jim looked to his left, where a red wall-mounted case held the extinguisher behind a glass door.

"Yes."

"Look on the right side."

Jim approached the case and scanned it. At first glance, he almost missed it completely; the small box protruding from the side was painted an identical shade of red. When he pulled at the box, it detached in his hand, revealing a magnetic backing. Eagerly sliding the top off, Jim peered inside to search for the tapes.

But there was only a prepaid cell phone.

He dumped the phone in his palm and then pocketed it before replacing the magnetic box.

"I must have checked the wrong fire extinguisher," he said bitterly, "because the tapes aren't here."

The computerized British voice continued, "At the risk of offending you, I do not trust you not to screw this up and lure the Sky Thieves to wherever you are. If you want the tapes, you will have to get them in a manner that will not be intercepted—which is almost certainly what would happen if I left them in a dead drop."

"Enough foreplay. I've got your phone; now what?"

"You tell me."

Jim shrugged. "Tell you what?"

"When I should call you on it. When you are somewhere secure, away from your office and car, and not wearing anything that you have worn to your work, including your shoes."

Jim checked his Rolex and said, "Fine. Thirty minutes from now."

"Done. I will call you with instructions—do not bother trying to trace it. The origin will be undetectable."

"I have no doubt," Jim said, but he was only midway through the sentence when the line went dead.

He put his phone away, striding toward his Suburban with a renewed sense of determination. When that call came, Wraith wouldn't be the one giving the orders.

72

BLAIR

Blair pulled the car into the warehouse bay, killing the engine as Sterling and Marco rolled the door shut.

She leapt out of the car, not bothering to close the door. "Sterling, you okay?"

Exiting the passenger side, Alec shouted at her over the roof of the car.

"That's *Doctor Defranc* to you. Don't you see the scrubs, woman? This man is a learned medical professional."

Blair reached inside the vehicle and retrieved the laser spotlight she'd used to subdue Sterling's pursuers, holding one end behind her ear as if she'd had trouble hearing.

"What was that, Alec? I couldn't hear you."

"Nothing," he quickly responded. "Nothing at all."

Blair tossed the laser onto the driver's seat, slamming the door shut as Sterling said, "I'm fine." He walked past the car without meeting Blair's eyes. "We knew the meeting was a risk, we took precautions, and everything turned out fine."

She stood for a moment of disbelief as Sterling dropped into his seat among a ring of foldout chairs, stretching his legs in front of him. He looked like he'd just crossed the finish line of a particularly grueling 5K race, and in a way, she supposed he had.

Storming over and taking a seat across from Sterling, she said, "That most definitely was not 'fine.' We had to expose ourselves and you were one slip on the ice away from being captured. Dembinski needs to pay."

"It wasn't Dembinski, it was Jim's mentor."

"How could his mentor have known Dembinski was the Fixer?"

Marco lowered himself into a chair. "The same way we did. By looking at who would bid for the tapes. And once he figured out it was Dembinski, you better believe there was a bribe or threat involved to lure Sterling into a trap."

She glared at him.

"Well, which was it? A bribe or a threat?"

"What does it matter?"

Blair blinked quickly, feeling her anger rising. "If he was threatened, he gets a pass. But if he took a bribe to sell us out, I want to steal every dollar in his account."

Blair cut her eyes to Sterling. "So, what did he say?"

He gave a light shrug, folding his hands behind his head.

"That he didn't have a choice. And that he was sorry."

Marco noted, "Sounds like he was threatened."

"Or," Blair shot back, "he is trying to cover up a bribe."

Alec arrived at the circle, taking a seat as he carefully unwrapped a candy bar.

"Blair," he began, taking a bite and chewing, "your blood-lust for vengeance is both glorious and terrifying. But I'm going to go out on a limb and say that we have to direct that energy toward Jim, or risk losing the only thing that matters to us—the tapes, period."

Alec took another bite of his candy bar as Marco

appraised him with disgust. "I hate to admit it, Blair, but in this isolated and extremely rare case, Alec is right."

Blair nodded her assent, saying nothing.

She still didn't really agree—Dembinski had to pay for what he'd done, whether it was his choice or not—but her teammates' rebuke served to inform her that she'd been taken over by her emotions, by a protectiveness toward Sterling that exceeded professional considerations.

And looking at him now, exhausted and disheveled in his medical scrubs, Blair realized she didn't just need to protect Sterling from the assaults of Jim and his mentor, she needed to protect her own judgment as well.

Finally she said, "So what's our next step?"

Bracing his hands on the chair and rising, Marco replied, "What I'm about to do now: make sure we didn't miss anything. I have to screen the CALEA data that's come in since our little diversion to rescue Sterling."

"Oh," Sterling said. "Well, sorry for the inconvenience."

Marco didn't respond—he was already moving toward his office, where he'd don headphones and review Jim's computer activity along with any accrued audio files at triple playback speed.

Alec continued chewing his candy bar, raising his eyebrows at Sterling and then nodding toward Blair.

Sighing, Sterling turned to face her.

"Look, Blair," he began, "all our countermeasures worked. The tripwire, you baking those dudes with your laser, the runner swap with Alec. I wasn't even pursued into the hospital, and the ER was too packed for anyone to notice me. We're totally clean...just back to waiting for Wraith to make contact, same as before."

Blair felt like she was sulking, and sensed as much from her teammates' reactions. It wasn't their fault that Dembinski had betrayed them, after all, or their fault they'd decided to accept the meeting in the first place—the choice had been made out of necessity.

"You're right." She straightened in her chair. "We need to stay focused. Jim is the target, not Dembinski."

Alec finished his candy bar, crumpling the wrapper into his pocket. "See? We're still in the game, unless..."

He stopped speaking at the sound of footsteps, looking up as Marco entered the warehouse bay with a particularly sober expression. Then he continued, "...unless Marco has some really bad news for us."

Marco said, "I've got good news and bad news."

"So start with the good," Alec cheerfully remarked.

"Wraith contacted Jim."

"How?" Blair asked.

"Over his personal cell. Wraith's voice was concealed using text-to-speech software, and he directed Jim to the dead drop of a prepaid phone in the parking garage."

"Great. So we missed Jim getting a burner from Wraith."

"Be grateful that the CALEA tap was still in place, or we wouldn't even know that. But it's the next call that should concern us, and—"

"And thanks to Dembinski's little trap," Blair continued, "we don't have anyone standing by with a parabolic microphone to intercept. Unless Jim calls from home, we have no way of knowing. If he goes anywhere else, pulling our physical surveillance tonight will have cost us the tapes."

Marco replied, "Unless I'm mistaken, it already has. And that's the bad news. Jim told Wraith to call the prepaid phone in half an hour."

"When?"

Marco checked his watch. "Thirty-seven minutes ago."

73

JIM

Jim paced the second-floor room, testing the handle a second time to ensure it was locked.

He checked his Rolex, then double-checked the time against the prepaid phone in his hand. Wraith was late, and if this was some attempt at a power play, then the thief would be sorely disappointed by the time the call was over.

If the call came at all.

This room was the farthest point in the house from his wife's wanderings, sufficiently removed from the bedroom for him to have a conversation with some degree of privacy. He doubted she would attempt to eavesdrop, but couldn't altogether rule out the possibility. Most importantly, the room wasn't his home office, the primary candidate for any listening devices. While the entire house had been swept and came up clean, Jim couldn't be too cautious—then again, he reasoned, he had precious little need to conceal the upcoming information exchange from anyone but his wife.

He turned to continue pacing, stubbing his toe on a moving box and then kicking it with his heel before continuing his march back and forth. Eventually this space would be a guest room; for now, it was a morass of unpacked moving boxes that had been sealed since LA, every uncut strip of tape a reminder of how much stuff he and his wife had accumulated that they didn't truly need.

Stopping to gaze out the window at his back lawn, Jim's eyes settled on the covered inground pool. That was one amenity he lacked in Los Angeles; now that he had one, there wouldn't be a chance to use it for months. Taking a moment to lower the blinds over every window in the room, he continued pacing.

There was enough to enjoy inside the house to keep him occupied until summer arrived. Whoever originally built this custom home had done everything right: the wraparound porch was exquisite, every interior feature from the cabinetry to the built-in bookshelves and stonework made with craftsmanship that he appreciated during what little time he spent there. The longer his hours at work, the more he craved a beautiful home to return to—an important consideration, given that his professional responsibilities would only increase once he was elected to office in November.

And after that...well, who knew how far he would rise. Jim had no intentions of the House seat being the final ladder rung of his career, though what awaited after that remained to be seen.

Finally the phone rang, the display flashing with the same stupid caller ID as before: *GUESS WHO?*

Jim decided that Wraith's assessment of his own humor was probably as overinflated as his ego. No matter, he thought, answering the call; Jim was about to put Wraith in his place, and signal the beginning of the end of these ridiculous exploits.

"I'm here," he said.

"Hello, Jim," said the familiar computer-generated British

voice.

"You're late."

A brief pause before Wraith replied, "I suppose I got sidetracked thinking about how I am going to spend your 25.6 million. Now are you ready to receive your instructions for the exchange?"

Jim smiled with the heady anticipation of flipping the tables.

"No," he said smugly, "this time, I'm calling the shots. No more museums, no more chances for the Sky Thieves to interfere. I've set up something ironclad, and you're going to play ball."

Another pause.

"You seem to forget that I have the tapes."

"And *you* seem to forget that I have the resources and connections to make things happen in this world. I raised almost twenty-six million for the tapes, and if you don't do exactly as I say, my backer will easily spend twice that amount for the sole purpose of hunting you to the ends of the earth for as long as it takes. So I suggest you listen carefully, do exactly what I tell you, and walk away a free man with your full payment, never to interfere with me again. Do we have an understanding?"

This time there was no pause, though he couldn't decide whether Wraith was truly becoming compliant or simply probing Jim for more information.

"What are your instructions?"

"Day after tomorrow there's going to be a fundraising dinner at a Manhattan restaurant called Byrnside. It's going to be attended by a number of prominent Republican officials, most notably the President of the United States."

"I cannot walk into that."

Jim found himself nodding slowly, as if Wraith were

present in the room and needed additional convincing.

"You *will* walk into it, and here's how. There's a player named Avery Williams who works for a major conservative think tank. He's got a ticket reserved for himself, along with the event's only unnamed ticket for a guest of his choice—and as far as the Secret Service is concerned, that guest could be a colleague or someone he owes a favor to. You're simply going to approach one of the two Secret Service checkpoints on either side of the block, identify yourself as Avery Williams's guest, and produce a New York State driver's license. You're going to tell them Avery wasn't feeling well and won't be attending. They will direct you to Byrnside's main entrance, where reception officials will hand you a sealed envelope with your ticket, and you will pass a security sweep before entering the venue and proceeding to the open seating tables for $15,000 plates at the back of the room."

"Then what?"

"I trust you can manage your own dinner conversation while providing a sufficient cover for your presence. I will make my rounds at the open seating tables and shake everyone's hand. You will place the tapes in my suit pocket, whether overtly or secretly I don't particularly care. Once I'm done with the meet-and-greet at those tables, I'm going to check my pockets for the tapes, and they had better be there."

"If I plant the tapes on you," Wraith said, "what happens next?"

Jim shrugged. "We go our separate ways. I destroy the tapes inside the venue, which is within so many rings of Secret Service protection that not even the Sky Thieves could get inside, and even if they tried they'd be arrested at once. I leave that dinner with the evidence destroyed, and you leave it with the knowledge that any action taken against you won't come from me or anyone I work with. We're both free men."

"What assurance do I have that you won't have me arrested?"

"You have my word," he said, "and the additional insurance that you either do this exactly as I've described, or you go on the run now and find out if I'm bluffing in two days' time. Because if those tapes aren't in my pocket by the end of the dinner, or if I ever find out there are copies, then there is no place on this planet where you will be safe."

Jim waited impatiently through the long pause that followed, hoping that Wraith was seeing the logic in this arrangement. Because his mentor wasn't bluffing; not this time. Already irritated by the numerous setbacks in regaining control of the tapes, and furious at Jim for their existence in the first place, his mentor was going to receive assurances that the tapes had been destroyed at the fundraising event, or ensure that Wraith was destroyed for not complying, completely devastating Jim's chances of a political future in the process.

But Wraith replied succinctly, sealing the issue from further discussion.

"I will see you at Byrnside."

Then the call ended, and Jim breathed a long sigh of relief. Provided Wraith delivered the tapes at that event, all that remained was to ride out the clock. Because Jim's mentor had explained the particulars of security surrounding the president's visit to New York, including how the venue would be secured from unauthorized access. And all those facts added up to one incontrovertible truth: no one was getting inside that building unless the Secret Service expressly allowed it.

At this point Jim could make a press release telling the Sky Thieves the particulars about the upcoming exchange—there was simply nothing they could do to stop it.

74

STERLING

Sterling was the last to arrive at the foldout table, having quickly changed out of his sweat-soaked medical scrubs to take his place on the only unoccupied side.

Blair, Alec, and Marco were already seated before their laptops, the clatter of keyboards and mouse clicks filling the room in lieu of any spoken words. What had begun as a delirious celebration that they'd intercepted the call in the first place was soon tempered by reality as they considered the primary obstacle—regardless of the venue, they'd ultimately have to penetrate Secret Service protection.

That fact remained unspoken for now, though Sterling could see it written on their faces as they began their hasty analysis of the target—each crew member had a laptop open, with Blair looking at the big picture and Alec at the specifics of the venue, Marco handling everything in between, and Sterling preparing to orchestrate the madness like a symphony conductor.

As Sterling took his seat, Blair began, "It's on the Upper East Side. Rest of the block has a few art galleries, a hotel and spa, and some fashion and jewelry boutiques. Central Park is two blocks to the west, and the East River is six blocks in the other direction. North and south are urban jungle."

Sterling asked, "Building?"

"Known as the MacGregor, and it sits on the corner of East 65th Street and Park Avenue. Fifteen stories tall, originally built as the MacGregor Regent Hotel in the twenties. Byrnside is on the ground floor facing 65th Street, and the rest of the hotel was converted to condominiums in the mid-nineties. So aside from the restaurant, the building consists of sixty-eight condos plus the amenities you'd expect: full-time doorman, concierge, valet parking, and room service from Byrnside."

As he considered this, Sterling was surprised that he didn't feel more confident. The larger the facility and its staff, the more layers of personnel and thus opportunities to slip in with a well-planned disguise—but instead of being comforted by this fact, Sterling felt a vague state of unease that elicited a prickle of sweat across his forehead.

"Venue?"

Alec looked up from his computer. "Byrnside is the flagship restaurant of a celebrity chef named Brendan Byrnside, was ranked by Forbes as the top restaurant in America, and holds not one but two Michelin stars. Over forty cooks on staff, and needless to say, jackets are required."

"Capacity?"

He consulted his screen. "Apart from the main dining room, there's a bar, lounge, and two smaller dining rooms. Total seated capacity is three hundred guests for dining, plus another ninety at the bar and lounge."

"I'll say the obvious: we buy a ticket."

This time Marco answered.

"And I will reply with the obvious: with plates starting at fifteen grand and ranging into six figures the closer you sit to the president, they have already filled every seat."

Undaunted, Sterling replied, "Fair enough. So we're looking at roughly four hundred guests, plus standing security and a wait staff in the dozens. What's access like from the condominium to the restaurant?"

Marco said, "There's a service access corridor inside the building. Door connects behind the concierge desk in the condo lobby and leads to a hall next to the restaurant kitchen."

"Perfect," Sterling announced. "We place a false order for room service from MacGregor, then disguise one of our crew as the delivery man on the return trip to Byrnside."

"Great plan other than the fact that condo staff handles the food delivery, and there's no room service the night of the fundraising dinner."

Sterling drummed his fingers on the tabletop, then asked no one in particular, "Street access?"

Blair responded, "East 65th will be shut down between Madison and Park Avenue, with checkpoints to allow ticketed diners on foot. But the restaurant has a service door, a one-way emergency exit onto the street, and the main entrance facing the street. On the Park Avenue side, there's a one-way emergency exit for the condominium, then the main resident doors."

Sterling frowned. "What about the backside of the building?"

"Better," she said, "but not by much. Service entry for the restaurant, plus an additional service entry and resident door for the condos. Security will be guarding all of them leading up to the event, so if we're going to use a cover it had better be bulletproof."

"What's on the roof?"

"A deck for residents, bordered on three sides by walled-off private gardens with French door access to master suites of a few top-floor units."

"So we infiltrate from the top. Entry through an unoccupied rooftop condo."

Marco yawned.

"Great plan, other than the adjoining buildings are about a hundred feet shorter than the MacGregor. To the south, there's a small four-story private townhouse. To the west, a five-story building filled with medical suites specializing in plastic surgery. The remaining backside of the building is ground-level resident and staff parking with street access on 65th Street. So unless you plan on free climbing up the side of the building in full view of the Secret Service, the roof is out."

"Balconies?"

Blair shook her head. "Just one, centrally located off an east-facing condo on the eleventh floor."

Sterling chewed the corner of his thumb. "We rent a condo."

Marco replied, "They start at five million and have a three-year waiting list."

This spurred Alec to shake his head mournfully. "We'd have better luck if Blair seduces a wealthy bachelor who lives there and leaves the door unlocked for the rest of us—"

"Moving on," Blair cut him off. "There's got to be a way. Remember when we started planning for the Supermax breakout and it seemed impossible?"

"The difference," Marco replied with a hint of irritation, "is that Supermax was built from the ground up to contain inmates. Half of the security is in the architecture, and the other half is in the technology. The presence of guards at every corner is just a bonus."

"So?" Alec asked. "Manhattan should be easier, not harder."

"You're wrong. Because the venue is not designed to contain inmates or cash, it's built like a regular structure—a basic level of security but nothing more. That means to protect the president, the Secret Service will have an army of people on hand, to say nothing of local law enforcement augmentation. We do our best work in the gaps where security is entrusted to physical or technological means that we can bypass. The presence of actual guards is our Achilles' heel. One or two? Sure, we could implement a distraction, or sleeping gas, or whatever. But three dozen guards and all the technology they bring along for the ride? Not a chance."

Blair huffed a breath and said incredulously, "No one's suggesting we take on the entire guard force. We just need to slip one person through unnoticed."

"Unnoticed?" he asked. "Blair, there will be so many layers of security that we won't be able to tell where one ends and the next begins. I hate to say it, but Jim is right. This exchange is as close to airtight as he can get—not even Wraith argued with that."

Sterling felt a wave of realization wash over him and looked up, announcing, "That's it."

He felt the others' gazes fall upon him in unison, and he cleared his throat before adding cautiously, "Wraith didn't even argue with Jim's plan. Remember at the beginning of all this, when we were trying to figure out who Fixer was? We realized we had to start thinking like Wraith. Maybe we penetrate the venue the same way."

Alec squinted at him.

"By...thinking like Wraith?"

"No. By walking through the front door with a ticket, exactly like Wraith will. Think about it: the Secret Service is protecting the president, but ultimately it's five- and six-figure diners who make massive donations to his party. These people will only be hassled so much on their way through security. If someone is on the guest list and presents their ticket and matching ID, they're in."

Marco sat back, folding his arms.

"If we steal someone's ticket beforehand, they're not going to shrug and forget about it. They'll report the loss to obtain another, and then we're burned. Or are you suggesting we simply kidnap them?"

"No," Sterling said, "we don't steal it beforehand. We *let* someone enter the venue, and find a way to get them—and only them—back out. A work emergency, something important enough for them to leave before dinner begins. Then we do what we do best: steal the ticket off them, and use it to pass security and get inside. After that, it's just a matter of hanging out at the bar and pretending to be on the phone until Jim makes his rounds, then conducting the dip."

Marco threw up his hands as if this was the stupidest idea he'd ever heard. "The Secret Service isn't made up of idiots. If Shaquille O'Neal walks out of the venue, then I can't exactly stroll back in carrying his ticket."

Sterling nodded slowly.

"That's why we stop chasing our tails over the security measures around the venue, and start taking a good hard look at the guest list. We're going to need a doppelgänger."

"Exactly," Alec agreed. Then he hesitated. "Which is what, exactly?"

"A lookalike. Someone with enough physical resemblance that one of us could pass for them—given some advance preparation, of course."

Marco asked, "And the odds of that are what, exactly?"

Sterling shrugged. "There's only one way to find out."

75

BLAIR

Blair sat cross-legged on the cot in her room, flipping through DMV photos on her laptop with an increasing sense of apprehension.

Marco had obtained the list of registered guests and correlated each to a registered photograph, then divided the pictures equally among the team members to complete the screening process as quickly as possible and determine if anyone on the crew could pass for a diner.

But Blair's segment of the list included a number of sober-looking individuals she took to be high-powered businessmen, their last names paired with younger wives who appeared to be a succession of plastic surgery spokeswomen. A majority of them could be ruled out due to age alone—the crew could only accomplish so much even with their impressive arsenal of disguise equipment—and those who remained were so far removed in appearance from herself, Sterling, Marco, and Alec that she dismissed them at a glance.

Still, she added those with even a passing resemblance to a folder on her computer desktop, hoping that her teammates were having better luck. It would have been perfect if Avery

Williams himself bore any similarities to someone on the crew. After all, his was the only ticket that they definitely knew would go unclaimed.

But Mr. Williams was a sixty-seven-year-old man with a shock of white hair, and between his wrinkles and liver spots, no Secret Service agent would buy into anything outside of a Hollywood studio-produced facsimile.

After the first thirty pictures yielded nothing but a trio of last-ditch candidates, Blair wasn't sure if the problem was the registered guests or the plan itself. Even if they managed to find a remotely possible choice, the risks in pulling this off were immense. Still, she saw no other option given the extremely limited time they had to put together a response to Jim's exchange, and if they failed at this, then every effort over the past two months had been for nothing and they may as well have resigned themselves to defeat in LA.

As her hopes dwindled to nothing, she heard a victory cry from somewhere in the facility that could only have come from Alec.

Closing her laptop, she rose and followed the sound into Marco's office, where the hacker sat beside Alec as both men remained hunched over the computer, chatting excitedly. To her surprise, neither man seemed to notice or care that she'd entered.

She approached them, still unnoticed, and instinctively scanned Alec's body for the tape duplicates he'd been carrying as part of her pickpocketing training.

The tapes were partially visible in the right pocket of his windbreaker, half-exposed and ripe for the picking.

Blair's next movements were automatic, fluid, flawless— she crossed the remaining steps to Alec's backside, then dipped the thumb and index finger of her right hand into his pocket to find purchase on the tapes. Using her left hand to tap his shoulder and direct his attention, she simultaneously removed the tapes and slid them into a pocket of her fleece.

"So what's the deal?" she asked him casually, scanning his face for any sign that he'd detected her dip. "You find a candidate?"

Bracing for the disappointment of the three dreaded words she'd heard on every previous attempt—*nice try, Blair*—she was pleased when Alec said nothing of the sort.

Instead, he leapt up from the chair and grabbed Blair's hand, sliding his other around her waist and guiding her around the room in a ballroom waltz.

Before she could summon an appropriate reaction, Sterling entered and said, "Alec, calm down and then sit down. What's up?"

Alec released her and dropped back into his seat as Marco said, "In spite of all obstacles to the contrary, I did it."

Alec socked his shoulder. "Oh no. Don't you dare take this away from me."

Marco shrugged. "Why? I'm the one who found it."

"Found it? Sure. But you're dead in the water without *this*." Alec spun a finger around his face. "The breathtakingly good looks of everyone's favorite safecracker, pickpocketer extraordinaire, the one, the only—"

"Guys," Blair said, taking a seat behind them as Sterling did the same, "care to fill us in?"

Marco cleared his throat and straightened in his chair, opening a browser window for them to see.

On it was a *Business Insider* feature dated two weeks earlier, complete with a picture of the main subject: a Wall Street finance manager named Ernie Young.

"Oh." Blair squinted at the picture before leaning back and speaking in a deeper tone. "Oh."

"'Oh' is right," Alec said triumphantly.

Sterling leaned over to nudge Blair with an elbow. "You have to admit, it's close."

Alec blurted, "Close? It's much better than close. It's fortuitous, serendipitous, a veritable gift from the heist gods. Not even Marco can deny that."

"I can," Marco said, "and I have. It's luck."

Blair looked at the screen again, feeling amazed that, for once, things had worked out in their favor.

Because Ernie Young bore more than a passing resemblance to Alec. If Alec had introduced the man as his brother, Blair wouldn't have doubted him in the slightest.

Like Alec, Ernie Young was a stocky Asian man—the shape of their faces was the same, as were the eyes. The most noticeable difference was a thin scar across Young's left eyebrow, an effect they could replicate given a bit of time and cosmetics.

Alec said, "Clean-shaven? Done. Hair's a little longer than my taste would allow, but that's nothing a wig can't fix. And besides, you whites can't tell us apart anyway."

Blair asked, "Height difference?"

Marco replied, "According to his driver's license, he's two inches taller than Alec. Nothing the right pair of shoes can't overcome."

Sterling looked at Blair. "Let's say we place a call declaring a work emergency. How can we disable Young's cell phone service afterward so he can't reach anyone to verify that the emergency was fake?"

She said, "The same way we handled Jim's CALEA tap: by accessing the provider and then freezing his service. It doesn't have to hold up forever, just long enough that he has to make a trip to the office." Almost in disbelief that she was agreeing to this plan, she continued, "I've got to say, this whole thing might just be stupid enough to work."

Alec clapped his hands together. "It's *way* stupid enough to work. Not even the Secret Service could envision something this dumb. Guy who looks just like me leaves, guy who looks just like me shows back up with the right ticket. Biggest problem will be matching the wardrobe—"

"Which we can mitigate," Marco said, "by analyzing every picture and security camera still shot of Ernie Young that we can find and having Alec prepare duplicate wardrobe elements down to the dress shirts and ties. He will be ready to dress as required, and we can always have one team member prepared for an emergency department store purchase if Young shows up with something we don't have. But from what I've seen in his media articles, he dresses fairly soberly...charcoal or navy suits with solid-color ties." He shrugged. "I think we can pull it off."

"See?" Alec cried. "Even the Negative Nancy thinks it'll work, and he hasn't fully approved of a plan in so long I'm not even sure why he's still on the crew."

"Hurtful," Marco said, "but true."

Sterling looked at Blair for a response. She turned a palm upward in resignation and raised her eyebrows in an expression that conveyed, *what choice do we have?*

Then Sterling said, "I can't believe I'm saying this, but...I think we've found our doppelgänger."

Alec slapped a triumphant hand on the table.

"One thing I forgot to add—to buy us a little time after I get the tapes from Jim, I'll replace them with these."

Reaching into his windbreaker, he retrieved the pack of tapes and wagged it toward Blair.

Her hand flew to her pocket—he'd stolen them back from her during his ballroom waltz.

Alec put the tapes away. "Your dip was good and the left shoulder bump was a solid diversion. But I saw your reflection in the computer screen, and you hesitated behind me just a little too long not to be suspicious."

Before she could say anything, Alec announced, "Well I'd love to stay and chat, but time is money and I've got a wardrobe to buy. Sterling?"

"Okay," Sterling began, "here's what's going to happen: Alec and Marco return the rental vehicles while Blair and I find a place to set up shop in Manhattan and pack up the Sprinters. It'll take us close to three hours to reach the city, so we continue planning while we're on the road. I'll ride with Alec in the lead van and start building a profile on Ernie Young. Focus will be on his business dealings and what kind of work emergency we can conjure that will get him out of the venue. Marco and Blair take the trail vehicle and start mapping out the area around Byrnside—once Young leaves, we need to know where he'll be headed and reverse-engineer a three-man pickpocketing pass off his route. Don't forget to figure out where Alec can stand by and how we'll pass him the ticket. Am I forgetting anything?"

"Sure," Marco said, leaning his head back to look at the ceiling. "You're forgetting about sleep."

Alec shouted, "NO SLEEP TILL," and then broke into a spirited air guitar performance before adding, "MANHATTAN!"

The outburst was sufficient to shock the other three crew members into silence, and Alec filled the void with a head-bopping recital of rap lyrics that continued—albeit with increasing discomfort—until he finally trailed off.

Clearing his throat, he explained, "It's the Beastie Boys, man. 'No Sleep Till Brooklyn,' off their debut studio album *Licensed to Ill*. But, you know, I had to change the Brooklyn bit because we're headed to...well, Manhattan."

Still, no one spoke. Blair felt the level of awkwardness

steadily climb as Alec sheepishly added, "Seriously, none of you guys listen to the Beastie Boys?"

Sterling was the first to rise from his chair. "Let's get going, unless anyone wants to stick around for Alec's next serenade."

"Nope," Blair said, rising alongside him.

Marco pushed his chair back with the words, "I'm good."

Alec was the last to stand, calling after the others, "When there's a job that requires karaoke, you guys will be lucky to have me."

76

STERLING

Balancing the laptop on his thighs in the passenger seat, Sterling said, "Ernie Young isn't just a finance manager, he's a top partner at the firm. This guy's tied to institutional trading, corporate lending, acquisitions, mergers, and IPOs—we'd have a harder time finding something that *wasn't* related to his work."

Alec said nothing, steering the Sprinter van with his eyes focused on the road as Sterling watched him for any input. But his features were hard to analyze on this stretch of highway free of streetlights or civilization, and from what he could make out in the soft glow of the dashboard meters, Alec's expression was completely neutral.

Though Sterling couldn't rightfully complain about the darkness, he thought. Traveling at night meant that he could sit in the passenger seat without assuming undue risk, even in disguise. If Alec was pulled over, Sterling would have plenty of time to duck into the back and slip into the vehicle's hidden floor compartment.

The odds of a traffic stop were minimal: both vans were identically marked with the logo of a legit security consulting

LLC, a cover that was fully backstopped by business cards and a website. In the event of a vehicle search, either driver could launch into a lengthy diatribe about penetration testing their clients' businesses, first discovering security gaps and then training the management and staff on how to rectify them.

But the primary level of protection from law enforcement was much simpler: don't do anything outwardly illegal.

And so the Sprinter vans proceeded down I-87 southbound with cruise control set at the speed limit, making an uneventful drive past sleepy upstate hamlets and villages with names like Selkirk, Ravena, and Hannacroix.

Sterling added, "But whatever we think of, it's got to be something big. This guy manages billions in mutual funds, and it's going to take a major event to pull him out of that fundraising dinner and back into the office. He's got to have cronies who handle almost everything, so our job will be finding something that he can't outsource the solution to."

After a few more minutes of analysis Sterling closed the laptop, rubbing his forehead with the very real sense that he was drowning in a sea of information available on the world of Wall Street finance management. It didn't help that they had precious little time to take their nascent plan from inception to a complete working strategy, but he tried to count his blessings—after all, it was nice just to be sitting down, letting his legs recover from the mad sprint through Albany. The only thing that would have made the drive to New York City better would have been sleep.

Cracking his neck, Sterling concluded, "I'm not sure how we'll manage it given the dwindling time we've got, but we'll have to determine his criteria for what constitutes an after-hours emergency. Then learn enough about his assistant's voice and speech patterns to stage a convincing call. This is all going to require a lot of data, and I think it's going to take another break-in. We can call it Jimgate, Part 2: The Resurrection."

He thought Alec would be particularly proud of that last part; but to his surprise, he was slowly shaking his head, glancing over at Sterling as if disappointed.

"Sorry, boss, but I think you're wrong about that."

"Which part?"

Alec shrugged. "All of it. Do you know anything about Wall Street?"

Sterling felt his jaw settle, and he shot back, "Do *you*?"

"Course I do," Alec replied easily. "I mean I've never worked there per se, but know how many times I've seen *Wall Street*? Or *Wall Street: Money Never Sleeps*? Or *The Wolf of Wall Street*?"

"I don't think those qualify as valid education—"

"And let's not forget *Trading Places*. How Dan Aykroyd and Eddie Murphy didn't star in more features together is beyond me. Together, they were pure comedy genius."

Sterling blinked.

"If there's a point to this, I must be missing it."

Alec explained, "Here's what I'm getting at: why go through all the trouble of faking an emergency notification when we could just create an actual emergency?"

Sterling remained silent for a moment, uncertain if Alec was about to deliver another punchline or have an epiphany, but sensing that one of the two was about to transpire.

"Keep talking," he said.

"I realize you don't have the education in Wall Street movies that I do, so I'll explain how this works. We analyze trade data to find some big stock buy that Young recently made—if he's as active as you say, it shouldn't take long. Then Marco makes a cyber attack affecting that stock value; maybe he tweaks the reporting data, or releases a fake news story about the company that would cause its shares to crash. Ernie Young gets called in to authorize after-hours trades on a massive scale, and we can pull the plug on the cyber attack as soon as I'm strolling out of Byrnside with the tapes in hand. The market sorts itself out by the time the New York Stock Exchange opens in the morning, and the media will probably just blame Russian hackers. Which, since Marco's doing it, isn't entirely inaccurate."

Sterling noticed that his mouth had fallen open sometime in the course of Alec's explanation, and when he mustered a response, it was with a tone of disbelief.

"Are you the same guy who was singing Vanilla Ice a few hours ago?"

Alec shook his head solemnly. "Beastie Boys. Huge difference, Sterling. Huge."

77

BLAIR

Blair shifted in the passenger seat of the trail van, analyzing her laptop screen.

"Ernie Young has two route options to get from Byrnside to his firm on Wall Street, and since East 65th will be shut down we can rule out one of them. That means he'll be walking to the corner, turning right, and following Park Avenue south until he can get into either a cab or a company car."

When Marco didn't respond, continuing to steer without moving his eyes from the road, she asked, "You have anything to add?"

Marco inhaled as if he was about to launch into a lengthy diatribe, then spoke a single word.

"No."

Blair felt her jaw tighten. Marco's intelligence was beyond reproach, as were his technical skills—however, he also had a silent brooding nature that she found infuriating at times. He could be silently agreeing with her or finding her assessment ridiculous; either was possible, though getting Marco to divulge his inner thoughts was like pulling teeth at times like these.

Undaunted, she continued, "So the first steer can be positioned near the corner of 65th and Park, waiting for a visual intercept."

"No."

"No?"

Marco sighed. "That's too close to the Secret Service checkpoint to hang out for long without drawing suspicion. I suggest that our visual intercept should come from a pre-positioned camera—remember, there will be four hundred guests going in, but Young will probably be the only one coming out early. We outsource his departure to surveillance, allowing us to spread our team further south along Park Avenue."

Blair found herself nodding. "That's smart."

"It will also," Marco continued, "allow Alec to remotely view Young's behavior as he leaves—how fast he is walking, whether he is on the phone, et cetera, and mirror those mannerisms on his way back to the Secret Service checkpoints."

Blair adjusted her seatbelt. "We'll only have three people for the pickpocketing effort—after all, we can't risk Young seeing his body double. So one of us takes first steer to ID and trail the mark, another makes the dip, and the third works as second steer to take the handoff and get the cargo to Alec."

Marco said, "Since there are only three of us, and we will already know where Young stored his ticket from surveilling the entry point, I propose a modified setup."

"I'm listening."

"You've got the least pickpocketing experience, so you take the slot as first steer and trail Young on his way down the sidewalk. Sterling will be the primary hook and approach from the opposite direction, making the dip as Young passes. If he fails to get the ticket, then I make the next pass as a second hook. Whichever one of us recovers it hands it off to you. There are contingencies, of course."

Blair agreed, "Like if Young feels the dip."

"Which is why it would need to occur out of shouting distance from the Secret Service checkpoint. But he'll still have his wallet, and if we engineer a sufficiently critical work emergency, the only logical move is for him to cut his losses and continue to Wall Street."

"But we'd still have to scatter," Blair pointed out. "And in the event of a radio failure, I think it makes sense to have a phone tracking app that allows us to see each other's locations. I trust that won't be a problem?"

"Child's play. All that matters is that one of us has control of the ticket, and from there it's a matter of getting it to...where will Alec be staged, exactly?"

Blair analyzed her screen.

"There's a Starbucks on 63rd and Lexington. Alec could wait there alone without drawing attention while he monitors the camera feeds, and there's no risk of Young seeing him. Once we get the ticket we could move to him or he could meet us on the sidewalk—we've just got to give enough time offset to not give the Secret Service any cause for suspicion."

After yawning, Marco added, "Then Alec re-enters the Secret Service checkpoint with an exact duplicate of Young's driver's license, which I can replicate from the DMV records. A word or two of apologetic explanation about a false alarm at work, the standard security sweep, and—"

"And he's in the door to Byrnside," Blair finished for him.

Marco nodded slowly. "And he's in the door to Byrnside."

"I don't mean to sound surprised, but...we could actually pull this off."

"Don't deceive yourself," he cautioned her. "It is risky to a degree that defies my ability to put it into words. But yes, in essence, it is a deception operation that will be quite elaborate to stage and then relatively simple to carry out."

Blair watched him closely.

"Marco, it's okay to admit you think this will work." Then she looked away from him, directing her gaze out the windshield and nodding toward the taillights to their front. "I won't tell Sterling or Alec. Your reputation as the team pessimist can survive this thing intact."

"Okay." He sighed. "Then between us..."

"Yes?"

He cut his eyes toward her for a moment, then looked back to the road. "I think this will work."

78

BLAIR

Blair gasped with pleasure as she stepped into the warm spray of water from the showerhead, letting it soak her body before fumbling for the tiny bottle of shampoo beside her.

Predictably, there was no significant warehouse or storage space available for immediate rent in Manhattan. They could have managed to secure an all-inclusive space in the Bronx, but the distance to the fundraising venue would have made timely response to any late-emerging intelligence impossible.

And so they'd settled on the next best thing: a hotel.

The Wenton Parkside was a scant two blocks from Central Park's southern border, placing them within fifteen minutes' walk to Byrnside and the MacGregor building. It wasn't an ideal setup by any means—with the vast majority of their team equipment locked up in the Sprinter vans in the adjacent parking garage, the hotel made hasty planning a challenge of coordinating meeting times in Marco's room, where his computer setup would serve as their de facto headquarters for the time being.

Blair, however, didn't mind in the least.

After two warehouse facility rentals, the simple amenities

of a hotel room were sheer ecstasy—even when the hotel's Four Seasons-grade website proclaiming "historic charm" translated to stained carpets, scuffed furniture, and bedsheets whose last laundering cycle was dubious at best.

Her focus remained on the reasonably stable climate control, the brief reprieve of personal space from the three men on her crew, and, most significantly, the steady supply of warm water at acceptable pressure. She finished showering and toweled off in the steam-filled bathroom, considering that all she needed now was sleep.

But that would have to wait.

After dressing and donning her auburn wig—Blair reasoned that Manhattan was as good a place as any to be a redhead—she left her room, ensuring the do not disturb sign remained on the handle as she headed to Marco's room, where she gave a quiet double knock.

Alec opened the door, his eyes ticking to her hair. "A good morning to you, Your Majesty." Letting her in, he turned to announce, "Princess Ariel has arrived."

Blair crossed the room with an appreciative nod to the space. Only one executive double room had been available, and since they were likely to spend most of their time planning, it had gone to Marco.

He was positioned at the desk beside closed window shades, glancing at her over his shoulder before returning his gaze to the computer with the words, "Good morning, Little Orphan Annie."

Sterling was seated on the couch, balancing a laptop on his crossed leg as he appraised her with a thin smile.

She asked, "Can we get started?"

Alec leapt onto the far bed, bouncing on the mattress as he replied.

"Take it easy, Raggedy Ann. I miss the devil-may-care attitude of Blonde Blair—you're so serious as a redhead. I guess it's true what they say: blondes really do have more fun."

Marco snorted a poorly suppressed laugh.

"Alec," Blair began, "I don't *want* to hit you in the throat as hard as I can. But it's four in the morning—"

"Four-thirty."

"Four-thirty," she corrected herself, "and if shutting you up gets me to sleep a few minutes faster, then I'm not above it."

Sterling cleared his throat. "Guys, that's enough. Let's level the bubbles and see if we've got a viable starting point."

"Thank you," Blair said. "Who's going first?"

Alec answered, "Why don't you take it away, Ginger Spice?"

She raised a fist toward him, and he quickly looked away.

Blair gave a brief outline of her and Marco's plan: the necessity of surveillance cameras outside Byrnside to track Ernie Young's movements, the pickpocketing zone along Park Avenue, and Alec's staging location as he waited for them to deliver the ticket. She was met with no objection from Sterling.

The real surprise came when it was Alec's turn, and Blair could tell from Sterling's look of self-assuredness that they'd come up with something special during the trip from Albany.

Alec began, "Sterling and I—or should I say, Team Sterlec—came up with something based on my inexhaustible knowledge of Wall Street representation in Hollywood. Step one: identify a major trade that Ernie Young has made in the recent past, something big that a lot of cash hinges on. Step two: cause the stock price to crash through some kind of hacking wizardry. Steps three through five: Young gets a legitimate crisis call from work, has to flee Byrnside to reach his office and personally oversee all the after-hours trading required to keep his firm from going under, and I stroll inside and get the tapes from Jim. Step six: Marco pulls the plug on the financial play, and the universe is restored to order by the time the stock exchange opens for business the next morning."

Blair was quiet after that, as was the rest of the crew. Alec looked like he was preparing to receive a standing ovation, while Sterling was watching Marco. "Can it be done?" he asked.

Marco's eyes drifted to the ceiling, a lazy smile playing across his face.

"Normally, I do not get to use my hacking powers for evil. But there are a few options."

"Such as?" Sterling asked.

"Using a botnet attack to distribute fake news on social media and trigger a panic."

"Told you," Alec quipped, and Sterling held up a finger to silence him.

Marco continued, "Typically, that kind of thing is called stock doxing—you short a company's stocks, then use the news to tank their price and profit from it. If properly targeted against the right company, that could create a landslide effect that would be quite easy to reverse after we obtained the tapes. Or we could trigger a market crash by fabricating an enormous volume of sell orders—that ploy wouldn't last for long, but as far as we're concerned, it wouldn't have to."

Sterling began to speak, but Marco wasn't done yet.

"Or a hack, pump, and dump: hacking investor accounts, pumping up the share prices through automated trading, and dumping the shares at inflated prices to Young's firm. That would create a legal crisis that he would have no option but to deal with at the first possible opportunity. Perhaps we do the reverse and short his stocks, then trade to a competitor."

Blair asked, "Anything else?"

"Sure," Marco added. "A DDOS, or distributed denial of

service, could disrupt the firm's entire network. And if I can gain access to the firm's trading algorithms, I could manipulate them to misbehave on cue and make it look like the company is going into a tailspin."

Alec held both arms out to the side, looking to Sterling for validation of his theory.

But Sterling looked skeptical. "If we go this route, how do we prevent financial repercussions to investors?"

Marco rolled his eyes.

"The New York Stock Exchange has protective measures in place. If there is too much of a drop in a twenty-four-hour period, they will stop all trading. And when fraud is uncovered, they immediately reverse all affected trades. Short answer is yes, I think we can come up with something localized that gets Young's attention without causing any permanent damage. The media will probably do what they usually do when these types of attacks occur, and blame the disturbance on Russian hackers."

"I said that," Alec cried triumphantly.

"Which, since it was me, isn't entirely false."

"I said that too!"

"But the option we select must be based on an exhaustive analysis of Ernie Young's firm holdings as well as a full vulnerability assessment. I'm going to need a lot of time plugged in and isolated from Alec to have a chance of getting it done in time."

Sterling nodded.

"You'll have it. Let's all get some sleep, and first thing tomorrow—"

"Today," Blair corrected him.

"—today, we'll get started. Alec, you're shopping for a full Ernie Young wardrobe. Whatever overcoat, dress shirts, ties, suits, and shoes he wears on a regular basis, pick them up.

Then find all the interview footage you can and start working on his voice and mannerisms—unless he's from Boston, that's going to take some work."

Alec replied in an exaggerated New York accent.

"Fuhgeddaboudit, bro. Real talk: I'm mad good at voices, na'mean?"

Blair muttered, "Trying a little too hard."

"Chill out, yooz, or I'm gonna take it there."

"I think two examples are sufficient, Alec."

Sterling interceded. "Me and Blair will take care of placing surveillance cameras."

Straightening in his seat, Marco said, "Before you go, I'll run a scan for traffic and security cameras in the area and pinpoint any blind spots. No need to reinvent the wheel when I can hack CCTV."

"Perfect," Sterling concluded. "Then we can reconvene in the afternoon to refine our plan. Questions?"

79

STERLING

After the crew returned to their rooms, Sterling waited by his door and listened for movement in the hallway. His father's Omega ticked off three minutes without so much as the shuffle of a passerby, and finally Sterling ruled himself safe to move.

He cracked his door open and peered both ways down the empty hallway before slipping outside and easing the door shut behind him.

Sterling jogged down the hallway—each second out here was exposure he didn't need, and the only people who would be awake at this hour were his own crew members, none of whom would be deceived by a disguise. He'd made it halfway to his destination before hearing the telltale *clunk* of a hotel deadbolt coming undone, and Sterling had time to take three quick steps toward the open nook containing vending machines, ducking inside as he cast a quick glance over his shoulder.

That glance revealed Alec backing into the hallway, pulling his door shut and testing the handle.

Now Sterling was trapped in the small vending room

with no way out as Alec's footsteps drew nearer by the second. There wasn't space between the vending machine and the wall to hide, and Sterling cursed himself for not taking the simple precaution of bringing an ice bucket or even cash as a cover—but it was too late, and he stuffed one hand into his pocket before muttering a curse under his breath in the final second before Alec rounded the corner and saw him.

Sterling's face brightened. "Hey, man, can I borrow a couple bucks? Left my cash in the room."

Alec looked from him to the vending machine and then back again.

"What do you want to buy?" he asked.

Sterling turned the question around. "What does it matter?"

"Because you don't eat junk food, that's why."

Touché, Sterling thought. He scanned the vending machine contents, finding a single ray of hope in slot B5 as he tapped the plexiglass with a knuckle.

"Almond Joy."

"Almond Joy?" Alec asked.

"Yeah." Sterling nodded with vigor. "Don't think I've had one since I was a kid, and you wouldn't shut up about them when you found the drawer full during Jimgate. I just thought, why not?"

Alec's eyes narrowed as he regarded Sterling suspiciously. Sterling gave a weak smile, trying to appear casual, and after a beat of silence, Alec shrugged and said, "Excellent choice."

Then he fed two singles into the vending machine, selecting the candy bar before feeding his change and an additional dollar back in for a second one.

He reached inside and recovered the two candy bars, handing one to Sterling.

Accepting the Almond Joy, Sterling said, "Thanks. Have a good night."

Alec blocked his departure from the room.

"What are you doing?" Sterling asked.

Alec pointed his candy bar at Sterling's.

"Go ahead."

"Go ahead and...what?"

Alec's eyes leveled with Sterling's, and he spoke in the tone of a drug dealer testing a new customer to see if he was an undercover narcotics detective.

"You wanted an Almond Joy so bad, go ahead and try it. Let me know what you think."

Sterling swallowed against a dry throat. He never had much of a sweet tooth, and avoided all the processed sugar crap that Alec seemed to live off of. But this was do-or-die time, and he tried to appear nonchalant as he ripped open the blue wrapper and removed one of two small bars inside.

Examining the candy, Sterling was dismayed by the unsightly lumps of almonds beneath the chocolate exterior. The sickly-sweet scent of coconut hit him as he raised the bar to his mouth, locking eyes with Alec.

Then Sterling did the unthinkable—he bit slowly into the bar, breaking it in half and chewing on a grainy dollop of coconut punctuated by the crack of a stale almond.

"Mmm," Sterling mumbled, swallowing the putrid mess and feigning a nod of appreciation. "They're really good. Even better than I remember."

Alec's eyes narrowed further. "That's what I thought."

Turning to leave, he stopped in the doorway and called over his shoulder, "You owe me a dollar fifty. And tell Dana Scully I loved her in *The X-Files*."

And with that final redhead reference, Alec was gone,

retreating to his room as Sterling leaned against the vending machine, letting his head thump off the plexiglass.

He waited for Alec's door to click shut, then tossed the uneaten remains of the bar in his hand into the trash. Sterling was about to throw away the remaining half of the candy bar still in its wrapper, then decided against it. No amount of mouthwash would get the smell of coconut off his breath, and it was too late to do anything but be completely honest.

Sterling finished crossing the hallway and quietly tapped on the door.

It opened a moment later. Blair had ditched the wig, her natural dark hair pulled back in a ponytail.

Sterling entered quickly, holding up the candy. "Want half an Almond Joy?"

"No," she replied, locking the door. "Who would?" Then she stopped abruptly, looking to Sterling with wide eyes. "Wait, you didn't—"

Sterling cut her off. "Alec says he loved you in *The X-Files*."

"Come on, Sterling. You couldn't wait five minutes for him to hit the vending machine?"

"I was afraid you'd fall asleep."

She walked toward the bed. "Though I do have to credit him on the Gillian Anderson reference. Did you know her real hair is brown?"

"I always thought she was a natural blonde," Sterling replied, tossing the candy bar on a side table as he followed her into the room lit by a bedside lamp. The faint scent of shampoo lingered in the air, along with a hint of lavender whose origins he couldn't pinpoint.

Blair stood next to the bed and pointed to the mattress.

"Lie down."

Sterling complied, adjusting the pillow behind his head

and eagerly watching Blair for an indication of where this visit was headed.

But she simply lay down next to him, pushing his arm aside to curl into him and rest her head on his chest. With the sticky taste of the candy bar still lingering in his mouth, Sterling resigned himself to being Blair's personal body pillow, which seemed to be her only interest in him at present.

She asked, "How do you feel about the plan?"

He responded without hesitation. "Not sure yet. We don't have much time, and our crew's model has never been to roll out half-cocked."

"Right," she agreed.

"We've always had a meticulous plan, even if the end result has been us shifting off that plan to achieve results."

"That's true," Blair murmured. "And things never go according to plan."

"Which is why we can't let our guard down."

"Exactly." She yawned. "We're not some gangbangers knocking over the local 7-Eleven."

Sterling smiled at the movie reference from *Heat* as Blair continued, "We'll make it work, Sterling. We always do."

But his grin faded when she said, "I've been having anxiety attacks lately."

He jolted to full alertness. "What?"

Blair shrugged against his side. "I just get this chest tightness, my pulse starts racing. I get this overwhelming feeling of dread and fear."

Sterling felt his heart sink at her words. He'd tried to integrate her into the crew as seamlessly as possible, but the truth remained that she'd come from a career that was not only legal, but grounded in enforcing the law. Sterling had practically been raised as a thief, and yet he'd been dragging Blair into high-stakes heists that pushed his own limits of risk acceptance.

He said, "We've been pushing you too hard. It took us years to get to the level we're at now, and you just jumped into the deep end."

"What's that supposed to mean? You don't think I'm capable?"

"Of course you're capable," he replied, "but that doesn't mean you don't have to pace yourself. You should take a break—we can run things without you for a bit. Just relax, take some time off."

She pushed herself up on an elbow and responded heatedly.

"Sterling. I'm not having anxiety attacks because I can't handle the job. I'm having them because I keep thinking about Jim getting away with this, just like he's gotten away with everything else. He's a bent cop and a near-pathological liar, and everyone's been buying into his story since he joined the FBI. Anytime he runs into trouble, his mentor bails him out. He's like the spoiled rich kid in high school, and he's about to enter the political stage at the national level. It's insane, don't you get that?"

"Of course. I mean—"

"Granted," she said, lying back down, "we're not exactly choir boys ourselves, and I get that. I mean, we're thieves in the purest sense of the word. Not out of desperation, but choice. There's no other job I'd rather be doing, and in the FBI I did the closest legal equivalent in TacOps."

He nodded. "That's true. I'm a little jealous that—"

"And another thing," she said. Sterling smiled in the dim light. Her words were slowing, becoming slurred with the onset of sleep. But she powered through regardless, determined to finish her point. "Yes, we steal. But we've never robbed anyone who couldn't take the loss through insurance if not morally deserving to be robbed altogether. That certainly doesn't make us saints. It *does*, however, make us better than Jim and the people like him. The power-drunk elite, clawing hand over fist for more money, more influence, and for what? They don't even know what they're fighting for. They're just...lost in the effort."

She finally went silent, and Sterling pulled her closer. Never before had he felt so proud, so certain that this woman he'd recruited into the heist crew was worthy of the nomination.

"Babe," he said for the first time, "I love you."

A beat of silence, and he squeezed her again. "I said, I love you."

He looked over when she didn't respond, seeing that her eyes were closed. Reaching for the bedside lamp, he turned it off. The room lapsed into darkness save the city lights filtering through the blinds.

Sterling felt the sudden emotional impulse of romance combined with professional resolve fade from his system as quickly as it had surged through him. He relaxed his grip on Blair, feeling her chest expanding and contracting with shallow breaths as he let out a long, slow sigh.

The sound of his exhale faded into the noise from the heating unit, which soon clattered to a halt as the thermostat regulated it. Sterling stared at the ceiling, listening to the car horns and police sirens trickling through the walls and window, a predator in the noisy urban jungle, until he closed his eyes and fell into a deep, dreamless sleep.

80

BLAIR

Blair shuffled along the sidewalk on Madison Avenue, threading her way between people and overflowing trash cans.

The streets were filled with midday shoppers toting bags from stores like Chanel, Armani, and Jimmy Choo, and every fifth vehicle she passed was a Porsche or Maserati. She'd even spotted a Rolls Royce convertible a few blocks back, her first sight of one since the team's Cullinan had been returned to its rental agency.

The air was close to fifty degrees, which together with a lack of snow felt virtually tropical compared to Albany. And she had to admit there was a certain beauty to the city, a dense conglomeration of people and architecture that LA's sprawl couldn't seem to match. But this was still New York, and the vehicle noise was both constant and aided by a steady stream of blaring horns and screeching brakes that echoed off the buildings. This was, of course, in addition to the constant ambient howl of emergency sirens. On the way from the hotel, she'd seen a fire truck and an ambulance pass each other in opposite directions, but as long as neither was a police car directed at her, Blair was happy with the opportunity to stroll in public.

She carried a large handbag and wore baggy sweatpants and oversized sunglasses, her auburn wig deliberately tousled beneath a black stocking cap. The idea wasn't to draw attention but deter it by looking like a hungover woman. So far, the effort had been successful: in a quarter mile of city walking, Blair hadn't drawn even a sideways glance from the opposite sex, much less a catcall.

Marco's assessment of existing CCTV coverage was instrumental not only in discerning the existing blind spots but also in preventing Blair's face from being filmed as she made her drop. She selected her walking route accordingly, making her way up Madison Avenue while taking care to keep her gaze downward when crossing in front of the camera ranges identified on her phone app.

Passing an Alexander McQueen boutique, she turned right at the corner to follow 65th Street southeast. The foot traffic abated as she left the shops and passed into the shade between buildings, the aroma of steak wafting from a restaurant across the street. After ten feet she paused next to a brick facade, pretending to respond to a text as she waited for a woman walking her dog to pass. Once that occurred, Blair tried to stuff her phone into the handbag, missed, and sent the device clattering to the sidewalk.

She knelt to recover it, dipping a hand inside her bag and peeling an object from its adhesive backing. Pressing the object to the wall, she snatched her phone and rose, glancing at the plant to ensure it had achieved the desired placement.

The exterior casing was an innocuous electric power box painted flat gray and bearing the typical embossed GE logos. It had the universal electrical symbol for danger, sufficient to prevent any unauthorized tampering: a small yellow triangle sticker bearing an exclamation point. Only in the case of this particular unit, the dot in the exclamation point was a tiny lens powered by the box's innards: a battery enabling ninety hours of continuous surveillance, and a camera unit with a 120-degree field of view that broadcast wirelessly in 4K resolution.

Blair put her phone away and resumed walking, nonchalantly glancing up to see if anyone had noticed her camera drop.

The only possible observer was on the opposite sidewalk, a man carelessly strolling along as he texted. He wore a dusty polo shirt and had a tape measure clipped to his belt and a pair of leather work gloves stuffed in his back pocket, with battered kneepads and concrete-stained boots completing the construction-worker image.

It was Sterling.

81

STERLING

Sterling walked past Blair without so much as a sideways glance, keeping his focus instead on the phone screen and its GPS app guiding him into the exact spot he needed to set his camera.

His device was a bit different from Blair's, owing to its destination at the corner. Because this was a much smaller blind spot, he carried an object small enough to stuff in his pocket—with a ninety-degree field of view, his camera didn't require a woman's handbag to transport. None of the existing camera angles would cover Ernie Young's potential approach from Madison Avenue southbound, and that was a disparity he sought to rectify in the next thirty seconds.

Sterling had slowed his pace to ensure he missed the crossing signal, and arrived at the corner to stop beside a black pole supporting the traffic light overhead. Kneeling with his palm cupped, he applied the device's adhesive backing to the north-facing base of the pole.

His left boot had remained untied for the purpose, and after emplacing the camera, he hastily threaded the laces back together as he glanced at his device. The thin block was matched with the same glossy black paint as the pole and virtually indistinguishable from it.

Sterling finished tying his boot and rose abruptly, bumping into a pedestrian who'd stopped at the corner beside him.

"Watch it," the man said, casting his arms aside like he was willing to fight.

Sterling's first glance was made with the fearful expectation that he'd just come face-to-face with an NYPD officer, but the man before him was anything but: in his fifties with a pricey suit and a haircut to match, he was probably on his lunch break from some corporate job that had put a late-model Mercedes outside his Upper East Side townhouse.

"Take it easy, pal," Sterling replied gruffly. "Don't want you to hurt your manicure."

But his blood pressure had spiked, and for good reason—virtually the only way he could be compromised was to be caught in the act, and that had quite possibly just happened.

"What'd you say to me?" the man shot back.

"You heard me. You wanna be late to your power lunch on Madison Avenue, I'd be happy to leave your teeth all over the sidewalk."

The man was momentarily stunned into silence, and Sterling appraised the sidewalk beyond him for any sign of an approaching cop.

But the traffic screeched to a halt with the red light, and in customary New York fashion, Sterling began crossing the street before the walk light turned on.

He shook his head as he walked, glancing around for patrol cars as he waited to be shoved from behind. Making a scene was the last thing he needed, and each blind step forward felt like an agonizing eternity.

He reached the far corner without incident, looking back

to see that the man had turned north while still muttering to himself about the careless construction worker. No sign of outward suspicion, though, and under the circumstances, that was the best outcome Sterling could hope for.

Continuing west to distance himself from the confrontation, Sterling began a roundabout path back to his hotel.

82

BLAIR

Blair heard the soft double knock at Marco's hotel room door and quickly opened it.

Sterling entered, still in his construction attire, and she locked the door behind him.

"How'd it go?" she asked.

He shook his head wearily. "Aside from almost getting in a street fight with some banker-type on Madison Avenue, no issues. How are the feeds looking?"

Marco was seated in front of his computer, flanked by Alec, who was leaning back in his chair, hands behind his head.

Blair and Sterling pulled up chairs next to them as Marco began, "Behold the miracle of surveillance." He reached for his computer mouse and tapped through a series of live camera feeds. Blair saw the view from the camera she'd emplaced, followed by Sterling's, followed by an image of round tables topped with flower vases, interspersed among grand columns rising to a vaulted ceiling with chandeliers.

"Whoa," Blair gasped. "Byrnside has cameras inside the restaurant?"

Marco continued flipping through the feeds. "And at the entrance, so we can pinpoint exactly where Young pockets his ticket. I also found a few security camera views from businesses across the street. We'll have a real-time view of the Secret Service checkpoint, and of course be able to see when Alec makes his dip on Jim—I'm going to record that moment for posterity. Maybe frame the screenshot back at the warehouse."

Sterling said, "Marco, this is incredible work."

But the hacker waved his hand dismissively. "The feeds were barely secured. It took me a half hour to get all this. And we've even got an existing full-color camera angle from the lobby of Ernie Young's firm, which allows us to see what he's wearing before the fundraising dinner. I can see from the security logs of when he badges in and out of the office that he usually puts in twelve- to fourteen-hour days, so it's unlikely that he'll go home to change before heading to Byrnside. That gives Alec plenty of time to dress in advance, and a minimal chance that a last-minute adjustment will be needed."

Sterling looked at Alec. "How's that wardrobe coming along?"

"Easy peasy," Alec replied. "Young wears solid-color suits in navy, charcoal, and medium and light gray, with a combination of peak and notch lapels. Dress shirts in white and various shades of blue, some classic collar but he usually favors an Italian spread. Solid-color ties worn with a Windsor knot, and his dress shoes are usually wingtip Oxfords but he occasionally mixes it up with plain-toe or whole-cut lace-ups."

Blair said, "How did you figure all that out?"

"He didn't," Marco said. "I did."

Blair raised her eyebrows, then realized how.

"Ah," she said, "the lobby camera from his firm..."

Marco nodded. "I correlated his badge-in times with

ninety days of archive footage and handed Alec the screenshots on a silver platter. All he had to do was go buy the stuff."

Alec bristled.

"*And* educate myself on the particulars of men's high fashion, *and* get fitted on a rush order. Plus, I've got my second fitting in"—he pulled back his cuff to check his watch—"an hour and a half."

Sterling's arm shot out. He grabbed Alec's hand, pulling it toward him as he hissed, "What is *that?*"

"Oh," Alec said nonchalantly, "this little guy? Well there's one wardrobe element none of you thought about, but I did: his watch."

When Blair saw the reason for Sterling's utter shock, she gave a gasp of awe.

Alec's wrist bore a glistening dress watch on a navy strap. She leaned over for a closer look, and Alec held it up for her to see.

"It's a Vacheron Constantin Cornes de vache in platinum. Young checks his watch every morning on the way into work, and this is the only one he ever wears. Honestly, I think we can all see why."

Sterling asked, "How much was that?"

Blair could tell by the way Alec breezed around the question that the sum was immense, and he cheerily continued, "The Vacheron boutique had just sold their last model. But, being the industrious little worker bee that I am, I managed to find a used one at a gray dealer in the Diamond District. Looks good on me, doesn't it?"

Sterling repeated, "How much was that?"

Clearing his throat uneasily, Alec muttered, "Oh, about sixty."

"Sixty *thousand?*"

"Well, if you want to round up, closer to seventy."

Blair's jaw fell open.

"What?" Alec asked. "You guys want me going eyeball-to-eyeball with the Secret Service wearing a completely different watch? It's made of metal, they're going to take a close look. Besides, it's a business expense."

Sterling momentarily looked like he was about to cry, though whether because of the cost or sheer unadulterated jealousy, Blair couldn't tell.

He composed himself and said, "I'm going to pretend I didn't just hear that. And for the sake of my sanity and everyone else's—except you, Alec—let's swiftly change the subject. Marco, talk me through the stock play."

"It's called a flash crash," Marco explained. "The major one occurred in 2010, partially due to a single home trader with severe Asperger's who spoofed the system by placing thousands of buy offers and canceling them at the last second. It contributed to a trillion-dollar stock market crash that lasted thirty-six minutes. Of course, there are now measures in place to prevent that, but I was able to scale down the concept specifically to impact Young's firm."

"Explain."

"Basically, a large sell order in equity futures causes an abrupt crash in stock prices. Liquidity vanishes. And the key is e-minis."

Blair said, "Sounds like a breakfast cereal."

Alec shook his head. "I was thinking a friendly Pixar robot. You know, the kind that can only say its own name." Adjusting his voice to a high pitch, he said, "E-mini." He tapped Marco on the shoulder, then pointed to himself and repeated with emphasis, "*E-mini*."

Marco swatted his hand away and continued, "E-minis are electronically traded futures contracts that run 24/7. They track the S&P 500, and represent the ultimate liquidity in US equities, allowing traders to hedge against major swings."

Blair looked to Alec and whispered, "You catch any of that?"

"Not even a little bit," Alec replied. "But he seems confident."

Marco continued, "I'll be hacking into Young's trading accounts to place a massive volume of buy offers, enough to impact stock price. But instead of canceling them, I'll let them proceed—the New York Stock Exchange will block them based on volume, but it will send Young's firm into total chaos."

"Permanent impact?" Sterling asked.

"None. It's so temporary, it will barely exist—the protective measures will put this to a halt within fifteen minutes, maybe twenty. But it will take Young's firm hours to figure out what happened, and there is zero chance that any high-level manager won't be recalled immediately to account for the issue. But there's absolutely no money to be made by doing this. It will very quickly be identified as little more than a malicious cyber attack, and there are no real victims."

Alec adopted a Russian accent and said, "Except for the falsely accused hackers in Mother Russia."

"Right," Marco agreed, "except for them."

83

BLAIR

Blair hurried down the hallway, seeing Sterling exit his room to her front.

He shot her a questioning look, and she shrugged in response without breaking stride as they converged on Marco's room. Apparently he didn't know anything more than she did—the fundraising dinner was set to begin seating in less than an hour, and Marco had just summoned everyone to his room due to a "major problem."

Whatever the issue, they'd both be informed in the next thirty seconds.

Together they walked wordlessly to the end of the hall, where Sterling rapped on the door with a knuckle. Alec let them both inside, closing the door as Sterling addressed Marco at the desk.

"What's going on?"

Marco turned to face them, his expression somber. "Ernie Young is out."

"What do you mean, he's 'out?'"

"He just got indicted on charges of fraud and tax evasion. Maybe he decided to stay out of the spotlight or maybe they pulled his ticket—it doesn't matter for our purposes. He's not going to the fundraising dinner, and the organizers have already given his seat to a lobbyist on the standby list."

Alec was already dressed in a charcoal suit matching the one Young had worn to work that day. Yanking his tie knot apart, he said, "Why can't these Wall Street tycoons just walk the straight and narrow so we can steal in peace?"

"Focus," Sterling said. "Any chance the replacement attendee bears a striking resemblance to one of us?"

Marco shook his head slowly. "Not unless you can gain four inches and a hundred fifty pounds in the next forty-five minutes."

"What about someone else from Young's firm who would be susceptible to the same play?"

"It was just Ernie Young from that firm, and it is far too late for me to set up a stock crisis with any other company. Otherwise I'd be doing it already."

Sterling swung his gaze across the group and asked, "Any ideas?"

Alec put his hands on his hips.

"Without being on the guest list, we can't even get close enough to the entrance to watch Wraith claim his ticket. Sure, we can pick him up on the security cameras, but he's probably just as disguised as we are, and it won't matter much, because once those tapes enter the restaurant, they're gone for good."

"So we walk," Marco said. "With the Secret Service on sight, this entire operation was flirting with disaster from the start. There is no justification to continue."

Silence fell over the group as Blair's heartbeat increased to a fever pitch. Everything had gone so smoothly in planning this, almost too smoothly, and now the world was collapsing around them. They'd barely had a plan to begin with, and even that owed itself purely to luck, which had just run out like grains of sand through an hourglass.

All the time and money they'd wasted, traveling the country and hunting the tapes for the sum total of ending up in position a few blocks from the exchange without being able to do a single thing to stop it. It was maddening; once again, Jim had managed to come out on top.

And yet Blair couldn't accept this defeat—she felt a pulling sensation in her chest, a staunch refusal to concede failure. Here they were, one of the most well-trained and proficient heist crews on the planet. Even the small fraction of equipment they'd been able to pack up in the two Sprinter vans represented a significant arsenal of tools waiting to be leveraged. Only now, they were useless. Wraith's moniker was oddly appropriate in this moment—he was a faceless ghost somewhere among the thousands of faces below, drifting unseen toward the venue to hand off the tapes to Jim.

Finally, Sterling said, "Then we're out. It's time to pack our bags and head back to LA."

Blair, who had been staring vacantly at the floor, looked at Sterling with renewed intensity.

"No. We can still do this."

Alec replied, "Well unless you've been keeping a master plan from us, we just lost the only option we had. So what do you suggest we do?"

"The one thing we can. We know the NYPD has shut down 65th Street between Madison and Park. Dinner attendees can approach from either side of the block, where the Secret Service will be checking tickets and directing guests toward the restaurant. That gives Wraith a possible avenue of approach from two of the busiest streets in the Upper East Side."

Marco lifted his hands and shrugged. "So?"

"So," Blair answered, "we split up our team to cover both streets, and rely on our instincts to spot a fellow thief."

Sterling asked, "You mean pick Wraith out of the crowd? Off instinct?"

"That's exactly what I mean. We find him, and we pickpocket the tapes. Maybe we succeed and maybe we fail, but we don't give up while Wraith is still out there. No technology or equipment will save us now; it's too late for that. Our instincts are all we have left, and we're going to have to trust them."

Sterling drew a long, discontented breath, and Blair quickly added, "I'd be lying if I said this was foolproof. But unless one of you has a better idea, it's the only play we've got left."

"Well," Alec said, "I suppose it's not any dumber than having me impersonate Ernie Young."

"This is true," Marco agreed, looking to Sterling. "It's not a great option, but it is an option, and that's something. Given a staggering lack of alternatives, I'm inclined to agree with Blair."

Blair watched Sterling for a reaction, but his only response was, "We'll need to split up in pairs to cover both streets. One fugitive per side, so if we have to bolt for some reason, there's still a team member in place. You guys want to flip a coin for assignments?"

"No," Marco said. "It's Blair's idea, so she gets to pick her position and partner."

Blair looked at him. "Then I choose you."

He gave a crisp nod. "And what side are we taking?"

She looked at the overhead view of the venue on the computer screen behind Marco, considering Wraith's most likely approach. Central Park was only two blocks west of the restaurant, but there were six blocks of urban sprawl before the river to the east. If she were in Wraith's position, she'd choose the extended concealment of buildings and people to the wide-open spaces of Central Park.

"Park Avenue," she said.

Sterling replied, "Then it's me and Alec on Madison. If anyone spots someone who could be Wraith, pickpocket first and ask questions later. We won't have time to consolidate into a four-man team before he makes it into the venue, so act fast. Questions?"

"We don't have time for questions," Blair said. "Let's go."

84

STERLING

Sterling headed east on 65th Street, passing an NYPD box truck labeled as a mobile command center parked on the curb. The sight elicited an odd pang of concern in his chest, and he kept his eyes forward as he followed the flow of bodies moving away from Central Park as the temperature dropped into the low forties.

The city's transition from daytime to nightlife was in full swing, with residents and tourists taking to the streets for dinner, drinks, or shopping in the Upper East Side. The area was best known for its upscale real estate and cutthroat prep schools, and Sterling had been pleasantly surprised by the beautiful architecture he'd passed. The stone facades to his right were engraved with elaborate flourishes as he passed the Consulate General of Pakistan. A few exceedingly brave bicyclists were taking their chances through the flow of cars as Sterling reached the end of the block, catching his first view of the initial reception point across three lanes of traffic on Madison Avenue.

The far side of the street was closed, blocked off by parked NYPD vehicles and detour signs. He made out two Secret

Service agents at first glance, both flanking a podium where a representative from Byrnside held a tablet with the full guest list. Once a patron gave the correct name, they'd be checked off the list and directed down the otherwise closed sidewalk on the south side of East 65th, where they'd undergo further security screening before being allowed inside.

Sterling had no intention of getting too close to the initial reception point—aside from the visible Secret Service agents, there was no telling how many uniformed agents and police officers were positioned in the surrounding area.

Instead he turned right and followed Madison Avenue south, negotiating the next crosswalk to the east along with a crowd that spilled out into the street a full two seconds before the walk light appeared.

Glancing at a Vacheron Constantin watch boutique on the far corner, Sterling felt a momentary pang of envy that no matter what occurred tonight, Alec was going to walk away from this with a watch fit for a king. He turned away from the boutique, passing a Chanel storefront before stopping in front of a jewelry gallery halfway down the western side of the block containing Byrnside and the MacGregor building. Then he produced his cell phone to receive an imaginary call, holding the phone to his ear and transmitting, "Southwest corner is covered—I'm in position south of Madison and 65th."

Alec replied, "*Northwest is good to go. I'm at the bus stop on Madison.*"

When he didn't immediately hear a response from Blair or Marco, Sterling transmitted, "East side, how are you looking?"

Marco came over the net a moment later.

"*I've got the northeast side, halfway up the block from 65th and Park Avenue.*"

Blair was last to check in, her voice sounding composed as

she casually replied, "*I'm getting into position on the southeast corner now, on Park Avenue just out of sight from the initial reception point.*"

"Copy," Sterling said, glancing at his phone screen to confirm his team's icons on the map before bringing it back to his ear. "Let's clear the net until one of us sees something."

Marco replied, "If *one of us sees something.*"

"Yeah. *If.* Happy hunting, everyone."

Sterling cut his eyes to the sidewalk stretching south, and his first thought upon doing so was that this entire plan was ludicrous.

He'd intended to scan pedestrians for formal attire indicating they could be headed to the fundraising dinner at Byrnside—the problem was, the denizens and even tourists of the Upper East Side weren't exactly known for being destitute. This was the wealthiest neighborhood in New York City, populated by the upper crust and the ultra rich. Even the waiters and doormen were wearing suits, as were the many couples and singletons heading out for a night on the town.

Even if that weren't the case, four people weren't enough to cover all this foot traffic. Wraith could approach from the north or south on both sides of the block, or from the east or west sides down 65th Street. That meant they had only four people covering six possible avenues of approach, hoping on a wing and a prayer that they'd be able to miraculously spot a needle in a haystack before executing a solo pickpocketing attempt based on a lucky guess of which pocket the cargo might be located in. It didn't take a math major to calculate that their odds of success were near zero, and that was before he accounted for the worst part: by the time someone definitively sidelined toward the initial reception point, it was too late to pickpocket them.

But devoid of options, Sterling kept the phone to his ear

and conducted a one-way conversation for the benefit of the passing civilians, periodically checking his watch and gazing at the street as if waiting for a person or car to meet him. The flow of foot traffic continued past him unabated, and he discounted the families with children or solo pedestrians with shopping bags, directing his attention toward the many other possible candidates.

Blair had made everything sound so simple—just use your instincts to spot a fellow thief. What's so hard about that? Except here on the sidewalk, it became painfully apparent to Sterling that he could no sooner see through a Hollywood-grade disguise than anyone else could see through his own, and any thief capable of accomplishing what Wraith had over the past few months wasn't going to risk a visual slip-up.

So Sterling stood in the cold, carrying on his fake cell phone conversation as he scanned the people moving north in the hopes that he could achieve the impossible.

85

BLAIR

After seven minutes in position along Park Avenue, Blair realized that screening for formal dinner attire was a lost cause—nearly everyone was well-dressed, some exceedingly so.

She resorted to her instincts instead, but found them ringing hollow with every pedestrian she examined. Would she even be able to spot a properly disguised professional thief, whether by instinct or otherwise?

Blair wasn't sure, and each passing civilian eroded her confidence further as she scanned for something, anything out of place.

She looked across Park Avenue where a wide, tree-lined median separated three lanes of traffic moving in either direction. Combined with an additional row of parked vehicles on both sides, the street presented a significant obstacle to her view to the east.

Blair looked back to the south, where the foot traffic toward her continued—but for some reason, she found her attention being drawn across Park Avenue, rather than down it.

On one hand, the north-south axis was the most likely means of approach, particularly if Wraith intended to step out of a taxi to minimize exposure. It didn't make sense for him to follow 65th Street in a direct line toward the initial reception point, placing himself in full view of the Secret Service agents on the blockaded section of road.

Regardless, Blair once again found her attention drawn east, and on a whim, she began striding toward the crosswalk.

She transmitted, "I'm displacing across Park Avenue to monitor westbound traffic."

Sterling replied, *"You see something?"*

"No. But this is supposed to be about instinct—I'm trusting mine."

He didn't bother responding, nor did he have to. Blair had done her due diligence in reporting her impromptu shift in surveillance position, and now she approached the uncomfortable juncture of passing directly in front of the agents stationed beside the Byrnside representative. She was in disguise but a fugitive nonetheless, and few things were more disconcerting than placing herself in full view of federal authorities.

Blair noticed that every pedestrian to her front swung their head toward the NYPD cruisers blocking off the street, quizzically examining if not gawking or outright photographing the Secret Service presence. Not wanting to appear out of place, she also glanced at the scene.

The Secret Service agents were discernible at a glance by their unbuttoned overcoats, their suit jackets below likewise left open for drawing a weapon. Aside from that, their only outwardly distinguishable features were a round lapel pin and, she noticed with a rising sense of an epiphany, their shoes.

Neither agent was wearing the typical leather-soled dress

shoe of someone who could afford to live in the Upper East Side. Instead their shoes were slightly bulkier, with rubber soles that provided traction in the event they needed to run; and as the walk light flicked on, she made her way across Park Avenue with the mounting realization that her crew didn't just need to check clothes, they needed to check *shoes*.

No self-respecting thief would approach a mission in footwear that wasn't suited to running, and while Blair's civilian attire lent itself to sneakers, she wasn't trying to get into Byrnside. Matching running shoes with business clothes was no easy task, and she realized their best bet of locating Wraith was by looking for a man with similar footwear.

She was already examining the footwear of pedestrians crossing Park Avenue toward her, and preparing to transmit this revelation to her team, when she spotted the first possible match: a pair of black loafers that stood out among the decidedly more formal footwear around her.

But these weren't men's loafers, and her sudden attention turned to surprise when Blair scanned the beautiful woman wearing them.

She was in her late twenties or early thirties, dark hair cut in a chic bob, a slim-fit trench coat pulled tight over her dress. Nothing about her confident walk was out of place among the wealthy New York elite, and she could have been the trophy wife of a finance mogul or a successful entrepreneur meeting a business partner for cocktails. Blair could envision one explanation as easily as the other, but for reasons unknown to her at that moment, her mind instead flashed back to New Year's Eve in the Bank District of LA.

On her way to steal the tapes from her safe deposit box, Blair was disguised as a utility worker when she collided with a civilian striding out from a gap between buildings. That woman had a long blonde ponytail, skull-and-crossbones earrings, black fingernails, and Converse All Stars; by contrast, the one approaching her on Park Avenue was dressed to the height of fashion, contradicting the blonde in every visual way save one: her skin color was the same dark olive brown, and that combined with a sudden gut instinct told Blair the woman she was looking at was the same one she'd seen in Los Angeles.

And that meant she was Wraith.

Blair's second confirmation came a split second later, when recognition registered in the woman's face—wearing a disguise herself, she was no stranger to changing appearances and seemed to recognize Blair.

The eye contact lasted a fleeting moment before the woman looked down with a soft grin, removed her gloved hands from her coat pockets, and turned to run.

Blair took off in a sprint behind her.

"I've got her," she transmitted, "eastbound on 65th, black trench coat and dress, dark shoulder-length bob cut."

Alec was the first to speak over her earpiece.

"Did you just say 'her?'"

"Yes," Blair panted, "Wraith is a woman."

His response was immediate.

"Is she hot?"

Blair didn't answer, partly out of a desire not to dignify Alec's inquiry with a response and partly because, at present, she desperately needed all the breath she could manage.

Wraith was a true runner, generating smooth, effortless strides that catapulted her forward as she weaved between the onslaught of pedestrians moving in both directions on the sidewalk. It was all Blair could manage to keep the woman in sight as she followed suit, occasionally shoulder-checking a civilian who blundered into her path.

She heard Sterling's voice over the team frequency and

could tell from his tone that he was giving orders to Alec and Marco, but the content was lost amid her surging breath. It didn't matter anyway; Sterling could monitor her location via the phone tracker, and Blair's only purpose in life right now was to keep Wraith in sight.

That job was complicated when Wraith turned right at the corner, darting out of sight as she turned south on Lexington Avenue.

As Blair cleared the final building and cut down the sidewalk, she continued running, trying not to collide with the obstacles in her path—trees, fire hydrants, trash bags piled on the curb, and most of all the people—while trying to locate Wraith.

And when she did, Blair realized how truly fast this woman was.

Wraith was already on the far side of the street, continuing south as she approached the next intersection. Blair sidestepped right to avoid a pedestrian who shouted at her, clipping her knee on a folding menu sign and stumbling for two steps before regaining her forward momentum.

Then she vaulted off the curb and into the street, exploiting a gap between a box truck and a taxi to cross amid the deafening blasts of car horns.

She alighted on the far sidewalk, looking up in time to see Wraith turning left on 64th Street. As Blair followed suit, locating her quarry running westward, she tried to discern where Wraith was headed. The woman was smart, and knew exactly where she was going. She doubtless had some carefully planned fallback position—a waiting car, an alley hideaway, a convoluted route through some underground parking garage—and she was moving there as quickly as possible.

But all Blair saw were the buildings, a sparkling array of towering spires on either side of the street. She passed a row of townhouses, tightly packed brownstones that left Wraith no avenue of escape. When Blair saw the sign for a public parking garage ahead, she was certain that the woman would dart into it, but she continued running toward the four lanes of traffic moving north on 3rd Avenue.

Wraith sprinted into the stream of moving cars with a vengeance, breaking stride only when required to avoid getting T-boned by a vehicle. Blair gained a few seconds when a red convertible refused to brake until the last second, one headlight bumping Wraith's hip before she scrambled past the car. That momentary advantage for Blair was lost when a delivery van refused to stop, *period*, forcing her to hover atop the lane marker until the vehicle had passed.

Then she was across, searching for Wraith and finding her in the middle of an action that Blair didn't fully comprehend.

On the corner was an otherwise insignificant one-story bank building. Wraith ran past its glass entrance, then rounded a Halal food truck parked on the curb. Climbing its bumper to the hood, she clambered onto the truck's roof.

Blair followed, albeit with ever-increasing confusion. There was simply no way Wraith could make the leap from the food truck all the way to the roof of the bank—and a moment later, Blair realized she didn't intend to.

Instead, Wraith vaulted from the truck to a tree branch hovering over the sidewalk, grabbing it with both hands before elegantly throwing a leg over the limb and hoisting herself upright beside the trunk.

Blair had barely made it to the food truck when Wraith pounced from the tree to the bank roof, catching the edge with her feet braced against the side. Then she pulled herself over the roof and vanished.

While Blair's worst fear was heights—even short ones— this was do-or-die time, and she had no choice but to mimic

Wraith's maneuvers as quickly as she could. She planted a foot on the food truck bumper, then scrambled atop the short hood before reaching over a sloping windshield to grasp the vehicle's roof.

Then she heaved herself upward, pouncing atop the flimsy vehicle roof and moving to the edge nearest the tree.

Locating the branch, Blair flung herself in a flying leap over the sidewalk.

Blair's negotiation of the tree was considerably less nimble than Wraith's—she managed to catch the branch, but swung in an awkward pendulum while raking one foot against the trunk below her before managing to pull herself up.

There was a moment of dizziness as she hovered over a leg-breaking fall to the sidewalk, forcing her eyes up to the bank roof. Steeling herself with a quick breath, she leapt once more.

Blair soared over the sidewalk with her arms outstretched, impacting with a grunt of pain as she caught the edge of the roof with both armpits. At that point, she realized that Wraith could be waiting for exactly this vulnerable moment, standing out of sight until the opportunity presented itself to deliver a well-timed kick to Blair's face to end the pursuit.

But her first glance over the edge revealed nothing of the sort—Wraith was running between the blocks of heating and cooling units on the long rooftop.

Blair swung a leg sideways and hooked it over the edge of the roof, straining to pull herself atop it and launching herself forward into a stumbling run.

Half of the bank roof appeared to be cordoned off by waist-high plastic netting, supported by temporary signposts at regular intervals. Wraith placed a hand on a signpost and vaulted the net, clearing the obstacle but knocking over the post in the process.

Blair aimed for the downed section of netting—every second counted, and if she could gain even a few feet of ground by not having to vault an erect section of netting, so much the better. She wasn't immediately concerned about the adjoining building rising forty-eight stories into the night sky; after all, Wraith was a master thief, not Spiderman, and she had a tangible escape in mind.

Instead, her attention was drawn to the signpost that Wraith had knocked over, and Blair got a decent-enough look in the ambient light as she hurdled it.

The sign was attached to a small orange post, and had a black-and-red *DANGER* icon above the text *SCAFFOLDING IN PROGRESS*.

That was when Blair felt the fear overcoming her adrenaline, every horrid suspicion confirmed when she looked upward to see that the bank roof ended in construction scaffolding, the metal framework layered in a stack that ascended as far as she could see up the side of the adjoining skyscraper.

Blair's fear of heights had begun in childhood and mounted to a legendary status in her mind—she'd never managed to overcome it, and ordinarily the chances of voluntarily climbing anything more than a ladder were nonexistent.

Wraith appeared to have no such reservations, mounting the scaffolding at some carefully predetermined point and scampering upward on the horizontal bars.

Blair continued running with an inward contradiction, the shimmering hope of denial in that she couldn't possibly be seeing what she was seeing. Wraith had no reason to be trying to escape *up* rather than away, and yet here she was, clambering hand over foot up the scaffolding with an eerie precision.

Then Blair reached the scaffolding's ground mounts, coming eye-to-eye with the first set of horizontal bars before looking up to see Wraith continuing to ascend. Her chest tightened and her palms grew hot despite the cold, her thoughts shuddering with the realization that she had to start climbing this instant or lose the tapes forever.

What welled up inside her then wasn't anger at the thief she pursued, because Wraith was almost a bit player in this drama. Instead, Blair felt an insurmountable anger toward Jim, the man who'd manipulated everyone around him, who'd stood silently by when she'd gone to jail without incriminating him, who'd taunted Sterling at Supermax with threats against his mother. Jim had built a castle of lies he now presided over, and with every step Wraith took away from her, that foundation was strengthened.

So Blair began to climb, grasping the first freezing metal pipe and then reaching for the next, pulling herself upward to gain foot purchase atop the framework. Then she repeated the process, successfully trading handholds for footholds as she forced herself to breathe.

The bars rocked slightly in her grasp, emitting a light metallic clanging that mirrored the sound of Wraith continuing to gain height above her. Each bar was close to three inches in diameter, larger than a pull-up bar and spaced far enough apart to remind her that this was no ladder.

She had started the climb shakily but soon gained speed and efficiency, suppressing her fear by immersing herself in her rage toward Jim. She thought of the endless nights in solitary confinement, of Sterling's arrest, of Jim's gloating speech while she and Sterling hid in his mother's house, powerless to intervene.

The fear of falling was still simmering beneath the surface, and she very quickly reached the point where a slip would be fatal. Rather than resist the prospect of death, Blair surrendered to it; she fully acknowledged that this effort could cost her life, but she proceeded regardless. Better to try and fail than watch her final chance to take down Jim slip through her fingertips, she reasoned, and at this point no one else on her crew could accomplish this but her.

Wraith continued to climb, enjoying a lead of twenty feet or so. Blair's palms were slick with sweat, greasing the icy pipes with each handhold as her fingers grew numb. She had no idea how high Wraith planned to ascend, only that no matter the height, Blair would follow. It wasn't an easy gambit —heights aside, she was leaving a steady trail of fingerprints, and someone was calling the cops this second if they hadn't already. Her only path of escape was now the same as Wraith's, the difference being only one of the thieves knew what that escape entailed. And it wasn't Blair.

Then, Blair made the mistake of looking down.

At first she was checking the location for her next footfall, and then the dizzying height she'd attained became apparent as the bank roof and street below swirled in her vision, seeming to rise up as if she were falling already.

She froze, clutching the bars with such force that her arm muscles quickly grew fatigued. The fear was too overwhelming for her to function, so Blair resolved to narrow her world to the horizontal axis, focusing her attention on the bars in front of her as she resumed climbing, transitioning her grip hand over hand in the desperate pursuit of Wraith.

86

STERLING

Sterling reached the corner of 64th Street and Third Avenue and reached for his phone, trying to determine Blair's position.

Marco was a block north and Alec was still heading east, all three men having run as fast as possible in the hopes of supporting their teammate in recovering the tapes. But Blair hadn't made radio contact since, and now Sterling checked his phone display, trying to reconcile the tracker reading with his current position.

He could see her dot icon hovering over a structure, but which one was unclear—there was a one-story bank across the street from him, but it adjoined a high-rise building and Blair seemed to be located between the two. Then he heard the excited murmuring of pedestrians on the sidewalk, and looked over to see that a crowd had formed, all staring upward at some single point, their expressions fixed in awe.

Sterling followed their gaze up the side of the high rise across from him, which was covered in a zigzagging framework of construction scaffolding—and then he saw something that defied comprehension.

A tiny figure was free-climbing up the side, lit by the building windows and located perhaps twenty stories off the ground.

And a few stories below that, a second figure was making determined progress upward—and that person, he knew, could only be Blair.

Sterling was rocked by the sight. Blair's fear of heights was crippling; for her to be overcoming it now reflected a scope of determination beyond anything he'd yet witnessed from her.

He transmitted, "I've got eyes-on. Blair is pursuing Wraith up the construction scaffolding, so they're either headed to the roof or going to enter through a window. We need to picket the block and wait for Blair's word. I'll take the south side; Marco, go north; and Alec, move to the far east side of the block."

Marco replied, "Got it."

Alec's response had considerably less brevity.

"Maybe my radio's malfunctioning, but it sounded like you said Blair was pursuing Wraith UP the scaffolding. Do I have that right? You sure this is our Blair?"

"I'm sure," Sterling replied. "She's about two hundred feet off the ground and I don't know whether to have a heart attack or get my vision checked."

"Just making sure. On the way."

Then Sterling whispered, "Be safe, Blair," and began moving toward his position.

87

BLAIR

Blair pulled herself up another rung of the scaffolding, coming face-to-face with a spectator behind the lit window to her front. It was an eight-year-old boy in his pajamas, eyes wide as he waved at her. She returned the wave with one hand, then continued to climb.

Each glimpse through windows with open blinds made her question exactly what type of building she was ascending. The interiors were too large to be hotel rooms but too uniform in decoration to be apartments, and each lit window seemed to reveal a luxury suite. Gradually Blair concluded that this was some kind of extended-stay hotel, and that her quarry had probably rented one or more units for such an emergency escape.

What she still didn't know was why Wraith had chosen this building for her escape. It stood to reason that she was going to enter a room arranged for the purpose. But as for why that room would be located so high off the ground, Blair had no idea. At this point it didn't matter; Blair was fully committed, so desperately entrenched in this chase that to lose sight of Wraith was to condemn herself to a panicked flight from the authorities who were surely converging around the building at this very second.

Blair tilted her gaze upward to find that looking up was almost as bad as looking down—a vertigo-inducing sheet of scaffolding and glass seemed to rise endlessly into the blackness. But there was simply no other way to know when Wraith departed the scaffolding for the building interior: even the clanging sounds of her climbing were drowned out by the noises of traffic and freezing gusts of wind that had been growing in strength the higher Blair ascended.

Then Wraith stopped climbing, tucking herself into the scaffolding as Blair continued her climb, trying to see what was occurring above her.

But all she could make out through the framework of metal bars was Wraith's shadow sliding open an unlocked window and pulling herself inside before closing the glass behind her.

Blair felt a surge of energy at the confirmation of a finish line to this seemingly endless climb, and she focused every effort on reaching it as quickly as possible. Whether Wraith would wait in ambush was a question that would only be answered upon Blair's arrival at the window.

After pulling herself up the final few stories of scaffolding, Blair finally came level with the window and saw that the room inside was a sitting area with a loveseat and chairs surrounding a coffee table. Beyond that she could see a kitchen island and the suite's main entrance.

To Blair's surprise, the main door was still in the process of swinging shut, despite Wraith's head start, and Blair could only assume that the delay was to don new clothes or otherwise change her appearance.

Great, Blair thought, now I have to spot her all over again.

But she wouldn't have the luxury of worrying about it until

she got inside, which became considerably more daunting when she tried to open the window and found it locked from the inside.

Blair slammed the heel of her hand against the glass in frustration. There were myriad ways in which a thief could open this type of window, but Blair didn't have the equipment or the time to turn this into a delicate operation. This was tempered glass, and she could have shattered it using the proper handheld tool if she had one—which, of course, she didn't.

But she hadn't come all this way just to give up, and Blair resorted to examining the scaffolding in a hasty search for anything that could help her.

She grasped a horizontal bar of scaffolding and tried to shake it loose, only to find that it was part of a fixed segment. So she turned her attention to a diagonal brace instead, finding the nearest attachment point to be a claw hook held in place by a small lever. Blair pulled the lever open on one end of the bar, then the other, and hoisted it upward, feeling it come free in her grasp.

Then she maneuvered the bar horizontally until it was over her shoulder like a javelin, the far end braced atop a horizontal pole behind her. Facing the window with both hands gripping the bar, she prepared for her first strike.

Contrary to popular belief, the most vulnerable part of the glass wasn't the center but the edges closest to the frame. Blair aimed the claw hook at the bottom left corner of the window, then thrust the bar forward as hard as she could.

The claw hook bounced back so hard that Blair almost lost her numb grip, leaving the glass still intact.

Clamping her hands into a death grip on the bar, Blair steadied herself and then rammed the claw hook into the window again, this time with a deeper thud that still didn't succeed in cracking the glass. She repeated the move again, then again, achieving a steady cadence of strikes with the bar scraping across the scaffolding behind her.

Blair's hands were stinging with the effort, but the sixth impact elicited a dull *pop* from the glass as a fist-sized spider web fracture appeared at the corner. Homing in on this new bullseye, Blair continued slamming the bar with savage ferocity, her next trio of strikes causing the cracks to multiply and snake further until the entire window was whitewashed with fractured glass.

Finally the claw hook plunged through, bursting past the window and into the suite. Blair slid the bar halfway inside, then braced it against the bottom of the window frame to turn the metal pole into a massive lever.

Turning her head away and closing her eyes, Blair pushed down on her end of the bar with all the bodyweight she could apply.

The bar arced vertically through the window, sending a spray of glass shards soaring outward to clatter against the scaffolding around her. Blair adjusted her footing and raked the bar across the window frame, clearing out the razor-sharp fragments that extended like icicles from all sides.

Then she dropped the bar and climbed inside, clambering over a chair covered in glass particles to enter the suite. The heated space was a welcome reprieve from the cold as she made a beeline for the main door. She briefly considered how embarrassing it would be if Wraith was either still in the suite or had staged an accomplice to take Blair out of the pursuit.

Still, she had no good options other than darting to the door and flinging it open before bursting out of the suite and into an empty hallway. Blair saw a dead end in one direction before taking off to the opposite side at a run. Turning the corner, she saw no sign of Wraith but continued running, feverishly searching for any clue to the next leg of the thief's escape plan. Wraith was sharp and she'd picked this floor of the hotel at great inconvenience for a reason—what was it?

Locating a wall-mounted sign, Blair got her answer.

The first two lines of text indicated the direction of room number segments. But the third line held a more definitive answer along with an arrow pointing forward: *ROOFTOP DECK AND POOL.*

Blair kept running, intuitively knowing that to be the answer to Wraith's otherwise inexplicable escape-by-ascent. Since she hadn't climbed the scaffolding all the way to the building's summit, this place must have had an intermediate roof atop a side wing. Based on the complexity of Wraith's escape so far, Blair guessed that the roof would lead to another elaborate leg of the journey—very likely where she'd disappear for good.

She forced her way through the door leading to the rooftop deck, where a cold breeze gusted over her. The roof corner to her front was taken up by covered seating areas, each empty in the wintry night temperatures.

To her left, rows of reclining outdoor lounge chairs were spread out before a glass-enclosed pool stretching across the length of the roof. The pool was occupied by a number of families with small children, splashing contentedly and completely unaware of Blair's presence beyond the steam-coated glass walls.

Searching the roof for any sign of Wraith, Blair spotted a single figure jogging toward the far side, dressed in construction attire complete with vest and hardhat.

Blair broke into the fastest sprint of her life, driving her legs with the maximum possible speed until she was only fifteen feet away. Wraith looked over her shoulder, momentarily dumbstruck by the sight of another thief charging toward her.

Wraith tried to sidestep the attack, but by then it was too late—Blair closed the remaining distance in three sprinting footfalls before diving forward and tackling Wraith to the ground.

The two women crashed into the concrete floor, their cries intermingled as they grunted with the impact.

Wraith's hardhat flew off her head and clattered across the ground, but her recovery from the attack was remarkably fast. In the time it took Blair to try and exploit her top position to pin Wraith to the ground, the woman was already writhing onto her back and slipping an arm over Blair's shoulder. She pulled Blair in tight, sliding away on the opposite side and planting a foot on Blair's hip.

Then Wraith extended her leg, forcing Blair's hip away before bringing her leg over the shoulder, pinning her knee against Blair's throat. The entire process had taken place in perhaps two seconds and before Blair could react—Wraith locking her ankles together behind Blair's head, applying immense force that cut off the supply of blood to her brain.

Blair couldn't breathe, could barely think, as Wraith held the position until the inevitable blackout. With only a partial lungful of air and her pulse hammering from the climb and the chase, Blair did the only thing she could against a well-trained opponent who'd anticipate Blair's every move. It was the same technique she'd applied to breaching the window minutes earlier: a ragged, desperate display of brute force.

Blair clutched at Wraith's clothes however she could, pulling the woman in tight before rocking back on her hips with all the force she could muster.

The effort in no way broke the chokehold on her throat, but it did succeed in lifting Wraith's back perhaps two feet off the ground, and Blair exploited that distance by falling forward as hard as she could.

Wraith gave a yelp as her spine slammed into the concrete, but she held tight with her legs locked around Blair's side and throat. Blair repeated the movement, rocking back to lift the woman off the ground and slamming her downward at maximum force.

The impact caused Wraith's legs to go weak for a split second, but she adjusted them and applied the choke as tightly as before. With seconds remaining until blackout, Blair rocked back, tapping into her body's final survival instinct to lift Wraith as high off the ground as she could, pulling both torsos vertical before plunging forward again.

This time Wraith's back struck the ground with such force that the air was expelled from her lungs in a wheezing, shrieking gasp, and Blair felt the pressure on her throat release.

She squirmed backward and out of the choke, buying herself a moment of reprieve as she cleared her lungs and inhaled, trying to scramble upright before Wraith could get the upper hand.

It was too late—the woman recovered from the repeated blows to her spine almost immediately, leaping up and approaching Blair with both fists raised.

Blair threw the first punch, a blow that Wraith not only ducked with ease but exploited by wrapping one arm over Blair's shoulder and the other around her back. There was a brief scuffle as each woman tried to achieve the upper hand, but Wraith managed to plant her leg behind Blair's, forcing her off balance before driving one foot off the ground.

Blair felt herself whipping sideways, legs askew as Wraith threw her down with ruthless efficiency. Now it was Blair's back slamming into the cold concrete of the roof, an impact that sent a shockwave through her entire body.

Then Wraith was atop her, straddling her torso with her knees tight against Blair's ribs, driving a flurry of head strikes that Blair fended off with both hands. It was no use—Wraith was an experienced fighter, and Blair had no hope of defeating her in hand-to-hand combat.

So she didn't try.

Instead, Blair resisted with one hand while sliding the other inside Wraith's open construction vest, probing with her fingertips to see if she could find the tapes.

Wraith suddenly stopped throwing blows, and Blair thought she'd been caught in her pickpocketing attempt. But instead, Wraith leaned in and hissed in a foreign accent that Blair couldn't place at the moment.

"I don't want to hurt you." She lowered her voice. "But I will if I have to."

Blair stopped resisting then, and held both palms open.

"You win," she gasped. "I give up."

The weight was gone as Wraith stood, took a step back, and then raced to the far side of the roof to continue her escape.

Feverishly pulling out her phone, Blair scanned for the nearest icon and saw Sterling somewhere just off the roof's southernmost edge. She struggled to her feet, preparing to make her radio call when the sounds of Wraith's footfalls stopped abruptly. Blair looked over to see the thief patting down her pockets, then whirling around with furious eyes that latched onto the package of cassette tapes clutched in Blair's hand.

And then the thief charged toward her with such speed that Blair would never be able to outrun the fight.

Instead, she turned to the roof's southern edge, took three

darting steps, and transmitted, "Sterling, incoming!" before hurling the tapes as far as she could.

The package had barely left her hand before she turned to receive Wraith, whose shoulder struck Blair's chest as she sidestepped, then grasped Wraith's shirt and flung her sideways.

Blair reeled but managed to catch herself by planting a foot down hard, and then she spun to fend off the next attack.

To her horror, she saw that the reflexive effort succeeded in redirecting Wraith's momentum in the worst possible direction—the thief stumbled forward, impacted the rail at the edge of the roof, and flipped over the side.

88

STERLING

Sterling was jogging along the building's southern boundary, checking his phone as he tried to align himself with Blair's icon. He had no way of knowing what floor she was on, which made his confusion all the greater upon hearing her radio transmission.

"Sterling, incoming!"

He looked up, expecting to see an open window along the side of the building, but instead, he saw an object falling.

From this distance it was little more than a pinpoint of darkness, spinning and reflecting ambient light as it descended toward him. Whether it was the tapes or a piece of debris, he couldn't tell, but Sterling took off at a sprint, trying to intercept the object in the desperate hope that Blair had prevailed.

The object arced toward the ground, and he lost sight of it when it crashed into a treetop. Sterling continued running at full tilt, hearing the object snapping through leaves and bouncing off branches above him. He tried to orient himself by the sound of its fall, tracking the noise until he stopped beside the tree trunk with both arms outstretched, scanning for any sign of it.

A dark shape appeared out of the branches like an acorn falling from the tree, and Sterling took a final lunging leap to intercept it.

The object struck his hands so hard that his palms stung with pain, and as he staggered to a brief halt, he looked down to see that he was holding a stack of four microcassettes wrapped together by clear tape.

He felt a mix of exhilaration and disbelief, both emotions fading to fear as he stepped out from under the tree and looked up at the building.

Below the summit of the high rise was an intermediate roof fenced in by a short rail, and hanging from that rail was a tiny figure, holding on with one hand.

Sterling was momentarily paralyzed with fear—he first thought it was Blair, and the haunting powerlessness at being unable to help her was almost crippling. He focused on the figure, able to tell even at this distance that it was wearing a reflective construction vest. That must have been Wraith, and if she didn't find a way to climb back up she was going to fall two hundred feet to her death.

Sterling had no time to watch—the wail of police sirens approached, red and blue lights flickering off buildings on East 64th Street. If he didn't get those tapes to safety, they were going to be captured along with him.

So Sterling ran, negotiating the sidewalk until the first gap between buildings appeared to his left.

89

BLAIR

Blair ran to the edge of the rail, looking over with the fearful expectation that Wraith had fallen.

Looking down, she saw that wasn't the case—though the moment was fast approaching.

Wraith had managed to grab hold of the lowest bar on the rail, supporting her full body weight with her left hand. The effort appeared to have injured her wrist, and Blair saw in the woman's fearful expression that she wasn't going to be able to hold on much longer.

In that second, Blair forgot about the tapes completely. Nothing was worth the loss of life, and if Blair didn't act now, that was about to occur. There was nothing in the world she wanted less in that moment than to expose herself to another horrific fall, but Wraith was barely holding on, and Blair had no choice.

She quickly vaulted the railing, planting both feet beside Wraith's hand and grabbing the lowest rail beam to squat down.

Then she reached her free arm downward, and Wraith swung her open hand to clasp Blair's as the sound of police sirens radiated up from the street. Blair ignored them; cops were the least of her worries. She and Wraith were both in a precarious situation—if either woman lost their grip on the rail, they'd both fall.

Gripping Wraith's hand, Blair slowly rose to a crouch, leveraging the effort with her opposite hand on the rail. The effort caused her hamstrings to burn, but Wraith held fast, and as Blair lifted Wraith upward, the woman was able to swing a leg atop the roof, her foot gaining purchase at the edge and distributing her weight.

Blair stood then, hoisting Wraith's arm upward as the thief assisted with her leg, abandoning her grip on the rail to wrap her injured forearm around the bar. Then she released Blair's hand, taking hold of the rail and pulling herself upright with Blair's assistance.

Both women struggled over the rail, and Blair had never felt so immensely reassured as when the concrete roof supported her weight. She wanted to kneel down and kiss the ground in infinite gratitude, but the red and blue whirl of police lights reflecting off the buildings below were a reminder that time wasn't on her side.

Equally discomforting was Wraith's smoldering glare. The woman was standing three feet away, holding her left wrist and looking at Blair like she was about to attack again.

This time when she spoke, Blair deemed her accent to be Israeli. And while what she said was, "Thank you for saving me," her tone sounded more like, *I'm about to kill you for taking the tapes.*

"You're welcome," Blair replied.

Then Wraith said, "Now leave me alone."

She was turning to leave, but Blair stopped her with a final plea.

"Your wrist is injured." She glanced over the side of the

building toward the police cars below and added, "I'll help you through your route, and you let me escape with you. After that, we can part ways. This is over—neither of us has to go to jail."

Wraith paused for a moment, glancing down at her wrist before speaking again.

"This way."

Blair followed the woman to the far side of the roof, noting that the occupants of the glass-enclosed pool on the roof beside them were no longer oblivious to the two thieves: spectators were lined up in their swimsuits, peering through the steamy windows without making any effort to intervene.

Wraith didn't seem to notice, or care. Instead she recovered her fallen hardhat, then jogged past the lounge chairs toward a cluster of covered seating areas. She turned left, negotiating a waist-high wall into a utility area with a maze of humming air conditioning and heat pump units.

The two women threaded their way between the rumbling units, emerging at the eastern side of the roof where Blair looked over the edge to see that Wraith's current disguise now made sense: perhaps ten stories down was the rooftop of another adjoining building, this one beside a fenced-off construction site. Then Wraith stopped before a pre-staged setup that made Blair's stomach uncomfortably queasy: there was a thick climbing rope attached to a tie-down point on the roof, its remaining length neatly coiled.

Wraith turned to Blair and gestured to her left wrist.

"Well," she said, "what are you waiting for? Throw the rope over. We have to climb down."

90

STERLING

Sterling discreetly removed his earpiece and radio, depositing them into a sidewalk trash can without breaking stride. He placed his hands in his pockets and continued walking down 2nd Avenue, keeping his head down, just another New Yorker traversing the streets and acting casual—but in reality, Sterling had rarely been so worried.

The streets surrounding the building that Blair and Wraith had entered were now a maelstrom of police response, and Sterling had only managed to make it out by ducking a flurry of plainclothes officers running there on foot. With presidential attendance at Byrnside just a few blocks away, everyone was on high alert and Blair's spectacle on the scaffolding had generated a firestorm.

As a fugitive, Sterling's first and foremost goal now was to gain as much distance as possible from the area. His greatest concern was a stop-and-frisk, a concern looming sufficiently large for him to have ditched his radio for fear of it being discovered. In another block he'd draw his phone, check on his team's positions, and text the code for everyone to switch to the alternate frequency as a precaution in the event his radio was discovered in the trash.

But for now, he just needed to get farther away.

His escape was complicated by the sight of two men coming down the sidewalk toward him. One looked like a linebacker with a ballcap and ear warmer, the other a slightly smaller linebacker with a watch cap. They wore dark jackets and jeans, their strides matching one another to the footfall. Sterling knew they weren't civilians, but beyond that they could have been anyone: NYPD, FBI, Secret Service, or even members of Wraith's crew.

But Sterling's instincts told him these were cowboys, off-duty cops for hire by whoever was willing to pay for the service.

And while he was prepared to throw the first punch the instant they recognized him, he had little chance of taking down both. His disguise was good—hair length, facial hair, eye color had all been altered from his mug shot, and the glasses provided a finishing touch in addition to his hipster wardrobe. But nothing could hold up to the close scrutiny of someone looking for him, and with Jim and his mentor running the show, that was almost certainly occurring.

Sterling glanced at his surroundings, looking for an out within the normal flow of people, but there were no side streets between him and these men, no shops he could casually duck inside. His judgment call now was whether to run, or continue as if he'd done nothing wrong. Cops had to watch untold numbers of civilians pass them every day, looking for anything out of the ordinary. If Sterling bolted, he'd ignite an instant predatory response; if he played the part of a normal pedestrian minding his own business, there was at least a chance they'd let him by.

So Sterling continued walking, and regretted the decision a moment later.

"You, stop. Police."

The smaller man stepped in front of him to block his path.

Sterling said in a New York accent, "What's your problem?"

The larger man pushed Sterling's back against the wall and immediately started frisking him.

"What is this?" Sterling shouted for the benefit of every bystander on the sidewalk. "I've done nothing wrong. Where are your badges?"

But the pat-down continued, the man ignoring Sterling's wallet and phone. This confirmed his worst suspicions—these men were clearly cowboys looking for the tapes.

Sterling raised his voice even louder, calling out to the pedestrians around him.

"I'm being detained against my will! My civil rights are being violated!"

Out came a few cell phones, the first reluctant bystanders beginning to film—but these men were undaunted, continuing to pat him down for the tapes.

Their search was coming to an end as the larger man swept his hands down Sterling's legs, reaching his ankles without result.

Then he rose and said to his partner, "He's clean."

"Have a good night," the other man said.

And then they were gone, sweeping up the sidewalk on their way toward the scaffolded building.

The bystanders quickly lost interest, putting their phones away and continuing on with their night. Sterling turned to watch the two men, knowing he should leave immediately but needing to see if they'd noticed his actions prior to being stopped.

The men strolled past the trash can containing his radio

and earpiece without so much as a glance inside. Sterling then watched them hurriedly pass the next object on the sidewalk, this one located at the street corner: a blue-painted post office collection box.

Smiling to himself, Sterling turned and continued into the night.

91

BLAIR

After a night of ludicrous events, Blair found herself in the most surreal position of all—the passenger seat of a car, with Wraith at the wheel.

The woman's escape, Blair had to admit, was pretty ingenious.

After sliding down the rope to the construction site—a descent that both women made while using their feet as a braking mechanism, Wraith more so due to her sprained wrist—she'd led Blair to another clothing cache where she swapped her construction garb for a hoodie and a Yankees cap, throwing the excess in a backpack and strolling into an adjacent apartment building using a fully functioning keycard.

Then they'd made their way to the underground parking garage, where a Honda Civic hatchback with New York tags and a building parking permit was waiting.

And then Wraith had driven away like any other apartment occupant, making her way to 1st Avenue and then heading north. Throughout the process, the two women had barely spoken a word; instead, both prioritized monitoring the police scanner now piping through the car speakers, ensuring they weren't the subjects of an APB that would require a drastic departure from their getaway-in-progress. Their only other concern was replenishing themselves with water bottles from the center console, one of which Wraith had offered Blair.

Bottled water had never tasted so good—Blair's lungs were still raw from the icy night air, and she downed the bottle in record time as Wraith did the same. The moment her thirst was quenched for the time being, Blair's attention turned to the pit of her stomach, which was howling for sustenance. But that was one area Wraith seemingly hadn't prepared for, which made the sight of the street ahead even more enticing.

Wraith piloted the Honda Civic down a row of bars and restaurants, steering with her right hand as she searched for an open parking spot. Upon finding one, she parallel parked with ease despite the fact that less than a foot remained between cars to her front and rear.

Putting the vehicle in park, she said, "This is your stop. Four hours until closing time and the bars will be packed until then. You can arrange transportation from here?"

"Maybe," Blair replied, transmitting into her radio. "Need pickup at my current location."

No one responded—at least, not verbally.

Instead, she heard someone key the mic five times in rapid succession.

Blair squinted in confusion—someone was signaling her to flip to the team's emergency frequency, which meant that someone had either lost a radio or been arrested. And while that explained the notable absence of radio chatter, it meant something had likely gone terribly wrong. She manually changed to a designated frequency, then transmitted, "I'm up on this freq. What happened?"

This time Alec answered.

"Sterling had to ditch his radio, but tapes are safe and we're all moving to linkup. Are you okay?"

"I'm fine, just need pickup."

A pause as Alec checked her location. *"We'll collect Sterling and be on the way. Going to take us at least fifteen, maybe twenty minutes."*

"Take your time." Then, to Wraith, she said, "They'll be here in fifteen or twenty."

"Good," Wraith said, waiting for Blair to open her door. When that didn't occur, she raised her eyebrows. "You can go now."

Blair found herself nodding but felt a deep resistance to stepping out of the car, never to see Wraith again. She reached for the door handle, then looked out the windshield at an all-night pizza place in front of them and asked, "You hungry?"

Wraith's stare intensified, then relaxed as her shoulders sagged. "Starving."

"I'll buy you a slice, okay?"

A beat of silence followed.

"Sure. I will wait in the car."

"Okay." Blair opened the door hesitantly and exited into the frigid night air. Her limbs felt stiff, the effort of walking a mild challenge after the exhausting race to pursue Wraith. She glanced over her shoulder as she entered the slice joint, seeing that the Honda was still parked with its engine running. When Blair emerged with two paper plates holding greasy wedges of NYC pizza, she half-expected the car to be gone, but it remained idling in its parking spot, and Blair re-entered to find Wraith warily eyeing the pizza.

"Pepperoni or cheese?" Blair asked, proffering both plates.

Wraith took the plate with the slice of cheese and said, "Thanks for the save back there."

"Likewise with the escape," Blair said. "You know, you aren't so bad at this."

"Neither are you."

Both women took their first bite of pizza, chewing in silence before Blair asked, "How many in your crew?"

Wraith swallowed. "You're looking at it."

"Really? You work alone?"

The woman gave a brief nod, taking another bite and speaking as she chewed.

"You know, New York pizza is good. Maybe the best. But just the same...I was really looking forward to dinner at Byrnside."

Blair gave a short laugh.

"With Jim's money, you can afford their takeout. Easier that way."

Wraith watched her closely, then offered, "I thought you'd try to extort me for his payment."

"Keep it—you've earned it. We were after the tapes. Though I do have to ask...how did you find them in the first place?"

"Data analysis is a specialty of mine. The fake identity you used to secure the safe deposit box was good, but not *that* good."

"Did you make copies?"

Wraith shook her head. "I'm many things, but not a liar. I stole the tapes from you, and you stole them back...unless you had duplicates, you've got the only copy."

"If we had duplicates," Blair said, "we wouldn't have spent the last three weeks chasing you across the country. And on behalf of our safecracker, how did you get into the LA bank vault?"

Wraith set her remaining pizza on the grease-soaked plate and held up her right hand, wiggling the fingers. "By touch. How did you?"

"Auto dialer."

Lifting her slice again, Wraith said, "That's the smart way. But when you work alone, you have to do what you can."

"By touch, though...that's impressive."

She shrugged and took another bite, speaking with her mouth half full of pizza.

"It was an old vault." Swallowing, she concluded, "Not so hard."

Blair thought for a moment, then asked, "Did you recognize me? I mean, in LA. When we ran into each other outside the bank."

"I have to admit, I ordinarily wouldn't have. But given the time and place...I knew it was you coming after what I had just stolen. It was difficult for me to maintain my composure."

"Why?"

"Are you seriously asking?"

Blair looked at her quizzically. "Yes. You don't seem to have difficulty with much else."

"Because you're a friggin' Sky Thief. You guys took down the Century City job, the Sky Safe, the...the Supermax, for crying out loud. I was starstruck, man."

Considering this for a moment, Blair replied, "Well now, so am I."

Blair's earpiece crackled with Marco's voice.

"*We're five minutes out.*"

"Got it," she replied, looking at Wraith.

"My crew will be here in five. We'd better part ways now if you don't want them to see your face."

"No offense, but I don't." She set her empty paper plate on the backseat. "Thanks for the pizza."

Blair said, "You know, you should reach out to us sometime. Never know when we'll need another man for a job."

"Or woman."

"Right." Blair smiled.

"How do I get in touch with you?"

Blair heard herself sigh, then felt a tinge of embarrassment as she forced the words out. "Theskythieves@gmail.com."

Wraith's brow furrowed. "You're kidding."

"Nope."

"I don't know why I didn't think of that to reach you in the first place. It's so stupid, it's brilliant."

Blair shrugged. "Sometimes stupid works."

"Sometimes it does," Wraith agreed, extending her hand.

Blair shook it and said, "And since we haven't been formally introduced, I'm Blair. It's nice to meet you."

"Let's stick with Wraith for me." The woman released Blair's hand and gave her a seated version of a graceful stage bow. "Until next time."

Blair opened her car door and agreed, "Until next time."

She stepped out of the car and closed the door, moving to the sidewalk and tossing her plate before Wraith expertly maneuvered out of the tight spot and accelerated up 1st Avenue.

Then she was gone—no puff of smoke, no dazzling disappearance up the side of a building, not even a graceful sprint away. The Honda Civic entered the flow of traffic, its taillights soon indistinguishable from all the rest.

Blair remained on the sidewalk, watching this master thief's departure with an odd sense of mournfulness. For some reason, this didn't feel like she'd narrowly triumphed over a worthy adversary. Instead, it felt like she was eight years old again, saying goodbye to her best friend before moving to another state. That friend had never responded to Blair's letters, and she likewise wondered if Wraith would ever bother to write.

As this thought crossed her mind, the Honda Civic rounded a corner and vanished from view.

92

STERLING

Sterling flung open the Sprinter door, holding it for Blair to enter as a car horn sounded behind him. He paid the angry driver no mind, instead watching Blair enter the van before he closed the door and Marco accelerated forward down 1st Avenue.

She looked frazzled but unharmed, as if she'd just come off an all-night bar crawl rather than an elevated fight to the death over the tapes.

"You okay?" he asked, unable to shield his concern.

Blair took the seat next to him, sounding strangely at peace as she replied, "I'm fine."

Sterling felt as if he could finally breathe again, the sight of Blair now safe and reunited with the crew a boon to his spirits in a way he'd rarely felt before. Never had he felt so powerless as when he saw her atop the scaffolding, and given the volume of law enforcement appearing on site immediately afterward, he knew she must have had quite the story on how she escaped.

Before he could ask, Alec launched his own inquiry.

"How'd you get the tapes off Wraith?"

Blair shot him a smug little grin.

"I made my first successful dip."

Alec high-fived her with the words, "That's my girl. Knew you'd get it one day."

She replied, "I had a world-class instructor. So where are they?"

"Where are what?"

"The tapes, man. Where are the tapes?"

Sterling rolled his eyes in advance, anticipating the response.

"Oh," Alec said, leaning back in his seat and adjusting his overcoat. "Turns out the old bring-a-self-addressed-stamped-envelope trick wasn't so bad after all."

"Really?" Blair asked. "They're in the mail?"

Sterling nodded. "The streets were crawling with cops, and I got nervous. Dropped the tapes in a post office collection box right before ditching my radio. And it's a good thing I did, because I got stopped and frisked less than a minute later."

"Who was it?"

He gave a slight shake of his head. "Best guess, some cowboys sent on behalf of Jim and his mentor. They patted me down while I was screaming about my civil rights, and as soon as they didn't find the tapes, they were gone."

Rather than praise Sterling, Blair turned her attention to Alec and said, "You're a genius."

Alec shrugged.

"If I had a dollar for every time I've heard that, I wouldn't have to steal anymore."

Marco looked over from behind the steering wheel.

"You would have one dollar. And Blair, you know better than to encourage him. How did you make it out of the building?"

"Well, it's kind of a long story—"

She stopped speaking as Alec leaned in, sniffed her, and asked, "Why do you smell like a cheap slice of New York pizza?"

Blair pushed him away.

"Because I ate a cheap slice of New York pizza." Then she added, "While having a nice chat with Wraith."

Sterling's head snapped toward her.

"Where is she?"

Blair shrugged. "Who knows."

Alec's query was considerably less urgent.

"Well, was she hot? You never answered my question over the radio."

"Yeah, Alec. She was hot. And in LA, she cracked the bank vault by touch."

"By touch?" Alec exclaimed. "My God, this is my dream woman. Why'd you let her go? Least you could have done was give her my number."

Blair sighed triumphantly.

"I did one better: I told her we might need a hand one day, and gave her your stupid email address."

"Ah, you mean my *genius* email address. Bet Wraith will never forget it."

Sterling cut his eyes to Blair and asked, "What was your impression of her—do you think she'll ever reach out?"

Blair sighed and slid down in her seat, looking as if the full exhaustion of the night's events had hit her in one fell swoop.

"I don't know, Sterling," she said, struggling to summon up a more precise response before giving a helpless shrug and repeating, "I don't know."

93

BLAIR

Blair sat in her chair in the crew's conference room, watching Marco's sullen face.

He checked his watch and said, "He should be here by now."

Beside her, Sterling spun his chair to face the hacker.

"Don't forget we're talking about Alec here. And we have to account for him getting distracted by one or more shiny objects."

Blair said nothing, instead reveling in her surroundings: with its long table, couches, and coffee maker beside the sink, the conference room was nothing special by objective standards. It was, however, ground zero for her crew's heist planning and, at present, the very embodiment of being back in LA after their cross-country travels in pursuit of the tapes.

And while that may not have meant much to the two men in the room, Blair had gone from a modest home in El Segundo to a prison cell, then been released to a run-down, one-bedroom apartment before meeting the crew. Now, being back at their warehouse hideout felt like a triumphant return to the only home she had left.

The truth was, Blair wouldn't want to be anywhere else. These men were her family now—save perhaps Sterling, who'd become something more—and there was no other job in the world she wanted to be doing. Even the weather suited her, the warm Southern California sun an intoxicatingly relaxing experience after the bitter cold Northeastern winter. Weighed against all that, returning to LA victorious in their quest against Jim was merely a bonus; that was, she reminded herself, if the tapes successfully made it back.

No sooner had this thought crossed her mind than the conference room door flew open and Alec entered, holding the sealed padded envelope in both hands, pumping it up and down like a hockey coach holding the Stanley Cup.

Sterling and Marco burst into applause, but Blair merely felt an immense wave of relief wash over her as she exhaled an audible sigh of gratitude. It was one thing to know the tapes were in the mail, but verifying they'd made it cross-country unscathed was another matter altogether, and the only thing Blair looked forward to more than bringing down Jim once and for all was tonight's celebration of this triumph.

Especially if it was with Sterling.

Ending his applause, Marco pointed to the envelope and ordered, "Give that to me. I'm going to transcribe the audio to digital format before you break them."

Alec took a seat and slid the package across the table toward Marco.

The padded envelope made a whooshing noise as it coasted down the table's long surface, but before it reached Marco, Sterling put out his hand to intercept it.

"First, we need to consider what we'll release from these tapes."

Marco recoiled. "What do you mean? We release all of it. If you're worried about affecting the democratic process, don't be. You heard Wraith—the contents affect both parties equally. If we want to do the best thing for America, we expose corruption wherever we find it."

"I'm not worried about America," Sterling said, setting the envelope on the table and resting a hand atop it. "America will be just fine no matter what we do. I'm worried about my mom —and us."

Marco shook his head. "Jim won't be able to hurt anyone, not once these tapes are released."

Sterling raised his eyebrows. "But his mentor could."

Marco folded his hands on the table and said, "We don't even know who his mentor is."

"What matters right now is that *he* knows *us*. The media coverage over Blair's chase in New York makes it pretty clear that Wraith tried to hold up her end of the bargain in delivering the tapes. That puts us in the mentor's crosshairs, not her. So we've got an enemy out there no matter what we do. But that enemy is concerned about what's on these tapes, seeing as he coughed up nearly twenty-six million to recover them. If we only leak the segments that burn Jim and hang onto the rest, then we've got some degree of leverage over the mentor. He hurts us, we can hurt him right back."

"Or," Alec proposed, "he takes our restraint as a sign of good faith and leaves us alone. The status quo is restored, and we go back to business as usual: conducting high-profile heists across the Los Angeles metropolitan area from the comfort of our home base." He rubbed one hand in an affectionate circle across the conference table, patting it twice as if it were a loyal dog.

Blair shook her head. "We won't be that lucky. Jim's mentor won't cut his losses—he'll want some restitution, and for him that means us in prison." Leaning back in her chair, she announced, "So I'm with Sterling. We incriminate Jim, and hang onto the rest of the cassette audio for when we need it. Then we figure out who Jim's mentor is and prepare to strike first."

Marco looked from Blair to Sterling. "We just spent a month running around the country to take down Jim, during which time we made *negative* hundreds of thousands of dollars. Are we in the heist business or the vigilante business?"

Sterling replied, "Right now, we're in the self-defense business. But this mentor has money, and a lot of it. He also deserves to be robbed blind. As for whether we're out for profit or justice, well"—he gave a light shrug—"I propose that we can accomplish both at the same time."

Alec nodded thoughtfully. "Once we figure out who the mentor is."

"Right," Sterling conceded. "Once we figure that out."

Marco leaned over the table and snatched the envelope from Sterling, rising from his seat as he spoke.

"Well I'm going to put these tapes in digital format, then transcribe them so we can decide what segments to leak to the press."

Alec rose with equal urgency.

"And I'm going to take a nap. Let's face it, genius ideas like packing a self-addressed envelope don't just grow on trees, and if I'm going to have to carry this crew through our next score, I need my beauty sleep."

Blair watched Alec and Marco leave the conference room, then spun her chair to face Sterling.

"And what are you going to do?" she asked.

Sterling gave an apathetic shrug.

"Doesn't matter to me. I'm just biding my time until Alec and Marco head home."

Blair held out her hand, and Sterling took it.

"I have some plans for after they do."

"Oh?" He leaned in. "Do tell."

"I was thinking we could move in together," she said, watching for his reaction.

His eye twitched. "We already live in the same warehouse."

"I mean, the same room."

Sterling gave a low whistle. "That's a big step in our relationship. I'm not sure I'm ready for that level of commitment."

"Lots of other options, eh?"

"You'd be surprised. You're not the only hot fugitive out there."

"Neither are you."

"Touché," he acknowledged. "On second thought, maybe we should move in together. Your room or mine?"

Blair looked into his green eyes and replied softly, "Mine. That way when I'm mad at you, it'll be easy enough to kick you out."

Sterling swallowed.

"That's fair. And until then, shall we get to work trying to determine the identity of Jim's mentor?"

"Lead the way," she said.

Sterling leaned down to kiss her hand, then released it to stand alongside her, and the two exited the conference room together.

94

The media room was a long space with modern, clean lines. It was reflective of the rest of the 27,000-square-foot house interior, whose sleek character was fashioned by a famed interior designer who had come out of retirement for the commission.

Floor-to-ceiling curtains ran the length of both side walls, blocking any view to the outside world. A long rectangular block of polished marble served as the coffee table, and beside it loomed two large couches facing each other—both empty save throw pillows that hadn't been creased with use in weeks.

The only occupant in the room sat in an Italian leather armchair facing the far wall, where a recessed electric fireplace spread a long, narrow swath of red-orange flames above the floor. Most of the remaining wall surface was covered by an enormous ultra-high-definition television that flicked to the image of a brunette reporter in a stocking cap and jacket, speaking into a microphone against the backdrop of a high-rise building.

She began, "This is Caroline Paquin, CBS 6 News, live outside the office of Jim Jacobson. Most Albany residents know Mr. Jacobson as a highly decorated FBI agent and current Congressional candidate for New York's District 20 seat in the House of Representatives.

"But just hours ago, multiple news outlets across the country received an anonymously submitted compilation of recordings that appear to incriminate Mr. Jacobson in widespread corruption during his time in the FBI. Now publicly available on the internet, the recordings feature a man with a vocal likeness to Mr. Jacobson admitting to the fabrication of evidence to close criminal cases, and coercing a subordinate to do the same. And while the investigation is just beginning, Jim's campaign manager, Chris Mitchell, has resigned from his position citing ethical concerns."

The screen cut to an indoor press conference, where a regal black man in a windowpane suit was issuing his statement to the chattering of camera flashes.

"I was shocked and saddened to listen to the recordings, as I suspect were many residents of Upstate New York. And while I never—I repeat *never*—witnessed any unethical behavior during my short time on this campaign, I cannot account for Jim Jacobson's activities prior to retiring from the FBI. In light of the recordings that surfaced today, I hereby resign as Jim Jacobson's campaign manager—"

He was cut off mid-sentence, the view flicking back to Caroline Paquin in front of Jim's office building.

"Also featured in the tapes is a woman's voice who investigators believe is Blair Morgan, a former colleague of Mr. Jacobson while he served as the head of a federal task force responsible for ending a series of high-stakes heists across Southern California. Following her imprisonment for filing a false report in an investigation, which the recordings indicate may have been at the behest of Mr. Jacobson, Ms. Morgan famously joined the team of thieves she was previously responsible for apprehending. Now referred to as the Sky

Thieves for their daring robbery of the Sky Safe in Los Angeles, the team's other notable exploits include the Century City heist and breaking one of their own members out of the federal Supermax prison in Florence, Colorado."

The mentor smiled at this line. There was no diversion quite so entertaining as a worthy adversary, and no victory quite as thrilling as prevailing after a lengthy game of cat-and-mouse. In the end, it was always better to be the cat.

Caroline continued, "Whether Ms. Morgan made the recordings and, if so, why she would wait until now to leak them to the press is still unclear. But the FBI has opened an investigation alongside local and state authorities involved in Mr. Jacobson's former task force, and prosecutors say that if the recordings prove to be authentic, they will pursue the maximum punishment afforded by the law, including potential prison time for the former agent and recipient of the Bureau's highest honor, the Medal of Valor."

At that moment, the reporter turned to observe the flurry of activity behind her—Jim was exiting the building to an immediate flood of cameramen and reporters converging on him, shouting questions with microphones outstretched.

Jim, for his part, made a good show of appearing unconcerned as he pushed his way through the crowd, perfectly dignified as if this were all a slight misunderstanding that would soon be rectified by his attorneys.

As he tried to negotiate the crowd, Jim withdrew a cheap prepaid cell phone from his pocket and began typing a text.

On the side table next to the armchair, an identical phone emitted a single buzz.

The mentor reached for it, examining the screen to see Jim's incoming text:

SOS. Please help.

With a wry smile, Jim's mentor typed and sent three brief responses in quick succession.

There is no place I can't get to you. Especially prison.
If I hear the slightest rumor of you speaking my name, the consequences of your failure will be the least of your worries.
You and I are finished.

After pausing a moment, the mentor wrote one final line of communication with former protege Jim Jacobson.

I am going to take care of the Sky Thieves myself.

Then the mentor opened the case back to the phone, removing the battery back before extracting the SIM card.

Setting each component of the now-disabled phone on the side table, the mentor lifted a remote and aimed it at the television. Onscreen, Jim Jacobson looked aghast as he stared at his phone in disbelief, and then, with the touch of a button, the screen went black and he disappeared forever.

The mentor set down the remote, rose from the armchair, and strolled out of the media room to make the first preparations for war.

THE FIFTH BANDIT: SPIDER HEIST THRILLERS #4

The Fifth Bandit is the final installment of the electrifying Spider Heist Thrillers series by USA Today bestselling author Jason Kasper.

They've broken into safes and out of prison, but their greatest heist may be their last.

The Sky Thieves have conquered their worst enemy. Now they face an even greater threat: the ruthless mentor who brought him to power. Uncovering the mentor's identity is their first step to staying out of jail and exercising their own personal brand of justice—by stealing from the mentor's incalculable wealth.

But they aren't the only ones looking for clues, as their new opponent activates a vast web of connections to hunt them down. The game is rigged against the Sky Thieves—until a last-minute partnership with an unlikely ally gives them the key to their enemy's most valuable assets.

In the race to free themselves from a powerful opponent, the crew must undertake their most daunting heist yet...with their lives hanging in the balance.

Get your copy today at severnriverbooks.com/series/the-spider-heist-thrillers

ABOUT THE AUTHOR

Jason Kasper is the USA Today bestselling author of the Spider Heist, American Mercenary, and Shadow Strike thriller series. Before his writing career he served in the US Army, beginning as a Ranger private and ending as a Green Beret captain. Jason is a West Point graduate and a veteran of the Afghanistan and Iraq wars, and was an avid ultramarathon runner, skydiver, and BASE jumper, all of which inspire his fiction.

Sign up for Jason Kasper's reader list at severnriverbooks.com/authors/jason-kasper

jasonkasper@severnriverbooks.com

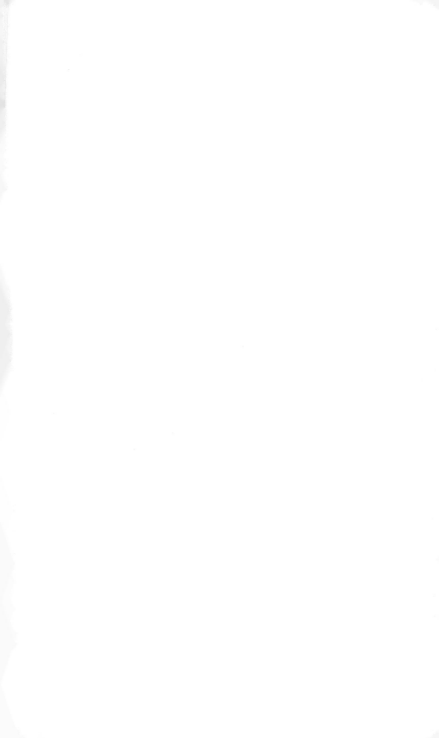

Printed in Great Britain
by Amazon